LOVE
in the Balance

Books by Regina Jennings

Sixty Acres and a Bride
Love in the Balance

LOVE in the Balance

REGINA JENNINGS

BETHANYHOUSE
a division of Baker Publishing Group
Minneapolis, Minnesota

Published by Bethany House Publishers
11400 Hampshire Avenue South
Bloomington, Minnesota 55438
www.bethanyhouse.com

Bethany House Publishers is a division of
Baker Publishing Group, Grand Rapids, Michigan

Printed in the United States of America

Library of Congress Cataloging-in-Publication Data
Jennings, Regina.
    Love in the Balance / Regina Jennings.
        pages cm
    ISBN 978-0-7642-0991-8 (pbk.)
        1. Texas—History—19th century—Fiction. 2. Christian fiction. 3. Love
stories. I. Title.
PS3560.E527L68 2013
811'.54—dc23   2012040439

Scripture quotations are from the King James Version of the Bible.

Cover design by Kirk DouPonce, DogEared Design

Author is represented by Books and Such Literary Agency

13 14 15 16 17 18 19   7 6 5 4 3 2 1

To my sisters,
who loved me enough
to spend their vacation touring libraries.
Trina, Becky, Meena, and Cara—
I owe you a shopping trip.

1

The pew creaked as another sinner rose to unburden her troubled soul. Molly Lovelace twisted around on the slick wooden bench, bunching her tiered silk skirt against her mother's, and watched as Louise Bradford stood. Bother. As if she had anything interesting to confess.

"After all God has done for me, I still can't live in holiness. This week I harbored thoughts of impatience toward my husband."

Molly cringed. Surely Mrs. Bradford's worst thoughts would bleach Molly's laundry clean.

Molly's transgressions, on the other hand . . .

Leaning forward to see around her father, Molly caught Bailey watching her intently. Her pulse quickened. With all the people trying to make decisions for her, she couldn't afford a misstep, but she hadn't expected to lose her heart so completely. What did Bailey Garner have to offer? Nothing, by her father's reckoning. If only his pockets were filled out as nicely as his homespun shirt.

Molly's sigh earned a stern glare from her mother. She

bowed her head, hoping to appear sorrowed over Mrs. Bradford's tedious list of near sins. How long would the woman ramble on? Bailey was waiting.

Every Sunday for the past year Bailey had escorted Molly to Lockhart, where she boarded for her job at the courthouse, but somehow on the twelve lonely miles between the Texas towns of Prairie Lea and Lockhart, Bailey's skills as a surrey driver diminished. For a cowboy, he let the horse wander off the road with surprising frequency, often failing to get the beast under control until it reached a sheltered grove out of view from the road.

That spot held a special place in Molly's heart. The bittersweet kisses shared between the thwarted lovers fueled her imagination, but until Bailey could keep dumplings on her table and silk stockings over her toes, she had to refuse his proposal. Her parents expected more.

But no one had ever delivered so reluctant a rejection. She braved a smile in his direction, noting his clean-shaven jaw and anticipating the smell of his shaving soap. Her father thought she was weak because she'd allowed an earnest young dreamer to disrupt his ambitions for her, when actually she'd never done anything braver than championing Bailey. Bailey was a good man who'd never had an opportunity to thrive, and Molly understood a thing or two about limited opportunities.

Mrs. Bradford's recital concluded.

From the raised platform, Reverend Stoker closed his Bible. "Thank you, Mrs. Bradford. We'll faithfully pray for you this week, won't we, church?"

Grunts and a few drowsy amens echoed over the heads of women itching to get their food on the tables before it cooled in the mild October weather.

"Then if there are no further—"

"I have something to say."

Molly's teeth rattled, she shut her mouth so hard. She turned quickly, her blond curls swinging straight out.

Not Bailey, Lord. Please, not Bailey.

He pulled himself up by the back of the pew and studied the floor. "Y'all need to pray for me. I've got a burden that's wearing me slick."

His silhouette blocked the sunlight streaming through the open window and stretched his shadow across rows of shocked parishioners. His eyes wandered in Molly's direction, held her gaze for an agonizing moment, and then turned toward the stained-glass cross in the window behind the pulpit. "God's convicting me, but I keep falling into the same pit. I'm still snared."

Molly's bonnet quivered. This wasn't part of their plan. She opened her mouth to protest, but her mother elbowed her sharply in the ribs. Holding her side, she looked again to Bailey. He'd never done this before. Only the elders spoke, and when they did, their stories were as bland as buttermilk. Terrified, Molly realized that Bailey's confession could be quite salty indeed.

He straightened his shoulders and shuffled his feet. "Anyway, guess y'all need to hold me accountable. God has something planned for me, but until I'm free of this . . . temptation . . . I can't move on to see what that is."

Freed from her? How could he say such a thing in front of all these people? In front of her parents? Molly's face went hot and her hands went cold. He couldn't mean it.

"I ain't blaming no one but myself, but if I'm serious about following God, I need to get my priorities straight, so pray for me. I can't do it on my own."

He plopped down next to his mother. Mary Garner's face shone scarlet. His father reached around to pat him on the back before turning forward. Everyone turned forward, but they didn't look at Reverend Stoker. They glared at Molly.

Had her parents been right? Was her relationship with Bailey a mistake? Well, she'd had enough. She wouldn't be tossed aside like last season's gowns. Her broken heart could wait as long as there was a comeuppance to be delivered. Tearing free of her mother's grasp, Molly popped to her feet.

"Reverend Stoker, I have a confession to make, as well." Her voice sounded as clear as a fork tapped against a crystal goblet. She shook her skirts out the best she could within the narrow row.

"Like all of us since Eve, I've made some mistakes." She wouldn't look in Bailey's direction. She would not. Instead, she looked at the parson and wished she hadn't. The horror on his face almost stopped her. Almost. "And like Eve, I was tempted, but I thought the fruit the serpent offered was healthy and wholesome. I didn't realize the snake offered me diseased fruit that wasn't nourishing. Rotten fruit from a tree that was unproductive and fallow. A tree that couldn't provide for a family or make a decent income—"

Bailey leapt to his feet, hands held out in appeal. "I told you I'm looking for a job. I'm moving to town next month."

Mr. Lovelace shot up. "Sit down," he bellowed at his daughter, but Molly could still see Bailey over her father's shoulders, if she hopped.

"Your employment, or lack of, is no longer my concern. How dare you impugn my character. You're upset because I won't—" Her father finally wrestled her to her seat.

"I didn't say anything about your character. No one would know I was talking about you if you'd kept your trap shut."

Reverend Stoker's throat clearing trumpeted with an authority that words couldn't merit. "That will be enough." His chest heaved in indignation. "This congregation would do well to remember that anyone may come to me for guidance anytime. Some issues are best discussed privately!" He ran his finger under his string tie. "However, we certainly will not forget to pray for you."

A strident *amen* rang out from the rear of the building, followed by snickers. Molly stared straight ahead, the stained-glass window blurring through her unshed tears. Her heart pounded, causing the lace ruff at her neckline to tremble. Did he mean to hurt her? She bit her lip. Bailey? The one person she thought she could trust?

Her parents stood with the rest of the congregation, and she had no choice but to follow as they pulled her up with them. She submitted, joined their hands, and followed the prescribed procedure to reach the end of the service.

How could she go outside for the potluck and pretend everything was fine? Impossible. She'd hoped against hope she could stall her father's plans long enough for Bailey to make his fortune. Never had she considered the possibility that Bailey might give up before she did.

Without him, her struggle was over. She'd fought for the freedom to make her own decisions, but without Bailey would she have the courage to continue?

The benediction ended and Molly dropped onto the wooden bench.

"Mr. Lovelace?" Russell James gripped the end of the pew in both hands as if it were a shield. He'd been her father's bookkeeper her whole life and was still naïve enough to believe it was his good fortune. "If I may be of assistance . . . Please don't worry about what people say. Their opinions are fickle at best."

Molly's father glared at him. "You should look after your own family, Russell, before you attempt to guide mine."

"Yes, sir," he stammered. "Please don't take offense. I was

trying to help. I didn't mean to compare your daughter to Michael."

"I'm getting the surrey," her father said. "If you'll excuse me—"

"We aren't staying for dinner?" her mother asked. "I had Lola make extra. . . ." His look of annoyance silenced her. "Well, I'm not staying in here." She rose to follow her husband out the door, Russell James trailing with a caboose of apologies.

Molly's thoughts whirled. What must everyone think of her? The picnic tables would hum with the story all afternoon. She winced at the laughter floating through the open window and wondered if it was at her expense.

The room grew quieter and quieter until Molly knew everyone had gone, everyone except the man sitting in the section to her left, fourth row from the front.

"And you think I'm going to let you escort me to Lockhart after that?" She kept her eyes on the pulpit.

"No, I don't. That's the point."

She heard Bailey take a deep breath.

"And even if you would, your father wouldn't. At least that's what I'm counting on."

She turned weary eyes to him, surprised to see concern etched on his face. If he wasn't mad at her, why'd he go and do that? She'd fought for him, defended him, and now he was abandoning her. Her arms still twitched with the longing to knock his head off of his broad shoulders. Without that baby face he wouldn't get far.

Bailey picked up a paper fan from the back of the pew and slapped it against his hand as he made his way to her. "I know you're mad, but this is best. I want to make you and your family proud, and it's gonna take some work before I'm good enough for you."

"That's what I don't understand. Why jilt me now that you're free to leave the ranch and make a name for yourself?"

"Because I want to do this right," he said. "I'm starting something new, and I don't want to mess it up. God can't bless my efforts when we're carrying on like we do."

Molly stood. "Then move to Lockhart. Get a job. You could've done that without calling me down in church."

"I didn't mention you, but it's just as well that you jumped in. I need some accountability, because no private decision is strong enough to keep us apart. We act like we're fixing to get hitched, and we both know it's going to be a spell before that's possible." His eyelashes, so thick Molly coveted them, lowered as he rotated the paper fan in his hands. "I think of you in ways a man shouldn't think of a woman unless she's his wife. You've got to give me some room."

Her toes curled. How could he want her so badly, yet be willing to give her up? Inhaling all that trail dust had addled his brain.

"The scales have never been in your favor, Bailey. I thought Father might relent if the business at the sawmill picks up, but how can I plead your case now? You've thrown the balance completely askew."

"Wait for me, Molly. I finally have my pa's blessing. He's even helping me find a position in Lockhart. As soon as I'm settled, I'll come calling, but I can't court you now. I can't keep stepping out with you until we're ready to wed. Will you wait?"

With an explanation to her parents looming, Molly wasn't in the mood to make promises to the man who'd humiliated her, no matter how regretful he might sound. "After this disgrace my parents will marry me off to the first gassy old man who wanders into our parlor. And maybe it's for the best. Maybe I'd be happier with someone steady." Molly tugged at the bottom of her bodice firmly enough that the stitches popped. Here she was, lying in church. Well, she might as well make it a whopper.

"Why would I want to marry a cowboy anyway? Stinking boots, barn manners, and rough . . ." She looked at his hands and couldn't bring herself to disparage them in any fashion. Not when she wanted nothing more than to feel them holding her close. "By year's end, my father will be marching me down an aisle, and it won't matter who's waiting at the altar as long as the arrangement benefits him."

"Then every kiss I take is stolen from another man's wife." He dropped the fan into the slot in the back of the pew before gracing her with a sly smile. "But you won't be bullied into marrying some old goat. Remember when you stood down those townies pestering my puppy? You were quite the little spitfire."

She remembered. Every childhood memory of hers included Bailey. He was like the comfortable old wing chair in her room—always there when she wanted him but not essential. Then last year her clumsy attempts to win his cousin Weston had changed their relationship and revealed that Bailey was who she really needed. In the year they'd been courting, he'd gone from a diversion to her mainstay, her future. She couldn't imagine going on without him, even if it was temporary.

Molly hadn't realized how close he was leaning until he straightened suddenly. She turned and caught Reverend Stoker peering in the window. He jerked his chin toward the door, and they both understood.

"More time, Molly. That's all I'm asking. I want to do right by you." His dark eyes traveled to her lips. "It'll be worth the wait. I promise." And he left her alone before the empty altar.

Molly twisted a blond curl to her mouth and chewed as

his footsteps echoed against whitewashed walls. If her parents would allow it, she would walk outside and say yes, and Reverend Stoker would see them wed before the pecan pies were broken out. The vision lingered a second longer than she'd expected, but her wistfulness was replaced once again by frustration.

She lifted her chin and straightened her bonnet. Even if it meant locking herself in her wardrobe, she wouldn't moon after him. How could she? He'd humiliated her in front of half the town. Prairie Lea gossip would be Lockhart news by Monday. No. He'd have to come to her—and not with empty pockets this time.

She'd been willing to accept a poor man despite her parents' dire warnings. She'd begun to imagine a life without the luxuries necessary for a lady. She'd grown less concerned with the latest fashions and coiffures. She'd even ventured out once on a promenade in mismatched gloves.

Molly shuddered. After waiting a year for him to be released from his familial duties, she'd known that she'd have to wait a little longer for him to get established—but not that she'd be waiting alone.

Waiting and bracing for a bombardment of parentally approved suitors.

Reckless man! Even if she did manage to resist her parents, how did Bailey expect her to carry on without him? How long before she stopped looking for him over every crowd in town, wondering if he'd managed to sneak away from the ranch to visit?

Only Molly's insistence and her parents' long-standing friendship with the Garners had prevented them from banishing Bailey outright, but now she'd be gussied up and sold to the highest bidder.

Did he have any idea what he had done?

"I have half a mind to make him marry you. It'd serve him right," said Thomas Lovelace.

Molly watched the stripes on her father's shirt expand and contract with every labored breath from her seat in the back of the surrey. This wasn't how she'd imagined her ride back to Lockhart. Usually the journey had more to recommend it—like a handsome, cheerful driver, for instance.

The grassland between Prairie Lea and Lockhart offered little to distract her parents from their tirade. They had no interest in the longhorns eyeing their trek across the barren winter fields or the jackrabbit bounding over the knots of dried grass. Rebuking their daughter would be their sole diversion for five miles yet.

"Thank goodness the boy's got more sense than I gave him credit for. You'd make a poor man miserable," her father said.

"It was this surrey, wasn't it?" Adele Lovelace's gloved hand caressed the leather bench. "Do you know how long I pleaded before your father would purchase it for me?"

Molly grasped the support from the second-row bench and thrust herself forward between her parents' shoulders. "Your surrey remains untainted, Mother. Of all the things to worry about after I've been humiliated before the whole world. We didn't do anything, or not much. Bailey's just upset I won't marry him."

"After all the music lessons and deportment classes, how could he imagine you'd squander your prospects on him?" Mrs. Lovelace shook her head and clucked softly. "I'm glad your brother isn't here to see your shame."

But Nicholas would hear about it, no doubt. Although his new business supplying lumber to the railroad kept him away from home, his partnership with his father's mill ensured frequent visits and correspondence. Which busybody's letter would reach him first?

The horse slowed its pace as if waiting for redirection. Molly looked up. The pecan grove. She kicked her boot against the bottom of the front bench, startling the horse and earning a suspicious glare from her father as he struggled to keep the horse from wandering toward the copse of trees.

"So now that Bailey Garner has removed himself from your consideration, are you prepared to entertain more appropriate options?" her mother asked.

Molly didn't make a peep. Her head churned with possible candidates and how to avoid them. What would it take to outwit her parents? How could she keep her freedom without an outright rebellion?

"It was our mistake pushing you toward Weston when he obviously wasn't interested," her mother said, "and now we need to make up for lost time. You aren't getting any younger."

Molly adjusted her bonnet as a precaution against freckles.

"Remember," her father continued, "your stay in Lockhart is dependent on your finding a husband. If you aren't becoming acquainted with the right sort of gentlemen, you might as well come home. No sense spending all that money on gowns if no one appreciates them. Besides, unless the sawmill does better, there won't be any money for gowns."

Molly's ears perked at the welcomed topic change. She scooted to the edge of her bench. "What's causing the mill to be unprofitable? Prairie Lea is rebuilding from the fire. Nicholas is sending railroad contracts our way. Lumber prices are stronger than ever."

"Just because you have a little job in the courthouse doesn't mean you understand enterprise." Thomas squared his shoulders.

"You mustn't allow your position to fill your heart with self-importance. It's unbecoming in a lady," her mother said.

"I merely asked a question based on solid information. I fail to see what role pride plays in this."

"You fail to see what a drought can do," her father huffed. "If the river wasn't low, we could float the logs to the mill. As it is, I'm feeding mule teams and paying drivers to bring in the raw material. Nicholas's railroad contract is locked in, so we're operating at a loss."

For all of Molly's life her father had claimed they were losing money. Made her wonder how rich he'd been in the beginning.

"If you want to help your father," her mother said, "go back to Lockhart and find a man with income."

"And connections." Thomas said. "Someone with capital who's interested in investing."

"And, of course, a society leader. We aren't completely merciless, Molly. There'd be something in it for you."

Molly frowned. This was no spontaneous discussion.

"Who is it?" She crossed her arms and settled in for a fight. "If you're going to stick a hook in me and throw me in the creek, I'd like to know for whom we're fishing."

Her father pressed his substantial weight back into the surrey seat, causing it to bump into Molly's knees. "The banker in Lockhart has a son."

"Mr. Fenton!" Molly covered her eyes. "Mr. Fenton is courting Prue McGraw."

"The blacksmith's daughter?" Adele *tsk*ed. "That's precisely the problem. His parents do not view the match favorably."

"You talked to them? No, I can't come between Fenton and Prue. She's my friend, the court reporter of whom I've spoken. She's been teaching me shorthand so I can take her job when she gets married."

Her father chuckled. "Don't let her fool you. The salary for the court reporter is chicken feed compared to your allowance as Mr. Fenton's wife."

Allowance? Molly clenched her reticule tightly. No other word could ruffle her feathers so. Every week she brought home her wages from the courthouse and handed them over to her father. Every week she returned to Lockhart with an allowance from him because he *allowed* her to keep a portion of her own money.

She suddenly filled her chest with a long draw of crisp October air. Would being a wife provide her with any freedom? She studied her mother's tightly wound coif in front of her. Probably not, but what other choice did she have? Anything was preferable to being treated like a child. A girl child, especially.

Stealing Mr. Fenton from Prue was out of the question. Molly wouldn't betray her friend. Besides, Mr. Fenton's devotion to Prue McGraw couldn't be shaken. He, at least, was safe from her parents' schemes, but whom would they settle on next?

Molly clasped her hands together. Would Fenton willingly stand in as a decoy? She needn't worry about losing her heart to him, and he definitely had no interest in her. Perhaps an understanding could be reached with the banker's son that would pacify her parents and give Bailey time to get established.

Would Mr. Fenton play along . . . and would Prue understand?

2

LOCKHART, TEXAS
NOVEMBER 1879

To Do List:

- *Write Mother a scintillating account of dinner with Mr. Fenton.*
- *Buy new tortoiseshell combs.*
- *Learn when Bailey is moving to town.*

Living in the cultural center of Caldwell County agreed with Molly. Ever since Mr. Myers led that first herd of cattle up what they now called the Chisholm Trail, cowboys and cattlemen had flooded the city. Businesses prospered and the streets bustled. Although the cowhands could get rowdy in certain areas of town, the ladies of Lockhart were moving it toward gentility and sophistication, and Molly wanted to be in on every step. To her mind, the only advantage that quiet little Prairie Lea held was a certain man who'd promised to relocate any day now.

Yet he hadn't appeared.

Mr. Fenton entered the dining room and scowled as the

waiter pointed in her direction. Molly had put off this rendez-vous as long as she could, hoping that Bailey would renew his suit, but it'd been three weeks, and she hadn't heard a word from him. She closed her journal and hid it in her reticule as the banker's son stalked toward her, taking long strides with short legs. Mr. Fenton barely halted before he collided with her round table.

"I suppose I must make an attempt at civility. If it weren't for my disdain for ungentlemanly behavior, this situation could certainly provoke me toward churlishness." He made a big show of looking around the hotel's dining room, rotating his shoulders as if his chin were fused to his chest. "Fortunately, the presence of witnesses bolsters my restraint."

Molly leaned her elbows on the table. "Please, Mr. Fenton, be seated. There'll be enough said about us dining together as it is. We gain nothing by feigning misery."

"You may feign. My pain is real." But he pulled out the chair and sat, doing his best to avoid her gaze. "The lengths to which we submit to pacify our families . . ."

Molly's eyes widened at the insult. My, what a tantrum he could throw. How dare he act condescending. He was court-ing the blacksmith's daughter, for crying aloud.

She fought the desire to retaliate. Less than a month had passed since her last public dispute with a man. She'd have to use a different approach.

"If it weren't for my parents, I wouldn't be here, and I as-sume you are in a similar situation. If you want to revolt, you have my blessing, but please spare me your unpleasantness. I am not your enemy."

Molly had spoken as sweetly as possible, and still his wide eyebrows rose. "I wondered why, despite your well-favored appearance, your parents felt they needed to sweeten the deal with part ownership in the mill. Now I understand. No doubt your sharp tongue has chased off several offers." He studied her as he waved the waiter over. "Miss McGraw would never accuse me of being unpleasant."

Molly smiled at the waiter, taking a moment to bask in the appreciation reflected in the man's eyes, but was she only attractive to poor men? Well, she'd promised her parents she'd give Fenton a chance. They couldn't fault her if the results didn't satisfy. Besides, knowing she had a suitor might build a fire under Bailey. It'd been weeks and she had no news of his progress.

"Prue is an angel, on that we can agree. And you've probably never had a reason to be unpleasant with her."

"True. She is the most gentle, most sincere woman I've ever met. It pains me to think of what this is doing to her." His jaw grew so tight that his ears moved.

"I've tried to explain to Prue, Mr. Fenton. I've promised her I'm not attempting to steal your affections and that you definitely have no interest in me, but she doesn't understand the pressures visited upon us." Molly slid her napkin off the table and spread it in her lap as the memory of Prue's tear-streaked face appeared before her. "Surely if we both reassure her, we'll make it through this trial without further damage. Then we can honestly tell our families that we became acquainted and have no interest in furthering the relationship."

"And hopefully such a declaration can be made before our association becomes noticed—"

"Mr. Fenton, I'd hoped to find you about today." Judge Rice's periwinkle eyes peered from a weather-lined face. Like a courtly gentleman, he bowed slightly to Molly before continuing. "It's come to my attention that my young stenographer is suffering from some form of distress, and I thought you might be able to enlighten me."

"She is?" Fenton sprang to his feet. "Where is she?"

"No, son, not of that nature." With a hand on the shoulder he guided Fenton back to his seat. "She's moping about, sighing as ladies are wont to do when grieved." His keen eyes rested on Molly. "I'm sure you understand, Miss Lovelace. Perhaps you would have insight as to what ails her."

Molly kept her chin lifted. Of course she knew, and so did the judge. "Perhaps her father is interfering with matters of the heart. That seems to be a frequent culprit these days."

"Mr. McGraw? I think not, but I hope that we, her friends, can ease her discomfort." He rapped his knuckles against the table with the same hand that usually held the gavel. "I won't keep you from your meal or your . . . uh, conversation . . . but I offer that food for thought should you be able to relieve her distress. Good day."

They both sat, chastened, until the keen gentleman left the room.

"Insufferable," muttered Mr. Fenton. "I'll admit you are a victim of the same parental ailment that plagues me, but how can we proceed?"

Molly's mouth lifted on one side. She needed to be alert to walk this tightrope, and holding grudges exhausted her. "We will proceed together, Mr. Fenton. That might be the quickest way to get apart."

Bailey Garner sat high in his saddle, enjoying the prestige of riding through Lockhart at his cousin's side. Tipped hats, deferential nods—people respected Weston Garner, and Bailey hoped someday to be as highly regarded as his eldest cousin, former employer, and mentor. No wonder Molly's parents had hoped Weston would favor their daughter. He'd been surprised that Weston had shown no interest in Molly, but maybe she'd been too young for the old man. Downright crotchety at times, he was. Still, Bailey was glad when his aunt Louise returned from Mexico with that beautiful widow, Rosa. The Lovelaces never would've allowed Molly to step out with him until Weston was spoken for. Now with a wife and a newborn son, Weston was well settled—another reason Bailey envied him.

The Lovelaces, as well of most of Caldwell County, held the Garner family in high regard. Coming from South Carolina before the war, the Garner boys had claimed a large spread that grew every year. His cousin Weston, old enough to merit the title "Uncle" from Bailey's little sisters, had prospered on his ranch, Palmetto. Weston's sister, Eliza, and her husband, Jake, were working the land that they'd purchased from his aunt Louise when her marriage to the shop owner moved her to town.

Bailey's parents, George and Mary Garner, lived nearby and ran sheep with the help of his brothers, but they never seemed to get ahead like the rest of the family and often relied on their relatives to make ends meet.

"Is your mother's family expecting you?" Weston asked.

"Yes, sir. Uncle Matthew's got me a job, and Aunt Frances is putting me up. I'm all set."

Weston swerved closer to avoid a wagon that pulled into the street. "I guess you've prayed through this, but it seems like a contradiction, if you ask me. You swear off Molly, and then you move to Lockhart. Don't know but what you aren't playing with fire."

"Believe me, I've wondered aplenty if I'm doing the right thing, but this seems best. There's no future for me on the ranch, not with two brothers who'll want their share. I've always known I wanted to move to town and have a career. Now that Samuel and Tuck can take up the slack, I'm free to make my fortune."

"So you're doing it for your gal, but doing it without your gal?"

"It's like to drive me crazy not talking to her, but we needed to take a few steps back to get on the right path again. Besides, I don't need any distractions, because until I can support Molly, it's clear that God has said, 'Not yet.'" He saw Weston's shoulders twitch with mirth. "All right, maybe Molly's parents said it, too, but I'll keep my distance until God changes their minds or my income, because I'm hooked. Ever since primer school when she whooped everyone at arithmetic drills, I knew she was the girl for me."

"Of all the credentials I've heard for a wife, that's got to be one of the strangest."

Bailey was no good at sums, but he could decipher Molly, and she knew it. Long ago she'd given up trying to keep secrets from him. She needed him. And he needed to be needed.

Bailey's knees tightened around the saddle as they approached the hotel. He couldn't keep the doubt from crawling back. Did Molly remember why he was leaving her alone?

"It's a brave move to risk losing your girl." Weston reined his horse toward the hitching post. "One caution, though. Don't get discouraged if you stumble. Sometimes we have to deal with the same temptations time and time again."

"We're supposed to be 'more than conquerors,'" Bailey protested.

"Conquerors can lose a few battles along the way. Just yesterday I was talking to your pa—"

Bailey dismounted and looped the reins tightly over the hitching post, trying to avoid a reciting of his pa's story. They'd almost lost their ranch and endangered his aunt Louise's farm because of his father's love of cards. He didn't need Weston to remind him of his family's embarrassment. George Garner was a fine man. His pa loved him like the dickens, but

Bailey was made of sterner stuff. Thank the Lord he didn't inherit the same weakness.

"I'm starved." Bailey nodded to the wide hotel with the real second story. "This place looks good." And smelled good, too. His stomach gurgled at the meaty aromas wafting out the swinging batwing doors. Aunt Frances wasn't expecting him until suppertime, and with her houseful of children he knew better than to show up unannounced and hungry.

Bailey followed Weston into the restaurant and nearly bumped into his back when he stopped abruptly. Weston turned around.

"Let's go to the Hungry Drover. It won't be as full."

"I don't mind. Got to get used to the hustle and bustle of a crowd if I'm going to live in town." Bailey stepped past his cousin, afraid he was about to dig in his heels.

And there she sat.

Molly spotted him at the same moment.

Bailey groaned as he took measure of the uptight man with the pinched face and beetle-brown sack suit. It didn't take a genius to figure what she was up to.

"No wonder you threw on the brakes."

"I tried to warn you." His older cousin avoided controversy like preachers avoided the Minor Prophets, and for once Bailey was grateful.

"Weston? Is that you?" The man's voice traveled over the din to lasso them.

The cousins exchanged weary glances, but Weston was trapped.

With one last dark look at him, Weston turned. "Hello, Mr. Fenton, Miss Lovelace. How y'all doing?"

Bailey had no choice but to follow as Weston did his duty. Molly's gown, the same dusky color as a rain cloud, suited his mood. He'd anticipated her parents would present her with new suitors, but not that she'd fold so easily. At least her companion didn't look pleased. If watching Molly talk to other men got this Fenton character riled, he'd better poke his eyes out.

"Mr. Fenton, my cousin Bailey Garner."

The man stood and offered his hand.

"Mr. Fenton works at the bank." Molly set her fork down next to her plate and wiped her fingertips on the napkin. "Our fathers are business associates."

He should've known. Bailey shook hands with the man and then tried to wipe off the contact on his canvas britches.

"Pleased to meet you." But he wasn't.

"I heard you're building a new house," Weston said.

"Yes, it's nearing completion."

"Is that the new two-story with the beautiful mansard roof on San Antonio Street?" Molly asked, leaning halfway across the table.

Fenton nodded.

"It's magnificent."

Bailey narrowed his eyes. Was she sincere or merely pretending for his benefit? It didn't matter. Mr. Fenton squirmed like a worm on a hook. He looked longingly at his plate of roast beef.

"Yes, well, if you'll excuse me, Weston, Mr. Garner. My dinner hour is nearly over, and I've yet to finish my meal."

Bailey looked up to see Molly scowling at him. She narrowed her eyes and then cooed to Fenton with the subtlety of an auctioneer, "It's a pity you don't have time to converse, but I guess the bank can hardly do without you. Perhaps we can visit with the Mr. Garners some other time."

She paused, offering them the opportunity to voice their regrets.

Boy, was she putting on a show, trying to herd them all

exactly where she wanted them. But Bailey wouldn't be led by the nose. Time to stampede.

He picked up an empty chair from the nearest table with one hand and slung it between his legs, dropping into it backwards. "There's nowhere in the world that I'd rather be than here, becoming better acquainted with Mr. Fenton."

Molly's eyes widened. "Oh?"

"Yes, I've long been fascinated with the banking business. I'm sure it's a breathtaking and dangerous venture. And your house, Mr. Fenton?" He batted his eyes and raised the pitch of his voice an octave. "Oh, I so admire everyone who lives on San Antonio Street."

Molly's attempts to incinerate him with her eyes failed. He was fireproof.

"Bailey," Weston warned.

Bailey cringed, not sure by which piece of his anatomy Weston might drag him out, but his mentor could hardly act as barbaric in the eatery as he would've on the ranch.

Weston nudged the leg of his chair. "There's not room at the table for four. Let them finish alone."

But Mr. Fenton blinked first. He smirked at Molly although he spoke to Weston. "No, please. Take my place. It's an honor I'm willing to relinquish. Please pass the seat on to the next man when he arrives."

"You must disregard him, Mr. Fenton. He is leaving." She got to her feet, but her protests were losing strength.

Fenton tossed a bill on the table, dipped his head to Weston, ignored Bailey, and left the dining room as fast as his rounded-toe shoes allowed.

"You ran off my escort. Father will not be happy," Molly said.

But she didn't look upset. Despite the hand on her hip, she seemed relieved. Her eyes sparkled and her pert mouth tilted.

"I'm trying to help you out," Bailey said.

"If you wanted to help, you'd be building a house on San Antonio Street instead of lollygagging about town." But the only work she was doing was twisting a blond curl around her shapely finger.

Then she noticed Weston.

Bailey couldn't help but be charmed by the change in her. He was captivated by the thought that she had expressions and mannerisms only he was privy to. Decorum replaced the eagerness on her face. She resumed her proper poise, but Weston didn't notice the difference.

"Won't you join us?" Bailey reclaimed his seat. "Weston can chaperone, so I should be safe from your charms."

She rolled her eyes. "I must return to the courthouse. Employment seems to be a rare commodity these days. I don't want to jeopardize my own."

With a nod at Weston, Molly clomped across the room so strongly that her square heels could've left indentions on the oak floor.

Weston took a seat across from Bailey as the batwing door swung shut behind her. Leaning back, he crossed his legs at the ankles and frowned at his charge from across the table.

"You're playing with fire, Bailey. Playing with fire."

The three-story sandstone courthouse looked like a castle, complete with turrets and a waving flag at the pinnacle. Entering through the red sandstone arch as the giant clock chimed, Molly could almost imagine that she was a princess returning to a celebration in her honor. Smiling, dipping her head, she could keep the fantasy alive until she crossed the golden tiles in the entry and reached the land office.

The wooden door eased open just enough for Molly to squeeze her lobster-tail bustle through. Open it any further and the movement would be visible from Mr. Travis's office, and getting caught meant—

"Miss Lovelace, did you not hear the courthouse clock chime one? There was a vacancy at your desk when the event occurred. Again." Mr. Travis's beard hung on sagging skin and hid his jaw completely.

"Yes, sir. I'm sorry." Molly untied her hat and exchanged it for her inky apron that hung on the pegboard. She pressed a hand to her rosy cheek, willing it to fade, along with the memory of her tumultuous dinner. Hopefully her father would think she'd suffered enough and wouldn't require her to make another attempt with the prickly Mr. Fenton. Dinner would've been a complete loss if it weren't for Bailey's appearance. And what was even better, he'd seen her with another man. Complete triumph.

"Being sorry doesn't get the work done. I answer to the taxpayers of Caldwell County, and I can't justify spending their funds on workers who neglect their stations."

Behind Mr. Travis, Molly's co-worker Carrie rolled her green eyes and flapped her hand open and closed like a duck's beak quack, quack, quacking.

". . . empty all the waste bins after hours—that means on your own time. And see that you aren't tardy again."

"Yes, sir," Molly repeated.

As soon as the latch on his office door clicked into place, Carrie slid off her stool and rushed to Molly's work station.

"How was dinner? What did he do? Did he talk about Prue?"

Molly unbuttoned four buttons on her right wrist and pushed back the cuff. If only her situation excited her as much as it did Carrie.

"I survived. That's all I'm going to say." Molly touched her neckline and straightened her hair.

Carrie's sharp eyes searched her face. "What happened? You're hiding something."

"It wasn't as bad as I expected. That's all."

"Do you think he'll leave Prue? He didn't make advances, did he?"

"Don't be absurd." Molly shuddered at the thought. How high a price was she willing to pay to please her father?

Turning her back to Carrie, she took the stack of letters delivered during the noon hour, opened the top envelope, and extracted the payment. The smell of ink and the newly bound ledger cleared her head. Numbers were faithful friends. They didn't expect you to waste your youth waiting. They didn't tempt you and then embarrass you publicly. They stayed on their paper until you had time for them, and they always followed the rules.

"Mr. Saul Nimenko, sixteen dollars and twenty-two cents." Molly dipped her quill in the inkpot and scratched the entry onto the page. Then she slid off the stool and followed Carrie to the wall of bookshelves. Land parcels in the northwest section of Prairie Lea—that was the volume she needed. Carrie took the heavy book for the south central region of Lockhart in both hands and stepped out of her way.

"Northwest, northwest," she whispered to herself. She'd never met Mr. Saul Nimenko, but if his property tax was a measly $16.22, she didn't need to meet him. She'd do just as well with Bailey.

The rat.

The office door squeaked open, and a sturdy brunette peeked around the corner.

Prue.

Molly ducked her head as Carrie silently waved her friend

over. Former friend. The lady would certainly never claim any association with her now.

"Prue, what are you doing here?" Carrie set the heavy book on her table without a noise. "Is court out of session?"

"The jury is in deliberations, so I slipped away." She smoothed her dark skirt, and with another furtive glance toward Mr. Travis's door, she leaned across the counter to whisper, "How are my friends in the land office doing?"

Molly lowered her eyes. She felt bad enough already. She mumbled a greeting, trying not to recount Judge Rice's words. Evidently Prue didn't believe that any association between her and Fenton was merely endured. She sighed. It *was* strange that a man like Mr. Fenton had become besotted with the blacksmith's daughter. Molly expected her to attract a nice humble boy—someone as good as gold and shabby as burlap—not a connoisseur like the banker.

"Your friends are doing quite well, thank you," Carrie said. "At least Molly is. She dined with Mr. Fenton today."

Molly groaned. Didn't Carrie understand how hurtful her comments were? Did she enjoy the discomfort she was causing?

Prue's large brown eyes rested on Molly. She pressed her hand against her olive shirtwaist and swallowed slowly. "Did he have his roast beef?"

Molly nodded.

"Good. If he eats anything else for dinner he suffers from indigestion. He'd prefer to eat at home, but his kitchen is under construction, and there's no one to cook for him."

"There will be soon, if Molly has her way," Carrie said.

"Carrie, stop," Molly said.

"Why? Prue's being a sport. If Mr. Fenton prefers you, it's best he realizes it before he finds himself bound in holy matrimony to the wrong person."

Prue's face turned gray. "I should go. The jury may have reached a verdict." She clasped her hands together in a martyr's pose. "But I have a favor to ask, Molly. If you have a free evening, would you come for a visit? Come for supper if you're tired of the fare at the boardinghouse."

Visit the McGraws? Did Prue really want her there, or was she trying to increase Molly's guilt? In the long run, it didn't really matter. She could hardly refuse.

"Thank you, Prue. I'd like that."

And she would if the weight of her father's schemes didn't rest so heavily on her conscience.

Carrie, being free from culpability, had no compunction about voicing her opinion, which she did on their walk home after work.

"Why doesn't Prue say what she thinks? She must be fuming. I can imagine how I'd feel if you'd gone after a beau of mine in the same way." The girls linked arms as they crossed the street in front of the courthouse and made their way to the boarded sidewalk of the square.

"But I'm not. Not really. It's all been arranged by our parents."

They made a pretty picture promenading before the storefronts, or so Molly thought as she watched their reflection in the windows they passed. She straightened her back so as not to appear slouchy next to Carrie's flawless posture. And did her charcoal ensemble appear drab next to Carrie's lemon shirtwaist?

"She should've seen it coming," Carrie continued. "I can't imagine why Mr. Fenton has put up with her mousy ways for so long. She should claw your eyes out. Who wants a spineless woman?"

"Believe me, I wish she'd fight for him," Molly said.

Carrie's long strides moved Molly too fast to produce the

correct swing in her skirts. Her hat bobbed as she tried to keep up, Mother's deportment lessons cast aside.

"I can't fault their logic," Carrie agreed. "What business does a blacksmith's daughter have with a family like the Fentons? She'd be better off with that cowboy, Bailey."

Molly skidded to a stop.

"Don't be ridiculous. Bailey and Prue would never suit. He's so . . . dangerous. Wild. He'd scare her knickers off."

"Bailey? He seems like more of a goody-goody. Too tame for me. Unless . . . unless Bailey has some potent charm you've kept secret."

The hair on the back of Molly's neck stood at an unbidden memory. Stunned, Molly dropped her handbag on the boarded sidewalk. Where had that chill come from? So startled was she that she swooped to snatch it off the ground before considering the right angle for her descent. Carrie didn't release her hold on Molly's arm until the last minute, throwing her off balance and causing her to fall on her hands and knees.

"Be careful," Carrie snorted. With a firm grip, she hauled Molly to her feet. She held the errant handbag while Molly dusted herself off and straightened her skirts over the boning underneath. "Don't look now, but we're being observed."

Molly's furious arranging immediately ceased, and she assumed an air of a queen inspecting her . . . what did queens inspect? Who knew? Molly didn't have time to read old books while a man like the one standing in front of the bank roamed the earth.

At first glance she was convinced he was golden. Perfection incarnate. But as she scrutinized him, she realized her opinion was formed more by his bowler hat and silk cravat than his physical attributes. His frock coat was fuller than any she'd seen before, and his trousers were heroically striped, making her workday dress look dull by comparison.

She couldn't see the color of his hair because of his hat but assumed it to be the same shade as his light-brown moustache, unless it was heavily waxed. Yes, the part above his full lips evidenced wax. She smiled. Good grooming meant good breeding. Between the hat, his gloves, and his spats, very little of him was actually visible—only lively eyes and an arrogant jaw.

A queen inspecting her noble courtiers. That's what Molly would inspect if she were queen.

Aware they couldn't return blatant stares, Molly and Carrie resumed their stroll, but not before Molly noted the cane and thick gold chain leading undoubtedly to a heavy pocket watch.

"An interesting development," Carrie said. "Not that he'll pay me any mind. He only had eyes for you."

Molly pretended to pick lint off her shoulder to get another look. He remained in front of the bank, folding bills into a thick wallet. "Let's pray my parents don't hear about him."

3

"Ow! That's hot!" Bailey dropped the tongs as his knuckle brushed against a smoldering bar of iron. He popped his finger into his mouth.

"It *is* a blacksmith shop," Mr. McGraw groused as he pumped the bellows. The flames in the forge burst from orange to white hot, radiating enough heat to keep the structure sweltering, even though the double doors were thrown open and summer had long gone.

Picking up his tongs, Bailey found the wooden bucket and immersed his hand. Ah, relief. But his hand would heal before his eyes would. His first day on the job and his eyes felt like he'd rubbed them with onions. Maybe the smell of manure back on the ranch wasn't so bad after all.

He took a swipe of the ointment offered by the thick blacksmith and smeared it on his knuckle, the blister already filling with fluid. "I'll work the bellows for you. It looks safer."

Mr. McGraw's muttonchops swung as he slid his jaw around. "Naw, go over there. That iron is ready. Draw it out on the anvil, and when it gets an eighth of an inch thick, bring it to me. Oh, and Bailey, use the tongs, not your bare hands."

McGraw's son laughed from his bench near the forge. The

younger McGraw stood half a foot shorter than Bailey and possessed forearms the size of hams and a schoolgirl giggle.

"Reckon I deserved that." Bailey swung the glowing iron his way and grinned as his eyes grew big. He had been so clumsy today the man had every right to worry. Positioning the iron bar on the anvil, he squeezed the tongs firmly and swung the hammer. The vibrations of the blow reverberated up his left arm. Renewing his grip, he struck again.

Satisfying. Sometimes a man needed to work out some frustration. Bailey wasn't a fighter, but the more he thought about Molly with Fenton, the more he could picture himself overturning tables, firing off a few rounds into the night sky, and maybe even kicking a dog. There he'd be—on the fringes of society like that no-account Michael James. If Molly married Fenton, Bailey might as well loiter outside the local saloon with Michael and harass passersby. He smiled in spite of himself, imagining the church folks' shock. Well, he'd raise a glass to them and . . . no, he wouldn't. Bailey possessed equal parts fear of the Lord and fear of his ma. The Lord would have the final judgment, but his ma might move up the trial date if he crossed her.

Bailey flipped the rod and banged on the other side. Molly would wait on him. She'd want him to worry over her, sure, but she knew he was trying to do right by her. And God would reward him, too. He was finally setting out on the right path. If he wanted to be successful like Mr. Lovelace, he needed to find his place in the world. As much as he loved his own father, he didn't want to follow in his footsteps. He didn't want to live season to season barely squeaking by.

The smoky air burned his lungs. He wiped his tears with his sleeve before young McGraw saw it and laughed at him again. The smithing job came available at the right time, but it might not work out after all.

"Howdy, Prue. Quitting time already?" Mr. McGraw called.

The young lady looked ill at ease in her olive dress, as if even the simple gown were too fine for her. She hurried to old McGraw's side and kissed him on the cheek. "Let me change, and I'll offer what little help I can."

"No hurry. Bailey is giving us a hand."

Prue straightened. "Then I'll get supper on."

She tarried at the edge of the shelter. Bailey swung his hammer twice more before she worked up the nerve to speak.

"Bailey? Molly's Bailey?"

Bailey lowered his hammer. Did Molly still claim him? He couldn't really say one way or another. "My hide doesn't carry her brand."

"Of course not," she stammered. "I didn't mean . . ."

"Molly?" Her brother growled. "Is this the same Molly who stole your Mr. Fenton?"

Now the unfortunate girl truly was speechless. Her mouth pursed. She blinked rapidly and studied the glowing coals in the furnace. "His hide doesn't carry my brand."

But three men at the forge were all eager to remedy that oversight.

Bailey's mouth twisted. The stuffy Mr. Fenton, huh? He'd done his best to nip that thistle in the bud. Bailey pounded on the bar, imagining it decked out in a beetle-brown sack suit. Between ringing strikes he heard Prue's timid voice again.

"Mr. Bailey, did you come to town looking for a job?"

He shot a glance at her father.

"He's got one here, if he can take the smoke. Pity such a strong back got paired with delicate eyes."

Junior giggled again and earned an impatient look from Prue.

"I've recently heard of one, actually. Bailiff. Pays decent, no smoke, and—" Prue paused until he met her eyes—"a charming co-worker in the land office next door."

A smile spread across his face as he recognized a conspirator. "I don't want to leave your father shorthanded."

McGraw spat into the sizzling fire. "Stay around till I get someone else. If you'll swing your hammer instead of swinging your jaw, that is."

Fair enough. He could hardly carry on a conversation over the ringing iron. Bailey watched as Prue disappeared into the house. Molly spoke of Prue with respect, and from her description, Bailey had assumed that Prue was older, matronly. What a surprise. Now, Carrie he knew well. She boarded with Molly and figured into many of her stories, but somehow he couldn't wrap his mind around the fact that Prue was perhaps even younger than the other girls. Not an old maid at all.

The woman in the olive dress reappeared to present her father with a tin pail of fresh drinking water before slipping into the house again.

The McGraws were respectable, church-going folks. Bailey's uncle had sent him to Mr. McGraw to ask for job, knowing the man would treat him fairly. Even his mother encouraged him to call on the McGraws. Bailey didn't know they had a daughter, but something told him his mother did when she and Uncle Matthew procured this job for him.

"Are you still taking customers?" a familiar voice called from the sunny road.

"Come on over, Reverend," Mr. McGraw offered. "What can I do for you?"

"I'm looking for some nails and two heavy hinges. We're sprucing up the Lockhart parsonage."

"You're leaving Prairie Lea?" Bailey asked.

Reverend Stoker took a second look. "Bailey? What are you doing here?"

"McGraw's letting me try my hand at smithing." Bailey wiped his irritated eyes.

With hands in his pockets, the pastor moseyed over to inspect Bailey's work. "Looks like you can swing a hammer." He winked at the blacksmith. "To answer your question, I'm splitting my time between the two churches, and Mrs. Stoker would rather live closer to the city than in the little Prairie Lea parsonage."

Bailey's iron bar had cooled. Careful not to impale young McGraw or the reverend, he carried it to the forge and thrust it in the coals. "I'd be glad to help when you move."

"Both parsonages are furnished, but there would be a trunk or two. Actually, if you have your evenings free, I could use some help fixing the place up."

"I have my evenings free." The smoke mercilessly aggravated his eyes. Who would have thought he'd be so sensitive? He wiped at them again.

"McGraw, do you mind if I have a word with Bailey? I won't keep him."

"Talking's what he does best," McGraw grunted.

Well, now he'd have to work late. Smoke or no, Bailey had negotiated for a day's labor. He'd see to it that McGraw got a day's work no matter how long it took him. Bailey followed Reverend Stoker out of the shop to stand in the pile of leaves donated by the bare sycamore overhead.

Stoker's eyes were filled with concern, peeking from beneath his full gray forelock. "How are you doing, son?"

Bailey sniffed, his watery eyes having affected his nose. "I'd feel a sight better not breathing in all that smoke."

"The reason I ask is because lately you've been the topic of several conversations between my wife and me, and she asked a pertinent question. Do you think you might be called to the ministry?"

Bailey put his throbbing knuckle to his mouth and then spit out the nasty-tasting salve. "The ministry?" He shook his head. "I'm not fit for the ministry."

"That's for God to decide, isn't it? You have a heart for the Lord and a way with people. Something to keep in mind as you search."

"My way with people got me in trouble. I can't be all holy unless I quit loving—" Bailey stopped. "Is this confidential?"

"Why are you concerned now? You've already unburdened your soul before the whole church." Stoker chuckled. "Caring for Molly isn't wrong. Only when you love her more than you love God does it become a problem."

"With God so far away and Molly so . . . here . . . it's hard to keep my sights on the target."

"And how about Molly? Where are her eyes fixed?"

Bailey caught a leaf floating down and twirled it by the stem, afraid to answer the question. He didn't know about her relationship with God. He was too busy trying to shore up her relationship with him, and the longer they were apart the more concerned he became.

But how could he be a good influence for her if she was with someone else? Had God taken that into account?

Molly's new gown with the mandarin collar was making its debut on the damp streets of Lockhart that morning. She'd waited until the leaves had scattered before breaking out the emerald taffeta, hoping that an infusion of green would bring warm thoughts to those she encountered, although she usually had to wait until her noontime break before meeting anyone interesting.

Was her digestion going to be ruined by the woebegone sighs of Mr. Fenton, or was her dinner unclaimed? She couldn't remember. Thoughts popped up in Molly's head as numerous as soap bubbles, and the only way to keep up was to record them in her blue leather journal. Since it contained her personal musings, she kept it close. Risky, but better to write her plans and achieve them than allow them to remain vague and unreached. She flipped to her daily reminders.

To Do List:

- *Take shirtwaist to Mrs. Leeth's to replace ink-stained cuffs.*
- *Buy Father a cigar and beg him to forget Mr. Fenton.*
- *Regretfully decline Prue's invitation.*

No dinner with Fenton mentioned. All was good. She returned the journal to her beaded bag and swung it against her skirt, throwing flecks of light on the damp gravel road leading to the town square. Was the rain from the preceding night enough to bring the river up? If her father could stop hauling the lumber across land, he wouldn't be so desperate—or so he claimed, but by now Molly had learned that her father's slightest whim was everyone else's emergency.

Down the quiet lane she meandered in zigzags, keeping her steps on the driest spots. She'd left the boardinghouse a little early, wanting to put some distance between her and Carrie. Boarding with her co-worker had seemed like a good idea at the time, but sometimes Carrie's harsh remarks stung. While they were probably meant in jest, continued exposure to her sarcasm affected Molly's spirits. Occasionally she needed to get away from Carrie's prying. The girl had noticed how Molly looked around every corner and jumped when the courthouse door opened.

"Expecting someone?" she'd laughed.

No, Molly didn't expect anyone to come looking for her, but if Bailey did, she wanted him to catch her having the time of her life.

She paused when she reached the mimosa tree in Mr. Hernandez's yard. The man strolling through the intersection didn't see her, his morning promenade being one of intense reflection. Molly squinted at the curiosity. Strangers weren't unusual in Lockhart. As the jumping-off point of the cattle trail, cowboys comprised a large chunk of the landscape, but the man passing before her was no cowboy.

She fell into step behind him after he'd traveled a respectable distance. Where had she seen him before? Medium build, perfectly tailored suit, bowler hat—at the bank, of course. As if reenacting her memory, he reached into his coat and pulled something out. The wallet wasn't distinguishable until he dropped it on the ground.

"Oops." Molly covered her mouth.

He didn't hear her. She watched as he pushed aside his coat and stood with his hands on his hips contemplating the wallet. Why didn't he pick it up? It had fallen into a depression of sorts and was surely getting wetter the longer it remained in the puddle.

The man kicked at the wallet and missed. Molly stopped walking to observe the gentleman's odd behavior. With his cane, he dragged the wallet to higher ground and squatted next to it. Carefully taking his gloved hand, he tried to flip it open but jerked at the contact as if it'd bit him. He might be rich, but he was evidently as crazy as a loon.

He straightened, studied the wallet a moment longer, and then walked away, leaving it lying in the middle of the road. What kind of feathers filled his head?

"Excuse me, sir," she called out. "You forgot your wallet." He turned, and she giggled at his sheepish expression. His perfectly parted moustache stretched above generous lips and straight teeth as he grinned.

"Yes, well. I think I'll do my best to forget it. It's dreadfully soiled."

"You're going to leave it there? Someone will take it."

"I do hope so. I came to tour the Wild West, and frankly, you people aren't living up to your reputation. Since I haven't been held up at gunpoint, I'll make a donation. Yes, that will suffice."

Molly bent to appraise the full wallet, not forgetting to arrange her posture to her best advantage. She tilted her head up to him and let her eyes do the smiling for her. "Surely you jest. This is rainwater. Your bills are probably cleaner now than after they've passed through the hands of our local residents."

He grimaced at the revelation. "I don't mean to insult your sensibilities, but since I have no interest in reclaiming it, and since you would loathe touching—"

Before he could say another word, Molly snatched it up. Holding it away from her new gown, she shook it, knocking loose a few stray drops.

"I'll dry this out and have it to you tomorrow. I can't bear the thought of leaving your property behind."

"I really don't want it . . ."

"It will wash out."

". . . but I would be pleased if our paths crossed again."

"Oh." Molly stopped. She hadn't meant to elicit an invitation, but she wasn't about to turn one down. "I'm afraid we've not been—"

"Edward Pierrepont, at your service." He removed his hat and bowed. His sandy hair was lighter than his moustache. She'd guessed it. Wax. "I apologize that there's no one present to make proper introductions."

"Molly Lovelace. Pleased to meet you." Goodness, but she was glad she left without Carrie. Keeping his wallet safely away from her skirt, she resumed her stroll, not surprised when he joined her. On impulse she turned left. It would take them to the courthouse—eventually. "From where do you hail?"

"My family resides in New York most of the year."

"New York? How exhilarating. You left New York to come here?"

"It's not as you imagine, not if you live there, anyway. The pretenses, the intrigues." He shook his head. "I yearn for new horizons and adventure, while my set expects to be pampered like the Czarina's lapdog. Not me. I want to see the world."

"And have you?" Molly turned right at the intersection, hoping Mr. Pierrepont wouldn't notice how their path meandered.

"Of course. I took the required grand tour of Europe and then traveled even farther for family business—Constantinople, Moscow, Tangiers—and this journey will culminate in the Alaskan tundra. I loved the exotic. The sounds, the colors. Not the smells, necessarily." His wrinkled nose relaxed into a genuine smile. He really was quite handsome.

Molly had to tear her gaze away. She shouldn't be making cow eyes at him. He was a nomad, not husband material. But even rich New Yorkers had to marry someone, didn't they?

"Surely you want a family, a wife? Doesn't domestic felicity appeal to you?" Her heart raced at her brazenness, but if he was merely traveling through, why not have her curiosity satisfied?

He sighed and studied the rising sun before answering. "I deeply desire to have a woman at my side. Someone who would travel and explore with me. Someone with whom to

46

share my adventures. Who says a woman must stay by the hearth and wait for her wandering man? With ample funds, travel can be luxurious, even out here."

Molly pondered as they walked. This new data needed to be organized and filed. Like her tax payments, every idea should fit neatly into well-established categories. She might have to open a new ledger for this possibility. *Touring socialite.* Would he meet the parental requirements? Would a dalliance with a rich tourist release Mr. Fenton and her from their painful association?

All too soon she realized the courthouse was looming before them.

"I've enjoyed our stroll, Mr. Pierrepont, but my destination is ahead. Thank you for escorting me."

"To the courthouse? It'd be my pleasure to walk you to the door."

"No, no. That's unnecessary." No use in piquing Carrie's curiosity. "But what about your wallet?"

"You may find me at the McCulloch Hotel, with or without the wallet, but please don't trouble yourself. Our paths will cross again."

Molly blinked at the certainty in his voice.

"Now, if you'll excuse me, Miss Lovelace. My morning wanderings have left me somewhat disoriented. Isn't the hotel a block down Market Street?"

He'd noticed. She blushed in what she'd been told was a charming manner. "Yes, that's the most direct route. Good day, Mr. Pierrepont."

He tipped his hat and performed a complicated pirouette to avoid another puddle as he departed.

Molly filled her lungs with the damp morning air and steeled herself for another day at the thin mercies of Mr. Travis. She hoped he was in a fair mood. She hoped the river was high again. And since hoping was free, she'd hope that Bailey had found a job—one that paid generously.

Another week gone by and she hadn't heard from him. He was making good on his promise to keep his distance, but what if his reasons weren't as noble or charitable as he claimed? What if he had tired of her but didn't have the heart to tell her?

The man in the spiffy suit disappeared behind the livery stable as he turned the corner. How many opportunities might slip away while she waited for Bailey? Was he waiting for her?

4

Broken pickets littered the walkway and slowed Molly's progress. After work, Molly had dawdled at the courthouse, delaying her trip to Prue's, but once on the seedy street she couldn't get there quick enough. She lifted her skirt to fit her foot precisely between the staves lying on the ground. Of course, if she would've said no in the first place, she wouldn't be in this predicament. On afternoons like this, Molly's lack of fortitude irked her to no end.

Would you like to buy the matching bracelet? May I have this dance? Are you hungry for seconds? Usually her weaknesses didn't leave her quite so distraught, but when Prue asked, "Don't you want to join us for supper?" Molly found herself traipsing across the canal to the smoky neighborhood of the tanner, the butcher, and the blacksmith. The further she walked from the town square, the smaller the houses and the larger the families grew.

Molly stood before the McGraws' house and evaluated it as accurately as Mr. Travis the tax assessor could. How had Mr. Fenton endured his visits to the McGraws'? The house on San Antonio Street belonged to a different realm. Molly couldn't imagine what had enticed him so far from his natural habitat. Perhaps he had trouble saying no, as well.

"Be sure and come around front," Prue had admonished—as if Molly would dream of walking through the hazy yard amid the clanging iron and sweaty men. No indeed. So what was she doing eating dinner with them?

The last time she'd visited, Prue's mother had concocted a feast that made Molly long for the cuisine of Lola, the Lovelaces' cook, but Prue's mother had succumbed to consumption last year, leaving the quality of the meal she was about to consume in question. She hoped Prue knew her way around the kitchen, or the evening would be a complete disaster.

"Come on in," Prue called through the open window.

Molly hesitated inside the doorway, unsure where to hang her hat and shawl. The tiny half-moon table crowded the entryway, and the vase of chrysanthemums left little room for anything else. Molly buried her nose in the flowers before remembering she didn't like their smell. Even so, she had to admit the arrangement was gorgeous.

One step into the parlor brought her to the settee against the wall. She quickly dropped her wrap there and joined Prue in the kitchen.

"Can I help?"

"Sure. Can you make the gravy?"

"Gravy? Sorry." Molly scratched her elbow. "I could set the table."

Prue nodded toward the cupboard with the plates. The efficient kitchen hadn't changed since Molly's last visit. Although the décor was less than fashionable, it still possessed a pleasing ambiance. A little oasis of peace in the boisterous neighborhood.

The whisking noise stopped as Prue turned to Molly. "I

don't want you to be uncomfortable, but before the men join us, I'd appreciate it if we could have a little talk."

Molly's hand froze on the plates. Goose bumps appeared on her arm. So much for peace. Without lifting her eyes she pulled the plates down and began to place them around the table, as mute as a ladybug.

"It's about Mr. Fenton. I don't wish for any awkwardness to fester between us. While I still esteem him greatly, I recognize that he might not be God's plan for me. If that's the case, then I'll be forced to adjust my expectations, plain and simple. I'll trust that God has someone better."

The plate was chipped, right through the painted rose, but Prue had probably never noticed. Molly walked around the table to set the next plate in place.

"Prue, I told you he doesn't want to squire me around, but we have no choice."

"He does have a choice, and I'm disappointed with what he's chosen." Prue twisted a dishrag in her hands. "Of course, I still have feelings for him. Those don't just vanish, you know. It'd be nice if they would, but Mr. Fenton is the first man I've ever loved. I don't quite know how to get over him."

The plate clattered on the table. Could one ever recover from love? Maybe if Mr. Fenton embarrassed Prue in front of the entire church, it'd help her forget him.

Maybe not.

Conflicting agendas warred within Molly. She wanted to promise Prue she'd never speak to Mr. Fenton again, but if she refused to see him she might as well pack her bags and hop into the first lumber wagon back to Prairie Lea. Besides, until the finances at the mill were secured, she'd be foolish to insult the family that could loan them enough to stay solvent another season.

"Perhaps I should court someone else, Molly. Someone

who's nothing like Mr. Fenton. I need to dwell on the qualities that he lacks."

"I don't think that's helpful. Mr. Fenton and you suit each other quite well."

"Oh, come now. He can be frightfully priggish. So uptight." Prue straightened her back and turned to survey the room with her gaze dripping off her nose. She lowered her voice to a midtenor and proceeded with a decent imitation. "'I believe we were to meet at noon. It's now two past the hour.'"

Molly frowned, panic rising in her throat. "He's not that bad."

"Oh, yes he is." Prue took Molly's arm. "'Allow me to escort you, Miss Lovelace, but please don't walk too close. We mustn't incite gossip.'"

Molly twisted her arm out of Prue's grasp. What was wrong with her? Molly thought Prue's regard for Fenton was unshakeable. How could Molly escape her fate if he became unattached?

Molly took cotton napkins to place around the table. "Mr. Fenton holds you in the highest regard. He's reliable and steady."

"Then perhaps I need to find someone different, someone impulsive and exciting, someone who laughs easily and drinks life to the lees."

"I don't know if I'd recommend—" But her caution was interrupted.

"What's for supper?" Mr. McGraw bellowed from the doorway.

"Ham and potatoes. Come and get it."

Counting the plates on the table, Molly panicked. She'd set a place for herself and the four McGraws, forgetting Mrs. McGraw's passing. Why hadn't Prue corrected her? She reached for the plate, but someone caught her wrist.

"You aren't going to let me eat?"

"Bailey?"

She blinked, not trusting her eyes. Had he followed her there? No one else seemed surprised at his presence.

"Nice of you to join us tonight," Bailey said.

"How did you know I'd be here?" She turned stunned eyes to Prue, who set the gravy boat on the table, as serene as ever.

Mr. McGraw smiled. "That's right. Y'all know each other, don't you?"

"Yes, sir. Molly and I are old friends." His eyes danced, although tears were running down his face.

Was he crying? What was going on?

"I . . . I'm not hungry." Molly held on to the back of the chair with white knuckles. "I think I'd better go."

"Nonsense." Bailey took her by the shoulders and directed her to a chair. "Prue's put together a fine meal, and she's quite the chef. Isn't that right, Cookie?"

"Please don't call me that," Prue said. "I don't appreciate being compared to your trail cook."

"The comparison's to your credit."

"But it shows a lack of . . ." She untied her apron and tossed it on the counter. "Maybe it doesn't matter. I was telling Molly I need to be more . . . what was it? Impulsive?" Prue carried the last dish to the table and then seated herself. Bailey took the seat next to her, opposite Molly.

Molly squirmed on the hard chair, unable to drag her eyes off Prue. It couldn't be. Proper, cautious Prue wasn't interested in Bailey, was she?

She had to get her wits about her. With a start, Molly realized she'd passed the food around the table without filling her plate. Bailey noticed, too. Silently he raised an eyebrow and nodded to her plate. He lifted the platter of ham and passed it her way a second time.

Molly scowled. She'd just as soon eat her leather boot as the slab of ham, but she must partake. She speared a thick piece and tried not to notice Bailey's approval. Molly tossed her curls. They wouldn't get the best of her. If eating could prove her unaffected by the ambush, she'd put food away like a sow at the trough.

"This is right nice y'all eating together," Prue's brother said. "If Mr. Fenton were here, we'd have a tableful."

His barb went uncommented upon, but nothing said could've rivaled the silence for discomfort.

Mr. Fenton. Molly wished she'd never heard of the man. Why had she allowed her parents to convince her to take after him? He belonged to Prue. She had half a mind to summon him before Prue became fonder of his absence. Molly's mouthful of meat seemed to expand the longer she chewed. She'd have to swallow it whole.

Junior spoke up again. "But at least you stopped crying, Bailey. Things must be looking up."

Molly had forgotten the tears. Could he be missing her? She looked at his now clear face, and just as she reached for her glass, he winked.

"Watch what you're doing," Junior cried, but it was too late.

Molly's glass tipped and a flood of tea rushed across the table and onto Bailey's lap.

"Whoa there!" Bailey jumped out of his seat, sending the chair crashing to the floor.

"Oh no." Molly threw her napkin on the table to stop the rivulets streaming off the edge onto Prue's clean kitchen floor.

General chaos broke out as Prue went for a mop and Mr. McGraw removed the dishes so the soaked tablecloth could be taken away. Molly dove onto the floor with the dish towel, crawling awkwardly with her bustle bouncing above her.

Bailey met her midway under the table. "It was only a wink," he whispered. "No reason to drench me."

Molly tilted her head up, inches from his face. Why, oh why, did her heart have to beat like a hummingbird's wings? Why couldn't her anger prevent the fluttering in her stomach?

Fluttering or no, his unsettling smile must be dispelled.

Lifting the saturated dish towel over his head, she squeezed it, sending a cascade of dirty tea rolling down his face.

"I have every reason to drench you," she cooed and willed the butterflies to calm before she rose to help her shocked hostess.

"But you mustn't walk by yourself," Prue said to Molly after supper as she gestured to the street. "This neighborhood isn't safe at night."

Bailey, stretching with his arms overhead and enjoying the early winter evening, almost missed his cue. "I'll see her home."

Was it wrong that he enjoyed the glower Molly shot his direction? He stepped off the porch and rubbed his belly. "It's the least I can do for my hostess after that bang-up meal. I couldn't eat another bite."

"Perhaps we could do it again." Prue leaned against the porch rail.

"Sounds dandy," Bailey said. "Aunt Frances won't miss having me at her supper table. That's a fact. You might check with your pa, though. I don't think I'm going to be working for him much longer. Not with the havoc the smoke plays on my eyes."

"Smoke? That's what's wrong with you?" Molly blurted.

"What did you think? That I was spilling tears over some heartbreak?" But Bailey couldn't be sure she'd heard, for she was already marching down the street unescorted.

Prue chuckled low. "You two make quite the pair. Better catch her before a vagrant crosses her path and she beats him senseless."

"You're right. Thanks again, Prue." He settled his hat on his tea-damp head and trotted after Molly, who was plowing a path through the scraps of former fences left in the walkway.

Instead of wasting time offering his arm, Bailey took Molly's and directed her to the street. She tried to pull away.

"What's wrong? We're in public. Are you afraid I've lost my convictions?"

"No, but your shirt is wet. It's getting my sleeve dirty."

He grinned and pulled her arm even tighter against his side. "It'd be dry if you hadn't baptized me under the table."

"I didn't think you'd mind—seeing how you've got so much religion these days." Her eyes flashed blue above rosy cheeks.

"Why are you worked up? You aren't still mad at me, are you?"

Her little chin jutted out like a billy goat's preparing to butt heads. Charming. 'Specially knowing that anger wasn't what ailed her. It was jealousy. Bailey couldn't hide his smile. Prue had been right, but would Molly admit it?

"I'm sorry to hear that you'll once again be unemployed," she said. "Can't say that I'm surprised, though."

"Thanks for the encouragement." He thought about winking but remembered the tea.

"Well, if you learned a skill like blacksmithing, you might accidentally stumble into an income. Then, if you weren't careful, you could find yourself in the uncomfortable position of having to marry me like you've threatened." The jutting chin disappeared beneath a smug smile.

"Believe me, if I find myself dangerously close to being able to support a wife, I'll be sure to call our families together and

56

see what they suggest. We'll meet at the church for a discussion. You should come, too. Show up in white—"

He didn't want to stop just as her confidence was returning, but the situation at a vacant house ahead of them demanded attention. Standing on a porch the size of a cowhide was a dingy little girl peering into the window.

"No one lives there." He frowned and went to the gate, trying to remember who the child belonged to. "Do you need help?"

The girl turned, took a bite of a sticky bun, and nodded solemnly.

Bailey held the gate open and motioned Molly into the yard.

The house stood abandoned, the flower beds brimming with winter weeds and blooms past their season. The girl's dress had seen better days, too. With grimy fingers wrapped around her treat, she walked out to meet them.

"I'm supposed to be home before dark, but my kitty ran into this haunted house." Her big brown eyes never left his, but she must've seen his amusement, for she set him straight immediately. "It *is* haunted. That's why it's for sale. Old Lady Ridens don't want to share her bed with a haint no more."

Share a bed? Oh boy. Bailey saw Molly dimple, trying not to laugh at the girl's story, and the movement drew the child's attention to her.

"Say, you're dressed up real pretty like." She took inventory of Molly's skirt trimmings of braid and fringe. "Like the pictures in the catalogs."

Molly gasped and pressed a hand to her chest. She peered triumphantly through her eyelashes at Bailey. He chuckled. As if he needed a ragamuffin to draw his attention to how Molly looked.

"Thank you, honey. And don't you have the cutest—" Molly's enthusiasm wilted.

Even Bailey could see the girl's plain frock sported only one strand of eyelet lace, broken loose and dangling. A ribbon that should've been retired years ago captured fewer strands of dirty hair than it released.

"Freckles?" he offered, and Molly threw him a grateful smile.

Bailey's heart warmed as she knelt and fished through her reticule for a handkerchief. He should've known she'd spiff up the child. His little sisters always begged him to bring Molly home, relishing the attention she lavished on them.

The girl slurped sticky bun off her finger but held still for Molly's attentions. "When I get big, will I look like you?"

"Only if you're lucky, sweetie," Molly said. "Lucky and willing to spend two hours at your dressing table every morning, scads of money on your wardrobe, and have the patience to religiously scour *Harper's Bazaar* for the latest fashions." After a few swipes at the glaze, she gave up and pulled the sticky handkerchief off of the girl's face. Sighing, Molly fished a three-cent piece from her bag and dropped it into the child's hand.

"Tomorrow morning you go buy yourself a fresh hair ribbon." Molly stood and tugged at her snug bodice. "And no more sticky buns. You'll regret every bite some day."

"Don't pay her no mind," Bailey said. "She does everything she can to disguise what God gave her. If she'd spend half the effort, she'd get twice the results." He really shouldn't be looking at Molly like that. What had Weston said about repeatedly falling into temptation?

"Now, let's get that cat of yours before the haint does," he said.

Pushing through the unlocked door, Bailey walked into the dark building.

The creaking hinges sent chills up Molly's back. She didn't believe in ghosts. Not usually, but sunset in the questionable part of town wouldn't be the time or place to learn she was mistaken. Boards creaked as she felt her way further into the house.

"Bailey, don't go by yourself." Molly tiptoed to the nearest window and slid the tattered curtains open, making use of the last of the sunlight. "Can you hear me?"

No answer came from the dark hallway.

The girl at the door peeked in. "He's d-dead. The haints got him."

"Don't be ridiculous." But why didn't he answer?

Molly crept closer to the giant stone fireplace, trying to hide herself between it and whatever lurked in the shadows of the hall. Footsteps sounded, coming toward them. The child's eyes grew large, and Molly backed into the fireplace to hide.

"Meow!"

Something landed on her neck.

"Bailey, help me." Molly streaked across the dusky room screaming and swatting at her back. "Some beast has a hold of me. Get it off." She touched something hairy and screamed again.

"It's not a beast," the girl cried. But if it wasn't an animal, Molly's ideas about the afterlife were shattered.

Bailey ran into the room and removed the life-threatening menace, but not before it hooked a slender claw in her neck.

Bailey handed the kitten to the little girl, who cradled it in her arms. She kept her grasp on the now fuzzy sticky bun, choosing to let the three-cent piece drop on the scuffed floor instead.

"You best keep your money, miss. If you don't know the difference between a kitten and a haint, you might should spend less time in front of the mirror." She spun on her bare foot and marched proudly out the door.

"The little ingrate." Molly was appalled but bent to retrieve her coin nonetheless.

Bailey chuckled.

"I don't expect you to be as insulted as I am, but would it pain you to hide your amusement?" she said. "Surely you don't approve of such haughty behavior in children."

"Absolutely not. Someone needs to take her down a peg . . ." Molly nodded.

". . . before she grows up and some poor fellow falls in love with her."

Molly drew a heart with the toe of her boot on the dusty floor and then rubbed it into oblivion. "I thought you'd sworn off talk like that—to me anyway."

He crossed his arms and leaned against the wall. "Talk like what? I'm merely discussing the failure of a child's mother to teach her values. I didn't say which child. There's many a lesson to be learned when confronted with ill behavior."

"You sound like Reverend Stoker." Molly reached up and gingerly touched her hat. "Did that churl destroy my bonnet?"

"I'm more worried about the scratch. Let me see."

He took her by the elbow and turned her from him. Molly felt his fingers trace a tender path from her hairline to her collar. She stood absolutely still, waiting until he was finished to breathe again.

"It's too dark to see, but it raised a line. You'd better get some iodine on that before it scars." He stepped away.

"Serves me right, venturing across the canal."

"It's not that bad. The McGraws have a nice house—and look at this place. Even a beginning blacksmith could afford this."

"But you aren't smithing anymore."

"There are other jobs. I hear they're looking for a bailiff."

"Too late. I met the new man today." It was the truth, but maybe she could've said it a little nicer.

Bailey seemed to pull from his inexhaustible reserve of optimism. "So I'll find something else—butcher, baker, candlestick maker—they all have houses and families. You don't have to live on San Antonio Street to be happy. There's nothing wrong with starting small."

Replacing an errant hatpin, Molly cocked an eyebrow. "Like this hovel? Where would the maid sleep?"

"We wouldn't want a maid, not when it could be just the two of us. Alone. Real cozy like." He didn't come any closer, but his voice reached out to her and pulled her into a warm embrace.

"You should see the kitchen," he continued. "It's the perfect size—everything at your fingertips. No hollering across a giant dining room. And for this parlor we could drop a nice sofa right here in front of the fireplace. Wouldn't that be perfect for days like today? Cuddling under a quilt until one of us decided it was time for bed."

True, the room did have nice trim and a pretty fireplace. A few simple pieces of furniture would finish it off. Medallion backed or cherub? While Molly couldn't decide which sofa would best enhance the space, she could clearly imagine herself pulled up against Bailey's chest, her feet tucked under a blanket, watching the fire spark and dance. To have the privacy the little house afforded seemed a dream. Surely even she could manage to keep a few rooms clean without a maid. So caught was Molly by the possibilities that she didn't realize she was alone until she heard a noise in the hall.

What was he thinking? Bailey wandered into a deserted room and made his way to the window overlooking the ramshackle yard. Daylight had all but disappeared and with it his good sense. Nothing about this house would appeal to her. He'd have to do better before he could make an offer. And why had he even mentioned the bailiff job to her before he'd checked it out? Another missed opportunity. Another reason for her to doubt him.

Maybe he could find a job in sales. His pa always said he could talk a fish out of water. Something with commission would be good.

"What would you put in this room?"

The twilight lit the room enough to see her in the doorway, and he had to look. Could it be that Molly still had hope for him? Could she truly be satisfied with something so humble?

"It's the bedroom." He stepped out of the way to allow her in, the darkness amplifying the scent of her lilac fragrance. Her skirt brushed against him as she turned.

"A large wardrobe would fit in here. Mother always said my clothes needed a room of their own, but this is spacious enough. Where would you put the bed?"

He gritted his teeth. Why had God cursed him with a conscience? They were alone. At dusk. Any other red-blooded man wouldn't hesitate, but he'd given his word. Whether she appreciated the sacrifice he was making or not, Molly was off limits.

Ignoring her question he trudged out of the house. Keeping your convictions had to be easier around homely women.

"Don't leave me in here." Molly ran to the front door and skidded to a stop when she saw him. Worry filled her blue eyes. "Are you angry?"

"Yes, but not at you. Come on. This is no place for us to linger."

She still cared. That much was obvious, but he couldn't do anything about it. Not yet. And he was no closer than he'd been a month ago.

5

To Do List:

· *Convince Mr. Fenton to let me peruse Father's account book at the bank.*
· *Buy powder to cover nasty scratch on my neck.*
· *Return the stranger's wallet.*

With her hands on her hips Molly surveyed the articles of clothing strewn across her sunny room at Mrs. Truman's boardinghouse. Tidying her wardrobe didn't suit her mood this fine Saturday morning. If she had an excuse to gad about town, she'd use it, but the bank was closed, and without getting some allowance from her father, a trip to the emporium was pointless.

That left a call at the McCulloch Hotel as her only option. Between inquiring after available positions for Bailey and mentally arranging furnishings for a cottage, Molly had completely forgotten the wallet and bills drying on her towel rack, but now that she thought about it, a trip to the McCulloch Hotel seemed horribly inappropriate. What business did she have making a call on a complete stranger?

On the other hand, she couldn't stay indoors on such a beautiful day. Tucking the bills into the water-stained leather,

Molly checked her appearance in the mirror above her wash-stand. Finding nothing unbecoming, she grabbed a wrap and hurried down the stairs, leaving her chaotic mess behind. One quick trip and she'd be done with it. She'd leave the wallet at the manager's desk and she would have the burden off her hands.

The street carried very little traffic—foot or hoof. Had her parents noticed that she was staying in town on the weekends now? Not that she'd seen Bailey much in Lockhart, but the long drive to Prairie Lea had certainly lost its allure.

Molly pulled her wrap closer against the cool morning air. The real question was how long could she remain in Lockhart if she continued to avoid Mr. Fenton. Word traveled quickly. One sighting of him with Prue on his arm and her parents would demand an explanation. Her days of freedom might be coming to an end.

She approached the two-story hotel and found it unmarred by the revel-makers' antics of the night before. A sigh of relief escaped, for there were no drunkards to step around, no broken bottles to avoid.

Maybe this was why her father didn't trust her to live on her own. She'd made her share of mistakes in the past, and visiting a hotel early in the morning might qualify as another. Molly didn't want to scandalize her parents. She didn't want to embarrass them or make them unhappy, but neither was she willing to give up her independence for their whims. Had they truly been needy she might consider a marriage of convenience, but she wouldn't walk the aisle with a stranger so her mother could preside over the wedding of the decade. She wouldn't marry a man so her father could invest in a new millstone. They weren't desperate.

The foyer of the hotel was as quiet as the outside. Good thing. Maybe she could go on her way without being recognized. She craned her neck to peer into the office, reluctant to ring the bell on the countertop.

Clearing her throat produced the result she sought. Feet swung off a desk and a corpulent man appeared.

"Yes, sir. I believe this wallet belongs to a boarder here."

The man took the offered wallet and flipped it open.

"Who does it belong to?"

"If you'll give it to Mr. Pierrepont, I'd be much obliged."

"What? Did I hear my name?" The voice from the balcony fell pleasantly on her ears, even though it meant she wouldn't be sneaking away undetected.

"Mr. Pierrepont, I didn't want to disturb you. It's not quite visiting hours."

He descended and took her hand. Wearing gloves indoors? An eccentric was he? Only the wealthy were allowed such indulgences.

"Far be it for me to set limits on our acquaintance," he said. "I'm 'at home' for visits at your convenience. Please allow me to escort you to my parlor."

He took Molly's arm, but as they approached the staircase, she gripped the banister.

"I beg your pardon, Mr. Pierrepont. I have no intention of going upstairs." Molly looked over her shoulder, relieved to see the manager had returned to his office. "You must be mistaken."

His reassuring smile instantly set her at ease. "My suite includes a drawing room, but I acquiesce to your superior knowledge of local propriety." He gestured to the front door. "Perhaps you would accompany me on my morning stroll?"

He'd taken her reprimand so graciously she couldn't refuse.

"I apologize for not returning your property sooner. I—" Molly halted. What was her excuse? *I've been mooning over my beau and forgot all about you?*

"Please don't. I didn't expect you to bother. Besides, I returned from a cattle drive only yesterday."

"Cattle drive? In November? No one in their right mind—" She covered her mouth.

"Perfect description of me, I fear. Not in my right mind. That's what the cattleman said, too, but when I adequately expressed my desire to experience this Western phenomenon, he arranged a short adventure. Even had his hands set up a camp so we could retire outside under the stars—for an extra sum, of course."

Molly lifted an eyebrow. "You paid a cowboy extra to sleep outside? I'm afraid someone's pulling the wool over your eyes."

"I disagree. I see well enough to appreciate the exquisite pointed Basque cut of your gown. I didn't expect the latest fashion in bodices down here. The Chantilly lace is a nice touch, as well."

Molly stopped in her tracks. No man she'd ever met noticed anything about her clothing beyond color (Bailey) and price (her father). She wasn't sure if this was a pleasing development or not.

"How did you come to know so much about women's clothing?"

His answer was cut off by the appearance of a wagon brimming with lumber, her father, and her brother.

"Molly Parmelia Lovelace, what are you doing out this early?" her father said.

She panicked. Too late to hide. Too late to disassociate from her escort. "Father, Nicholas, may I present Mr. Edward Pierrepont?"

But her father ignored the introduction. "What's this I hear about Mr. Fenton? Have you refused to see him?"

"Of course not, Father. I've been occupied this week."

66

"We'll have plenty of time to talk on the way home," her father said. "You pack your trunk while we make this delivery, and we'll meet you at the boardinghouse in an hour. If you're going to let Mr. Fenton slip through your fingers, you have no reason to live in town."

Molly was speechless. Just like that? Her job, her friends, her room—it was all to be taken away that quickly? Nicholas, looking much too dapper to deliver lumber, shot her a look of sympathy but didn't intervene.

If only there were some way of mollifying her father. Her mouth went dry. *Mollify*. What a word! Had her parents named her with a view toward their expectations?

She wouldn't go down without a fight.

Molly gripped Mr. Pierrepont's arm tightly and prayed he would understand. "Father, I thought perhaps you might rather stay in town and dine with Mr. Pierrepont. He's a friend of mine, a businessman all the way from New York."

Nicholas leaned forward, his eyes merry. "New York, you say? What type of business?"

Quick as a wink she turned to Mr. Pierrepont. Truthfully, she had no idea what his answer would be, but she needn't have worried.

"I have trusts I manage personally. Funds, investments— that sort of thing. My family has been very successful in land speculation, large tracts in particular."

"Molly's in the land business herself." Nicholas gave Molly a lopsided grin. "It says so right on her door at the courthouse—Land Office."

Her father's eyes glinted. He was obviously intrigued. She hoped Mr. Pierrepont didn't mind being dangled as bait.

"Dinner." Thomas Lovelace yanked his watch out of a too-tight pocket. "Maybe we could make it a second breakfast. I don't want to wait around until noon."

Molly turned to catch Mr. Pierrepont's response, fearful he would balk at her insinuation, but his eyes met hers in a gaze that was surprisingly familiar considering their brief acquaintance.

"That would be delightful. Haven't I been telling you, lovey, how much I wanted to meet your parents? And you were worried that we might not get an opportunity with them living all the way out in . . ."

She swallowed. "Prairie Lea."

"Ah, yes. Good old Prairie Lea." If he didn't wipe that syrupy smile off his face, he would draw flies. He turned to Molly's father. "But I do hope you aren't going to deprive me of Miss Lovelace's company by taking her home. I fear I'm growing attached to having her here in town."

Oh, my stars. Molly feared he was overshooting, but judging from the look on her father's face, he'd hit the bull's-eye.

"Naw, she's got an important job to do here. I wouldn't cart her off. Just a little playacting on my part. Molly knows I'm funning her." He forced the watch into his pocket. "Be at the diner in an hour? Good day."

Molly's feet were nailed to the ground. As the wagon creaked away, Nicholas looked over his shoulder and wagged his eyebrows at her. Now her brother had a whole hour to think of ways to crack her story. And they had an hour to prepare.

But first things first.

"Lovey?" She removed her hand from his grasp and crossed her arms.

Unabashed, Mr. Pierrepont smiled. "Perhaps the endearment was bad taste. In my eagerness to replace the unfortunate Mr. Fenton, I might have overstepped my bounds, but come. We have an hour in which to concoct a fascinating account of our relationship, and I can think of nowhere better to plot and plan than at the millinery."

"You're going to buy a hat?" He was insane. She'd thrown her lot in with a moonstruck fool.

"Yes, because that monstrosity on your head should've been put in the missionary barrel with the rest of last season's clothes. Never commission a new gown without a matching hat. Didn't you know that?"

Molly covered her hat with one hand, her mouth a perfect O.

"When I'm in a good mood, I spend money," he continued, "and I find that while I generally have a cheerful temperament, today's performance has put me in . . . What was it the cowboy said this week? In clover?"

"But you can't buy me anything. We've barely met," Molly protested, even as she directed him to the preferred milliner.

"Money is completely impersonal. What difference does it make if I buy a hat for you or a harness for a horse? There's a need and I have the funds. Not complicated in the least." He narrowed his eyes at her. "Complicated would be an intelligent, competent woman allowing someone else to make her decisions for her. That would be incomprehensible."

He waited for her reply. The door to the milliner's wasn't going to open itself. Molly reached for the handle, but Mr. Pierrepont stopped her.

"Tell me, Molly, and I must call you Molly if we are going to successfully mislead your father, are you satisfied with your lot? Do you want to go through life being nothing more than a cunningly painted marionette?"

She jerked on the handle. "You, *Mr. Pierrepont*, are insulting."

"If I thought you incapable of setting your own course, that would be insulting. But why would you replace your dreams for his? Is it possible you have no ambitions of your own?"

It was a fair question. Did she have no ambition beyond outmaneuvering her parents? Was her goal of financial independence any loftier than her father's? Still, it rankled to have a stranger identify the heart of her problem so effortlessly. Maybe there was more to Mr. Pierrepont—Edward—than she'd expected.

Bailey didn't mind spending the long winter evenings helping Reverend Stoker with repairs, but going on home visits was even more interesting than patching the parsonage roof. Between Prairie Lea and Lockhart there were many who relied on Reverend Stoker when they needed more than a weekly sermon.

"Thanks for coming with me." Reverend Stoker hopped across a small gulley that had washed out the path. "My wife was right. You have a heart for ministry."

Bailey chewed the straw in his mouth into submission before answering. "If this is what you call ministry, then maybe I do have a knack for it. I always thought parsons just preached. Never been keen on that."

"What are you keen on, if you don't mind my asking? I heard you're quitting the blacksmith."

Bailey grunted. "Not sure what's next. I really thought it'd be easier than this. That God would be clearer in His directions."

Their path took a sharp incline before they reached the Schmidt home. Reverend Stoker huffed with the effort.

"Remember the Hebrews," the pastor said. "They wandered forty years before they reached the Promised Land."

"I don't think Molly's going to wait forty years."

Mrs. Schmidt watched their approach through checkered curtains and met them at the door before Reverend Stoker could knock.

"Come in. He's in the bedroom."

For a woman with a husband on death's door, she seemed remarkably composed. Bracing himself for what he might see, Bailey followed Stoker inside. As promised, there lay Mr. Schmidt in his nightcap, reading comfortably before the window.

"What are you doing here? Oh no." His eyes flashed as he slammed the book down on the nightstand. "Is this Gretchen's doing?"

"Mr. Schmidt, we're here to visit and pray with you if you'll allow us."

The reverend didn't need to go any further, because Mr. Schmidt was on his feet, barreling out of the room.

"Where's that wife of mine? Gretchen!"

Bailey backed into the parlor, unsure if they were witnessing a miracle or a crime.

"I told you I would send for the preacher. You wouldn't listen." She poured a glass of milk and took a sip, indifferent to his ire.

"This is preposterous!"

"Any man who stays in bed and makes his wife chop firewood must be on death's door," she said. "Two days with a fever, not so much as a cough since then. You tell me what's wrong."

The man flung himself into the rocker and pulled on his boots. Bailey looked away to spare himself more flashes of the hairy legs beneath the nightshirt.

"Mr. Schmidt, while I'm glad you're feeling better—"

"You want firewood, then I'll get firewood, but if I catch another cold, my blood will be on your hands. The parson's my witness. My blood on your hands." And he stomped out to the woodshed, nightshirt billowing in the breeze.

Bailey chewed the inside of his lip to keep from smiling. Mrs. Schmidt set her glass down and stood with hands folded.

"Thank you for stopping by. Seems like he's on the road to recovery."

"I don't approve, Mrs. Schmidt." Stoker's white eyebrows lowered over reproving eyes.

"I apologize, but very few avenues were available to me."

"Besides patience?"

She raised her chin but didn't possess the nerve to meet his gaze. "Once again, I'm sorry to disturb your evening."

Clearly unrepentant, but what was the good reverend to do? "Excuse me, ma'am. I think I'll give your husband a hand with the firewood," Stoker said.

Bailey was on his heels to follow when Mrs. Schmidt stopped him.

"I haven't had a chance to tell you, young man, but I was impressed by the stand you took at church."

He didn't have to ask her to clarify. His repentance had garnered all sorts of unwanted attention. "Thank you, but I wasn't trying to impress anyone. Just trying to settle with God."

"And that's the fastest way to it. There's some who'll lead you astray. Some who don't care about their souls."

Bailey's neck grew hot as he discovered sympathy anew for Mr. Schmidt. Where did Mrs. Schmidt get the misguided idea that Molly was the problem? He hadn't insinuated that, had he?

"Ma'am, I'm afraid you misunderstand. I had no grand plans. I was scared to death and knew I needed to do something about it."

"If everyone had the courage to correct wrong when they see it, like you and me, the world would be one step closer to glory." She looked out the window at her husband swinging the ax in his nightshirt.

As distasteful as the woman's attitude was, she had stumbled into some truth. While his actions with Molly grieved the Lord, surely his willingness to address his sin pleased Him. His decision to stand before his parents, his church, and Reverend Stoker had been one of the most difficult of his life, but he'd done it. And although it still wasn't easy, missing Molly and leaving his family while he tried to establish himself, he was shouldering the responsibility. He was persevering.

Maybe God could find a use for someone like him.

"All week her father has boasted about the gentleman from New York who dined with Nicholas and him." Adele Lovelace beamed at Edward as she directed the waiter to add cream to her tea. "And I had to wait until today to meet the man who convinced Thomas that Molly must stay in Lockhart. For days my curiosity has been denied, but I must confess the pleasure of your acquaintance was worth the wait."

The candelabrum sparkled, scattering its reflected light across the sapphire walls and the cherry buffet. Who would've thought the private dining room at the McCulloch Hotel would be so elegant? When Molly's mother began to press for an introduction to their most promising candidate, Molly had stalled, but once the practicality of furthering their ruse became clear, she feared that Edward would not be up to the task of impressing her more finicky parent.

She needn't have worried.

The paste jewels in her mother's plumed hat clinked against each other with each nod as Edward shared tidbits of New York society gossip. He spoke with a quiet authority, the power of his voice being all that was necessary to knit together a world completely foreign to them. Molly could almost forget that her interest in him was contrived, for he possessed the knack of turning words into reality. Music seemed to swell above the sound of the rowdy Friday dinner crowd in the public area. The scent of lilies filled Molly's head, although the Chinese vases held odorless silk flowers.

Long after the waiter had removed their empty plates, after the proprietor had asked if they required any further service, Edward continued his tales as Adele pretended to recognize the names he dropped like shimmering gold coins into a marble fountain.

"The opulence I can only imagine." The flames from the candelabrum reflected in Adele's eyes. "You must think us entirely gauche—riding up to meet you in a lumber wagon."

Molly's father roused himself from his after-supper nap, the cushion of his seat hissing under the pressure. "Russell had to make a deposit at the bank, and we had planks to deliver. Three birds with one stone." His eyes closed again drowsily as his head tilted to his shoulder.

From the corner of her eye, Molly could tell that Edward had turned his golden gaze toward her. To blush would be to acknowledge his lovelorn expression. She looked to her mother instead and was shocked to see more warmth, more appreciation in her smile than she'd ever witnessed before. All because of the approval of a stranger.

Her father was no better. Thomas Lovelace had followed the conversation closely during the meal. After reflection, he had admitted a familiarity with the Pierrepont family—not that he knew them, really, but he had heard of them, something to do with foreign affairs in Washington. Whatever the case, he was impressed, and once Edward's suitability was established, Thomas's interest waned. They might as well call Reverend Stoker and settle the matter.

Edward was still looking at her. Molly's heart hiccuped. Edward Pierrepont was the real McCoy, connected to the best families of the land. Could life in New York truly glitter as he described? She folded her napkin and laid it on the table. He told good stories—that was all. If she wasn't careful, she'd believe the rest of his tale—that she was the sole reason for him to stay in town, that he couldn't bear to leave without her. Foolishness, but a tantalizing foolishness at that.

"Thomas, wake up," her mother said. "Russell is probably waiting on us."

"He can wait." But her father grunted and strained to rise out of his chair. "It's been a real pleasure, Mr. Pierrepont. You'll come out to our place next time, won't you?"

Edward held Molly's chair as she rose. "I'd love to, Mr. Lovelace, but my time here is uncertain. I'm on my way north and would like to get as far as possible before the weather prohibits further travel. I've already delayed longer than prudent."

"Alaska isn't going anywhere. You might as well tie up your business here before running off." The waggling eyebrows did nothing to hide her father's meaning.

"Come, Thomas," her mother said. "Don't frighten the man away. We wouldn't want to break Molly's heart."

Good gravy! "Mother, why don't you and Father wait inside? Edward and I will see if the wagon is back."

She beamed. "That's a fine idea. Ask the waiter to bring our wraps."

Even with the doors closed, Edward kept to her side, dutifully playing his part. "I'm in a conundrum."

Molly lifted an eyebrow.

"This subterfuge has begun to weary me."

He wanted out? "I understand. You can't keep me safe from their plotting forever."

"Perhaps I can," he said.

He wore the same expression that had impressed her mother, but why? There were no parents observing them now.

Molly was pressed against his side as they squeezed out the doorway, crowded by a line of cowboys entering. She banged into the frame of the door as Edward was jostled by a dusty straggler wearing his slouch hat indoors.

"Hear, hear," he said. "Take heed of the lady."

A sterner reproach was on her lips until the man turned. His puffy, bloodshot eyes were proof that Michael James had conquered more than one bottle of whiskey that morning and would be in a foul mood until he'd bested another.

He sneered. "Are you talking to me?"

"Yes, sir, I am." Edward pulled her behind him and squared his shoulders. "I'm willing to overlook your carelessness, but you owe the lady an apology."

What was he doing? If Edward Pierrepont wanted a taste of the Wild West, he was about to get it, along with a belly-ful of his own teeth.

"I'm fine, Edward. Let's go." She pulled at his sleeve.

Michael James leaned into Edward's face. His sour breath drifted over Edward's shoulder to assault Molly's nostrils. "Sounds like your woman is worried you might get hurt. She knows I could mess up her pretty little friend."

"Michael James," Molly warned. "Your father will be along any minute. Please don't embarrass him in front of everyone."

"There's no shame in running off fancy-pants fellows who don't belong here. Varmint control. That's all."

Edward tugged on his glove, tightening it over his fist. "Push me," he said.

"Edward!" Molly couldn't believe her ears. He couldn't know that Michael James was a notorious brawler. He couldn't know that he spent more Sundays in jail than a parson spent in the pulpit, but couldn't he see the obvious size difference? Before she could explain to Edward the folly of his actions, Michael James shoved him on the shoulder. The sneer on Michael's face didn't disappear, but suddenly his eyes widened and his head snapped. And Molly saw that his nose was bloodied, his lip split.

"Edward, you broke his nose," she gasped.

"That's the only move I know, lovey. If he has any fight left—"

"Why you . . ." Michael James lowered his head and charged at Edward, arms spread wide. Molly screamed and jumped aside. He did have fight left and more than Edward was equipped to handle, but he was determined to give a good account for himself. With a powerful swing upward, Edward connected with Michael's unprotected face before he was tackled, but once on the ground beneath the bigger man, he could hardly escape a pummeling.

Molly's screams brought men running from every direction. Thankfully, the besotted attacker wasn't in his finest form and was quickly restrained by a couple of drovers. Hauling him to his feet, they pulled him away—right into his father's path.

"Michael!" Russell James searched his bloodied face. "You weren't harassing Miss Lovelace, were you?"

"Of course he was." Thomas burst through the doors, somehow considering himself an expert witness, even though he'd been inside. "Your no-account son attacked my daughter and her escort."

"He didn't attack us, per se." Edward sat up. "I wouldn't go that far."

But Michael didn't stay around to appreciate Edward's balanced report. He'd vanished between buildings before the law could be summoned.

"I apologize, sir." Russell passed his handkerchief to Edward, who dabbed at a cut above his eye. "When Michael is in his cups, he doesn't know what he's doing. It's no excuse, but—"

"When has he ever known what he's doing?" Thomas bellowed. "It's a bad reflection on me when my employee is involved in a brawl in the middle—"

"Russell wasn't involved." Molly knelt to aid her hero, but he would need nothing more than a cold compress and a new pair of gloves.

"Still," her father continued. "I can't have you dragging my name through the mud. Go tend to your son, and I'll tend to business." And with that, Thomas Lovelace marched to the wagon, leaving Russell at a loss before the gathering crowd.

Edward extended his hand to Russell and used his help to rise. "Thank you for your assistance."

"I . . . I'm mortified at my son's behavior. He could've seriously hurt you."

"Yes, he could've, but as long as Miss Lovelace isn't inconvenienced, there's no harm done." His eyes twinkled. "I traveled many miles for such an adventure."

6

Despite Thomas's tantrum, Russell James did return to work the next week, and Molly's mother was grateful, or so her letter said. As much as Thomas claimed to be disgusted with the Jameses' family situation, Russell was a loyal employee, and Thomas would be hard-pressed to replace him.

Molly tucked her mother's letter into her reticule and turned her attention to the man sitting across from her at the picnic table on the courthouse lawn, but she was too late to catch his words.

"I'm sorry. I wasn't attending," she said. "Could you repeat that?"

Edward's indulgent smile belied the words. "I'm leaving soon. The porter is preparing my railcar for the trip north even as we speak."

"Ah, the infamous railcar. You've never shown it to me. What's it like?"

"It's more ornate than the dining room at the McCulloch Hotel." His eyes twinkled. "But I love it anyway."

"I can't imagine traveling across the country in luxury. I rode from Luling to Austin once, and I was so sore I couldn't walk down Congress Avenue without hobbling. And the places you must see, how sophisticated compared to Caldwell County."

Molly slid her hands into her new mink muff and pulled it tight against her stomach while she imagined herself on a velvet sofa watching the world fly by her picture window. It was fortunate that her parents didn't know about the railcar. They'd be furious enough when they learned that Edward Pierrepont had slipped the net. Molly frowned. It was of no consequence what her parents thought. She would miss Edward. The winter sun looked a bit brighter every time he called, and he never called empty-handed. If Edward left, would she be forced to choose the comfortably rich Fenton over the richly uncomfortable Bailey?

"I'm not leaving today, pet, but I appreciate that woebegone expression."

"When must you go?"

"We have to prepare first, but it shouldn't take long."

Molly's back straightened. *We?* Surely he didn't mean it, but Edward's face carried the same imperturbable expression as always.

Her parents would be thrilled, but what about Bailey? Had he heard about Edward? Part of her wanted Bailey to realize she didn't have to wait on him, but she wouldn't seriously consider leaving him.

"Molly, I'm not ready for our relationship to end. While this may have begun as a ruse, I find it's grown into much more." His moustache twitched once before settling over determined lips. "I can't bear to leave you here under your father's thumb forever. It's not my place to judge your family, but I don't think they appreciate the intelligent woman you are. With me, you'll have the freedom to express yourself, to be the woman you want to be."

"I've spent a fair amount of time imagining my future, but never did it take place outside of Caldwell County."

"But you'll consider it? I could certainly use your help investing my legacy. My family has been after me for years to take more interest in the family finances, and I think I could learn to enjoy the dreadful task with your help." Before she was ready, Edward stood. "But now for a treat. I want to make another purchase on your behalf."

Molly stroked the mink. "I must refuse. It's unseemly." Good thing she wasn't under oath. The chilly wind had pinked her cheeks and made her blue eyes sparkle. At least that's what she'd been counting on when she'd let him purchase the powder blue frock coat. Present such a pretty picture that Bailey would find her irresistible.

"Unseemly?" He laughed. "The taxpayers will question county salaries if you don't admit the source of your new duds."

"Maybe it's acceptable in New York, but this is Texas. A man doesn't buy clothing for a woman unless . . ." She lowered her eyes. She didn't want to encourage him further.

Edward took Molly's elbow and assisted her to her feet. "Isn't there a cobbler on Market Street? Let's get you measured for climbing boots. Shoes should be exempt from your warped sense of propriety."

"Climbing boots? There aren't any mountains around here."

"You never know when they might come in handy. Go on, unless walking unescorted will soil your reputation. I must send a wire, but I'll be there directly."

Molly pushed a curl behind her ear. She could only imagine the nature of his wire. Was he notifying his family? Was he sending for more money? She felt his eyes follow her as she made her way across the dried yellow lawn and the busy street.

Her thoughts raced ahead. Why did she need climbing boots? She generally disliked all manner of physical exertion, but his secretive mien intrigued her. She walked past the barber shop and the mercantile, her breath quick and shallow. Was he going to propose? Already? They hadn't known each other long, but he seemed to be an impatient man. He'd probably never been refused anything in his life. Would she be the first?

And was he truly besotted with her? Edward's eyes didn't burn with the same intensity as Bailey's. She couldn't imagine him getting sulky when she tarried with another man. For her part, Molly didn't miss the possessiveness she felt whenever Bailey spoke to an eligible lady, the fear and uncertainty she suffered, wishing they could be together, wondering if they ever would.

Edward was warmth while Bailey was fire. Edward was pleasant, civilized. Bailey's excitement often threatened to sweep her along in the current, dragging her away from her family's carefully structured plans, but maybe that had changed. For all she knew, Bailey burned for Prue now. From Carrie's reports, they'd been seen around town enjoying each other's company.

The bell jangled as she entered Mr. Hernandez's shop.

"Have a seat," the shoemaker's lilting voice called out. "Someone will be with you in a minute."

Molly chose a high-backed chair and turned to watch the shoppers passing by the window. She breathed deeply of the leather scent. Did the seats in the Pierrepont private railcar smell this good?

Marrying Edward could give her father the financial stability he desired. No longer would their fortunes depend on the amount of water in the rain gauge. As far as her mother was concerned, Edward's social connections placed him far ahead of anyone in their acquaintance. Of course, Molly wouldn't live in Caldwell County any longer, but think of the places she'd go and the people she'd meet. Her parents would pass around her letters describing her adventures from family to family, everyone awed at how far in society their little Molly had risen. Climbing boots might be the perfect accessory after all.

The stool before her creaked. Molly straightened in her chair to face the attendant.

Like a prairie dog, this man popped up everywhere.

"What are you doing here?" she asked Bailey.

She gripped the arms of her chair. He never left her thoughts. Not a moment passed that she wasn't wondering where he was, what he was doing, but little had she expected him to appear at her feet.

Bailey smiled, as if he expected her pleasure to match his own. "Miss Lovelace, how nice to see you." Without pausing for permission he reached under her hem and pulled her foot out to hook her heel on the edge of his stool, his leather apron hanging between his knees spread akimbo on either side of her. "I'm new to shoemaking, but I think these boots need to come off to measure you."

"Is there someone else who could help me?" She swallowed as his fingers brushed where they shouldn't. Explaining Edward was going to take finesse. She didn't have time to spare.

"I'm doing what Mr. Hernandez pays me to do. Besides, you're the one who keeps showing up at my place of employment." He untied the lace that crisscrossed halfway up her shin. With sure movements he ripped the strap through the eyelets at the top and worked his way down to her ankle.

"What kind of shoe are we commissioning for you?"

He was cheerful. Too cheerful. Molly ground her teeth together, knowing the situation could explode like a powder keg.

"I'll do that." She pulled her foot down and bent to finish the job he'd begun. "I need climbing boots."

Bailey frowned. "When have you ever stepped off the board-walk?"

"I didn't ask you." She kicked the boot off her foot. "Where is Mr. Hernandez?"

Molly jumped when the bell rang again. She pulled her skirt down primly as Edward entered the building. He eased himself into the empty chair next to her and crossed his leg. Pulling out his watch fob, he frowned and then returned it. "Continue, please. Don't mind me."

Edward's foot tapped lightly against the floor. A mallet pounded somewhere behind the red velvet curtain, but Bailey was silent.

At her feet he remained motionless. He didn't move until she raised her face to meet his brown eyes. Unbelief. Hurt. Not until he'd inaudibly communicated his reproach did he reach behind him and produce a sheet of heavy white paper. Pulling out a short pencil tucked behind his ear, he made some notes on the bottom corner, the scratching noise of the soft lead audible in the still room.

"Climbing boots, you say?" His tone had lost the cheerfulness it'd had before. Molly missed it, hating that she'd destroyed it. "What specifications, exactly?" His head was bent over the page, pencil poised.

"I don't know," she croaked. Why was her throat so raspy? She looked to Edward, whose face grew thoughtful.

"Oh, they need to be tall but flexible. Sturdy, low heel for a good grip."

"You mean for real mountains? Moccasin looking?"

"Precisely." Edward beamed. "That's exactly what I mean."

"Are you planning to accompany the lady? We could make you some, if I can find a man's form in such a small size."

Edward laughed easily. "No, my friend. I won't need any, but if you are going to try to sell extra pairs, it doesn't do to insult the customer."

Molly bit her lip. She didn't like this. It seemed impossible that the two of them could be in the same room. They occupied different spheres, different arenas of her life that should never overlap. Edward was fantasy, an apparition that served a temporary need. Bailey was her future, although an uncertain future.

She squared her shoulders. She couldn't allow Bailey to humiliate her again. Not in front of Edward. "We're in a hurry. Please measure me so we can be about our business."

Bailey's eyes smoldered, but he laid the paper flat on the floor. Rising, Molly stepped with her stockinged foot onto the paper. On his knees went Bailey. He covered her foot with his left hand without hesitation—a warm and steady pressure—and pressed the pencil against her instep. Molly glanced at Edward's spotless gloves. Naturally Bailey didn't pause before touching her. Only on unfamiliar ground did one proceed with caution.

Once again Molly couldn't see his face—or hardly his head—over her billowing skirt as he leaned in closer to judge the pattern as he traced.

How could she be so conflicted? How could she want to draw Bailey to her, run her fingers through his hair, and talk for hours about all that had happened? All that had happened? Edward's offer was what had happened, and Bailey wouldn't want to hear about it. The burden she most needed to share, the situation she could most use advice on, she had to find her way alone.

She forced herself to breathe as his pencil worked its way around her toes and along the outside of her foot. Molly didn't dare look at Edward but sensed that he was messing with his gold watch again. What was taking Bailey so long?

"Are you about done?" She wished he would look up to see the impatience in her eyes that she didn't have the nerve to express with her tone.

The pencil finished its trek behind her heel and back to the beginning point. Not allowing his hand to linger a moment longer than necessary, Bailey sat back on his heels. Molly moved her foot so that Bailey could examine the sketch. "That'll do."

Edward nodded. "All right, lovey"—Molly winced at the endearment— "remove your other boot and let's get your left foot traced."

"That's unnecessary. We can reverse the pattern and use it for both." Standing, Bailey turned his back to them and started toward the red velvet curtain that led to the workroom.

"How soon will they be done?" Edward called.

"You can give them to her for Christmas." Bailey's steps never slowed as he slung the curtain behind him and disappeared from view.

Bailey spread the paper smooth and leaned heavily against the work table, elbows locked, shoulders up around his ears.

She belonged to him. How could she sit within arm's reach—in his grasp, even—and allow another man to call her *lovey*? Molly knew better.

He squeezed the tabletop until he thought it'd crumble in his hands. She didn't love that man. Impossible. If she loved that other fellow, wouldn't she be following his every move with those blue eyes? Wouldn't she spark when the city dandy took her arm the way she trembled while he traced her foot?

Bailey straightened and pounded the table with his fist.

He'd hurt her when he broke off their courtship, but his ardor hadn't cooled. Was she testing him? Trying to make him miserable in hopes that he would get his act together more quickly? Well, she was doing a fine job plaguing him, but did that other fellow understand she wasn't available?

"See to the man up front." Hernandez sped by, snatching his awl off the workbench.

Bailey left his sketch on the board and headed to the storefront. How much more cash did he need before he could resume their relationship? How much before God opened the chute and set him free again? His commissions on shoe sales were adding up. 'Course Christmas came only once a year, but he'd have enough to set up housekeeping if Molly could be content with something similar to the little house in Prue's neighborhood. Would it be soon enough?

"Mr. Garner, just the man I'm looking for." Mr. Fenton stood, stance wide, arms crossed, as if daring Bailey to try to push him over.

"You found him." Bailey removed the pencil from behind his ear and tossed it onto the countertop. "How may I help you?"

"It's come to my attention that you are mooning for a woman who is far superior to you."

Bailey shrugged. "I don't deny it. What's on your mind?"

"I came to appeal to your sense of decency. I can better provide for a wife. I'm already established and offer a secure living for a family."

Bailey held up his hand to interrupt. "So if another bloke showed up with deeper pockets, you'd step aside?"

"I don't think that's likely."

"Hate to tell you, but you're beating a dead horse. I'm not the one standing in your way."

Fenton's mouth twitched. Bailey could tell he wanted to know more, but he restrained himself from asking.

"I don't fear the future, Mr. Garner. Not when happiness is within my grasp. If you'll excuse me, I must be about my plans."

Bailey almost choked. Drivel. Unless he was on a stage, a grown man didn't voice such ridiculous sentiments. *Happiness within his grasp?* Maybe Fenton would go home and stitch it on a sampler. He'd need something to fill his lonely nights, because Molly sure as shooting wasn't interested in him any longer.

 7

No lamp from within the modest yellow house shone to light her way through the dark yard. Molly crept close enough to spot the wash line tied to the porch-swing chain. According to the courthouse records, this was the address, and if she remembered correctly, she'd heard that Bailey's aunt Frances let her children swing after she hung the laundry in the hopes that the movement would dry it faster. With all the washing she took in, those children must have unflappable balance.

Now, how to find the correct window? All were opened to take advantage of the cool weather. Molly crept to the left and heard unabashed snoring wafting over the sill. If that was who she thought it was, she'd turn around and sneak back to Mrs. Truman's boardinghouse immediately. She wanted nothing to do with any man capable of such offensive noises.

Bracing herself against the wall, she paused to gather her thoughts.

Edward would be leaving soon, and his invitation to her had been clear. Although it wasn't accompanied by an engagement ring and a nervous speech from one knee, he wanted to marry her—and soon. She'd tried to keep the news from her parents, but they sensed that a culmination was imminent.

Letters arrived daily from her mother asking for updates. Her father actually snubbed Mr. Fenton at the barbershop during his last visit to Lockhart. They smelled victory.

She saw defeat.

Molly gathered her skirt out of the crackling leaves. Without the bustle to fluff it out, it hung as flat as a cow's tail and tangled around her ankles. No matter. She could hardly have crawled out the kitchen window with additional padding. Tight enough fit as it was. Besides, no one would see her this time of evening, and even if they did she wouldn't be recognized wrapped in her old cloak. With her hand against the clapboard siding she worked her way to the back porch, around the kitchen windows, to the lone room on the other side of the house.

There she heard him. Tentatively, gently, the guitar strings released a melody, one note plucked at a time. Molly crouched under the window and listened to him drowsily croon the ballad. That voice meant so much to her. Teasing, encouraging, adoring—the most precious words ever said to her had been spoken by that voice, and she wanted to hear more.

Molly pulled her hood back and adjusted her hair. No reason to be unprepared. Considering how much trouble she'd gone through sneaking out of Mrs. Truman's, she might as well make an impression.

Molly stood and peered through the open window. The music stopped. She couldn't see in, but obviously he could see out.

"Who's that lady, Uncle Bailey?"

Oh, fickle pickle! Molly dropped to her knees, but it was too late.

The slow, drowsy voice she'd been listening for answered. "Probably Slue-Foot Sue. Was she riding a catfish?"

"I didn't see one," a boy's voice replied.

"Well, I'll check. You stay in bed."

The metal frame creaked, and Bailey's head appeared above hers. "I'm sorry, ma'am. Pecos Bill doesn't live here. You have the wrong house."

"It's really her?" The bed bounced again.

A quick frown and he vanished into the dark room. "Appears so. No lady I know would be sneaking around at night unless it was that brazen Slue-Foot Sue. Now you get to sleep. I played you the moon song like I promised. I'm going to sneak to the kitchen for a drink, but when I come back I want to hear you snoring like your pa."

Something rustled inside and Molly heard the distinct snap of suspenders. A tiny shock ran up her spine. Good thing she couldn't see in the window. She hadn't considered the peril of peeking into a man's bedchamber at night.

Trying not to rustle the leaves, she reached the back porch just as Bailey eased the door closed behind him. No wonder the suspenders had snapped so loudly. They'd hit bare skin.

He crossed his arms over his chest and came to the edge of the porch. Not wanting to raise her voice, Molly started toward him. Her foot hit the porch step, but with an outstretched hand he stopped her.

"No you don't. Get over there." He motioned to a spot on the other side of the rosebushes lining the balustrade.

"My goodness, Bailey. Are you that scared of me?" But her voice shook. There was so much of him. Skin everywhere she looked.

"Don't you have this confused?" he asked. "In the fairy tales isn't the prince supposed to come to the sleeping maiden's window?"

"I don't read fairy tales. In real life, nothing good happens while you sleep, only wrinkles."

"Then say what you have to say. We shouldn't be alone at

night in a place like this." He motioned wide to the moonlit yard, his complete naked span from fingertip to fingertip exposed.

Her breath caught. Until now she'd only guessed what he looked like, based on the hard muscles she felt through his clothing. If she had known . . .

"Don't look at me like that. I swear, if anyone deserved to be kidnapped and dragged to the parson, it's you. If your father had any idea how you go looking for trouble, he'd lock you up."

"It's your own fault. How am I supposed to forget?"

A hoot owl startled them both. Molly waited until the bird finished its call, waited for the sparks between them to calm, before she spoke.

"You really hurt me, pushing me away like you did." She pulled a stem from the rosebush and began breaking off the thorns. "I understand why, but it still hurt."

"I know." She could feel his heavy gaze on her as he spoke. "I thought it was for the best."

"This doesn't feel best."

"Amen, sister."

Him and his religious talk.

Come to think of it, she had a confession, too. "Since then, I've acted shamefully. I've tried to upset you and make you jealous." A thorn stuck her finger. She squeezed it until a dark drop appeared. "No matter what happens next, it's not out of spite. I want you to know I wouldn't go that far."

The wind moved the bushes, scratching the banister and sending the cloying scent of old blooms into the air.

"Have you already decided what happens next?" Bailey bent at the waist and rested his arms atop the simple wood railing. "Mr. Fenton told me he's ready to declare his intentions. I have to applaud you. Looks like you've been successful."

Molly blinked and then waved that suggestion away like a horsefly. "Fenton? Never. I'm not interested in that pompous goat."

"You played interested not too long ago. Has someone else caught your eye?"

She squirmed. Had Edward Pierrepont fulfilled all her aspirations, or had he made it clear that no one would replace Bailey?

"How's your job with the cobbler?" she asked.

"Sales couldn't be better, but I've been a disappointment to Mr. Hernandez in the workshop. He tried to teach me to make those tiny stitches, but they're impossible to see. Once the Christmas rush slows down, I'll most likely be looking for another position."

"That's too bad." Molly wrung every drop of disappointment out of the words until they were left dry. "Do you think you'll be unemployed again?"

He nodded.

"Mr. Pierrepont—that man who bought me the boots—he's leaving soon."

"'Bout time."

"He wants me to go with him."

The balustrade creaked under Bailey's weight. Molly looked away, unable to bear the hurt on his face. The crickets chirped. She pulled her cloak around her tighter, wishing she could creep inside and hide.

"And you don't know what you're going to do?" His voice fell gently, almost sympathetically.

"You don't understand. Every dance lesson, every music teacher Mother hired was to prepare me for an advantageous marriage. My parents raised themselves from obscurity to prominence. For me to marry poorly would be a reversal of fortunes for my family. Still, I'd do it for you—if you were ready."

"Wait for me, Molly. There's no hurry."

"I waited on Weston, and he married someone else. What if you do, too? What if you fall in love with Prue? In the meanwhile, my corset's getting tighter, my cheeks are getting paler—"

"I haven't noticed."

"But I'm not young anymore. Besides, once Edward leaves I won't have that opportunity again."

"If he loves you—" Bailey's voice caught, but he forced the words out— "he'll come back."

Molly didn't answer.

"He loves you, right?"

Did he? Edward must or he wouldn't offer marriage. With his riches and position, he wasn't desperate. Any girl would be lucky to catch him, just as any girl would be lucky to secure Bailey's regard.

"That's not a requirement according to my parents. You know my situation."

"And I'm doing everything I can to get you out of it." Even in the dark she couldn't miss the longing in his eyes.

Molly moved toward him and stepped into the rosebush.

"Ouch!" She pulled away, snatching her cloak from the grasp of the thorns she'd missed.

"My hedge of protection." He chuckled. "Those church folks are praying for us. I hope while they pray for my defense against your charms, they remember to pray for my financial situation, as well."

His efforts to cheer her weren't lost on Molly. Her frown relaxed into a smile that he shared until their gazes deepened, and then he broke it off. Just as well. At least one of them had some sense.

Bailey straightened and surveyed the dark homes around them. "No one can tell you what you want, Molly. You're a big girl and will have to live with your decision. But for now, I'm going to do everything I can to help you, even if it means sending you to your room. You really shouldn't be out alone at night."

"Fiddle. These streets are as safe as Grandmother's parlor."

"Not hardly. If you want to talk, don't wait until dark—unless that's the only time you can escape your escort."

She shrugged a shoulder. "You get to bed. I won't keep you up any longer."

"Yes you will."

And even after Molly reached the alley she could still make him out, standing on the porch behind the rosebushes.

December eighteenth marked the one-year anniversary of the reopening of Bradford's Mercantile, and it was swarming like an anthill drenched in lemonade. The cobbler had given Bailey a half day off to travel to Prairie Lea for the celebration, and the trip was worth it. His entire family would be in attendance. Even Molly's brother, visiting from Garber, had stayed to congratulate the proud shopkeeper.

"There's no finer store between here and Austin." Nicholas Lovelace slapped a beaming Deacon Bradford on the back. When Deacon's mercantile burned down a couple of years earlier, many wondered if the customers lost to the bigger towns of Lockhart and Luling would ever return to little Prairie Lea, but they had proved loyal to the kind shopkeeper. "Your one-year anniversary and everything still looks brand-new. What do you think, Mol?"

Molly surveyed the smart displays, the pyramid of tin cans, and the notions arranged beneath the glass counter. Bailey knew she wouldn't be caught dead wearing any of the fabric, and goodness knew she had no use for the housewares and farm equipment, but she wouldn't let her brother outdo her in anything, especially flattery.

"I love Mr. Bradford's store. The shop exudes confidence while still possessing a welcoming atmosphere. You've put together an amazing selection in the past year." She turned an effusive smile to the gentleman. "First rate."

Bailey shook his head at Deacon's pleased stammering. Were all men so easily hoodwinked? Seeing through the exaggeration wasn't difficult when you weren't the target. 'Course he was no better.

"Molly can spot quality," her pa said, "but she wouldn't know a whisk from a rug beater."

Molly's eyes tightened, but her smile didn't falter. Laughter filled the room, and hers was the merriest of them all.

Bailey wasn't fooled. Something needed to be said in her defense. "Hey, Tuck," he called to his brother, allowing his voice to carry. "You said you needed help on your ciphering. You should ask Molly to look at your sums. She's a whiz at figures."

Mr. Lovelace's laughter twisted into a cough. He pointed at Tuck. "That's a fine idea, son. Women are helpful when it comes to making it past the schoolmarms. Don't know what good it does them later, but don't turn down help when you can get it."

Tuck scowled at Bailey and ducked out the door to join Samuel and the older boys, where there was less talk of ciphering and schoolmarms.

His mother, Mary Garner, left the refreshment table to join Molly. "Did you bring any food, or are you begging off everyone else?"

Bailey shook his head. He agreed Molly needed to make some effort when it came to bringing grub, but he grew defensive when his mother got involved. Between his ma and her pa, she was taking a beating.

Molly kept her chin up. "I'm sure Mother brought something. She said Lola was working in the kitchen until late last night."

"Lola has a husband, doesn't she?" Mary flipped a dish towel over her shoulder. "Yes, a good cook doesn't stay single long."

"Mother, what does Mrs. Lovelace's servant have to do with anything? You're fishing for trouble."

"Don't you talk that way to your ma." Bailey's father, George, shuffled between the aisles holding one of Bailey's little sisters by the hand. He winked at Molly. "At least not where she can hear it, or she'll make me do something about it."

"Oh, stop," Mary huffed. "It's no secret Molly wants to get married, and as far as I'm concerned, the sooner she does, the better. Adele is my dear friend, and if her daughter can't catch a husband, she won't mind me helping. I'd want someone to do the same for Susannah and Ida if, heaven forbid, they got to her age without a trip down the aisle."

Molly's smile faded. Bailey looked to his father for help. Once Mary Garner got started, it took a team of horses to redirect her.

"Now, dear, men marry for more than meat and taters. Miss Lovelace is so elegant that none of the bumpkins around here are up to snuff, but enough with this tomfoolery. You might want to check on Ida. She feels warm and says her throat hurts. She won't even try the sweets."

His mother knelt and placed the back of her hand against his sister's forehead. With a wrinkled brow she led the little girl away, allowing Bailey an unobstructed view of Molly. Her blond curls were swept up, exposing her delicate but stubborn jaw. Her black brows and lashes framed grateful bluebonnet eyes that turned toward him.

Reverend Stoker had said he could love her, hadn't he? Mighty generous of him, 'cause there was no way around it. Even knowing the trouble she could cause him, was already causing him, he couldn't help himself.

Before he could accompany her to the refreshments, Deacon asked his cousin Weston to pray a blessing on their gathering. With head bowed, Bailey breathed his own prayer. *I'm trying to do right, Lord. Have I done enough? Have I waited long enough? She's going to make a decision soon. You wouldn't let her leave, would you?*

Standing in lines had never appealed to Molly. It seemed like a waste of time. She'd much rather follow Bailey to a bench and wait. Whatever it took to avoid Mary Garner. Although Molly had known Mrs. Garner all her life, Bailey's mother frightened her. How could the woman speak plainly when Molly had to hide behind layer after layer of inflection and suggestion to get her meanings across?

"You'll have to excuse Mother. She thinks you've got me plumb hornswoggled." He patted the empty space next to him.

Molly sat. "Really? As far as I can tell I have no effect on you at all."

"Don't pretend that you need the situation explained again," he warned. "I know you're smarter than that."

"Don't be so sure." Thomas Lovelace stood before them with a plate laden with treats. "We all know she doesn't have a serious thought in her head. Isn't that right, sweetie?"

Bailey sat taller. "Molly's thoughts, when she chooses to share them, are usually quite interesting."

"Like whether to buy the green cloth or the yellow?" Thomas laughed.

"I was imagining a weightier decision," he said.

Molly met his dark eyes. She noticed the patient set of his mouth as he waited for her to defend herself, but she'd given up on that long ago.

"Now that I've had time to consider, I don't think I want either fabric. Gingham simply isn't being worn in town anymore."

She looked away to avoid his reproach. Why couldn't he understand? She wouldn't entertain pretenses of intelligence. Nothing could throw Thomas Lovelace into a foul mood more quickly.

Her father relaxed. "Before you leave, remind me to give you some extra funds. If Mr. Pierrepont wants to see you in a new gown, we'll consider it an investment." He tossed a gingerbread cookie into his mouth and ambled away, obviously pleased with himself.

Molly closed her eyes. As if she needed a reminder of Mr. Pierrepont's plans.

Then again, perhaps she did.

"Amazing how you can find room for all those numbers when you have a brain the size of a catfish's," Bailey said.

Molly shrugged. Intelligence wouldn't take her anywhere new—only force her to be discontent with her lot. And the discontent was growing. She'd taken a holiday from work to attend the event, and her father had ruined it.

Bailey elbowed her gently. "Don't think about him," he said. "Tell me about the courthouse. Are you still working on your shorthand?"

But even that topic couldn't cheer her. "Yes, but I've had to practice on my own. Evidently someone has been keeping Prue busy."

Bailey ignored her prying. "If you were the court stenographer, you'd have a decent income right in Lockhart. With a highfalutin job like that, you wouldn't need a rich husband."

A throat cleared. Molly's mother strolled past and raised her eyebrows. Bailey's father was watching, as well. Evidently their families thought their conversation treaded dangerous ground. They were probably right.

"Molly, don't let him keep you from the *comida*." Rosa, Molly's friend and former rival for Weston's attention, swayed as she spoke. Molly tapped the nose of the adorable dark-haired infant she was rocking in her arms. Maybe Bailey's mother was right. She could at least make an attempt at domesticity. It hadn't hurt Rosa any.

"I'll bring you a plate," Molly said to Bailey by way of reconciliation.

"What?" His mouth dropped open. "You're going to serve me refreshments? You're not sick, are you? Did you catch Ida's cold?"

Rosa giggled as Molly rose, and they squeezed their skirts down another crowded aisle. "How has the big city of Lockhart been treating my *amiga*?"

"I don't want to think of the big city. I want to enjoy my old friends today." She shot a glance at Bailey, but he was engrossed in the shorthand book she kept in her purse.

Rosa followed her gaze. "You want him back, no? Bailey is a good man."

"Yes, but my parents don't think he'll make a good husband. They would be devastated if I married him." Using the silver tongs, Molly lifted colorful petit fours and cookies and filled two plates, then added a piece of pecan pie to Bailey's.

With her free hand Rosa balanced a cup of punch on Molly's plates. "Everyone told me that Weston and I should be together, and I wished I'd listened sooner. So much advice people give, but only God knows."

"Fie on you, Rosa. Getting all serious. Trying to take Reverend Stoker's job?" Molly gave her a peck on her stunned cheek. "Don't you do any matchmaking. I've got enough trouble as it is."

She returned to the bench and sat next to Bailey, aware of the whispers that followed her. Well, her conscience was clear. Bailey hadn't so much as laid a finger on her since . . . oh, bother, since he'd seen to her scratched neck in the dark vacant house. Her heart fluttered at the memory. But besides that, well, he did touch her when he measured her feet, but that was necessary. He had to unlace her boot. Her eyes closed as the delicious thrill of his hands on her ankle revived. Maybe not completely necessary but excusable under any circumstances.

Molly startled. She found herself leaning against Bailey with both plates still in hand. She tried to scoot away.

"Careful there!" Grabbing her arm, he pulled her toward him and took his plate. "You're about to run out of bench. What's wrong with you?"

Now they had another contact to repent of.

"I was remembering . . ." What could she say? She popped an entire petit four into her mouth and shrugged. No answer necessary.

Bailey leaned forward to peer around the stack of canned goods between them and the nearest listener. "I'm glad you're here, Molly. I'll admit you got me worried the way you were talking the other night. Have you decided what you're going to do?"

"What is there to decide?" she asked. "I haven't had any proposals presented to me, have I? And besides, why are you trifling with me? If you were out of the way, my life would be—" she pursed her lips together—"simpler."

"Molly, come on over." Nicholas's head appeared above the pyramid of canned goods. "We need your courthouse knowledge."

"When have you ever liked simple?" Bailey asked as she slid

a sugar cookie onto his plate and went to join her brother across the room.

"Be sure and let us know how Ida is doing," her mother called to Mary as Molly walked past.

"She'll be fine. Probably the cold air getting to her." Bailey's mother wrapped her own coat around the little girl. "Now where did Samuel and Tuck go to? Are your brothers already in the wagon?"

Ida squirmed away. "I want to tell Bailey good-bye."

"Go on, then." Mary smiled. "The girls miss their big brother, what with him working in town and all. Samuel and Tuck are always after us to visit him, too."

And he was in town because of her. Molly straightened her cuffs as Ida wandered past her. She hadn't asked him to move to Lockhart, but was it wrong of her to wish he'd stay?

"Here's Molly. She'll know what's going on." Nicholas turned to her. "We were wondering about Anne Tillerton. Has she been cleared?"

"Yes. They completed the hearing last summer. The district attorney isn't interested in prosecuting her."

"I should think not." Rosa bit her lip. "She saved my life."

Which had surprised them all. Although Anne Tillerton had lived in Prairie Lea for a couple of years, she had remained a mystery. Her husband, Jay, was well known about town, but she never made an appearance. Only when Rosa and her mother-in-law, Louise, moved to the adjoining farm did the situation become clear.

Bailey's cousin Eliza broke off a piece of cookie and handed it to the child on her lap. "To think what she endured, living with that monster. I would have shot him myself long before he attacked another innocent woman."

"We can't judge," Rosa corrected her. "I'm thankful she acted when she did."

"Of course," Eliza amended. "Every woman in the county owes her for her bravery. If he were still around I wouldn't be safe in my own house."

"Yes you would." Molly wasn't surprised that Eliza's husband, Jake, spoke up. He wasn't one to miss an opportunity. "Don't imagine I'd cotton to that no-account dawdling around our place, but I have seen someone over the fence doing lots of target practice."

"Is that what the ruckus is?" Eliza fed their daughter, Cora, another bite of cookie. "I've seen the man traipsing through their property, still smooth-cheeked and slight. How old would you say he is?"

Weston frowned. "A man is living there? You don't suppose she's got a brother, do you?"

"Maybe her kin came down from Ohio," Jake said.

"Sounds like it bears checking into. Last thing Mrs. Tillerton needs is more man trouble." Weston stood and took Rosa's empty plate. "Maybe we could swing by on the ride home."

Eliza beamed at her brother. "Yes, do. Invite them to come over to our house. We could have a sing-along. I can't think of a more delightful way to spend an evening."

"I can." Jake grinned at his wife, who wisely chose to ignore his comment.

"Molly, you must accompany us." Eliza stood and lifted her daughter to her hip. "You haven't been to our place for ages, and I need your help with the soprano line. Nicholas can take you to Lockhart later."

Molly caught her father's eyes on her. A job could be a blistering nuisance, but it was her only excuse not to live at home. "Father will take me. I have to be at work early tomorrow, and it looks like the weather's fixing to turn. Perhaps next time."

Eliza graciously accepted her regrets and then worked her way through the friends and family, inviting them to the impromptu social.

Wraps were gathered, purchases were loaded into wagons, and the crowd dispersed early in search of another location to continue their fellowship. Molly watched as the last carriage full of young people rolled away from the hitching post, leaving her with her parents and the older set to tidy up.

Deacon's wife, Louise, rattled off a list of things that needed to be done in order to close the shop, but after "bank the fire" was "wipe down the counters," and Molly knew she'd found her job. Maybe she couldn't cook, but she'd stay and give a hand when everyone else her age was out for merriment. Well, almost everyone.

Bailey stood behind the counter shaking out an embroidered tablecloth, sewn by Rosa, no doubt. The tablecloth snapped like a bullwhip, flinging the crumbs in all directions. Molly could still picture his corded arms and bare chest, but she shouldn't. Instead, she thought of his family . . . and of her family's struggling sawmill. If he was determined to wed her, he needed to get his chicks in a row. Time was running out. Dare she encourage him? Molly straightened the small cap perched atop her curls. When it came to Bailey, there wasn't much she hadn't dared to do.

"Do you need help?"

"No, ma'am. Just cleaning up." He flung a sheet over the cashbox, causing the receipts to scatter in the breeze.

Molly knelt and dragged the closest papers toward her. "I hear you've been helping out at the church. I didn't realize how much it took to maintain the property."

"Reverend Stoker rides the circuit between here and Lockhart, but there's a lot to be done besides preaching." He turned serious, businesslike. Molly rarely saw this side of him—the side that belonged in the office more than the parlor. "Visiting people, keeping the grounds up, unlocking the building for meetings, Stoker can't keep both churches going without help. I fill in wherever he isn't."

Molly tidied the receipts and held them out to him. "You've been busy. Seems like everywhere I turn, you're working."

A crash sounded behind them. By the time Molly turned, all she saw was Deacon Bradford holding one end of a bench and her father crumpled on the floor under the opposite.

Bailey rushed past her. He lifted the bench off Mr. Lovelace and tossed it aside. What was wrong? The bench wasn't heavy enough to crush him, but her father wasn't getting up. He lay on his side, one arm straight, the other held to his chest.

"Get Dr. Trench," Louise called.

Bailey ran out the door.

Her mother cried as she raced across the room. Adele loosened his cravat and fanned his egg-colored face. Molly watched in horror as he gasped for breath, his eyes bulging, sweat running through his thinning hair. She was helpless, too stupefied to even pray.

Louise and Deacon joined hands and did the praying for her. Good thing. Why would God listen to her now? Shaking, Molly stumbled to her feet and ran for a water pitcher. Sloshing water all over the countertop, she filled the punch cup and ran to his side.

Before she could lift his head to the rim, she could tell that her father's struggle was alleviating. His breathing evened and his eyes closed more peacefully. Trembling, he sought his wife's hand. She snatched it and pressed it to her chest.

"Thomas, dear. Can you talk? What happened?"

"So sorry." He tried to swallow. "I'm afraid it's all over."

8

The kerosene flame flickered eerie shadows on the embossed wallpaper of the bedroom. Molly gripped her father's hand, wishing he'd match her strong grasp.

"You're sweet to stay with me while your mother talks to Dr. Trench. I don't want to die in here alone."

"Nonsense. Your spell is over and you survived. You'll be on your feet in no time." Taking her handkerchief, Molly mopped the sweat from his cold brow, stunned by how suddenly her world had been upended. It only took seconds for her father to change from a blustering choleric to an invalid. What other changes loomed?

"You have a good head on your shoulders," he said. "I know I don't give you credit often enough, but I never knew how to parent a girl. I tried to make you into something you weren't. Can you forgive me, honey?"

Molly squeezed his hand as tears sprang to her eyes. "Of course, Father. You had my best interests at heart. I know it's hard for you to understand how I could be happy without—"

Now his hold intensified.

"Listen to me, Molly. Your mother needs you more than ever. We need you. What if I can't work? What if I have another episode? We'll lose everything. That's a lot on your shoulders, but your brother is busy in Garber getting us new contracts. You are a reasonable woman. You understand it'd be counterproductive for him to return. We're relying on you to do your duty. We're trusting you to do your part."

Molly's eyes dimmed. "You need water," she whispered and extracted herself from his grip. Turning, she reached for the ceramic pitcher.

Her father couldn't force her to do anything. He couldn't drive the wagon to Lockhart and cart off her trunks now. He couldn't bully Mr. Travis into firing her while lying in his sickbed. In fact, her courthouse salary was more important than ever, but it wasn't enough. Not enough to replace her father's income.

And he trusted her.

She caught sight of herself in the mirror hanging over the bureau. Her blue eyes glowed, determined. How hard had she worked to prove herself to him? How long had she dreamt that he would someday acknowledge her intelligence and sense of responsibility?

And now it was up to her.

The door opened silently on oiled hinges. Doctor Trench looked from the bed to her and held the door open wide. Obediently, she rested the glass of water on the nightstand and left the room.

When she entered the parlor, Bailey pushed off the mantel he was leaning against and swung his hands behind his back. Nicholas was standing behind the sofa, patting her mother's shoulder as she cried into a dainty handkerchief. At Molly's approach her sobs burst with fresh strength.

"Did Dr. Trench tell you?" she asked. "The next attack will be stronger. Thomas must give up the business. No excitement. No competition. Nothing of the life he loves so. What will we do?"

"We'll do what the doctor says." Nicholas squeezed his mother's shoulder. "Keeping him calm will be of the utmost importance. The fewer disruptions for the family, the better."

"I suppose that's what he'd want." She sniffed. "You know your father. Take care of business and the rest will take care of itself."

Molly nodded, although she knew in her heart it wasn't true. What happened at the courthouse between eight and six had little bearing on the rest of her life, but she certainly didn't want to cross Mr. Travis now. "If you want me to work tomorrow, then Nick will have to take me. It's getting late."

Adele faltered. With a glance toward her son she said, "I'd hoped he would stay to help with your father tonight."

"I'll take her."

Molly had almost forgotten that Bailey was in the room, and when he spoke he didn't sound like her young man—just a man who would do what needed to be done. He didn't look away even as Mrs. Lovelace cast an uncertain glance toward Nicholas.

"You shouldn't have to worry about your daughter tonight. You have your hands full as it is, and I'm headed that way." He held his hand out toward Nicholas. "You can trust me."

Nicholas let out a big breath and took the offered hand. "Thanks, Bailey. Dr. Trench will be leaving soon, and I don't want Mother here alone. Besides, that wind is brutal." He turned to Molly. "If Dr. Trench is right, Father will be raring to go in no time. That's when life will get difficult. Until then, it's best we carry on."

Bailey slipped out to prepare the surrey while Molly gathered her valise and a lap robe. The fashionable parlor was designed for a game of charades or a musical evening, but sorrow seemed to settle into the room quite comfortably once there. Molly shuddered. What else would change before she could make her way home?

"We'll pray that Dr. Trench is wrong." Adele stood to wrap one arm around her daughter and the other around her son. "I don't know what will happen to us if Thomas can't work. We could put the mill on the market, but who would want to buy a business out here in Prairie Lea?" She patted Molly's shoulder. "Unless someone with means had a powerful attachment to this family, we couldn't hope to get enough out of it."

Molly stepped back. "Don't worry, Mother. You'll be fine. Everything is going to work out for the best. I promise."

The bare branches etched stark lines against the clouds. The horse kept his head low in defense against the sharp pellets of precipitation that fell against the lap robe in droplets. From the way they struck Bailey's face, he could've sworn they were ice.

Molly's left cheek was red from the pelting, but she didn't blink even at the gust of wind that nearly blew Bailey's hat off.

"What am I going to do?" she said at last. "Father is worried about the business, worried about the money, and he's counting on me to take care of Mother."

Bailey's neck tensed. "He's desperate. He's clutching at straws."

"But I *could* help. I'm not some emotional miss who faints away at trouble. I can do what needs to be done." The space between them grew as she tucked her lap robe beneath her. "I can, can't I? I can make myself do anything for my family."

How could he be so proud of her and so afraid for her in the same moment? "You don't have to. I won't let you."

"But what is right? What is noble? Do I sacrifice you, or do

I ask my parents to forget all the sacrifices they've made?" She looked at him through tear-stained eyes, the blue startlingly clear. "How can I turn my back on my parents when they need me? I won't be any help married to—"

She stopped, her lips already formed around the word *you*.

Bailey flexed his fingers. The promises he'd made to her family, to his church, and even to God didn't fit the situation. Everything had changed. He'd waited too long for the perfect circumstances. He was out of time.

"You can't sell yourself on their behalf. You mustn't listen to them." His voice grew raspy as he prayed that his words would have the desired effect. Never before had the stakes been so high. "I love you. I will always love you, Molly Parmelia Lovelace. We will get through this together."

She looked down, lashes fluttering on her cheeks. "You're the only man who has ever told me you love me, maybe the only man who ever will, but I have to consider everything. My decision affects more than the two of us."

He started to protest but closed his mouth with resolve. He'd been a gentleman, and he'd spun precariously close to disaster. He'd lose Molly if he didn't do something to overcome her objections, and they both knew what would wipe them clean off the map. Even the horse had veered off the road onto the familiar detour. His heart hammered as he came to his decision. Molly needed his reassurance. She asked for his love. What boundaries wouldn't he cross to save her for himself?

Moving the reins to one hand, he wrapped his arm around her shoulders and pulled her to his side. Molly looked up, her lips rising beneath his. "Molly, I . . ." Words failed him. All he had to do was lean close enough to inhale her lilac scent. Close enough to feel her warm breath.

Was he too late? Had she already decided against him? At

the first sweet taste of her lips, he realized it didn't matter. This heat between them, this connection would carry them through their doubts. He gave in to the force pulling him, deepening their kiss and speeding his heart. Ignoring the cold, Bailey dropped the reins and leaned her back against the surrey seat. Her bonnet caught on the bench and held until he untied the ribbon and tossed it to the side.

"I don't know what to do," she said. "I feel so alone—so afraid I'm going to fail."

"I'll take care of you. I promise."

"I don't see how." She brushed his hair out of his eyes. "Saying it doesn't make it so. I wish—"

But he had wishes of his own. Instead of following a set of rules he'd invented, he had to listen to his heart. Reaching to his side, he set the buggy brake. He moved the lap robe out of his way and pulled her against him, enjoying the gasp she uttered before he took her breath away. He wasn't playing. He was fighting a battle—turning a mighty tide. As much as he wanted to slow down, he couldn't. Her weak protests did nothing to discourage him. How far was he willing to go?

One lone prophet, some righteous remnant deep in his soul cried for sanity, for intervention, but he snuffed it out. There was too much at stake. God would have to forgive him, because he couldn't lose her again. Only that was unacceptable.

And now instead of pushing against him, she pulled him closer and held on as if she'd never let go.

And he knew he'd won.

A thrill raced through him as her hesitations vanished, and soon her porcelain skin was flushed with heat instead of cold. His fingers reached the buttons on the back of her bodice, and he contemplated the best way to proceed. He hadn't wanted it to be like this, but it would still be special between them. As long as they were together, nothing else mattered. As long as she could never leave him.

A twig snapped.

"May I be of assistance?" A thunderous voice cut through the cold night air.

Bailey yelped in surprise and bolted upright. Divine intervention? He fully expected to see an archangel, but the figure atop a horse lurking in the shadows little resembled anything celestial. If it was supernatural, it hailed from a realm warmer than the one to which Bailey had appealed, and he suddenly became aware of their isolated location.

Dangerous on many accounts.

 9

Molly gasped. The deep evening shadows hid the speaker from her view. Fearfully, she clutched at Bailey as he fumbled for a gun that wasn't there. Good thing, for as the man rode toward them she could see that Sheriff Colton already had his pistol out.

"Mr. Garner, Miss Lovelace. I didn't expect to run into you so far off the road. Did your horse get away from you?"

Molly pressed her hand against her chest, trying to rein in her runaway heart. Long seconds passed before Bailey could answer.

"She's fine now, but you gave me quite a scare, Sheriff." Bailey took to his side of the surrey, leaving Molly to squirm into a more dignified position unaided. "Don't like being caught unawares."

"I reckon not." The man's bushy brows rose over rheumy eyes. "You gotta keep your wits about you. No telling what kind of trouble you could stumble into."

The sheriff holstered his pistol as Molly fished her bonnet out from under the seat and crammed it onto her head. Even fully clothed and covered with the lap robe, she felt as exposed as Eve searching for fig leaves. With swollen lips and flushed face, there was no disguising her recent activity.

Would Sheriff Colton tell her parents? It would kill her father.

Poor Bailey pulled his coat tight, trying to cover the mess she'd made of his shirt.

"I'll ask again, do you need any assistance?" the sheriff growled.

"No, sir," Bailey said.

"I wasn't speaking to you. It's the lady that's my concern."

Molly cringed under his steely face. "I'm fine, thank you." But she wasn't.

The sheriff nodded, pulled at a plug of tobacco, and situated it inside his bottom lip. "Why don't we get you on the road. I don't mind accompanying you to town."

Molly shot Bailey a sideways glance as he released the brake and chucked to the horse. What a dreadful ending to a disastrous day. She'd tried to escape from the memory of her father crumpled on the floor, but now he'd die for sure when he learned of her behavior. And what would've happened if the sheriff hadn't intervened?

All of her worries returned tenfold. Her father's condition shifted even more responsibility to her shoulders. But who did she want at her side during this crisis? A stranger who knew no one and was unknown, or Bailey, whom she'd known since childhood and whose family had stuck by hers through thick and thin? If she didn't decide tonight, the decision would be made for her.

The night sounds, the howling wind scolded her. Irresponsible. Impure. Ungodly. All true, but also true was the love behind her weakness.

Sheriff Colton's mount fell into step next to the carriage. Bailey's attempts to engage the sheriff in casual conversation were successful, but Molly wasn't fooled. Despite his brave show, he was as overwhelmed as she.

She shivered, once again feeling the cold and smelling a freeze in the air. The safety of her room called, but Molly knew she'd find no comfort there. She'd rather be humiliated with Bailey than banished alone until morning. If only he could stay with her. He was her best friend, and she needed him. No, he was more than a friend. Her heart belonged to Bailey, and it was time they do something about it.

Before the wheels reached the ruts of the main road, Bailey had eased the sheriff's concerns so that the man gave no indication of remembering the circumstances of their meeting.

"The fish were biting, you say? I've never fished Mr. Schmidt's pond. Does he stock it?" Bailey stole frequent glances her way. She gave him a half smile. He hadn't forgotten her, although it would behoove both of them if Sheriff Colton did.

"Yes, so don't get caught out there without permission. That German gets angry."

"I'll keep that in mind. Don't want to make any trouble."

"I'd appreciate it. Stepped into a hornet's nest already this morning." The sheriff's mount nipped at their horse and was rewarded with a tail swipe in the face. "A man's body was found just south of the creek on Tillerton's land. A shooting."

"Shooting?" Molly gasped. "Who?"

"Saul Nimenko. He moved here recently."

"Saul Nimenko?" She leaned forward to look at the lawman. "Saul Nimenko, northwest part of Prairie Lea? Sixteen dollars and twenty-two cents annual property tax?"

His badge reflected the moonlight.

"How well do you know Mr. Nimenko?"

Bailey narrowed his eyes. "Yeah, how well do you know Mr. Nimenko?"

117

"Never met him, but his tax payment was delivered to the office last month."

"And you happened to remember the amount?" Bailey wasn't buying it.

She sighed. "Does 324 Cibilo Street mean anything to you?"

"That's my address!" Sheriff Colton said.

"Twenty-five dollars and fifteen cents." She smoothed her skirt.

"You're wrong there, ma'am. It's twenty-four something."

"That was last year."

The sheriff let a stream of tobacco fly across the dead grass. "I best have a talk with Mr. Travis."

As curious as she was about the body found on Anne Tillerton's land, Molly had faced enough tragedy for one day. The freezing rain was going strong by the time they reached Lockhart. Looking for warmth, Molly moved closer to Bailey, but he scooted in the opposite direction and stayed there until they reached the boardinghouse.

Would Carrie see her driven home in disgrace? Molly watched the windows of Mrs. Truman's anxiously, knowing the girl must wonder what had kept her so late on a Wednesday night. The horse halted in front of the gate, and as expected, a lamp appeared through Carrie's parted curtain. Molly blinked back the tears that threatened to reappear. Her rival would offer her no sympathy. Her father's attack would hold no interest for her nosy friend compared to her conspicuous arrival.

Bailey said his good-byes to the sheriff, but the man refused to depart.

"I think I'll wait to see Miss Lovelace safely inside."

So he hadn't forgotten. Bailey climbed down and lifted her valise over the side. Taking her hand, he helped her find her footing and escorted her to the porch, all under the watchful, bloodshot eyes of Sheriff Colton.

Bailey didn't release her arm until they stood before the door.

"Are you going to be all right?"

"Don't leave," she whispered.

"I don't have a choice." He stole a glance over his shoulder.

"I need you. Come back after he's gone." Molly rung the handles of her valise, dreading the empty room she'd be exiled to until morning. "Or even better, I'll sneak out and meet you."

"You'd better not. I've been rescued from my folly once already. Let's not test God any further."

She hung her head. Once again she'd soiled his conscience. He was right to keep his distance. Trouble followed her like goslings after a goose. But what did he mean? Was he giving up? They might have been foolish, but her decision remained intact. She chose Bailey, no matter what the circumstances. They would find a way. They must.

"You best get inside. You've been in the cold too long already."

Should she tell him, right there on the porch? Right in front of the sheriff and an eavesdropping Carrie? Should she beg him to marry her before she made a mistake worse than the one the sheriff had saved them from?

When she didn't move, he twisted the knob and held the door open. Carrie hopped back, barely spared a hit when it swung wide.

"Is that Bailey? Molly, where have you been and what's the sheriff doing?" She held her wrapper tightly together, slippered foot tapping.

Molly groaned. With one last searching, pleading gaze at Bailey, she straightened her shoulders, lifted her chin, and marched inside to take her medicine.

The next morning found Bailey at Reverend Stoker's, wishing he'd volunteered to help out at the local saloon rather than with the parson. It would have been easier on his conscience. He hadn't spilled his guts yet, but shame was eating away at him.

"Glad the cold spell blew through quickly. That kind of weather isn't compatible with my old bones." Reverend Stoker removed his coat and stretched under the tentative afternoon sun. "Once we get this step rebuilt, my wife will have no trouble getting off the porch. Every time she walks out the door, I'm reminded of my shortcomings." He laughed. "And those papists think clergy shouldn't marry. Cowards, that's what they are."

Cowards? Bailey took the plank the reverend held out to him and found the pencil mark showing him where to saw. He had the courage. Nothing he wanted more than a little wife and family. Nothing he wanted more? Was that his mistake?

"Talked to Deacon today," Stoker said. "He told me about Thomas's attack. You were there?"

Bailey leaned into his work and wondered how he was going to sidestep the stinking piles of the conversation. "Yeah, I was there. Figured he'd be walking the streets of gold today, from the looks of it."

"God is merciful."

I hope so.

Bailey plied through the board, sending sawdust flying in all directions. The scrap end of the plank dropped to the ground. Surely helping the reverend would absolve some of his guilt in God's ledger.

Stoker pushed his white hair out of his eyes and straightened. "How's Molly doing?"

"She's taking it hard, no doubt about it." He didn't say any more. Bailey dropped nails into his palm and nodded at the hammer. "We can chew the fat later. Don't want to keep you from your work."

A sly smile played at the corners of Stoker's mouth. "You are aware of my calling, aren't you? This is my work." The man watched him a moment before kneeling again and taking up the hammer. "Whenever you're ready. Something's bothering you, and I'm guessing it's more than concern over Thomas Lovelace's health."

Taking a board from the scrap pile, Bailey stood with handsaw in position. What could he say? How could he confess the same mistake twice? Dropping the saw and board, Bailey dusted the sawdust off his trousers, unsure what words were fixing to come out of his mouth.

"I should've known better, but I volunteered to drive her home."

"Aww," Stoker's eyebrows rose, "but you wouldn't lay a hand on a lady under those circumstances. No, the Lovelaces trust you, and for good reason."

Bailey turned away, unwilling to meet his eyes. "I don't know about that. Even with Mr. Lovelace stricken, Mrs. Lovelace still had reservations. I had to give my word." The handshake with Nicholas. Bailey's stomach turned. He'd looked the man square in the face.

"Don't be upset with Mrs. Lovelace. It takes time to earn trust. You might be eager to restore that relationship, but you can't blame her for being careful. Besides, she gave you another chance, didn't she? Prove yourself trustworthy and the next time won't be as hard for her."

Bailey turned desperate eyes to him. He had tried to seduce a woman while her father lay on his sickbed. What kind of man would do such a thing? He sat on the sawhorse. His throat tightened painfully. Pulling one knee to his chest, Bailey bowed under the guilt.

"But I was tempted." He shook his head. "Here she is crying and worrying about her pa, and I . . . I wanted to kiss her."

Wanted? His cheeks flamed at the half-truth, but even that tidbit was humiliating. The whole story would be unbearable. Bailey waited, hoping Stoker would bring the fire and brimstone, hoping the man would make him pay.

"Son, resisting temptation is a victory. You were in a delicate situation. The fact that you managed to withstand is admirable."

"No, I didn't . . . I mean . . ." His foot hit the ground. He picked up a hammer and swung it into his palm. "I feel rotten over the whole deal."

"I don't think you should be so hard on yourself. You're a good man."

"No . . ." He looked into Stoker's honest face and couldn't bring himself to destroy the trust he saw there. "If I'm good, then I'd hate to know what the bad ones feel like, because I'm miserable. I've tried to forget her. I've tried to stay away from her, but I can't. Must be why the Bible says it's better to marry than to burn."

"Will she marry you? I thought she had objections."

Oh, Bailey could recite her objections like the Lord's Prayer, but when they made their appearance last night, he'd done his best to drown them out.

What did she think today? Did she hate him for his advances? Did she have the same regrets?

"Not sure which way she's leaning. 'Course, she's tore up about her pa. She's worried about his health, and then there's the business, too. Dr. Trench says he can't work anymore. You know Mr. Lovelace. How long will he live if he can't go to the sawmill?"

Reverend Stoker wiped his brow. "How's your stint at the shoemaker's going?"

"It's slowing down. Mr. Hernandez can't fill any more orders before Christmas, so there isn't any commission coming in." Bailey shrugged. "Fine with me. Boots are necessary and all, but if I wanted to fit shoes I'd do farrier work for the blacksmith."

"Sounds like the Lovelaces could use a hand."

Bailey chewed this over. Sure enough. Nicholas couldn't stay in Prairie Lea forever. Someone needed to keep an eye on the office while Mr. Lovelace recuperated. Someone he could trust. Someone who was almost family.

"That's not a half-bad idea. Kinda shamefaced I didn't think of it myself. Of course, it's not going to help me forget Molly."

"You're not going to forget Molly. Not until you've made an honest attempt at winning her. You seem to think God's brought you together. Maybe it's time to buckle down and find out. Besides, I know an empty parsonage in Prairie Lea that a fellow could claim as long as he keeps lending a hand at the church there. It's only half a mile from the mill."

Would Stoker be matchmaking if he knew what a lowdown snake he was talking to? But maybe he was right. Maybe working for the Lovelaces would convince them that he could take care of their daughter. It couldn't hurt to try. And the sooner he got a ring on her finger the sooner he could make amends.

10

To Do List:

 · *Buy some lozenges for sore throat.*
 · *Send money home to Father.*
 · *Find Bailey.*

Heat poured out of the woodstove next to Molly's desk. The winter might produce days cold enough to justifying wearing her new wool walking suit, but inside the building she was suffocating. That morning she'd felt so chilled she feared the goose bumps would permanently pucker her arms, and now she could barely breathe. She loosened the straps on her clerk's apron and tried to fan herself with the bib, but the effort increased her discomfort. She'd failed to convince Edward that the Texas winter would not get any colder. For such an amiable man, he wasn't easily swayed. Every time she commented on the heavy clothes he'd commissioned for her, he laughed and hinted that she would need them soon.

Molly dipped her pen into the inkwell and neatly scripted the next tax payment on the appropriate line in the ledger. She wasn't going anywhere. Seeing her father nearly die made home more precious to her. Traveling the world in Edward's private railcar didn't hold the allure it once had. Molly would cling to the familiar and hope the security she'd always known as a child wouldn't vanish.

Until last week she'd been taught to think of security in terms of riches. Security meant getting what you wanted. Security meant having the funds to solve your problems. But sitting in her parents' room, watching her father fight for every breath, she realized that the security she sought had little to do with business and everything to do with relationships.

Molly had tried to catch the eye of wealthy men and had been moderately successful, but something was missing from the exchange. Just as her parents targeted Mr. Pierrepont for his wealth, she sensed that Mr. Pierrepont viewed her as an accessory, as well. He didn't love her. How could he? She did her best to hide who she was when he was around. Would he still come courting if she'd railed at him in church like a tinker's wife? Would he be insulted if she found mistakes in his ledgers? Would he kiss her when her cheeks were chapped and her nose was cold?

Molly slid off her tall stool and went to fetch the correct ledger from the shelves. Hugging the heavy book to her, she inhaled the newly bound scent that still lurked within the pages.

Where was Bailey? Every time the door creaked, she jumped in anticipation, but he hadn't made an appearance yet. What was keeping him? Could she have sent him a clearer message? She glanced at Carrie, fearful that she could read her thoughts, but Carrie was paying her no mind.

Molly eased past the girl's desk, amazed Carrie hadn't ferreted the complete saga from her. If only Bailey would marry her quickly, before she had second thoughts. Her love for him might be a liability when written down in fresh ink, but she was done with calculating. It didn't matter who you married—one wrong step and you could still end up as poor as a church mouse. You might as well marry for love.

Molly had just plopped the heavy volume onto her desk when she heard footsteps in the hallway. Out of habit, she whirled, but it wasn't Bailey. Carrying a hand bouquet of pansies, Mr. Fenton was stalking down the hall, looking as nervous as a bull at a calf-fry festival.

Oh, fiddle-faddle. Molly's throat lurched to the roof of her mouth. With all her concern over her father, she'd forgotten about Fenton. Bailey had tried to warn her that Fenton was coming to propose. And here he was—a man on a mission.

Taking her skirt in both hands, she ran out to intercept him before he reached her desk. "Mr. Fenton, can I talk to you outside?" How could she be so thoughtless? She knew that he'd buckled under his parents' demands, and she'd done nothing to correct him.

Mr. Travis's door swung open. "Miss Lovelace, may I ask what's caused you to abandon your work station?"

Mr. Fenton fumbled as he tried to shake Mr. Travis's hand. "Sorry, sir. I don't mean to disturb your office."

"Let's go outside, Mr. Fenton," Molly pleaded. "I have something to say."

"No, I've put this off long enough, and nothing you say is going to sway me." He shot a nervous glance up the staircase as Carrie joined them in the hall.

Mr. Travis crossed his arms. "Well, if you're going to bring the whole office to a halt, it better be important." No smile threatened to break through his bristly beard. "A proposal of marriage, at the least."

"You don't give a man much wiggle room, do you?" Fenton swallowed hard. His eyes skimmed over Molly and went to the ground.

Carrie waggled her eyebrows at Molly and leaned forward.

"Please," Molly begged her supervisor with hands pressed together in supplication. "Can't I take him outside? We need to talk privately."

"Miss Lovelace, you are as shy as a politician on Election Day. Why feign timidity now? Are you going to marry him or not?"

"M-marry me?" Mr. Fenton stammered. "I wasn't going to ask—"

"Then get out," Mr. Travis ordered. "No courting allowed here. She is currently occupied."

"Thank goodness." Molly pressed her hand to her forehead. "I didn't want to hurt your feelings."

Fenton's chin hardened. "Don't flatter yourself. Why would any man prefer you over Miss McGraw? She is the dearest, most sincere"—his voice lowered—"most *forgiving* woman God created, and I'd be blessed if she would consent to be my wife."

"Prue?" Carrie cried.

"Yes, I'm coming." She must've been listening from the landing above them, for Prue flew down the steps like a dainty brown wren and jumped into Mr. Fenton's arms.

Molly couldn't help but covet her radiant smile. She must have practiced it for years to make it look so natural. Well, her efforts were paying off, and the smile Mr. Fenton returned was just as blissful.

"These are for me, then?" Prue extended her hand to receive the bouquet. He nodded, speechless once again.

Mr. Travis's mouth opened and closed like a fish out of water. "Miss McGraw, eh?" He snickered at Molly before turning toward his office. "You other two get to work. This doesn't concern you."

Arm in arm the happy couple strolled out the double doors, leaving Molly and Carrie in shock.

Imagine! Prue, the banker's bride? Had the world gone

mad? Had Bailey misunderstood Fenton all along? Her throat tightened. What a fool she'd made of herself—in front of Carrie and Mr. Travis, too.

"What a fine how-de-do," Carrie called from over the counter. "Who would've thought Prue would've beaten both of us? And with Mr. Fenton, of all people. I guess his uppity family has decided she'd do their receiving line just fine."

Molly grimaced. Or they'd heard about her father's attack and saw no future for her. She might be in worse financial straits than Prue at this moment. Prue's father had a trade while Molly's did not.

But she would cast aside her bruised pride. Bailey was her man. She'd decided on him, and she wouldn't change her mind. Her parents could live simply—healthily—like the Garners. Of course, she had to admit Mary Garner's appearance was marred by the brutal Texas sun. Without her French potions and creams Molly would be as wrinkled as a granny, too, but that didn't mean she couldn't be happy.

Molly bit her lip as she made her way to her station. Was Mrs. Garner happy? The woman seemed as coarse as Molly's pumice stone. What would Molly look like after a few children? She already had trouble keeping her corset strings from stretching.

But it was worth it for love, right?

Molly somehow managed to survive the rest of Carrie's caustic remarks. The pain behind her eyes wasn't imagined. Just half an hour until quitting time. While she wanted to rip out her hairpieces and hide underneath some warm quilts in her room, her first priority was finding Bailey. Whatever evil fairy was playing havoc in her skull would be soothed by a reassuring word from him.

"Are you feeling all right, Molly?" Prue entered with her wrap on and pansies in her hand. "You can go home now."

Molly lifted her head. How had she missed the chimes? "Thank you. I have some peppermint oil in my room. Perhaps if I take to my bed, I'll be improved by tomorrow."

She stood, wincing as she landed on her feet. She should go home. Real home. Not her rented room. If Bailey offered, she'd let him take her to Prairie Lea. She wanted to be with her family and to get their blessing. She wanted to convince them that they would survive. The situation might be different, but they'd all be together.

And most of all, after the day's debacle, Molly wanted to go far away from the courthouse. No more Mr. Fenton.

Although not frigid, the cool air stabbed at her already sensitive eyes. Luckily the cobbler's shop lay across the square. Keeping her head down, she walked as quickly as her polonaise would allow.

The leather scent greeted her at the door, and Mr. Hernandez wasn't far behind.

"You are here for the boots?" He wiped his hands on his apron.

She blinked. The boots? "Actually, I came to see Bailey."

"Bailey doesn't work here anymore. Is there anything I can help you with?"

Molly pressed her hand to her forehead to keep it from exploding. He told her that, right? She vaguely remembered something about him messing up her shoes. Goodness, where was he? She'd go to his aunt's house. That's what she'd do. If she could find it in the dark, she shouldn't have any problem in broad daylight.

Molly slid her hands into her walking coat, glad for the extravagance as a cool breeze from the door blew past her. "Keep the boots. I don't think I'm going to need them."

"But they're paid for. You might as well."

Soon she found herself with her arms full of boots walking toward Bailey's aunt's house.

The distance seemed to multiply along with the weight of her parcel. If she didn't find Bailey soon, she might be beyond his help. Instead of searching for a sympathetic shoulder to cry on, she should be looking for a doctor.

Then suddenly she was standing at the door.

"You want Bailey?" His aunt snapped clothing down from the line without pausing to look at Molly. "He left late this morning. Said he was going home. Probably missed those cows of his. Don't know when he'll be back, or if he'll be back. He hightailed it out after talking to the reverend."

Reverend Stoker? Oh no. Molly hugged her boots tightly. Not another confession. What must Reverend Stoker think of her? She wished she could talk to the pastor and find out where Bailey had gone, but something restrained her. Reverend Stoker, as God's agent on earth, would extend no help to her. Just disapproval. As shallow and frivolous as she was, she could expect no understanding from a man like Reverend Stoker, or from God, for that matter.

Hadn't her father taught her that?

Thanking the woman, Molly dragged herself toward her room, too tired to be humiliated. He'd said that he had regrets. How much of their relationship did he want to undo? If he still wanted to marry her, she needed to know.

As she crossed Blanco Street she heard her name called.

"Miss Lovelace, it's a pleasure to see you." The young Mexican cowboy reined his horse to tarry at her side. "We've missed you at the ranch."

It was Rico, a hand on the Garner ranch back in Prairie Lea. Maybe she was clutching at straws, but she saw a possibility.

"Rico, are you going to George Garner's tonight?"

"*Sí, señorita*, I am on my way at this moment."

"Wonderful." Tucking the boots under her arm, Molly fished through her reticule until she found her journal and pencil. With shaking fingers she found an empty page. "If you could take a note to Bailey . . . ?"

Rico raised his eyebrows. "It is true? Bailey has captured your heart? But it is of no matter. Bailey is not on the ranch."

Her pencil moved furiously over the paper:

To Do List:

- *"I Do" List:*
- *Find Bailey—immediately.*
- *Tell him that I want to be his wife.*
- *Live happily ever after.*

There. She read it again. Not a typical response to a proposal, but the best she could do under the circumstances.

"He should be there by now. Please see that he receives this tonight. It is of the utmost importance." She tore the sheet from the binding and folded it with crisp creases. "Please, Rico. As a believer in true love, make certain he knows he must respond by morning."

Her appeal to his romantic nature hit its mark. Rico straightened in the saddle and placed one hand over his heart and the other palm up before her. "As the river delivers fresh water day after day, so I will deliver the life-giving words from your heart."

With barely enough energy to bat her eyelashes at him, she kissed the letter tenderly to ensure the man wouldn't forget their encounter and placed it in his hand. She'd barely told him thank-you when he spurred his horse, kicking up dust with his departure.

Would Bailey answer? He had to. He knew what was at stake. She managed to drag her aching limbs to her house, but rest would remain elusive.

"You're going to need those boots, and soon." Edward rose from the swing on Mrs. Truman's porch, pulled open the door, and escorted her inside.

The house looked empty. Molly called for Mrs. Truman, in desperate need of refreshments to help her survive a caller, but there was no answer. "She can't be gone long. Please make yourself comfortable." She motioned to the parlor and removed her gloves and bonnet. "That is, if you have the time. I thought you'd be gone already."

"Not yet. My car is being coupled for tomorrow's afternoon train. That is the reason I'm here—to say that I'm not leaving without you."

A sense of justification flooded over her. After Mr. Fenton's harsh rejection and Bailey's disappearance, Edward's approval comforted her. Despite the tragic turn her life had taken, she hadn't been wrong. This relationship had proceeded as planned, but her plans had changed.

"Thank you for the offer, but I'm afraid I have to decline. As much as I'll miss your company, I'm needed here. You'll get along fine without me."

His moustache twitched. "I disagree, but I'm more concerned about you. It troubles me to think of beautiful, intelligent Molly being reduced to a mindless ornament, polished and presented on special occasions."

Dread crept over her like fast-growing ivy. "I won't allow it."

"There's an even worse option," Edward said. "You could become extremely utilitarian—cook, clean, farm, nurse. There's no end to the demeaning chores a poor man will find for you." He sat on the red sofa.

"If running a household were so simple, you'd think I'd be better at it." She propped herself up against the curio cabinet. "Besides, I'm beginning to suspect that who you are working for is more significant than the manner of work."

Pushing a cushion aside, Edward made room for her next to him. "I agree. That's why you must come with me. Up until now I've only lived for myself, and I want you to make life meaningful. I want you to be my companion, to share the world with me—and I do mean the world." He unwrapped her boots and inspected them. "We have no limits. You want to see Paris, we'll go to Paris. You want to see Panama, Panama it is. All in the finest style imaginable. Arrangements have been made for my departure—and yours. You should have collected a suitable winter wardrobe by now."

He spoke the truth. Piece by piece, he'd given her the coats, gowns, and wraps for their journey. He'd prepared for a wife in under a month. Bailey still hadn't managed, and he'd had a year to do so. Molly rubbed her forehead. If Edward's railcar were at her door, she might just climb in. Anywhere she could lay her weary head. Anything that would ensure her parents' future.

"I haven't told you about my father."

As Molly told the story, Edward expressed his concern with characteristic appropriateness. "He can no longer work at the mill? But your father thrives on success. I know many like him, and financial ruin will kill him." Edward took her hand and studied the fire a moment. "How about this? My family would be elated if, for once, I invested money instead of squandered it. What if I bought the mill? We could come to a settlement that would keep your parents comfortably idle, especially if I took a rather costly daughter off their hands."

The throbbing behind her eyes eased. "Truly? You would do that?" She shook her head. "No, I've always dreamed of a big wedding. White silk gown. Pink roses—"

"A big wedding?" The sofa creaked as he leaned into it. "Unfortunately, that is out of the question. Perhaps if there were some other way to soothe Daddy's conscience."

If he could be spared the expense of a costly wedding, her father's conscience wouldn't utter a peep. Her objections were stronger. "It's not only my parents' feelings I must consider. I have an opinion of my own."

How could she think of marrying a man she'd never even kissed, when yesterday with Bailey . . . Her breathing sped at the memory. She swallowed and felt a soreness already spidering across her throat.

Edward straightened, as if reading her thoughts. "Please don't judge my appreciation for you by my restraint. I'm a private man." He looked around the boardinghouse parlor. "As of yet, this is the closest we've ever come to being alone."

Yes, he treated her like a lady, but could she love him? She searched for an answer and found nothing disagreeable about his appearance. His lips were well shaped. His face kind and mature, not given to rages or passions. A smile played at his lips as he watched her evaluate him.

"You're not convinced?" He leaned forward and cupped her cheek. His eyes widened. "You're burning up. Why didn't you tell me you were ill?" With a grimace he removed a glove, the first time she'd ever seen him without one, and pressed the back of his hand to her forehead. "Poor dear. It's early yet, but you must retire. Let me get you a draught for the night. I'll check in on you tomorrow. Once we board you won't need to leave the car. I can have a doctor brought to you in San Antonio."

"It's too sudden. I must send word to . . ." She faltered. How long before Bailey received her note? "To my parents."

"If you weren't ill, I'd hire a buggy to take you to them. If you'd like I could go."

"Not with Father's condition. He shouldn't receive visitors."

"Then I'll send a post to alleviate their worries and present my offer. I'm confident they'll understand the benefits of my proposal."

Molly brightened at the word. It was one of her favorites. The only other proposal she'd received came with laden with caveats—"when the time is right," "if I find a job," "when your parents approve." If she compared Bailey's offer to Edward's money, prestige, and availability, the scales were definitely in Edward's favor. Sure, love tipped the balance toward Bailey, but was Bailey's offer still good, or had he rescinded it?

On wobbly knees, she rose and Edward understood the suggestion.

"Hopefully after a good night's sleep you'll feel like getting your things together. The train leaves tomorrow afternoon."

"I haven't said yes," she said.

He smiled. "Yes is the easiest word in any language."

A filled canteen and a stack of quilts. Bailey's very survival depended on those items, and as far as he could determine, nothing else in the world existed.

He rolled onto his side and curled his legs up to his chest under the blankets, thankful that Mrs. Stoker had left the empty parsonage with a clean straw tick and bedding. A fire would be nice, but he suspected his ague was responsible for the chill more than the temperature outside. Whatever bug had attacked him was ruthless. He hoped he hadn't passed it on to Molly. He didn't want to imagine her stuck in town without any family looking after her.

Had he been thinking, he would've sent word home before he holed up at the parsonage for the night. What he wouldn't give for his mother's cool hands and warm soup right now. As it was, he'd skirted the ranch and headed straight for the abandoned house in Prairie Lea. Going to the Lovelaces' was out of the question. The last thing they needed was for Mr. Lovelace to catch influenza in his weakened condition.

Besides, they weren't expecting him. He hoped they would accept his offer, but he wouldn't be any help till he was back on his feet.

His sore eyes opened, spotted the canteen hanging on the bedpost, and closed again. Bailey fished around blindly until he snagged the strap and brought the open vessel to his parched lips. The cool water eased his mouth, but he had to brace himself for what was to come. Grimacing, he forced a swallow and whimpered at the pain as his throat constricted. What a sissy boy he'd turned into, lying in bed, crying for his ma.

With effort he hung the canteen over the post and searched for the warm spot he'd lost. If someone would skin him alive, they'd be doing him a favor. Every inch of his hide had puckered, prickling like he'd been dropped naked into the icehouse.

He drifted and wondered how much the fever had twisted his memories. Molly's words spun in his head until he couldn't remember exactly what she'd decided, but by following Stoker's suggestion to help her pa, surely he would remove any further objections. All he needed was a few days to sleep off this illness and get everything in place. Then he would head to Lockhart and return with his girl.

11

The pounding on the door shook her bed. "Go away," Molly groaned and pulled a pillow over her head.

The doorknob clicked and skirts swished. "Molly! What are you doing? Mr. Travis is going to have conniptions if you're late again." The bed sagged where Carrie sat on it. "Did you sleep in your clothes?"

Molly pulled the pillow away and stared at the woman through red-rimmed eyes. "It's morning?"

Carrie's eyes narrowed. "You're not hiding from Prue, are you? You know if you don't show up she'll think you're crushed over Mr. Fenton."

"Feel my forehead. I can't counterfeit a temperature."

Carrie pressed her hand against Molly's cheek and shook her head. "Convenient. You're lucky even when afflicted. All right. I'll pass word along to Mr. Travis, but you might want to send for the doctor. Your story could require collaboration." Carrie lingered at Molly's dressing table and fiddled through some jewelry. "Were you going to wear this today?"

Molly waved her consent and Carrie slipped out the door, earbobs in hand.

So morning had come. Bailey had not. Molly sat up slowly

to find her balance before she attempted the chamber pot. She wouldn't leave her room. The day had just begun, and there was no way she'd take a chance on missing him. He was getting his shot. If he wanted to marry her, he had to make an appearance soon. The longer she waited, the more loath she was to turn down Edward's offer to buy the mill.

Mrs. Truman appeared with hot tea and a biscuit with strawberry jam. Molly choked it down, wincing with every swallow. She wondered how her mother would respond to Edward's letter. Would he mention her illness? Would Nicholas be sent to fetch her home? Wiping the crumbs from her mouth, she pushed the china plate across her vanity and crawled into bed.

She must have drowsed, because she didn't hear Mrs. Truman reenter. The woman stood striped by the bright sunlight peeking through the shutters, her apron already splattered with dinner preparations.

"What time is it?" Molly licked her swollen lips.

"Nearly noon, sweetie. I've been up to check on you, but you were sleeping so hard, I didn't want to wake you. Your gentleman has come by a few times, too. He's getting antsy to see you."

He was here? Molly lowered her feet to the floor. Gingerly she stood, tried a few steps, and looked in the mirror. Oh, bother. One look at her and Bailey would turn tail and run. She tried to ply a brush through her matted locks, but her head was too tender. On the other hand, her cheeks had never looked rosier or her blue eyes brighter. Even her lips were full and red. As pretty as the painted china dolls at the mercantile. Hopefully, he'd appreciate her florid complexion and not notice her rumpled gown and fuzzy hair.

Mrs. Truman followed her down the stairs, clucking all the way to the parlor.

"Edward." Molly faltered at the threshold. There stood the man of her ambitions with a cane and a bowler hat, but he wasn't the man of her heart.

"Yes, love. You seem surprised. Did you forget I was returning?" He took her by the arm and gently led her to the sofa. "My poor dear. You've had a miserable night, haven't you? We'll get you settled into my car, where I can take care of you."

"What are you talking about?" Mrs. Truman's hands went to her hips. "I run a respectable establishment here. No young ladies will be carted off from under my nose."

"Nothing to disrespect your establishment. I have written to Miss Lovelace's parents, and it's been settled. Your mother sends her best." Edward smiled as smooth as butter and produced a folded note.

Molly wanted nothing to do with the letter. If she hadn't already been seated, she would've fallen down.

"If you're not going to read it, I suppose I will." Mrs. Truman took the offered paper and read it with creased brows. "I see. Beg your pardon, sir." She handed it back to him.

"No offense taken. If I could trespass on your kindness, though, it seems unlikely that Miss Lovelace can pack her trunk without help in her present condition. Is there a chance that you could lend her a hand? I'll have a wagon sent around at one o'clock."

Molly's head spun. Was this really happening? While Edward and Mrs. Truman discussed their plans, she pulled the letter from his hand.

Molly,

I can't express how delighted I am with your news. Truly, this seems the very solution that we sought. There is no reason to delay your departure, as I'm confident

*your father would not want his health hindering your
happiness. Mr. Pierrepont has assured me of his care
for you, and when your father has sufficiently recovered, I will present Mr. Pierrepont's offer for a possible
partnership in the business. We both know how pleased
he will be.*

*We look forward to your return and wish you every
happiness.*

*Your mother,
Adele Lovelace*

She couldn't move. Her mother's scented stationery hung
from her limp fingers. How foolish to hope that her mother
would protest. If the balance amount on the bottom of the
ledger would improve, Adele Lovelace was willing to forgo
the niceties.

Molly was exhausted. She'd scrambled to stay ahead of
their plans, but finally they'd caught up with her. The delays
and distractions had failed to get her what she wanted. Bailey
had failed her, too, and now, through the haze of disillusion-
ment and illness she saw no alternative. Molly allowed the
letter to flutter to the floor.

"I'm afraid Miss Lovelace is overwhelmed, Mrs. Truman."
Edward sat next to her and took her hand.

"Don't worry, Molly," Mrs. Truman said. "I'll get your
duds packed up, but you might want to change into a fresh
gown first."

Her tears splashed onto the dress she'd worn since she'd
made the trip to Bailey's aunt's and heard that he'd left town
without saying good-bye. He wasn't coming. He didn't want
her.

She squeezed Edward's hand, too tired to fight any longer.

She was a practical woman. He was a good man. No obstacle would prevent their union.

Bailey made it outside to the pump handle, quite an accomplishment, to his thinking. It took some effort before he could thrust both hands into the stream and splash the refreshing water onto his face. He couldn't show up at Mr. Lovelace's smelling like the devil's outhouse, but he didn't have the strength for a proper bath yet. He stood and expanded his lungs with the crisp December air. The last traces of the illness lingered, but he'd kicked it enough that he could walk across town and round up some vittles. Anything more and he'd be laid low again.

He pulled his hat over his wet head. By sunrise tomorrow he should have his legs under him. Then he'd take a dip in the river, clean up, and offer his services. One more day wouldn't hurt anything.

Her bed swayed, rocking her like a cradle one minute and making her nauseated the next. How long had she slept? Molly plucked at an unfamiliar gown, recognizing it as silk but unable to remember from where it came. Struggling, she tried to set her jumbled memories into order but wasn't up to the task and surrendered again to oblivion.

Deep voices awakened her. The movement had ceased and with it some of the vagueness that had clouded her thinking.

She was on a train. She remembered that much. She remembered parts of the ride to the station in Luling, remembered watching from the buggy for Bailey, thinking she was going to meet him, only to discover that Edward Pierrepont was with her instead.

Molly pulled a pillow from her face to see Edward and a man in uniform—the conductor, perhaps? Their voices echoed nonsensically in the small room. She pulled the luxurious sheets up to her neck. Why were men in her room? Molly began to tremble, for even through the haze of her fever one memory was clear. Edward had been in her bed.

She tried to swallow, but her throat was too parched. The voices stopped, and then she felt a hand on her forehead.

"If there's no physician here, we won't disembark. It's imperative that we get her to San Antonio as quickly as possible." Edward cradled her head and lifted a glass to her lips.

Yes, he'd been there all night with her. Vaguely she remembered a man holding her as she tossed fitfully. What else had happened?

"We have to get married," she rasped as soon as the water freed her voice.

She didn't hear any words for a moment. Edward withdrew.

"The delirium has been quite intense at times," he said.

"This isn't your wife?"

Where silence should've fallen, a strange ringing filled her head. After what seemed an eternity she barely heard Edward's answer.

"No, sir, she's not."

"You're mistaken if you think I'll transport a lady for illicit purposes. We will uncouple your car, and you can sit here in Marion."

"That wouldn't be helpful. She needs a doctor."

"Sounds like she wants a parson," the conductor said.

Molly tried to sit up. "A parson. We need a parson, Edward. You've already stayed here one night with me."

"I'm afraid there's been a misunderstanding," he said.

But the conductor interrupted. "Forget the parson. I'm sending for the sheriff. I don't like the sound of this."

"No sheriff, please. Surely we can come to some manner of agreement."

Molly fell into the pillows, curious about the fear in Edward's voice. He'd said that a big wedding was impossible, so why did he care if they got hitched at some little way station? She lost focus as another current of exhaustion pulled her under.

When she floated to consciousness again, she found that she and Edward were alone.

"Where'd the man go?"

"To get a parson, as you requested." He ran his fingers through his hair as he paced the narrow room. "It's not that I don't *want* to marry you, but a marriage will be complicated. There are certain legal implications I wish to avoid."

She ran her tongue over dry lips. "Your family will object?"

His laugh was not pleasant. "Very much. You have no idea what this could cost me."

Molly felt like a wet noodle. A hungry noodle, if that were possible. Had she any strength she would've pointed out the absurdness of the situation.

Of course, his parents wouldn't be happy that he'd married a nobody from tiny Prairie Lea, Texas, but it was a little late now. Why worry about his folks back East when the conductor was threatening to send him to jail and haul her tainted petticoats back to Caldwell County?

Surely his parents wouldn't cut him off. She motioned for another drink of water. What if she'd forsaken Bailey to marry a penniless Edward? What would Carrie call it? Divine irony?

"I'm hungry."

"Forgive me. The current dilemma has caused me to be unmindful of you. I'll have Freida bring you some breakfast."

"Freida?"

"Your lady's maid. The one who helped you to bed. You don't remember?"

Molly fiddled with the lace on her nightgown's sleeve as he left the paneled room to find the maid, her thoughts clearing. A lady's maid? She should trust Edward. He wouldn't have taken advantage of her, but didn't he understand that his presence was enough to compromise her? True, they were getting married, so it wasn't unforgivable, but she wouldn't go another mile before they set it aright.

By the time Molly had blinked again, a grisly-headed woman was arranging a tray of food next to her on the bed.

"There's some pretty eyes. Began to wonder if you had any. Here, eat some toast. It'll be a good start. Pity getting married when you're feeling sick as a dog." She tore off a piece of toast and climbed right up on the bed beside Molly.

Molly grimaced as she tried to swallow. "You must believe that I'd never have allowed Mr. Pierrepont to stay in my room had I been cognitive of the situation."

Freida laughed. "Don't you worry, missy. I ain't one to tell tales. Besides, I thought it was so romantic. He crouched by your bedside, giving you sips of water, changing out your cool cloths. And you clung to him, holding on to his shirt, begging him not to leave. It was sweet as syrup."

If Molly's face hadn't already been beet red, she would've blushed, but Freida didn't seem to mind. She hummed a happy tune as she fed her another bite of toast, followed by a sip of tea.

"You two will make a lovely couple, but it is a pity you won't get to walk down the aisle."

Molly attempted gratitude but only managed a grunt. When she felt better she'd be sure and tell the woman what a comfort she was. Having a lady's maid suited her. Maybe Edward would let her keep Freida.

"It can't be helped. I won't pass another night without being legally wed, even if it means giving up on a fine wedding." Molly ran her tongue over her teeth. Ugh. She must do something with her sour breath before he returned with the preacher.

"Impatient, are we?" Freida laughed and wiped her nose with the back of her hand. "Don't you worry. By the time we pull out of the station, you'll be man and wife—Mr. and Mrs. Bailey Pierrepont."

12

"Bailey Pierrepont?" Molly mustered every ounce of strength and sat up to stare in amazement at the maid. "Did you say 'Bailey'?"

The woman smiled slyly, revealing a mouth with half the teeth God intended. "I told you, I'm not one to tell tales. Mr. Morgan has a different Mrs. Morgan every time he travels this stretch of track, but do I say anything? No. I'll keep your secrets to the grave."

"Who said anything about Bailey?" Molly persisted.

"You did. Last night you wouldn't quiet down until Mr. Pierrepont held you—brought a tear to my eye, no less—and you were crying, 'Hold me, Bailey. Please don't leave me.'"

Molly could feel the chill start at the base of her spine and work its way up. She groaned and clutched the blankets. Why hadn't Edward thrown her out this morning? Instead he'd gone for a preacher. No wonder he was reluctant.

She gritted her teeth together. She'd make it up to him. She couldn't school her dreams, but she could discipline her behavior. Her actions would never cause him to question her loyalty. She owed him too much.

"Like I said, I'm not a tale teller. Mrs. Carver has pads

sewn into her corset cover and Mrs. Treadwell is practically bald, but do I say anything? Never. Couldn't pry my mouth open with a crow bar."

The idea of having a lady's maid had lost its appeal.

A knock at her door sent Freida scurrying to gather the dishes.

"Come in," Molly croaked and smoothed the duvet over the sheets. She still hadn't brushed her teeth.

Edward stuck his head into the room and, seeing nothing amiss, allowed a red-faced clergyman and the conductor to cross the threshold.

"Miss Lovelace." The man doffed his hat to reveal a shiny dome atop a tomato-colored face. "Reverend Snow at your service. Mr. Postmont has informed me of your tragic condition. I was taken aback by his suggestion, but I understand your circumstances are most unusual."

"Reverend Snow, may we start the ceremony before her strength fades?" Edward dropped his hat on the dresser and pulled a chair next to the bed. Keeping a respectable distance between them, he reached for her hand.

Her eyes blurred as the parson flipped through his prayer book and began the words she'd longed to hear. Never would she have thought to have them spoken over her while lying in bed aboard a train. Through her fever-weakened eyes she saw Edward, as pale as dry bones, rub his bare ring finger. Obviously, he hadn't prepared for this ceremony, either.

He allowed a wan smile in her direction. Molly squeezed his hand. He was holding up his end of the bargain. She would do no less. Looking up at the parson, she tried to assume the countenance of a bride blissfully happy to marry the man of her dreams.

Under normal circumstances Bailey would've loved to chew the fat with Rico, but he was on a mission. Regardless, the horseman had spotted him and wasn't letting him go without a greeting.

"We've been looking for you, Bailey. Where have you been hiding?"

Bailey gestured over his shoulder. "I was feeling puny. Stoker let me ride it out at the parsonage, but I should have sent word to Ma. Kinda lonely getting sick solo."

Rico wagged his dramatic eyebrows. "Unless you're more foolish than I thought, you won't be alone much longer." He pulled a note from inside his leather vest and handed it to Bailey. "From your señorita *bonita*."

Bailey's boots didn't move another inch. He unfolded the note with lightning speed, flipped the paper over, and caught his breath.

Rico laughed at him. "It's good tidings, no? Sorry they did not reach you sooner. Miss Lovelace was searching for you desperately. Even your *madre* was concerned."

"Just under the weather. Tell Ma I'm all right. I'll tell Molly in person, right after I have a little chat with her pa."

Bailey almost ran before he caught himself. His uncertain mission now looked brighter than new spurs. With remarkable self-control he strode down Mill Street until he reached the Lovelaces' fine abode on the river.

Nicholas opened the massive oak door. "Didn't expect to see you until the weekend."

Always more of a city boy growing up, Nicholas had truly become a man of sophistication since winning his own business contract with the railroad. Bailey wished he'd been as successful, but if Nick continued to connect Thomas Lovelace with railroad barons, he'd be helping them all.

"I came to check on your pa. How's he faring?"

Nicholas stepped aside to allow him entrance. "He's doing well. Itching to get back to the mill, but Dr. Trench is adamant. I don't know that Mother will be able to handle him."

"That's what I came to talk to him about."

Nicholas waved Bailey on toward the parlor, but not before Bailey caught a cinnamony whiff of snickerdoodles. He followed Nicholas and found Mr. Lovelace sitting morosely before a checkerboard, and it looked like he was winning. His canvas pants and sturdy shirt spoke of a man heading to work, but his stockinged feet said otherwise.

"What they're doing to me is unconscionable. I'm in the prime of my life, and they're coddling me like I'm in my dotage."

"Nice to see you up and around, Mr. Lovelace." Bailey offered one hand and removed his hat with the other, but Thomas waved it off as Nicholas made himself comfortable on the sofa.

"It can't be nice to see me. Not in this temper. Either I die happy at work, or I'm going to make everyone wish I would."

Lola entered with a tray of mugs. Ah, warm cider. Even better than snickerdoodles. Bailey had to force a few swallows down his sandpaper throat before he went on.

"That's what I came to talk to you about. I wanted to offer my services."

Thomas Lovelace narrowed his sunken eyes. "I heard you've been blacksmithing, shoemaking, and ministering. Have you taken up doctoring, as well?"

"No, but I'd like to try my hand at working a saw."

Nicholas's face lit up. He bounded to his feet. "That's a capital idea. I've spent more time here than I should. If you could take over—"

But the elder Lovelace wasn't convinced. "What do you know about managing a sawmill?"

"Managing? Is that what you need? A manager? I thought Russell James would take your place."

Thomas huffed. "Can't trust a man with a scalawag son."

"Russell James is honest," Bailey said. "You can't hold him responsible for Michael. He did the best he could."

"Then he failed, and it'll only be a matter of time before he sinks to the level of the boy."

"Father, I agree with Bailey. Russell has been a loyal employee for years. Each morning and evening he comes by and gives a full account of every cent that crosses the till. Why don't you promote him?"

"He does the billing, and that's bad enough. I have to verify the numbers every night. If Bailey was any good at figuring, I'd give him that responsibility, but what I need worse is someone to sell to the customers and settle disputes. Russell fawns and simpers like they're doing him a favor. I need someone with more confidence to chew the fat with my regulars."

"Chew the fat?" A slow smile spread across Bailey's face. His thumbs slid under his vest and stretched it as he rocked on his heels. "There's two things I'm good at, and talking up people is one of them." At the black scowl from Mr. Lovelace he quickly added, "Playing the guitar is the other."

"What do you say, Father? Wouldn't you rest easier if Bailey was your front man?"

Mr. Lovelace crossed his arms and looked Bailey up and down. Bailey expelled a tension-filled breath but couldn't draw another one through his chapped lips. How he wished he hadn't aired his dirty laundry in front of the church and Molly's parents. What a dimwit.

"I'd like to have someone I could trust if Michael James starts poking around. I reckon it'd beat selling the whole kit and caboodle to that Pierrepont fella."

"Pierrepont?" Bailey's jaw set. "What's Pierrepont got to do with it?"

"He sent an offer. Adele won't let me know the terms until I can consider it calmly, but if it was a decent bid, I think she'd have shown it to me by now." He grunted. "It doesn't matter. I'm not selling to the likes of him. If he had funds to invest, then we'd have a deal, but I'm not going to let him run my life's work into the ground on a whim."

"Absolutely not." It was Bailey's turn to pace. "He's merely passing through. Why would he want to be tied to Prairie Lea?"

The ticking of the grandfather clock grew deafening. Thomas swept all the checker pieces off the board and onto the table. "I'm done playing." He moved the card table and got to his feet.

"Wait, Father." Nicholas stepped into his path. "Don't you have something to tell Bailey?"

The man blinked and rubbed his recently distressed chest. His eyes darted to Bailey, and then to the floor.

"He deserves to hear it here and not in the papers," Nicholas said.

But that was enough. Bailey knew.

Carefully Bailey balanced his hat on the mantel over the fireplace between a candlestick and a tintype picture of the family. There sat a younger Molly with her golden curls proudly cascading down her shoulders, nearly to her elbows.

"He's going to propose." Fear rose in his throat before he could remind himself of her letter.

"Yes, and I didn't get nearly what I wanted. If Adele's afraid of my reaction when I see the offer, then it's not promising. Evidently he's the black sheep in a family of golden fleeces. He'll probably sell out at the first opportunity, maybe even to my competitor Merriweather in Luling."

Bailey whirled. "So the mill won't profit from Molly's marriage?"

"Not unless he can throw some business this way. He might have contacts, but none around these parts. She would've been better off to have stuck it out with Fenton's son."

Bailey stepped forward. "Mr. Lovelace, I'd like permission to marry Molly."

He could feel Mr. Lovelace's eyes burning through his hide. Bailey hoped he saw a man who loved his daughter. For all his failures, he hoped Mr. Lovelace at least credited him that.

Mr. Lovelace harrumphed and the floor creaked beneath him. "If you could convince her to marry you on a manager's wages, then you're a better salesman than I thought."

"Does that mean I have your blessing?" Bailey snatched his hat from the mantel and moved toward the door.

"To be honest, I need a manager more than I need a son-in-law. You aren't going to let that simpleminded daughter of mine interfere with our arrangement, are you?"

Bailey was on his toes, raring to go. "Tomorrow I'll start working for you, engaged or not. I'm anxious to get started."

Mr. Lovelace's face eased. Before answering he stomped and shook out the deep creases in britches that hadn't been straightened all day.

"In that case, I won't tell you no, although I wish you no luck. We've raised that girl for finer society, but if she can't discern between you and Mr. Pierrepont, there never was any hope for her."

Bailey would waste no more time. He saw Lola preparing supper as he passed by on his way out the door. "Keep two plates warm," he called to Mr. Lovelace, "and I'll be back, but not without your daughter."

13

"She wouldn't leave town with him!" Bailey shoved himself away from Reverend Stoker's simple oak table and scrambled to his feet.

The reverend grasped his arm. "Steady, son. There's no way around it. Those are the facts."

"But it's not true. It can't be. She told me to come get her. She promised to marry me." Bailey laid his hand across the vest pocket that held her folded note.

"If I hadn't verified it myself, I wouldn't have gone looking for you," Stoker said. "I spent the morning hunting down all the information I could."

If it weren't for Mrs. Stoker, sitting at the table with bowed head and folded hands, he'd have stomped out. Her lips were moving silently, talking to God about him, no doubt. Praying for what? That it was a mistake? That Molly would return unharmed?

As if reading his mind, her voice rose. "Please, Father, tend to your injured child. Help him find your will in this. Help him to forgive those who've betrayed him."

Bailey shook off Stoker's hand and moved to the solitary

157

window. Her voice continued, softly interceding for him, but he wasn't listening. She might as well pray for manna to fall from the sky as pray that he'd find acceptance.

The weak winter sun threw gray shadows over the yard, delineating every blemish in the bark of the oak tree. The dead grass waved listlessly under the pale scrutiny with no growth, no life. Just waiting until boots treaded across it and wore it down. Waiting until it was free of the roots that held it to the ground and it could blow away. Disappear.

Bailey leaned against the glass. He had nowhere but here. As much as he wished he could sink into oblivion, his roots were so intertwined that he couldn't be uprooted without damaging others. And he wouldn't do that.

But Molly's roots were shallow. She'd never had the space, the room that she needed to thrive. Why hadn't he recognized it earlier? For all her brave words and heartfelt promises, she'd left him as she'd threatened all along. How had he dreamed she could do otherwise?

He pounded the plaster wall with his fist.

"Prue McGraw saw her riding on the road to Luling with her trunks and Mr. Pierrepont," Stoker said, "but they didn't go to the courthouse. There wasn't a marriage license filed. We shouldn't assume."

Bailey shook his head. "She's married. That's been her goal all along."

Where was she? What was she doing right now? Bile rose in his throat. Thoughts like these would drive him mad. He pounded the wall again.

"Why don't you stay here," Mrs. Stoker suggested. "We can put you up for a spell."

"I can't." He pressed his fist against his head, wishing he could push out the memory of his conversation with Mr. Lovelace. "I've got a job at the mill. I gave my word I'd be back tonight." He faltered as he remembered the last promise he'd made in that parlor. Molly had made it safely home, no thanks to him. He'd do better this time.

The sun was setting on the worst day of his life, and he still had to face Mr. Lovelace and admit that he was correct. His daughter had rejected him. She'd eloped and played him false.

Please, God, working for the Lovelaces is the last thing I want to do. Show me a way out. Don't make me stay with them. How can I forget Molly while spending every day with her family?

The familiar ride between Lockhart and Prairie Lea allowed him ample opportunity to relive every kiss, every caress they'd shared. He'd thought their intimacy would unite them. He didn't realize it would leave him broken like the bond they'd had, a bond she now shared with another man.

And it could've been much worse.

Throughout his sickness Bailey had sought to justify his attempt to seduce Molly. He loved her. They were meant to be together. They'd marry soon enough.

Turns out she did marry. Without him.

Too soon he reached the Lovelaces' house. Too soon he found himself before the giant oak door with the door knocker in hand.

Had Molly shared the story of Bailey's behavior with her husband? Was Pierrepont furious, or were they ridiculing him?

Silently he eased the brass ring down. Images of the innocent girl in the tintype floated before his eyes. The long golden hair wasn't so beautiful now. More like a net spread to trap the unwary.

Why had she sent the note? Was it a cruel jest? Had she written it for Pierrepont's amusement?

Bailey lifted his hand to the door knocker for the second

time, and for the second time set it gently against its base without making a sound.

He didn't know if he had the courage to stay and do the work he'd promised. Someday she'd return in a fancy dress clutching her husband by the arm, and he didn't want to be here, of all places, when it happened.

But his lot was that of a poor man without options. He wasn't Nicholas, who could turn a piece of tin into a silver dollar. He didn't have a father like Thomas Lovelace, who ate dinner with the banker and played checkers with the mayor, and honestly that suited him fine. He didn't want to hobnob, but their worlds overlapped in one place—Molly.

Wanting to forget the whole episode, Bailey dropped the brass ring. Molly's desertion made him the victim, not the perpetrator. No reason for that night to ever be discussed again. However ill he'd misused her, she'd paid him back. They were even.

Outside of Denver, Colorado
January 1880

The snow-covered mountains shimmered under the full moon and grew larger with every passing mile. Although she'd begun her recovery more than a week ago, Molly couldn't break through the odd layer of detachment that separated her from her surroundings. By the time she and Edward had left San Antonio she was on the mend, although weak, but once she was in no physical danger, they'd pushed on, flying through Texas, Indian Territory, and Kansas. They headed north until they'd reached Salina, Kansas, and then they blazed toward the setting sun, straight at the mountains of Denver.

The scenery flew past the newlyweds watching silently from the square platform of the Pierrepont railcar. Molly held her mouth open and exhaled a warm, damp puff of air. A white cloud appeared but was whisked away by the cold wind rushing around her.

She could imagine Saint Nicholas's sled gliding over the foothills, but Christmas had come and gone while she recovered in bed. Getting out a week ago was the best gift she could've received.

Molly shivered, although Edward was unfazed. He loved the frigid temperatures and claimed to find them invigorating. She'd never been so cold in her life, but her husband did his best to warm her up.

Another shiver and Molly turned her thoughts back to the mountains.

"I can't believe they're real," she said. "You could hide whole cities in a crag."

"It may appear so, but disappearing isn't as simple as you might think. Even on those mountain trails it's likely you'll cross paths with an acquaintance. Alaska Territory is different. You might be recognized, but who's to care? No report will make it to civilization."

"What an odd thing to say." Molly laughed. "When did this obsession with anonymity develop? You weren't concerned in Lockhart."

The train lurched over a rough patch of track. Molly pulled her hand out of her stole quickly enough to steady herself on the rail, but before she could return it, she had to submit to Edward's ministrations.

"You really should carry your own handkerchiefs." With bent head, he thoroughly scrubbed each of her fingers that had come into contact with the iron rail.

"I only stepped outside the car. It's probably healthier out here than in my room after my illness."

"You, my dear, are spotless. By contrast, the general populace contaminates everything it touches." He turned her hand this way and that, and finding nothing objectionable, he smiled. Holding the handkerchief at arm's length, Edward let the wind tug a moment before he released it.

Over the rail Molly leaned and watched the sad white spot abandoned on the dead prairie grow smaller and smaller. Good gravy, she hoped he wasn't as demanding on the servants. She thought of Lola, capable by all means, but unless she followed Molly's every move, there had always been a path of destruction delineating Molly's progress through the house. Discarded jewelry, dropped brushes, half-eaten sweets, misplaced belongings—she rarely went back to retrieve them. Maybe they could afford two maids.

"Edward, where will we live?"

"We're living now, aren't we?"

She looked quickly to gauge his temperament, but he looked as eager for her approval as ever.

"You know what I mean. Where will we settle?"

"Together. That's all that matters."

She raised an eyebrow. "Your riddles tire me. Be serious or I'll touch the rail again."

"Oh, no you don't," he laughed. He caught her wrists and playfully pinned them behind her back, pulling her close to him. "I don't know when or where we'll settle. There's so much of the world for you to see. I insist on Alaska first, and then it'll be your turn to choose."

Molly tugged her wrists free and wrapped her arms around his waist. He liked it when she was affectionate. "Must we go any further? It's already colder than I thought possible. My curls might freeze and break off if we don't turn back."

"I'll not deny you often, but Alaska has significance for my family. My father helped broker its purchase, and I want to see if it was worth it."

She allowed him to wrap his opened coat around her. "Seward's Folly? I don't see what all the hubbub was over. I know land, and the price sounds marvelous."

"You have no idea how much it cost me."

Molly lifted her head, confused by his words. His wistful golden eyes bore a fleeting resemblance to those of a young man from Prairie Lea—not the shade, but the emotion, the yearning for something out of reach. But what could Edward long for? He had everything Bailey lacked—connections, money, and her.

Distressed by his sorrow she brushed his cheek with the back of her hand, prompting him to share a warm kiss.

He was nice. He was sweet.

But he wasn't Bailey.

"Is this enough fresh air?" he asked. "Are you content to retire for the night?"

She released him and tried to hide her hands in her stole, but her new ring of Colorado gold snagged in the fur. Would this disquiet ever be replaced by peace? By her own choice she'd become his wife—legally and physically—but when would the sense of betrayal disappear?

"Go on without me. I'll visit the dining car for some warm milk first. Maybe it'll help me sleep."

"You've not disturbed me."

Molly tried not to. She really, really tried. "But I need my beauty rest. It might be a year before I meet your family, and I don't want to be wrinkled like a prune by then."

Edward opened his mouth as if to say something but changed his mind. He helped her over the connection between the platforms and then returned to their home on wheels.

Molly waited until the door closed behind him before she entered the next car. Taking a deep breath she dropped her shoulders and let her head droop forward. Amazing how much effort it took to be presentable around the clock. Now when she could finally shed her miserable stays, she still had to mind her posture and carriage even in her quarters.

The green Pullman sleeper she'd entered was being prepared for the evening. Porters pulled the backs of the benches upward, forming upper beds in each berth while the passengers crowded the aisles, waiting to settle in. She shared a sympathetic grin with a woman holding a lanky sleeping child, who'd no doubt be crowded into the narrow bunk with her. Briefly Molly considered offering her sofa to the harried mother but knew Edward wouldn't approve. He'd burn all the cushions. She sighed. Maybe she'd rather sleep out here.

For over a week now, she'd gone through the motions. She responded and answered correctly. On the surface she played the role of a newlywed bride, but she felt like a fraud. Even the transitory nature of their quarters contributed to the bizarre. This wasn't real. The true Molly Lovelace was sleeping off an infirmity back at Mrs. Truman's boardinghouse. She'd awaken when Bailey bounded up the stairs with her letter in his hand.

Molly bit the inside of her lip in contrition. Sinful. A married woman shouldn't pine for another man. She'd said "I do." She couldn't fault anyone but herself. Well, Bailey could bear some of the blame. He didn't come through for her, and Edward did.

She turned and jostled her way out of the crowded car toward her duty. No use in crying over spilled milk. She'd made her choice and she'd stand by it. She'd always been a loyal employee.

14

PRAIRIE LEA, TEXAS
JANUARY 1880

The high-pitched buzz ringing in Bailey's ears had grown familiar. So had the sweet smell of sawdust. He offered a mug of coffee to the local carpenter, Mr. Mohle, while he looked over his invoice once again.

"We'll have you loaded before you know it. Is there anything else we can help you with?"

"Nope. That's enough to finish this job. Sure glad you're helping Thomas out. Right kind of you, especially after that nasty business with his daughter and all."

Bailey slid the pencils into the trough that kept them from rolling down the slanted desktop. It'd been two weeks since Molly had left, and he still hadn't thought of a good reply. He couldn't speak freely while on her father's payroll, and he didn't have the heart to defend her, so he let the comment ride.

"Do you want to go out to the yard and count the boards on?"

"I trust y'all."

But Bailey wanted out of the office. "Come on. We might as well enjoy the sunshine before another storm rolls in."

"Naw, I think I'll wait here." Mr. Mohle lowered himself to the bench with a grumble.

Bailey looked again at the pencils. Usually he had no problem with small talk, but some people were more of a challenge than others.

"Well, looky who's standing behind a desk."

George Garner stepped into the office, followed by Bailey's two younger brothers, Samuel and Tuck. His father was a welcome sight. Mr. Mohle didn't rise but offered hearty greetings. Thank goodness he shook Samuel's outstretched hand. The boy still wasn't sure when to offer it. Tuck ambled to the counter.

"Pa made us finish branding before we could come see you at work. Ma's at the parsonage now."

"What's she doing there?" Bailey asked.

His pa pushed his hat back until it popped up like the lid of a tin can. "She and the girls are working it over so it's fit for you to live in. They brought you victuals, too."

Bailey's eyes brightened. "Sure could use some of Ma's cooking. I eat supper with the Lovelaces when I take the accounts over at night, but Lola can't cook like Ma."

Tuck's eyes got big. "You eat with the Lovelaces? Even after Molly done runned off on you?"

Mr. Mohle shifted his weight on the pine bench and leaned forward, his eyes alert. George cuffed his youngest on the head.

"Boy, you gotta learn when to keep your mouth shut."

"Nothing I haven't heard before," Bailey said. And would hear again as soon as his mother got ahold of him. "You boys want to see the waterwheel? I was headed out there myself."

"The waterwheel? Yee-haw!" Tuck cheered. Even mature Samuel couldn't hide the interest that lit his face. They took out like two freshly branded calves—Tuck running and Samuel walking stiff-legged until he could no longer keep up with his little brother and had to finally break into a trot.

"How are you doing, son?"

Bailey was proud that his demonstrative pa used some restraint. He didn't need a hug in front of the crew.

"After Mr. Lovelace's attack, I thought Molly and I had reached an understanding. I don't get it. Guess I never will."

"I don't know, either. To be honest, your ma and I read the note she sent with Rico. We thought there might be a hint as to your whereabouts in it. Ma was of a mind to burn it, but I put my foot down. You're an adult and are responsible for your decisions—as is Molly."

"Reckon you should've burned it. I'd still be hurt, but maybe I wouldn't hate her so much."

"No use in hating. She can't hurt you again. Take your lumps and learn from them."

They walked past the piles of planks toward the angular building hugging the riverbank. Perhaps it'd all work out for the best, and if Bailey kept telling himself that, maybe someday he'd believe it. Molly had her flaws and he'd loved her despite them, but now he tried to rehearse them like the catechism to ward off the memories.

"You like this work?"

"Yeah, I do. Mr. Lovelace has noticed that sales are up. Couple that to the river rising and fewer shipping costs, and things are looking good." He scanned the teams loading, lifting, and sawing. "Could be this was where God had me headed all along. It suits me. I got bored out in the fields, and working in Lockhart had its own problems."

"I can see why this job appeals to you. You're getting paid to talk to people. They ain't looking to fill another position like that, are they?" George's wide smile stretched from ear to ear.

"It's not all that simple. Tricky part is to smooth over what the customer expects and what the customer gets. Sometimes that's two completely different animals. Then I take the books to Mr. Lovelace when Russell has them balanced up. My only paperwork is the inventory."

"You haven't seen James's son around, have you?"

"Michael? No. I hope he's staying sober—for Russell's sake," Bailey said.

"I pity the man. Can't imagine what it'd be like to have a son you were ashamed of."

Bailey had to look away. His father had made some mistakes, but he didn't deserve a hypocrite like Bailey for a son. Bailey shoved his hands into his pockets. It shouldn't matter now. As far as his pa knew, he'd kept his promise about Molly. Now that she was married, she wouldn't tell anyone the truth.

Treading the worn path between the wheelhouse and the riverbank, they caught up with Samuel and Tuck, who'd run downstream for a better look at the revolving waterwheel.

"Incredible what's accomplished when we use God's power," his pa said. "Imagine how many men it would take to saw those planks, day and night. But here's a river, running like it was designed to, without any effort. You can ignore that power, you can buck against it, or you can see where it's going and join along."

Bailey's eyes didn't leave the wheel. Didn't even blink. "We see two different lessons. You see the benefit of submitting to fate. I see a different story. I see those blades go through their cycle. They go up, higher and higher. Then they get cold water thrown in their face and are knocked back down until they're submerged. If they were smart, they'd stay down, but no, there they go climbing again, hoping that someday they'll get to stay on top."

George laid a work-roughened hand on Bailey's shoulder. "Guess you can tell stories like your old man. Hopefully you'll find some more happy endings. Are you still helping Reverend Stoker?"

"Yes, sir. It does me good to go visiting with him. Helps me remember my problems aren't the only thing God's got to worry about."

George whistled and waved his boys over.

"Are you coming out to the house this weekend? Susannah and Ida sure miss you."

"I miss them, too." Their childish flattery would go a long way toward soothing his vanity. "Depends if the reverend needs any help."

Bailey eyed his approaching brothers and saw that Samuel had broadened considerably during the few months he'd been away from home. He'd have to remember how stout he was before he picked a fight with the young man.

"How's ranching going?"

Samuel brightened. "Weston said I can go on the trail with Willie and Rico this spring."

"You can? That's fine news. What about the sheep?"

"I'm handling the sheep." Tuck's chest puffed out. George snuck a wink at Bailey as the boy continued. "Yep, those woolly-headed beasts ain't nothing but trouble."

"That's what I hear," Bailey said.

"Did you hear about Mrs. Tillerton?" Tuck asked abruptly.

Samuel fell back a step and guffawed, until a stern look from his pa silenced him.

"We were going to call on her after the celebration at Bradford's store, same night Lovelace was struck."

"She's dressing like a man," Tuck jumped in, "wearing buckskin."

Samuel's eyes danced, waiting for his brother's response.

Bailey had been the brunt of enough gossip lately. He didn't rejoice to see someone else in hot water.

"Tuck, you weren't even there," his father admonished.

"Good thing or she might've shot me."

"What?" Now Bailey was intrigued.

George shook his head. "There was a big to-do when we got there. Sheriff Colton had just found a man shot dead on her property—a new neighbor, it turns out. He didn't arrest Mrs. Tillerton, but it's no secret that he suspects she's involved. One thing for certain, she's a different breed. Wearing trousers, toting a gun—it's no wonder the sheriff is keeping his eye on her."

Anne Tillerton figured into one of the most harrowing days of his life. When Weston's wife, Rosa, disappeared, Bailey tagged along as a lark, little suspecting the gruesome scene he'd find. Bailey had never seen a man shot to death before, and the fact that Mr. Tillerton had been plugged by his own wife made it even more appalling. Not that he blamed her. Even if her husband hadn't attacked Rosa, he deserved shooting. Mrs. Tillerton's battered face spoke testimony against him.

"I can't imagine that she'd shoot someone again. I took her home that day, after that business with Mr. Tillerton. She was so shook up, so distant . . . but come to think of it, she might've been living like that for a while. You'd have to pretend you didn't care to survive the pain."

The compassion in his father's eyes embarrassed him. His pa had recognized the similarities before he had. Surviving the pain? Barely. Hopefully no one else caught on to his hurt, because Bailey was having a hard time pretending not to care. And while he was hoping, he needed a decade to pass before Molly came home, for his indifference needed more practice if he was ever going to fool her.

15

CHEYENNE, WYOMING TERRITORY

To *Not* Do List:

· *Do not shop without Edward again.*
· *Do not walk more than a half a mile in the winter—*
unless in Texas.
· *Do not keep calculating how high our expenditures*
are.

Molly had wondered how far north the trains could go before
the snow blocked their path. After watching a snowplow
explode through the drifts, the power of three engines at its
back, she wouldn't be surprised to hear that the track was
cleared all the way to Alaska. Nothing would stop them from
going farther and farther from everything she knew. It was
unbelievable that her one connection to her old life was the
husband she'd met for the first time in November.

Molly slid her way toward the depot. At least they'd had
two days off the train to enjoy the icy streets of Cheyenne.
After weeks on the rolling hotel, it was good to have firm
earth beneath her feet again . . . or at least firm ice. Thank
goodness for her climbing boots. The moccasin-like soles

helped her feel her way across the slick surfaces. She'd be on her backside in a snowdrift by now if she'd worn her high-heeled, thick-soled shoes.

That Bailey made them wasn't forgotten, but she couldn't allow her thoughts to linger on that painful fact. She had to look forward.

But not literally. Molly couldn't raise her head and keep her balance. Every step had to be chosen with care, but something besides her feet was afoot. When they'd first arrived in Cheyenne yesterday, a man had approached them—a stranger, judging from Edward's demeanor—and had requested a private word. Always worried about finances, Molly wondered if their wire request for more funds had been denied.

Her fears were relieved when Edward continued on to the bank and was able to withdraw a stack of bills.

Sitting in the waiting area, Molly had watched him count the lump. She noted the look of astonishment on the young teller's face and felt a sense of pride. She was a rich woman. What did it matter that her husband wouldn't touch the dirty money without the protection of his gloves, she could spend it just the same.

Taking his arm, she'd whispered, "So everything is fine? That man worried me."

Edward had slid the wad of notes into her handbag. "Never worry. No matter what happens, you'll be taken care of. That I can promise."

Odd words, but not as odd as his decision that morning to send her out alone—the first time on their journey that she'd ventured away from the train solo. Molly smothered a squeal as a chunk of snow slid off an awning and dashed against her collar. Usually Edward couldn't wait to escape the confines of the little house on the rails. If he thought the weather too harsh, he should've allowed her to stay. On the contrary, he'd booted her out like a stray cat.

Molly looked directly at the weak sun, a privilege not allowed back home without dire consequences to one's sight. The white disk lay far to the south but equally between the two horizons. Dinnertime. She'd see if Edward wanted to join her at the only diner in town.

The western train departed at 2:00 p.m. They would be attached to a new engine. There'd be different sleepers, diners, and observatories, but her home in the railcar would remain constant. She mustn't be late.

Attaining the platform, Molly searched for the now familiar private coach. No markings designated it as Pierrepont property. Only the windows identified it. There weren't as many as a passenger coach had, but they were much larger, offering better views of the scenery.

She spotted the car and blew air out of her lips in a most unladylike fashion. It sat three tracks over. How did they expect passengers to board over there? Thanking Bailey once again for her comfortable boots, she hiked her skirts and hoofed it across the ties.

Not until she'd climbed up the steps did Molly realize the car wasn't connected to anything. No wonder it'd been left on track three. It wasn't going anywhere.

"Edward?" She called into every room along the corridor. "Edward, why aren't we connected?"

He wasn't in his office or the bedroom. She stepped into the parlor and about collided with an expensive suit.

The man's arms flew up to protect himself and grasped her by the elbows.

"What are you doing?" Molly exclaimed. "This is a private coach!"

"My apologies, miss. It was not my intention to startle

you." It was the stranger who had spoken to Edward earlier—the one who looked as if he frequented the same tailor as her husband. Molly almost expected him to wash his hands after touching her.

"Of course I'm startled. You're trespassing. Where's my husband?"

"Your husband?" His high brow creased. "I've never had the honor—"

"Oh, stop with all your shilly-shallying. You know who I mean. Edward Pierrepont. You spoke to him yesterday."

The man stared at her, his face as blank as the snowcaps on the mountains. "And who might you be?"

"Mrs. Edward Pierrepont."

He stroked his moustache. "Now who's shilly-shallying?"

Something about his manner irked her. Molly had seen her mother snub people often enough to recognize the look. Edward would put this dandy in his place soon enough.

"I am Molly Pierrepont. My father is Thomas Lovelace, a well-respected businessman and leader in Caldwell County, Texas."

"That explains the unfortunate accent."

"How dare you!"

"Miss Lovelace—"

"Mrs. Pierrepont!" Her explosion caught him off guard. "I see the general consensus of Yankees and their manners has not been an exaggeration. I am a lady and expect to be treated as such. Do I make myself clear?" She threw her stole on the chair and stood her ground with flaming eyes.

Mr. Fine Airs must have had second thoughts. "Yes, ma'am. Perhaps there has been a misunderstanding." He motioned to her to have a seat, but she refused. The horsehair seats didn't belong to him, presumptuous man. "This car is the property of the Pierrepont family, and they have requested its return.

It will be connected to the eastbound train this evening and begin the trip home."

Home? To meet his family? "Oh, why didn't you say so? Does Edward know?"

"Yes, but he is not returning with it."

Now Molly dropped into the seat. Here was the perfect opportunity to visit his family, and he wasn't going to take advantage of it? The glamour of New York appealed to her infinitely more than the tundra of Alaska. Maybe she could change his mind.

"Where is Edward? Maybe I can get him to return home. I so dearly want to meet his family."

The man's eyes narrowed. "You want to meet the family?" He looked her over from head to toe. When his eyes returned to her face, he had to have noticed her discomfort. Although Molly didn't cower, didn't flinch, she couldn't help the blush that resulted from the obvious appraisal.

"Where exactly did this wedding of yours take place?"

Why was she getting defensive? This man meant nothing to her. "In Marion, Texas, right here on the train. I was ill and Edward brought a minister on board. Reverend Snow, I believe."

"Was the license filed at court?"

Molly hesitated. She remembered Edward's warnings of what could happen should his family find out. Too late now. And yet, something kept her from producing the certificate she had tucked into her jewelry box. "Certainly, but not by me. Like I said, I was ill at the time. I never disembarked at that stop, but it was all proper." Besides Edward staying at her bedside and her calling him Bailey. The man didn't need that tidbit of information.

"I see." He turned and played with a stopper on a decanter, as if he was trying to reach a determination. "This car will be transported through Nebraska tonight. If you have any personal items on it, I suggest you remove them. If you should see Mr. Pierrepont again, please inform him of our conversation."

"If I should see him?" This interview was not progressing as Molly had expected. "We're leaving on the two o'clock today."

"Just so. I'll find a porter to transport your trunks. Your situation is unfortunate, but there's not much that can be done."

"You can't toss me out!" But the man strode out the exit at the opposite end of the coach.

Molly fumed. Edward would set the man aright when he returned. Who did he think he was, treating her so shabbily? Her husband was probably securing suitable accommodations for them at that minute. Considering how hurriedly he swept her out of Lockhart, she shouldn't be surprised if he expected her to pack up at a moment's notice again.

She grabbed her stole and a favorite parasol from the parlor and headed toward her quarters. Molly rubbed the back of her neck. Her Grecian coils were twisted too tightly. If she could find Freida, she'd have her loosen the coiffure before the train started moving again.

From the disarray in her room, she surmised that Freida hadn't finished tidying from Molly's toilette that morning. Molly slid the scattered brushes, pins, and hot iron from her vanity and into a case with a crash. The glass perfume bottles and jewelry had to be handled more carefully. Running her hand along the table, she herded together all the earbobs and brooches she'd decided against that morning. She flipped open the lid to her jewelry box and paused.

There on top of her bangles and brooches was an envelope with her name printed in Edward's careful script across the center. With foreboding she eased it out of the fine embossed envelope and read words that forced the wind out of her.

16

The daffodils were already blooming in the early Texas thaw—bright spots of yellow in a winter-weary land. Riding alone in the passenger car, trying to sleep with strangers leering at her, making train connections, and haggling with porters, Molly hadn't found the courage to telegraph her parents before she arrived home. What could she say? The words on the marriage certificate and the words in Edward's letter seemed to contradict each other. They were married, but he said she was free. He would try to return, but she shouldn't wait on him. She was paralyzed by the hope that Edward would appear, would contact her, and her circumstance would be clarified. She'd prefer anything above facing the questions awaiting her at home, but he hadn't intervened. She had been left to face them alone.

Molly stood on the front porch of her parents' home and surveyed the mill she'd sacrificed to save. The wheelhouse, the office, the night watchman's quarters, and the mule barn were latched up and quiet after a full day's work. The river rolled peacefully on, filling the air with a humidity that the lands she'd crossed up north lacked. It hadn't changed, but she had.

While flying across the frozen plains, Molly dreamt of returning with fistfuls of money to save her family's pride. Instead, she'd returned today nearly empty-handed and had become the greatest threat to their undoing.

Molly stepped off the porch and wandered down the drive. Her parents had accepted her return with more grace than she'd expected, but she'd spared them her worst fears and doubts. She'd convinced them that Edward was indeed coming to get her. She'd convinced them that their separation was necessary and temporary. No reason to paint the news any blacker if there was a chance of light.

When she reached the gravel road, Molly turned toward town, unsure of her destination but certain that the less time she spent with her parents on her first night home, the less defeated she'd feel. She'd sacrificed her dreams to save them, and if Edward didn't return, she would lose much more than that. Her father might have signed hundreds of contracts during his life, but she could only sign one license of this nature.

The burrs and goat heads growing high along Church Street clung to her soft moccasin boots. She kicked her foot against the stone marker designating the border of the churchyard. Ugly things. She'd never wear them again. She didn't need them here in Prairie Lea, and there was nowhere left for her to go.

The musical scale stretched from the bullfrogs' note to the robins' pitch. With a damp rag wrapped around his index finger, Bailey swiped each one of the keys on the piano, catching the dust that'd sifted through the imperfectly fitted windows.

His Thursday night chores at the church completed, he lingered, having no reason to hurry back to the lonesome parsonage.

He sat on the rickety bench and pecked out a melody. The piano wasn't anything like his guitar, but his ear for music made up for his lack of experience with the instrument. Friday after work he would head home to help at the ranch and visit his family. Funny how life went on. When Molly left, he didn't think he could continue living, so great was his hurt and anger. But despite his predictions, the sun still came up over the gentle swells of the horizon. Once Molly's parents had stopped tiptoeing around him, he'd even found satisfaction working at the mill, and of particular surprise was his relationship with Thomas Lovelace.

Now that Bailey knew him better, his opinion of him was more realistic. Before, Bailey had positioned Mr. Lovelace somewhere between Midas and Solomon. He compared him with his own father, and if his thumb was on the scale, it was to Thomas's benefit. Now, after working with him, Bailey had a more accurate assessment. He admired the man while recognizing his flaws: critical, controlling, and unrelenting when he sensed a weakness. Working for Thomas Lovelace under other circumstances could've been torture, but their contact was limited to looking over the bills and ledgers at supper. Bailey could enjoy his company for a couple of hours a day. Living with him would be another story.

He hated to admit it, but Bailey had a new respect for the pressure Molly had stood against. He understood her resolve to live in Lockhart, even if it meant pretending to step out with Fenton, and he understood why she wanted to leave Caldwell County behind.

A foul odor wafted in the still air. Another dead mouse? Ugh! Bailey located the broomstick in the closet and followed his nose back to the massive upright piano. Removing the stack of hymnals and sheet music from the top of it, he propped the heavy lid open and fished the broomstick inside.

To be honest, Bailey was looking for excuses to loiter at the church. In the last month he'd found a balance that'd been missing before, and he attributed it to the quiet time he spent in prayer while doing his duties on the property. Finally he could sense God's leading and was free to follow. Even the way people treated him had changed. Respect hadn't been offered before, but he tried the yoke on and liked the weight of it.

Through the long opening Bailey could see the deceased rodent curled up at the bottom of the box. With a crash, he let the lid drop and crawled underneath the keyboard. He unsheathed his knife and used it to pry open the bottom panel. There it was. Bailey was reaching for the broom when he heard muffled footsteps coming down the aisle.

With one hand holding the panel board and one grasping the broom, he couldn't hop up but didn't want to surprise his visitor.

"Be with you in a second," he called out.

The footsteps halted.

Sweeping the dead mouse out of the box, Bailey replaced the panel, hammered it into place with the soft side of his fist, and stood.

So startled was he that he blinked, looked away to clear his sight, and looked again before he believed his eyes.

Molly stood empty-handed in the aisle. Above a blue satin gown her face bloomed with heat, her normally perfect coiffure fuzzed and frizzed. Her round eyes betrayed her shock. So she hadn't come looking for him.

Bailey ground his teeth. His knees shook as he tried to accept that it was really her standing before him in the flesh. The last time he'd seen her, she'd been just as disheveled, and he'd been the cause. Was she here to expose him? Would she and Pierrepont tell everyone about his attempt on her virtue?

He leaned against the keyboard to steady himself. The dissonant chord that resulted crashed through his shock and gave him a voice.

"Where's your husband?"

Her chin rose and she smoothed her skirt. "I don't know."

His mouth went dry. Bailey could read her as easily as bear tracks, and he could see the admission cost her dearly.

He forced his voice to be even. "Where'd you lose him?"

But Molly was having none of it.

"Oh, Bailey," she whispered, refusing to mimic his flippancy. "He disappeared in Cheyenne, leaving me at the train station with fare for the ride home and a note. Said he would miss me and might come for me someday, but I shouldn't wait for him." Her black lashes fluttered down to her cheeks as she folded and refolded a lace handkerchief that'd seen better days. "Said I should plan my life without him."

The muscles in his neck tightened. Abandoned by her husband? Never in his most bitter moments would Bailey have predicted this. How could the man leave a woman who'd left her family, left everything, for him?

But there she stood. Still beautiful, still married, and still the woman who'd promised herself to him a couple days before boarding a train with another man. Forgetting his dastardly behavior, Bailey set his jaw. All the understanding he'd gained during her absence vanished. He'd save his compassion for a more worthy recipient, like a rattlesnake.

"Don't worry. He probably didn't mean it. Not too long ago, I got a letter filled with base lies, too. Broken promises shouldn't surprise you."

He'd hit his mark.

"Those weren't lies. I wanted you to come get me. You didn't answer."

"Rico didn't find me in time. I was sick, too." Bailey's voice echoed off the empty pews. "Your love has shallow roots if it can't wait a day before withering up and dying."

She stuffed her handkerchief into her sleeve. "I thought I was helping my parents. I didn't want to leave you."

"But you did, Mrs. Pierrepont, and your father doesn't let any opportunity pass without boasting of the rich family you married into. Your mother goes on and on over the adventures she imagines you're having—her little Molly traveling the world. Meanwhile, I've stayed with your family even though they preferred a man who'd toss you into his railcar and then toss you out of his bed." Bailey prayed she'd contradict him, but she didn't.

He'd secretly held on to a childish fantasy that her disappearance was not what it'd appeared. He prayed there was a gentler explanation, but she hadn't been spared his worst fears. In that second, he felt his heart shrivel up and go sour. "Your parents survived, Molly. We made it through together, and now you're back with no husband and no money. It was all for naught."

Molly bowed her head and clasped her hands together. "Maybe Edward will come back. Maybe he went to get things straightened out, to raise funds. Say what you want, but please forgive me. I need your friendship."

Bailey found himself at the center of the platform, gripping the pulpit. "You are married. Do you know what people will say if they see us together?" He struck the pulpit with a force Stoker never used on Sunday. "You've made your deal with the devil. I won't burn for it."

She didn't look up as he stomped past, ashamed that she'd had the nerve to ask for his help, as if he owed her something. Remembering he didn't care would be difficult—just as difficult as remembering that she didn't care for him.

Molly sat, closed her eyes, and leaned against the firm back of the pew. Bailey had spoken the truth. If he aided her, his reputation would suffer. She'd already hurt him once. She didn't want to do it again.

But who could she turn to? Her father's health was teetering on the brink. Her mother would rather remain under the delusion that Molly had nabbed the husband of the century. She didn't want them to bear the brunt of their shattered dreams, but there was no one else to share her burdens. Had she turned her back on everyone who cared for her?

The silence of the church filled her ears and pressed against her, pinning her to her seat. She didn't want to move. She'd caused enough disturbance as it was, and to interrupt the peace that suffused the room seemed a sacrilege.

She was alone. She'd chased after security and certainty to no avail. While Bailey hadn't sacrificed his freedom, she'd tied herself to a man who didn't feel compelled to honor their vows.

The shadows lengthened across the sanctuary as she sat paralyzed. Where had she gone wrong? Would God let her life be ruined by a hasty decision made while deliriously ill? It didn't seem fair.

But her accusations were weak. She shouldn't have given up the fight against her parents' expectations. When the testing arrived, she'd surrendered. She'd allowed her head to be turned with promises of an easy and glamorous life. Was it too late to change course?

Molly stumbled to the altar, feeling as dim-witted as the cow in the manger scene. What good would this do? Had she trespassed so far against God that He'd washed His hands of her? Was He embarrassed and, like Bailey, couldn't afford to be associated with her now? She had to find out.

"God, I don't know what to pray, or if you want to hear my

prayer, because until now I haven't had much time for you. When I think about it, perhaps we've never been properly introduced. I figured we knew each other since we frequent the same circles, but I want to make this official. So, pleased to meet you."

She waited in silence, letting the step she'd taken catch up with her. It was pretty low of her to come to Him after she'd made a mess of everything, but nothing was going to improve without His help.

Molly rolled off her knees, feeling rather foolish, and sat on the step, bunching her skirts around her ankles. "What do I say? That I'll do whatever you want? We both know how quickly I'll fail, but maybe if you help me, things could be different."

She rested her chin on her knees. "Take Bailey, for example. He's not the man he used to be. He was as big of a rascal as I, and he decided to follow you. Now he's helping my family and helping the reverend. He went from a cutup to a gentleman while I sank deeper and deeper. No wonder you saved him from me. I've done my best to ruin your plans for him." She tugged at a dingy ruffle on the hem of her skirt.

"I give up. I don't even know what to ask for. I guess for starters, Edward should take care of me and Father like he promised—that's a good one—and keep Father safe. Let him not be too disappointed. As for me, the biggest request I can think of would be that you'd take me in and be my God, too. That you'd guide me and change me like you did Bailey. I'm tired of the Molly I've been. I'd like to see what you can do with me. I'm willing to let you try."

She studied the grassy toes of her boots. No lightning flashed. The earth didn't shake, but her world shifted. The load on her shoulders eased to a more manageable burden. The silence in the room felt more like a warm quilt than an oppressive weight.

Darkness fell as she lingered. Too soon it was time for the inmate to return to her cell. She would survive one hour, one minute at a time, but what to do with her growing fear, the suspicion that even worse news awaited her? Why did she feel as if she'd missed a debit on her ledger and she wouldn't have the capital to cover it when the payment came due?

She couldn't delay any longer and started the walk home. As she passed the parsonage, a jagged voice halted her.

"Molly?"

She gripped the papery trunk of a sycamore tree, wincing at the pain she heard in Bailey's voice. "Yes?"

"Go to Lockhart. Mr. Travis hasn't hired anyone to fill your position at the land office. You've always wanted to show your pa that you could take care of yourself. At the very least, you wouldn't be crowded in the house with your parents."

Why did she leave this man? After all she'd done to him, he was there for her. She turned and leaned her back against the trunk. "I should've known you'd help me, Bailey."

His voice grew tight. "Maybe I need to keep you as far away from me as possible."

For the first time she was glad she couldn't see his handsome face, shadowed as it was under the brim of his hat. His words were painful, but she would face her share of pain and would have to plan beyond it.

"Mr. Travis won't let me return, not if I'm involved in a scandal."

"Refuse to believe there's a scandal. Hold your head high. Don't act ashamed. There'll be questions aplenty, but you have to be above reproach until he returns."

She hugged her sides. "And if he doesn't?"

Something fierce seemed to build in Bailey. His profile hardened, and his figure seemed to tense.

"As far as you know he could be on the next train that pulls into Luling. You've got to live like you believe that. We both do."

17

LOCKHART, TEXAS

To Do List:

- *Pray. And pray more.*
- *Convince Mrs. Truman to lease me my room again.*
- *Write home every day inquiring about Father's health.*
- *Avoid unnecessary expenses.*

The massive courthouse on the square had never looked so imposing. No longer did Molly feel like a queen as she approached the portico. She'd abdicated her throne, and no one would welcome her back.

Molly tightened her gloves and wished her black gored skirt didn't have the pink striped panel in the train, but she couldn't find a more somber dress in her trunk. Moved by the needs of her unfortunate fellow passengers, she'd given away most of her more serviceable, less fashionable clothes, never dreaming she'd need employment again, but Monday found her in Lockhart, itching for an ink-stained apron to call her own.

She'd left without a good-bye and was returning without warning. Although curiosity would be high, her one comfort was that no one knew her story. By carefully sharing the smidgen of hope left in Edward's cryptic letter, she could keep her doubts private.

It wasn't only her pride she was protecting, but her livelihood. An abandoned woman had no place in society. Molly had always accepted that custom without questioning, but now on the other side of the coin, it seemed terribly harsh. Poor Mrs. Weems back in Prairie Lea struggled to raise her son alone and was treated like a pariah. What had she done to deserve the snubbing? Molly had no reason to believe she'd be spared similar treatment, and there was only so much time before Edward's absence garnered serious speculation. She needed to establish herself in a career before the shroud of disapproval settled on her.

As she pulled the door open, Molly fortified herself. *Hold your head high. Don't act ashamed.* No use in believing the worst. There'd be plenty of time for eating humble pie if Edward never returned.

"Look what the cat dragged in." Carrie was seated next to Prue on a bench in the main vestibule. Carrie set aside her dinner but made no move to greet her. "We thought you were gone for good."

Prue hopped up and scurried across the tile floor to Molly. "It's good to see you." Her blue calico gown and crocheted collar gave way when pressed against Molly's stiff taffeta.

"It's good to see you, too." Molly accepted the hug, then held Prue at arm's length and considered the lady, perhaps for the first time. "You look happy, Prue. I suppose wedding plans are progressing."

Prue squeezed her hand. "Yes. Mr. Fenton and I will wed next month. I do hope you and Mr. Pierrepont will attend."

Molly's smile faltered. "Thank you for the invitation."

"It's more than you offered us," Carrie protested. "You pretended to be sick and then snuck out of town the very same day. You didn't even tell us good-bye."

What could she say? To tell the truth would be to admit she didn't want to leave, that she'd waited for Bailey and only got on the train when he failed to appear. That story could never be told.

"I'm sorry. I was ill and not thinking straight."

"*Humph.*" Carrie jerked her chin down and tore a piece of bread off her loaf.

"I'm glad you decided to visit," Prue said. "I want to hear all about your journey. Will you and Mr. Pierrepont be staying in Lockhart long?"

"I hope so." Molly cast a furtive glance toward the land-office door. "Is Mr. Travis in?"

Prue nodded. "My break is over. I better return to my desk. Do come by after hours." She slipped to the staircase.

Molly studied the door with the etched glass. She would have sworn she'd never knock on it again. Her heart hammered as she approached, but she schooled her features to show confidence and poise. She'd been as nervous the first time she'd interviewed with Mr. Travis, and she'd done splendidly.

As she raised her fist, she saw a dark form move on the other side of the glass. Before Molly could knock, the door swung open to reveal the scowling face of her former supervisor.

"Mrs. Pierrepont, I presume. To what do we owe the honor?"

"I couldn't come to town without calling. How have you been?"

Mr. Travis didn't appear to trust her friendliness and stared with suspicion. "As you know, we're shorthanded, so I need to make the most of every moment."

Molly looked over her shoulder as Carrie entered the room.

"Since you're shorthanded, I'd be glad to fill in—temporarily, of course."

Carrie gasped. "Mrs. Midas wants a job?"

Mr. Travis shook his head, sending ripples through his jowls. "Why do you want to work? Does Mr. Pierrepont approve?"

Molly steadied her voice and spoke clearly. "He's out of town. I'd work until he joins me."

"Your newlywed husband sent you home to find employment?" He folded his arms across his chest and rocked from toes to heels, apparently enjoying her discomfort.

Mr. Travis wouldn't hire her. She saw that clearly now. He wanted her to grovel, but there was no reason for her to humiliate herself any further.

"On the other hand, thank you for your consideration, but I think I'll rescind my offer." She almost dipped a pert curtsy. "I'll be going now."

Molly could feel her stomach tightening. Not only had she lost a husband, she'd also lost her job. With a flash of her pink-and-black-striped train, she hurried out the door—directly into Judge Rice's path.

"Mrs. . . . er . . . I'm sorry, Molly, I can't recollect your married name. I hope you've returned to good tidings over your father's health. I am on my way to dinner. Would you like to accompany me so I can hear how my old friend Thomas is doing?"

Dining with men was unacceptable now that she was married, but that shouldn't include the honorable septuagenarian. The gentleman's sky-blue eyes twinkled, causing Molly to smile. If he remembered her interference with Fenton and Prue, he didn't hold a grudge.

"Thank you for the offer." She took his arm as they made

their way to the restaurant. "Father is not well, I'm afraid. His first bout of heart spasms left him weak, and this weekend he's had a setback. We worry that any spark of excitement might be detrimental."

The judge patted her hand. "The line between health and death seems a fine one at my age. One misstep and you've suffered a broken hip, one frigid night and pneumonia has bound your lungs, but I'm not convinced the situation is as haphazard as it seems. Your father isn't at the mercy of an ill-timed word or startling noise. He's in God's hands."

He opened the door of the restaurant and allowed her to enter before him. At times like these Molly appreciated every etiquette lesson her mother had forced on her. During most meals with local families, her comportment went unappreciated, but such skills were never noticed as much for their display as for their absence.

The judge ordered for them and then turned his kindly attention to her.

"So the bride of the year has returned to our inconspicuous corner of the world. Tell me, dear, where all have you been? Did you visit the family back East?"

"Do you know the Pierreponts?" Molly leaned forward, not wanting the women at the next table to overhear their conversation.

"I know of them. I admit I'm surprised their son was allowed to wed without a substantial to-do, but perhaps they are more sensitive to the impulsiveness of true love than they've been portrayed."

Molly straightened the silverware on her napkin. What had she expected? Did she think she'd walk into town, reclaim her job, and join the dance as if she'd never missed a step? She picked up her fork and toyed with the greens placed before her. Turns out, leaving had been the simple part. Coming back was proving to be much more difficult.

"Ah, there's some controversy with the family, I assume?" The judge laid his napkin on his lap. "It's none of my business, but you might find me a sympathetic listener. Between my age and my profession, not much surprises me."

She studied his lined face and kind smile. First things first.

"More than sympathy, I need a job."

Judge Rice's head popped back and a bushy eyebrow rose. "I was wrong. You did surprise me. Go on."

"Since Father's spell, he's been unable to work. I thought marrying Edward would give us the money to save the business. That has not materialized as I expected. A . . . er . . . a family friend is helping Father at the mill, but I don't see how that can be a long-term solution. I'd like to find employment, at least until Edward returns and perhaps we can better fund my parents. At the very least, I don't wish to be a burden on them."

Taking a sip of water, his eyes never left hers. He handed his salad plate to the waiter to make room for the entrée. "And when is this Edward Pierrepont returning?"

"I don't know."

His fork froze, pinning the filet to his plate. "Being a judge, and a lawyer before that, taught me that to find the correct answer, one must ask the correct questions. Did he tell you to expect his return?"

She slid her hands under the table and picked at her fingernails. "On the contrary, I'm to forget him. He said perhaps he'd find me someday, but he left little hope that his plans included a reunion." She shrugged, opened her mouth to say more, and then closed it again.

"And so you bravely carry on and pretend your rich husband will return at any moment. After all, to share your fears for the future would strain your father's health."

She nodded.

"See, I *am* a good listener." The older man tore a piece of bread from his roll and chewed it thoughtfully. "And yet, there's something amiss. A family like the Pierreponts would honor their son's commitments, even if they disapproved."

"I'm sure they are unaware. He said at the time that he risked their displeasure, but by then we—" Molly stopped. By then she'd been compromised? She wouldn't test Judge Rice's unflappability. "By then our course was set."

His silverware clicked delicately against his plate, reminding Molly that she'd yet to touch her food. Her stomach rumbled. As little as she wanted to eat, she didn't know when or where she'd get another meal. The money Edward had left her wouldn't last forever.

Finishing before her, Judge Rice tapped his fingers on the tabletop, as if playing an invisible piano. "Your story interests me. It's one I'd like to do some research into, if you don't mind. It'd be a simple thing to contact the Pierrepont family."

"I'm not sure. We were traveling in the family coach, and it was commandeered in Cheyenne. I never saw him after that. I hope Edward is mending rifts. I hope that he'll win their approval and then come for me, but I don't want to interfere with his plans."

The judge's eyes softened. Molly didn't like it. She knew him to be brilliant, shrewd. Of all the cases he'd presided over, all the pleas directed toward him, she didn't like the thought that her situation merited his pity.

She pushed her plate away. "As I said, the course I choose to follow is that of the dutiful wife and daughter. My husband is beyond my assistance for a time, but my parents are not. If I heard correctly, Prue McGraw won't be the stenographer for long. Have you found a replacement?"

"You know stenography?"

She nodded briskly. "Prue taught me."

He looked doubtful.

Molly dug into her bag and pulled out her trusty journal. She flipped to an empty page and grasped her pencil stub. On the train, when she'd gotten bored, she'd practiced in the passenger car. She'd gained confidence since her last lessons. An ornery smile worked its way across her lips, and she even dared to wink at the old judge, earning a startled chuckle.

Next to their table sat two women, one whom Molly recognized as a local horse trader's wife. Tuning out the background noise, she let her pencil skim the page as the ladies prattled rapidly.

"We have a hard enough time making ends meet without someone stealing our colts. They should string him up."

"And they caught him red-handed?"

"*Um-hum.* Now I don't feel an ounce of pity for him, but what about his wife? She has five children to take care of without his help."

"He'll be served three meals a day in jail while his family starves."

Molly didn't have to look to know a pitying shake of the head had accompanied the last statement.

"It's too bad the whole family suffers."

"Especially the children."

When her page was half filled, Molly wordlessly slid it across to the judge. He pulled out a pair of spectacles and squinted over the curious squiggles.

"This appears to be the genuine article. Unfortunately, we have a man completing the training that would certify him as a stenographer. He might not be as skilled as you, but he'll be certified."

"How long before he can begin?" Molly leaned forward. Her days on the train had been filled with such uncertainty that having a place to go each morning would seem an inex-plicable comfort, even if it wasn't permanent.

"Not for a few months, but he isn't guaranteed the job. You could perhaps intercept him—that is, if I can convince the commissioner that we're desperate."

Placing his napkin on the table, the man scooted his chair back. "If you aren't otherwise engaged, we could test your services this afternoon. Sheriff Colton and I have an inter-view you could record for us. Transcribe the notes and have a report ready by tomorrow. I'd consider it a half day's work, and then we'd go from there."

Molly beamed. God hadn't forgotten her. He'd even pre-pared her with the skills she needed to survive.

"An interview?" She widened her eyes. How she loved being in the know. "Another job applicant?"

The judge waved her suggestion away. "Oh no. Nothing like that. It's a deposition with a murder suspect—and I think you know her."

18

Cold chills ran down Molly's back as they approached the squat stone structure. The prisoners' friends and family were milling around the prison yard, gathering before the barred doors that lined the outside walls and waiting to visit with those detained. What did a family do when the breadwinner was removed? Could one of these women be the unfortunate mother of five she'd heard about at the restaurant? Molly hadn't forgotten the terror of having no provider for her family. Look how desperately she'd acted.

She ducked through the entry to the jailhouse, even though the rock opening was ten feet high. Oh no. Stinky. Molly pressed a lilac-scented handkerchief to her nose to combat the dank smells of unwashed prisoners.

A cursory inspection of the room revealed no one of Molly's acquaintance and definitely no women. A young ruffian sat on the wooden bench next to Sheriff Colton's desk, and the two men in the iron cages had their backs turned toward the outside door. Her curiosity overpowered her fear. Having never seen someone in the state of incarceration—only manacles in the courthouse—Molly peered through the dim light. She didn't realize she was staring until one looked over his shoulder and pulled a face at her.

"Oh!" Embarrassed, she covered her mouth before any more unplanned utterances could escape.

Sheriff Colton laughed and offered his chair to her. "So you want to try your hand at stenography? We'll let you practice. I think you know Mrs. Tillerton."

Easing her bustle between the arms of the sheriff's chair, Molly didn't even look up. "Yes, I've met Mrs. Tillerton, but I don't know that she would claim my acquaintance."

A woman's voice sounded from the bench, tired but clear. "I haven't met a lot of people here, but last I checked, keeping to yourself isn't a crime."

Molly froze. Did that boy speak to her? Confused, she looked for another possibility. There was no one else. She sputtered.

"Beg your pardon, Mrs. Tillerton. I would have spoken to you directly had I seen you."

Buckskin clad, wearing a loose green duster and a bandanna bunched over her neck and chest, Mrs. Tillerton didn't answer. Her hands twitched as her eyes lingered on the pistol lying on the desk in front of Molly.

"You'll get your gun when we're ready," Colton said, "and not a moment before."

Since entering, Judge Rice had been observing the woman from the doorway. Now he stepped forward and presented himself. Even Molly couldn't miss her flinch as he extended his hand. Strange behavior for a woman who was brave enough to dress like a man. Molly would rather fight a mountain lion than be caught in britches, yet Mrs. Tillerton's reaction didn't seem to be the manner of someone who was avoiding pain, merely preparing for it.

"Mrs. Tillerton, since finding the body on your property,

we've given you ample opportunity to come in for a deposition," Judge Rice said. "Unfortunately, you've chosen to ignore our summons."

"I told you everything I knew about it already, which is nothing."

Her delicate features and voice were at odds with her general appearance. Colton cleared his throat and nodded at a blank pad of paper. Goodness gracious! Molly had forgotten why she was there. Pushing the pistol aside, she straightened the paper before her and caught up on the interview.

"You can't disregard a court summons, and Sheriff Colton doesn't appreciate having a gun pulled on him when he goes to serve court papers," the judge said.

Mrs. Tillerton shuffled her feet, causing Molly to wonder what kind of shoes she wore. Men's boots?

"A woman living alone doesn't like to be caught unaware."

Sheriff Colton spoke up, requiring Molly to use a new symbol to designate him as the speaker. "And if you're saying it's legal to protect your property, you're right. It's also legal to shoot a man to defend yourself or another person, which you did last summer."

"I was cleared," Mrs. Tillerton said. "There were witnesses."

"But when another dead man is discovered on your property, we wonder if you might've taken protection to a criminal level," Colton said.

The bars of the cell rattled. "I know why the poor sap was sneaking to her place. It was probably his wife that done him in."

Molly wrote the comment before she realized it was spoken by a prisoner.

Colton hollered at the man. "Stay out of this or you won't get your supper until it's nice and cold."

"If it's your wife's cooking, temperature can't help it, either way. A noose won't kill me as fast as her succotash."

"Strike that." Colton said to Molly as he pulled a Bible from a shelf behind her. Molly scratched through the scurrilous critique while Mrs. Tillerton took the oath, her white hand looking fragile against the large black book.

"Did you know or had you ever met Saul Nimenko?" Judge Rice asked.

"I've seen him around. Never spoke to him."

The pause allowed Molly to sneak a peek at the room. Sheriff Colton was sitting on the edge of his desk but wasn't blocking her view of Judge Rice leaning against the wall or Anne Tillerton staring at the floor.

"Why was he on your property?" That was the judge speaking.

"Can't answer that. As far as I know, he'd never been to my place before."

The look Colton shot Judge Rice could only be described as skeptical.

"Mrs. Tillerton, where'd you learn to shoot?" the judge asked.

"At home in Ohio. I've got five brothers." She paused. "Are you telling me no one else in Caldwell County knows how to shoot?"

"Besides your husband, have you ever killed anyone?" he continued.

"Yes, sir."

The papers Colton was sitting on rustled as he leaned forward. "Who?"

"My mother," she whispered, "when I was born."

The room was silent. Even the jailbirds stilled. The judge pulled at his chin. "We realize that your actions last year saved Mrs. Weston Garner's life." His footsteps echoed off the thick stone walls as he came closer. "And yet your behavior since that incident has been erratic, to put it mildly. You've been through a traumatic experience, one of the worst imaginable. It's possible that it'd leave an impression on your psyche, perhaps arousing furies you're unable to control. Maybe you have fears that are irrational?"

Her voice didn't grow an iota louder, but it sounded stronger. "My fears have never been irrational. I lived with a monster, and his last act proved it. If you're on a hunt for uncontrolled fury, find other women with bruised faces and limps and ask them. They could point you in the right direction. You won't find any misdirected anger here."

Such pauses followed her pronouncements that Molly would've had time to write the conversation out longhand. She tapped her pencil on the desk, waiting for the next wave. Sheriff Colton launched first.

"Where were you December seventeenth?"

"I don't know. Chances are at my farm."

"Were you aware that your property tax is overdue?" Judge Rice asked.

"No. That's going to cause me trouble. I haven't done too well with the cattle. It seems like I'm losing them left and right."

"Is someone stealing from your herd?"

Anne shrugged. "I've got my suspicions, but they had nothing to do with Mr. Nimenko."

"Who do you suspect?"

She scanned the cells. "You think I'm going to say right now? In front of a dozen curious ears? That wouldn't be wise, Your Honor."

Sheriff Colton slid off the desk. "But you are about to lose your farm. You think someone is rustling your cattle. Would you say you've found yourself in a desperate situation?"

Mrs. Tillerton turned gray eyes on him. "Of all the situations I've been in during my life, this one feels the least desperate."

"Explain, please," the judge said.

Molly watched as Anne pushed her bandanna away from her face. "What's money? What's a ranch? No one is hurting me. No one is tormenting me. It's peaceful."

"Could that sense of peace come from possessing a Galand-Sommerville pistol? Belgian made?" Sheriff Colton asked.

"No. Why?"

"Mrs. Nimenko swears her husband carried that model, and it wasn't on the body."

Anne leaned forward. "You think I wrestled Mr. Nimenko's gun from him and shot him with it? Me?"

Colton's nostrils flared. "I don't know what to think, but since we have no other leads, we're hoping that you are connected in some manner. It'd make our job much easier."

Molly about dropped her pencil.

From the looks of it, Judge Rice was shocked, too. "That's not what he meant to say."

"Easier?" Mrs. Tillerton interrupted. "You hoped I was the murderer? That's not impartiality, is it? Bring someone in and hope they don't have an alibi?"

Colton had nothing left to say, but the men behind bars did.

"Don't be surprised, ma'am. That's Texas justice for ya. They decide who's guilty so they don't have to find the real culprit."

The judge sighed. Straightening off the wall, he rolled his eyes skyward and shook his head.

"All things considered, we're going to insist that you remain in custody."

Mrs. Tillerton sprang to her feet. "In jail? You're keeping me in jail?"

"You have no family, no ties. It'd be too easy for you to disappear."

"And you ignored our earlier summons," Colton said. "You've not cooperated up to this point."

Mrs. Tillerton's tough façade was crumbling. She cast a doubtful eye at the jail cells and then caught sight of her gun belt on the desk.

Colton snatched it before she could think twice. He reached over Molly to set it high on the shelf and then took the large ring of keys off their hook. The iron door screeched. Mrs. Tillerton obediently entered the empty cell, jumping when the door closed with a crash. Even the other prisoners sobered, seeming to regret her imprisonment more than their own.

Judge Rice reminded Molly once more of her assignment and made his departure. But Molly stayed. How could she leave a woman here alone? She didn't believe for one moment that the frightened girl was a cold-blooded killer. Had she been heartless, she wouldn't have saved Rosa.

Before Molly could speak to her, a man's voice rang through the open door.

"Sheriff! We need you at the cattle yard. Michael James drove a herd in with some sloppy rebranding. Someone called him on it, and he took off. They're chasing him now."

"Maybe we shouldn't catch him," he grumbled. "I'm running out of cells."

Molly left his desk to give him access to his gear. "I'd think Michael James would be a more likely suspect for this murder than Mrs. Tillerton. You can't hold her based solely on the location of the body."

"Your job is to take notes, not to interfere with an investigation." The sheriff jammed his hat on his head. He blustered to the door, took another look at Molly, and snagged the key ring before he left.

Anne had seated herself on the metal bed and turned away from the rest of the room. She wormed a shaking finger in and out of a buttonhole on her oversized coat.

Molly approached, feeling doubly foolish in her pink finery. How vain and frivolous her problems must appear to someone like Mrs. Tillerton. If only there was something she could do for her.

"I wonder if any of the cattle he brought in are yours," Molly said.

"If Michael James rides a roan and wears a slouch hat pinned up at the side, those are my cattle. I've seen him lurking about."

Molly grasped the cold bars as inspiration struck. "What if Mr. Nimenko saw him lurking about, too? What if he confronted him when he caught him rustling your cattle?"

Anne turned to face Molly, her gray eyes deadly serious. "Those are fair questions, but how are we going to prove our answer?"

19

Nothing Bailey had experienced while assisting Reverend Stoker had prepared him for what he encountered the next day at the sawmill. News of Michael James's theft and flight were all over town. Posses had formed to hunt for him and posters were probably being printed that very morning. What did one say to a man whose son was wanted for cattle rustling? Should he offer his condolences, or would silence be more appreciated?

Russell was late arriving. Through the office window Bailey watched him pause at the crest of the hill overlooking the riverbank. He removed his hat and wiped a shaking hand across his high forehead. That walk to the mill had probably never seemed so long before. Bailey set aside the stack of orders he was assigning to the crew and went to meet him.

"Morning," Bailey said.

"Are you here to ask why I'm late, or do you know already?" Sweat glistened on Russell's brow even though the morning was still cool.

"I heard about the cattle. How are you and your wife doing?"

Russell's chin puckered. "We tried our best with that boy, but it's easier for people to think they could've done better. It's easier for them to figure that we're all cut from the same cloth."

"People know you don't condone what Michael did," Bailey said. "You still have your reputation."

"Not according to Thomas Lovelace." Russell removed his hat for a second swipe at his forehead as they entered the lumberyard. "I've worked for him all my adult life, never shorted him a penny nor cheated him a minute, and it's no use. Nothing makes his day like hearing about Michael's crimes. The more my son disappoints me, the more Thomas is delighted. He'll never allow me to live this down. It wouldn't be any worse if I'd stolen those cattle myself."

The looks coming from the men at the saw varied from curious to hostile. Bailey met every one, staring until they turned away.

"Don't let Mr. Lovelace get to you. He hasn't been down here since his spell. Whatever he's thinking, he'll have to keep it to himself."

"Russell! Bailey!"

Bailey turned to see Thomas descending the ridge, recklessly gathering speed on the gravel path.

"So he finally did it, did he?" The man's impatience prohibited him from catching his breath before throwing his barbs. "Cattle rustling? And I'm the fool who lets his father have access to my accounts."

No wood screeched through the saw. Everyone had stopped to hear the exchange.

"Let's go inside." Bailey opened the door to the office to give Russell the benefit of privacy, but it was not to be found there. The customers in the waiting room leaned forward when they saw him walk in.

"The brawling, the drunkenness—I was willing to overlook your son's faults because you managed to stay sober at work, but having a thief in the family is another matter. Makes me wonder if that's why we've been behind all year. Maybe Michael was practicing what he learned from his old man."

Didn't Mr. Lovelace realize that Russell had nothing to lose? Why cross a man with an outlaw son on the lam? Sounded like a good way to wake up dead. But Russell didn't respond. Instead of defending himself before his customers, he stood with feet spread broad and head bowed. Even Thomas seemed disappointed that the game had ended without a fight.

"Does he still have a job here or not?" Bailey asked and wondered why he couldn't keep his mouth shut.

"If it weren't for Dr. Trench and his doomsday predictions, I'd send him packing, but—" Thomas frowned—"but I guess out of the goodness of my heart, I'll give him another chance."

That Russell hadn't done anything to jeopardize his first chance wouldn't be debated. Giving the poor man an escape was the important thing.

"Russell, can you take Mr. Berg to his wagon? I bet the boys have it loaded," Bailey said.

Russell allowed Mr. Berg to go through the door and then pulled it closed softly behind him.

"Are they sure it was his son?" Mr. Kimball asked from his seat on the bench.

A man released a stream of tobacco to ping in the spittoon. "Yep. Those cattle are from several different herds. He was even too lazy to disguise the brands, only burned over the top of them."

"Now they wonder if he killed that man out on the Tillerton place. Maybe James got caught liberating Mrs. Tillerton's cattle," Mr. Meneley added.

"Maybe Mrs. Nimenko caught her husband liberating Mrs. Tillerton," the spitter said.

Bailey cleared his throat. "Sorry to keep you waiting. How can I help you gentlemen?"

"Ah, industry." Thomas inhaled long and hard. "I don't know how I've survived without breathing sawdust. A rooster can't spend all day in the henhouse."

Guffaws erupted from the men. Bailey smiled. You wouldn't catch him sitting inside for days, either. Perhaps if Thomas could leave Russell alone, the visit would do the man some good.

"Hey, Thomas. Saw your daughter in Lockhart yesterday. What's that son-in-law of yours up to?" Mr. Meneley asked from the bench.

Bailey wiped his palms on his trousers and picked up a pencil, feeling all eyes on him. He pretended to fill out a receipt as Thomas Lovelace answered.

"Something significant, that's for sure. We should've warned Molly that an important man doesn't have time to coddle a new bride, but she's a trooper. She's playing house until he gets things ready for her. You know Molly. It better be fit for a queen."

Bailey's pencil snapped. Without raising his eyes he grabbed the next closest one and tapped the lead against the blank page.

Could hardly call Mrs. Truman's boardinghouse a palace, and Molly was lucky she was allowed a room at all. But Mr. Lovelace forged ahead, letting his pride paint a victorious portrait of a spoiled wife and a doting husband.

"Come on, Mr. Meneley. Let's look the yard over. Maybe you could help me decide which building I should update next. My new partner, Mr. Pierrepont, is looking for a project to spend money on."

Bailey watched as the two men walked out the office door. There wasn't any money coming from Pierrepont. Thomas surely had to suspect that by now. Poor Molly. The longer Bailey worked with her parents, the more he understood the pressures that drove her into Pierrepont's arms. No longer could he despise her with a clear conscience, but he was finding it easier to hate himself.

"I don't believe a word of it," Mr. Kimball said after they'd left the room.

"Me neither." The spitter fired again. "I heard that Pierrepont fellow left unpaid bills in Lockhart. Half the pretties he bought for the gal haven't been paid for."

Bailey looked up. Truly? Had he left her with debts?

"That's what I heard, too. And yet Thomas pretends she's married into money. Where is the man, anyway? Can't imagine leaving your bride for this long," Mr. Kimball added.

Bailey had heard enough. "Mr. Kimball, looks like we owe you a refund on that last load. Do you want cash or a credit on your account?"

"Don't let us get under your skin, Bailey," he said. "I know you were sweet on the girl, but you're better off without her."

"My wife agrees," the spitter chimed in. "She was saying how she was proud to see you working around the church, making visits and all. If you'd got messed up with Molly, you'd be sunk as low as she is."

"Fellas, don't badmouth her on my account," he said.

"'Course, we know you don't have a dog in the fight. You're smarter than that. It's a good thing you steered clear of that mistake. You set a good example for all the young men hereabouts," the spitter said.

"Jesus should be their example, not me," Bailey said, but their approval grew.

"That's what we're talking about. Such a humble spirit . . ."

Misery, pure misery. And no relief in sight.

He did his best to hide the rest of the day, there being no safe place to turn without hearing either Michael James's or Molly's name. Odd how opinion was formed. Odd how people thought they could sum up a person's character by the news of the day.

After delivering the ledger to Mr. Lovelace and enduring supper at his table, Bailey headed down the path to his home at the parsonage.

Gravel crunched behind him. Bailey turned to see his Aunt Louise hobbling toward him.

"Good evening, Aunt Louise. How's life at the Bradford house?"

She wiped her forehead with her hankie. "I'm glad I caught you, Bailey. These new boots have me so aggravated I don't want to go a step further than necessary."

"What do you need?"

"You, of course. Reverend Stoker isn't around and the Mohles could use a visit. Mrs. Mohle had another miscarriage this afternoon, bless her heart. I'm on my way home from there."

"Miscarriage? I didn't know she was expecting."

"They don't let on until they have to because it's happened before. Don't want to get their hopes up, you know."

His heart went out to them. Bailey had a soft spot for children. He remembered how protective he was of Susannah and Ida when they were born. He'd fight a bear armed with a spoon for his little sisters.

"I'll head straight over." He took her thanks and a peck on the cheek and started to the Mohles' home on the other side of the school.

Perhaps he should prepare what he'd say to them, dredge his memory for appropriate Scriptures and sentiments, but instead he used the time to wade into their grief. What would he feel if he'd lost a child of his own? And to suffer this grief in silence? Mr. Mohle's carpentry business meant he frequented the sawmill, yet he'd never breathed a word about his loss. Would he want to talk now?

Mr. Mohle met him at the door, dry-eyed and solemn, all his usual bluster set aside. He ushered him into the dim bedroom where Mrs. Mohle sat propped up by pillows. A simple white handkerchief covered her head, and she was praying, mumbling words he couldn't understand while rocking like she did while playing the piano on the Sabbath.

Although both were several years older than Bailey, they were looking to him for something. But what? Wisdom? Comfort? All he had to offer was shared suffering. Mr. Mohle pulled up a chair and motioned for him to sit. He did. Closing his eyes, he discarded his own troubles in order to present the Mohles' sufferings to his Lord. No words, just trusting that God understood his heart groanings of pain for these good people.

Interceding was all he knew to do for them, yet he felt they expected something more. What would Reverend Stoker do? Bailey's bag of tricks ran pretty light. He was more apt to say something to offend than to soothe, another reason he'd rather speak silently to God.

Bailey opened his eyes. Mrs. Mohle wiped the tears from her face and smiled bravely at her husband.

"I'm ready," she said.

Ready?

Mrs. Mohle moved toward him. Bailey leaned forward on his elbows and reached to help her up, but instead she placed a tiny wrapped bundle in his hands.

In a heartbeat, Bailey's world became very small.

His troubles at the mill vanished, his worries were wiped clean. Who he was, why he was there—forgotten. The only thing in the world that had any meaning was the soft weight in his palm.

So perfect. So very tiny.

The bundle wasn't any bigger than his fist, but he cradled it carefully against his chest, wondering what the child would've done with ten years of life. With twenty. He was amazed to think that this fresh soul was already in Christ's presence and already knew his Savior more intimately than he did, despite all the sermons he'd heard.

With a sigh, Mr. Mohle rose and held out his hands. Bailey relinquished the bundle to the father and followed him into the kitchen, where a wooden jewelry box sat on the table.

The carpenter faltered when he saw the box. "Every time I make one, I pray we won't need it for this, but I keep one in the shop just in case."

He wound the ends of the blanket tightly together and placed it in the box. Covering the small bundle with his hand, his lips moved silently. Then he lowered the lid and fastened the latch.

In a daze, Bailey followed him outside, where the comforting sounds of a spring evening filled the air. A shovel was leaning against the tree, already dirty from the day's work.

"When she started having pains today, I went ahead and got it ready. Been here too many times before to be surprised."

Along the dark fence line stood four azalea bushes—the closest being half the size of the others.

"I had no idea," Bailey said.

"Not something people want to know."

"Is it something you want to talk about?"

Mr. Mohle shrugged. "There's no comfort in telling people what they don't want to hear."

After the burial Bailey stayed to pray with the bereaved couple once more, but Mr. Mohle's words would haunt him for the rest of the night.

Lying in his bed, studying the undersides of the wooden shingles above him, Bailey had to wonder who else was troubled by stories that no one wanted to hear. Was he strong enough to bear their heavy knowledge, or would he become jaded? Had God called him to share the burdens of His people?

20

The first time Molly visited the jail, her curiosity had blinded her to the despair and hostility caged within. Every time since, she'd desperately wanted to flee. It took all her resolve to stay while Sheriff Colton unlocked the door to let her join the woman who'd been there since the deposition.

Anne raised her head out of the curl she'd made in the corner of her bunk. "I don't know why you keep coming back."

"Now that I've got the stenographer job, it's easy to stop in after work to see how you're doing." Molly looked around the tiny space. "A silly question, I suppose. There's not much good that can happen here."

"They let me out a couple times a day. That's more than the men get." Anne swung her feet to the ground. "I've done my best to avoid male attention, and here I am locked up with the worst of them."

"They don't harass you, do they?"

"Not if I stay clear of the bars."

Molly took a step toward the middle. "You'll be pleased to know that they recovered your cattle. Sheriff Colton is going today to search your property again and look through your house. If they don't find any evidence, they'll have to release you. Judge Rice said they would've let you go sooner, but he was afraid you would've fled at the first opportunity."

"I would have. I should've left this place when Jay died. There's nothing here for me."

"I wish you didn't feel that way."

Anne removed her hat. The brown ringlets beneath it sprung up at the release. "Unfortunately, I don't know anywhere that's better, but I'll have time to think it through while I sell off my property. At least I'll have enough to get me set up somewhere new."

"Perhaps you're right. I hate to say it, but once people form an opinion of you, it's nearly impossible for them to change it."

What wouldn't Molly give for a fresh start? It hurt too much to think about.

The barred window opposite them provided a view of the street—children staring in open curiosity at the incarcerated, women scurrying by, refusing to look up. Socially, Molly had already sensed a change in the way people behaved around her. Errant whispers of speculation quieted when she entered a room. Sometimes she was avoided. Sometimes she was studied—much like the prisoners.

Molly wasn't a prisoner behind bars, but there were barriers nonetheless. Would she be released, or had she been given a life sentence?

The day of Prue's wedding arrived sooner than Molly had expected. She sipped punch from the Fentons' crystal and watched as her friend made the rounds through the crowded ballroom of her new home on San Antonio Street.

Prue was the perfect blushing bride—devoted, innocent, and eager to please her husband.

Molly had been, too. She was a practical woman. She'd known what to expect as soon as she recovered from her illness. All part of the bargain. But now what? Edward hadn't kept his end of the deal. Her parents were still in danger of losing everything. And what if he did come back? Could she give herself again to a man who could do without her?

She downed the rest of the punch and set the glass on the empty table at her side. Taking a seat would make it more obvious that no one chose to share her company. Molly sighed. Who would've thought that being a wife would be so lonely? Most women her age were married, but she didn't feel welcome in their circle, as if they feared her conjugal woes were contagious. She scanned the room. There was Bailey. But he was worse than a stranger to her. With a stranger the potential existed that they might become friends. Bailey already knew everything about her and kept his distance. And she couldn't blame him.

That left Carrie.

Lately Carrie had grown increasingly antagonistic toward Molly. Frequently she asked Molly how Edward was, if she'd heard from him, if there was any news, but with every negative answer Carrie grew more smug until her inquiries seemed less out of concern for her friend and more like Molly's misfortune was somehow gratifying.

Molly picked up her empty glass and headed to the punch bowl. She had no right to feel sorry for herself, not when she compared her plight to Anne's or to some of the other women she saw at the courthouse. She wasn't wanted for murder, and neither was her husband . . . as far as she knew. At least she had a veneer of respectability left.

She lifted her chin as Carrie approached. Bailey's words

had been her refrain since returning to Lockhart. *"Refuse to believe there's a scandal. Hold your head high. Don't act ashamed."* She was doing her best, but it was hard—especially alone.

Carrie smiled and waved, but not at Molly. She was waving Bailey over. It was too late for Molly to escape. She tried not to notice how nice he looked in his Sunday best. She also didn't want to see the disgust on his face when he realized he'd been lured into a grouping with her.

"Bailey," Carrie purred, "thank you for offering to be my escort. It would be bad form to show up at a wedding unaccompanied."

As Molly had.

"Prue asked me to escort you. Nothing more." Bailey must have found something fascinating through the doors into the salon, because he couldn't bring himself to look at anything closer.

"But I hope Molly doesn't mind seeing her old beau enjoying the company of another lady. If so, this wedding would be doubly painful." Carrie turned to address Molly. "And what about your husband? Did this ceremony bring back memories of your own wedding, or have we stopped pretending that there was a real ceremony?"

Molly's lips parted in surprise at the hurtful comment. "I *am* married."

"That's what you claim—that Mr. Fancypants was so besotted that he swept you out of town. But where is he now? Has the loving groom even inquired after his bride?"

What could she say? Carrie spoke the truth, and Molly was as scandalized as anyone at Edward's behavior.

"Carrie, I think Prue wants to introduce you to someone." Bailey gestured to the bride, waving frantically at her.

Carrie's eyes glinted like hard emeralds. She knew when

she was being routed. "Of course. If you'll excuse me, my friend requires her bridesmaid's assistance."

He should leave. Bailey couldn't get messed up with her, but it was the same old story. Even if he didn't care a jot for her, his feet rested under her father's table every evening. He couldn't walk away from Mr. Lovelace's kin.

Before he could make up his mind, she spoke. "You were wise to tell me to move to Lockhart. If I were home, my parents would've realized by now that Edward and I aren't corresponding. Carrie's right. It's been a month now and I've had no letter, not a single telegraph or note since he left. He's not coming back, Bailey." She bit her lip with perfect teeth.

Bailey felt the dread of a hundred spiders crawl up his back until he reminded himself that whether present or absent, she had a husband. His location didn't change the truth of his existence.

"You wanted freedom. You wanted to prove to your father that you could make it on your own. You can't unburn the bridge now."

"Freedom meant the chance to earn Father's respect. I wanted him to be proud of me. Discarded woman, abandoned wife—what I've become will crush him. Yet if Edward returns, how can I honor and respect a husband who left me?"

Bailey had tarried too long already. The conversation had wandered into dangerous territory. Maybe someday he'd have the experience and wisdom to offer counsel, but not anytime soon.

"I've made you feel uncomfortable." Molly set her glass down, her hand lingering on the stem. "It was terribly gauche of me. I didn't mean—I should go." And quietly she vanished from the assembly of Lockhart society leaders so he could breathe freely again.

To Do List:

- *Find a boardinghouse far from Mrs. Truman's and Carrie.*
- *Send an inquiry to Edward's family in New York.*
- *Plead Anne's case to Judge Rice again.*

Molly brushed off her best gown and hung it in the wardrobe with a last fond caress. The gown never made it to a New York ball as she'd hoped. She slipped her arms into her white housedress, confident she wouldn't be leaving for the rest of the day. Wouldn't leave her room if possible. As soon as supper was on the table, she'd make herself a plate and disappear. She'd rather grow a beard like President Hayes than see Carrie tonight.

Carrie had always been critical, but never had Molly suspected the animosity that must fill her veins. Had all Carrie's ribbing been purposely aimed to hurt her? Now that she'd seen the mask slip, Molly couldn't laugh off her jibes with the same carelessness. She brushed her hair with swift strokes. People had finally stopped asking about her absent husband, and Carrie had to stir the pot. What indignity would she be subjected to next?

If she knew for certain that Edward wasn't coming back, she'd buy herself a house in Lockhart, away from Carrie. Even the little place she and Bailey had wandered into would do. Molly slid her shoes into the row at the bottom of the wardrobe. Now that Prue had retired and Molly worked all the cases, she made enough to set up housekeeping on her own.

A knock at the door and Mrs. Truman could be heard making her way through the house.

"Molly, you have guests."

No one at the reception had wanted to speak to her. Who would call now?

She checked the buttons on her housedress and descended the stairs.

21

"Reverend Stoker, Judge Rice, to what do I owe this honor?" The words were calm but her emotions were in turmoil. Legal and spiritual? Was she in need of both types of counsel?

The men doffed their hats. Judge Rice smiled kindly while the reverend passed his Bible from left hand to right.

"May we come in?"

"Yes. Please follow me to the parlor." Molly led the way, forcing down the lump in her throat. "I suppose the reception is over?"

"Most likely," Judge Rice said. "We were unable to stay for the duration."

"You came to see me instead?" She could feel the blood leaving her face as she lowered herself onto a rocking chair, allowing them to share the settee.

"We have news that couldn't wait." The judge paused for Stoker to grunt his consent before continuing. "Despite your reservations, I made some inquiries into Edward Pierrepont, and what I found was unexpected."

Molly didn't move. The elderly judge's blue eyes held hers. She knew he was waiting for some response before he continued, but she was paralyzed.

"Go on," she finally managed.

"I queried every courthouse between here and San Antonio, and there were no marriage licenses filed for a Pierrepont. Are you certain—?"

"Yes!" Molly sprang to her feet, eager to squelch the doubt his question introduced. "I have a license." Without asking for leave she exited the room, skimmed up the stairs to scatter jewelry across her bureau as she pulled the folded license from the bottom drawer.

Smoothing it, she read the two signatures. Edward's angular thick strokes crowded into each other, her own small loops drawn unevenly from her sickbed. Proof.

From the time her foot left the bottom step until she sailed into the room, she held it outstretched and opened, afraid the all-important autographs might disappear if let out of her sight. "Here it is."

Judge Rice reached it first. His eyes flickered up immediately. "This says Edward Postmont. Do you know for certain he's a Pierrepont?"

"Of course. The pastor may have printed his name wrong, and his signature is illegible, but he's a Pierrepont, all right." Molly dropped into the rocker and clasped the arms of the chair to steady her trembling hands. "He had the private car on the train, and Freida, the maid, knew him. So did the man in Cheyenne who came to take the car away. He's legitimate, but that explains why you couldn't find a license. An honest mistake."

"Unfortunately that leaves us a situation that isn't honest at all." Judge Rice tapped the license with his long finger. "If he is Edward Pierrepont, then you aren't his wife. Mr. Pierrepont is already married. His wife is a member of the European nobility—Contessa Anatasia of Moscow."

"He was married?"

"*Is* married."

Molly's insides felt like they were being tumbled in a butter churn. "He's married to me, so that's impossible."

Reverend Stoker pulled the carnation boutonniere from his lapel. "Either he's not Edward Pierrepont and you've married a confidence man, or he is a Pierrepont and there is no valid marriage."

"But I . . . we . . ." Her gaze fell to the baseboards. "I have a license. I was his wife."

She turned toward the window in an attempt to manage the revulsion rolling across her in waves. Another woman's husband? She'd been with another woman's husband? But even as her emotions rioted, her analytical mind found evidence to verify their words. The conductor had forced Edward to marry her in Marion. He'd said that his family would strongly disapprove. He promised to show her the world but refused to take her to his home. She dug her fingernails into her palms. Why didn't he tell her? Why didn't he bring her back instead of going through with a ruse?

"Molly, dear." Judge Rice placed a cool hand over hers. "This is quite a shock, and we want you to take your time. You mustn't feel rushed to make a decision."

"I don't have a say, do I? I can't annul a previous marriage."

"No, but you must decide if you want to press charges," he said. "He's going to be brought to Caldwell County regardless of your decision, but the other charges wouldn't involve you."

"How many women did he marry?"

Reverend Stoker laid down his Bible. "No others that we know of, but some of our merchants have unpaid accounts that he defaulted on."

The rest of the conversation was beyond Molly's comprehension. All her hopes of a tidy resolution were gone. She'd been duped, ruined . . . and what had begun as a glorious solution to her problems had turned into a disaster from which there was no recovery.

Bailey passed through the receiving line, kissed the bride, and congratulated Mr. Fenton but stepped out before reaching the hateful bridesmaid. One more snide comment about Molly and he might lock Carrie in an outhouse with a wasp's nest.

He lifted a whole piece of cake off a glass plate and headed for the door. Why was it that his most unselfish impulse would bring the most condemnation? Yes, he was hotter than a two-dollar pistol that Molly had left with Pierrepont, but he couldn't stand to see her suffer. And as he tried to decide whether to come to her aid or stay away, Bailey couldn't help but think of those who were watching.

Despite the busybodies, he should check on her before he saddled up and headed home. It was the right thing to do. Didn't Jesus talk to the woman at the well? Jesus could've hurt His reputation, but He was willing to risk it to minister to a fallen woman. Bailey rubbed his neck as he neared Mrs. Truman's boardinghouse, still unsure of his intentions. Were they pure? Was he caring for a friend or giving in to temptation? Trying to know his heart was like balancing on a weathervane.

The one consolation Bailey clung to was that Molly was married. Their relationship could never be resumed, and even he wasn't so foolish and ungodly to wish that it could. He mourned what might have been, but the future held no possibilities for them. He was safe on this side of the barrier, forgiving her from afar.

The front door was ajar and swung open further as he rapped against it. He immediately recognized Stoker's voice.

Thank the Lord. Stoker would keep him accountable. Bailey followed his voice to the parlor.

"I think we need to consider the social implications in addition to the legal. Molly has much to lose if this case goes to trial."

"But if she doesn't prosecute, she'll be implicated in the scandal. No one will believe there was a ceremony or that she was wronged," Judge Rice said.

"What's this about?" Bailey asked as he stepped into the room.

Molly looked as green as a grasshopper.

Reverend Stoker placed a hand on her shoulder. "Bailey, perhaps you should go. This isn't the time."

"It's Edward," Molly said. "He's . . . he's . . . Oh, I can't say it."

Bailey's heart lurched. "He's coming back?"

Molly shook her head and raised stricken eyes. "He's . . ." She covered her mouth with her fist.

"Married," Stoker and Rice said in unison.

Bailey blinked as he tried to comprehend what they were telling him. Married? Edward? The Edward who came into town and left with his girl?

He swallowed hard. "But not to Molly?"

They both nodded.

"I was explaining to Molly that his marriage came about as his father and the count, his wife's father, negotiated the Alaska Purchase," Judge Rice said. "According to my sources, he left shortly after the wedding and hasn't returned to New York since."

"Already married?" The room turned red as understanding dawned. "String him up."

"Not a legal option," Judge Rice said. "Molly does need to determine what charges she wants to bring, although a settlement by the family would be more profitable than a conviction."

Molly sputtered. "I would never take money. I'm not some floozy he leased."

"Molly, your language—" The reverend adjusted his string tie.

"They'll use stronger language than that to describe me if I don't send him to jail. He should pay, not his family."

Could she be as blindsided as the rest of them? Her rocker swayed in short jerky swings as she turned toward the window, her face crumpled in a scowl.

Bailey scowled, too. How could she not know? But then again, what had any of them known about the man? That foolish, rash decision would cost her.

"Pray over your choices," Stoker was saying. "Talk to your parents if it won't distress your father."

"And if you have questions concerning the legal aspects, see me between trials. We'll be bringing the man in anyway, so there's no reason for you to spread the story until he arrives."

The men stood. Stoker placed a hand on Molly's shoulder. "I'll see the judge out. Bailey, will you stay with her for a minute?"

He nodded, although his head felt heavy enough to snap his neck and smash his foot.

Unmarried?

Bailey had come to accept the fact that Molly was off-limits. It broke his heart knowing that they would never be together, but the courtly idea of loving and caring for her from afar was safe. Now unmarried . . . having never been married . . . where did that leave them? What did she expect from him?

He needed space. He needed to think. Bailey thought he'd forgiven her until he was reminded of what she had done to offend him in the first place. She'd stolen their chance of happiness. He'd buried all his hope. Digging it up, corroded and musty, was still a loss. It wasn't the same.

"I can't stay in here with you," he blurted.

Molly looked away. Her lashes fluttered downward. "I don't expect you to."

"I mean . . . I just can't. As much as I'd like to be a friend for you . . . I can't. Not right now."

"Go, then," she said. "I'll be all right."

She was fibbing, but he wasn't strong enough to challenge it. He stalked out, catching sight of her pain-stricken face. The compassion that threatened to draw him to her side would have to be squelched. If he was going to help her in any way, it must be with the understanding that she was off-limits. Whether or not she was legally wed didn't alter the fact that she had been . . . and that she'd chosen another man over him.

Bailey headed to the livery stable, although he hardly knew where his legs were carrying him. He tried to untangle the implications, but his first instinct was to pretend that nothing had changed. Whether she regretted her decision, she had still decided and there was no going back.

Besides, he had to think about his work with the church. Molly was a fallen woman. No church in the country would allow him behind a pulpit if he married Molly. God couldn't call him to a vocation that required a spotless reputation—not if he and Molly were to be together.

He found the stall holding his father's horse and leaned his arms and chin atop the high wall. It was cruel, really, because although the barrier of a marriage had been removed, the stain of the scandal had just begun to spread. Word would travel fast and so would judgment. He hoped that Edward Pierrepont's punishment would be swift and severe enough to satisfy the inevitable outrage. The people would need a villain to despise, and Bailey prayed it wouldn't be Molly.

22

MARCH 1880

"It's nice to see I have one relative who isn't completely unbalanced. Who would've thought we'd turn out to be the sane representatives of our family?" Nicholas wrapped his sister in a bear hug, mindless of the observers in the courthouse waiting room, and kissed her on the cheek before releasing her. "I'm sorry I won't be here for the trial. Some railroad track washed out around San Marcos and needs to be replaced."

Her brother's business was the one bright spot in the family's saga, but his success meant that he traveled the tracks from Garber to Galveston and was rarely close enough to offer a sympathetic ear.

Molly wondered what she could've accomplished had she been given the freedom that Nick enjoyed as a man. Oh well. There was no use being bitter. She'd messed up the one choice she'd made.

"My railroad contacts tell me that Mr. Pierrepont arrived on the train Wednesday," Nick said. "They found him in Montana Territory waiting for the snow to clear off the track before he crossed into Canada. You're lucky they caught him when they did."

"How are Mother and Father coping?" Molly led him down an empty corridor and hoped the bailiff would be able to find her when Judge Rice needed her to return to her post.

Nicholas, never willing to stand upright if there was an obliging partition available, leaned against the wall and crossed his arms. "I stopped in to see them on the way from the train station in Luling. When I asked about the trial, Mother cried, wailed, and tried to blame Father. Father swore constantly and threatened to kill the man. Jiminy! I can't blame you for wanting to get away. I'd forgotten how loud the two of them could get." He pulled at his starched cuffs so they peeked the prescribed half an inch from his coat sleeves.

Molly lowered herself onto the bench and tucked her feet beneath it. "I'd hoped that he would've found some peace by now. Do you think his health was affected?"

"He seems stronger than ever. Making the Pierreponts pay has given him an incentive to live." Nicholas pushed off the wall. "He'll be fine. I'm more concerned about you."

Molly leaned forward. "I don't know what to do, Nick. I wish I could flag down every buggy on the square, go door to door and clear my name, but I have to keep moving forward. My future employment is uncertain. I don't think Judge Rice will allow an adulteress to work in the courtroom, and somehow that's a bigger shock than Edward's lies. I've already accepted that he'll never return. I've given up on a husband and family and plan to pursue a career. I could end up without either."

"Rubbish. Judge Rice knows you were lied to. Edward Pierrepont will be found guilty and you'll be cleared."

"I pray it's so. This court case could salvage my reputation. Someone is guilty here. If Edward isn't, then what will people say?"

"What if Edward comes back and you learn that your marriage is legal? Could you be happy?"

Molly plucked at her sleeve. Happiest would be Edward Pierrepont never having laid a well-shod foot on Texas soil. But nothing could alter the past. Beyond that she wasn't sure which would be worse: always carrying the stain of adultery or being at the mercy of an unscrupulous man. Given time, would Edward humiliate her again?

"If he returned, I'd try to be content with the situation for Father and Mother's sake. They'd keep their rich son-in-law to help with the business, and I'd have met all of Father's expectations."

She shook her head. She couldn't break down here in the courthouse, not on a workday. The next session could start at any time, and Judge Rice needed her there transcribing the case. "Enough about that. Tell me all the Prairie Lea gossip, the little that doesn't involve me, that is."

The side of Nicholas's mouth rose, but he didn't deny her assumption. "For starters, there's Michael James. It's whispered that he's lurking about, but the law hasn't been able to catch him—and they're trying. Knowing that he's been rustling cattle makes you wonder if he didn't kill the man by the creek."

"That'd be good news for Anne, but not for his father. I hope people show Russell some compassion."

"I saw Russell yesterday, and I hate to say it, but he looks like he's aged a decade. And the way he slinks about—it's as if he's the criminal. It's a pity, but at least Anne Tillerton has been released, but I suppose you knew that. She's an odd bird, that one."

"Anne's not as brusque as she wants people to believe. Maybe if I'd start wearing buckskin trousers, people would stop pestering me, too."

Her brother studied her. "Mol, why don't you come home, even if it's for a few days? I'm sure Mother and Father want to see that you're all right."

"But they didn't say that, did they?"

Nicholas suddenly spotted a place on his cuff link that needed polishing. "If it makes you feel any better, the mill seems to be doing well. As much business as Bailey's bringing in, he'll have it turned around soon. And with his ferrying messages and paper work, Father's content. He's even made it out to Bradford's Mercantile a few times for checkers and coffee. I'll tell you what, that Bailey has been a godsend. If only . . ."

Molly rose and walked to the window at the end of the corridor.

"I'm sorry," he said. "It's awfully poor taste, but I can't help thinking that you and Bailey might get your chance after all. Don't forget, he asked Father for your hand the day you left with Edward. Surely he'll renew his suit once Pierrepont is behind bars."

She could still hear Bailey's words from two days ago. He couldn't bear to be in her company. If he was kind, if he was helpful, it was only out of charity. Having Pierrepont accept responsibility for his actions would go far toward redeeming her reputation, but if she was going to have a future, it'd be one she chiseled out herself.

Not a week had passed since Nick's visit, and the trial was at hand. From the courthouse antechamber, Molly could hear muffled voices in the courtroom. Drowsy, conversational, nothing concerning her yet. She flopped into the leather chair and took as deep of a breath as her stays would allow. Her fingers were cold, and dampness crept through her bodice under her arms as she waited for the trial to start.

She jumped when the door opened and Sheriff Colton entered.

"I'm surprised to see your father here," he said.

"Mother couldn't keep him away." She hoped they'd made the right decision. Physically restraining him seemed more harmful than letting him sit through the deposition. "Is Edward here, too?"

The sheriff polished his badge with his thumb. "Yes, ma'am. Already been ushered into the courtroom. Bailiff will be calling you directly."

Molly folded her hands primly in her lap and tried to unknot the dread growing in her stomach. She would see him today, see the man who'd promised her the world and left her with nothing. But worse than facing him was facing her own folly. She could've chosen differently. She could've bucked against her parents' expectations and found other means to help them. But she'd given in.

The bailiff opened the door and motioned for her to follow. Usually the plaintiff was seated before the defendant, but nothing about this hearing was typical. There'd be no stenographer, since Prue was on her honeymoon and Molly would be seated at the plaintiff's table by Mr. Collins, the district attorney.

The massive judge's bench in the center of the courtroom had never looked so intimidating. This was the first time Molly had ever walked before it as a party to an action. Thankfully, this hearing was private. No indolent onlookers were allowed inside.

She recognized Edward's back, although he was wearing a suit she'd never seen before. Evidently his finances were still liquid. She faltered at the wooden gate leading from the galley when a rustling at her side caught her attention. There her parents sat, her mother straight-backed, her father squirming and seething. Finally they'd found someone who had earned more of their disapproval than she had.

Judge Rice acknowledged her with a dip of his head, and she went to sit on the right and faced straight forward.

"Your Honor," the stranger at Edward's table said, "Mr. Pierrepont would like to have a private word with Miss Lovelace before the proceedings."

The judge's blue eyes turned cold. "I think that time has passed. I would advise Mrs. Pierrepont against such action. Mrs. Pierrepont, are you content to begin?"

What could he have to say to her? If he was whisked to jail after the proceedings, she might never know.

"He may speak, but not in private. Let him have his say here," she said.

The judge nodded and the small gathering quieted as Edward stood. Molly studied his empty chair, being the closest to his person she would allow her eyes to wander.

"First off, let me remind you that these are words I'd rather share in private, but since that avenue is closed to me, I want to assure Miss Lovelace that, although not responsible for her situation, I am deeply sympathetic and would alleviate her suffering as much as possible."

She recognized her father's snort from the galley, but Edward continued.

"I think it would be in her best interest to curtail these proceedings and reach a more profitable arrangement. I'm prepared to settle a generous sum on Miss Lovelace for any inconvenience our relationship has caused."

The room was so still Molly could hear a horse whinnying on the square.

"Molly?"

Without intending to, she met his eyes and saw the man on whom she'd pinned her hopes. He was supposed to have been her savior, not her destroyer. But he didn't look sorry. He looked as he always did—as if he admired and appreciated her, as if he couldn't be dirtied by the squalid mores of the bourgeoisie.

"Molly, please spare yourself. This won't be pleasant. The lawyer's arguments are out of my control. I care for you, and I don't want—"

"That's enough," Judge Rice interrupted. "Anything you have to say should be said under oath. Unless Mrs. Pierrepont has an objection, we'll proceed."

"Did Mr. Pierrepont propose matrimony to you?"

Molly hadn't fitted her skirts into the witness chair before the question was asked. The bailiff was still removing the Bible she'd sworn on.

"What kind of question is that? I wouldn't have gone with him if we weren't getting married."

"What were his exact words?" said the man with the spectacles and vulpine whiskers. "Did he promise you a ring? Did you speak to a parson? Were any arrangements made for a wedding?"

Her flesh crawled as she tried to remember. "He talked about spending our lives together. He said he wanted me to travel with him, be his companion."

"But he never suggested that he was free to marry."

"Free to marry?" With a roar her father leapt to his feet. "He wouldn't dare invite my daughter to accompany him otherwise."

Judge Rice banged his gavel on his bench. "Mr. Lovelace, I will not suffer outbursts in my court. Do you understand?"

Molly closed her eyes in silent prayer. Her father must control his temper or his life could be at stake. Why didn't Judge Rice remove him before he became unmanageable?

Edward's lawyer addressed her again. "Please answer my

question. Did Mr. Pierrepont at any time ask you to marry him?"

"But he did marry me and that's illegal. If he would've explained himself, I would've returned home immediately."

"Miss Lovelace, about the ceremony, if that word can be applied to what happened—you were sick, were you not? Very sick, according to Mr. Pierrepont."

"Yes, and displeased."

"I want to remind the court that your memory of the event might be suspect due to the extreme condition of your health at the time, but would you please share what you remember?"

Molly sat up straight and clutched the banister. "I remember quite clearly. I awoke to find that Mr. Pierrepont was in my room while I was in a state of . . . well . . . dishabille."

"I've had enough!" Thomas Lovelace was on his feet again. "That you would submit my daughter to this indignity is unconscionable!"

"Bailiff." One word from Judge Rice was all it took.

Sheriff Colton and the bailiff each took an arm of Thomas Lovelace and dragged him backward through the double doors, the man yelling protests every step of the way. The doors closed, muffling but not quite drowning out his voice.

"Mrs. Lovelace," Judge Rice said, "you might want to fetch a doctor to tend your husband as a precautionary measure."

Her mother sniffed and stalked out. She could pretend to be disappointed, but Molly knew that she'd wanted to distance herself from the proceedings from the beginning.

And now, with her mother gone, she was the only woman in the room. As humiliating as her testimony was, to have to give it in a room full of men made it even more so. And the way they were twisting her words, she'd even begun to doubt herself.

Once Sheriff Colton and the bailiff returned, Judge Rice

nodded to her. What she wouldn't give for a glass of water, but she continued unaided.

"As I was saying, I woke to find Edward in my chamber. This was unacceptable. I insisted that we get married immediately, and he agreed."

"Under what circumstances, ma'am?" The lawyer's voice rose. "He agreed to marry you after he was threatened with detainment, right? It was imperative that he get you to a doctor, and the only way for him to help you was to go through a fraudulent ceremony using a false name. He acted to save your life, even though it was against his best interest. Is that not correct?"

The room swam before Molly's eyes, but Edward didn't move. There he sat, as kind and accepting as ever. He looked as if he'd welcome her into his arms and call off this evil lawyer if she'd let him. Yes, he surely would. He'd take her on the train, and they'd put Caldwell County far behind them, but without the benefit of holy matrimony. Until his family cut him off again, he'd care for her as a mistress. That was all she'd ever been to him. All she could be.

Molly released the banister and settled her back against her chair. She took a shaky breath and prayed God would give her the courage to speak the absolute truth.

"What you say is true. Perhaps he didn't intend to marry me when we left. Perhaps he was forced into that situation, but he should have told me once I recovered. He knew he had a wife already." Her eyes bounced from person to person, finding nowhere safe to land. "But he didn't tell me. Instead, he lived with me as my husband. I wouldn't have consented."

All eyes turned to the bespectacled lawyer.

"That will be all, Miss Lovelace. We'd like to call the next witness, Your Honor."

Molly gripped the rail tightly to steady her steps out of

the box. Edward had tried to warn her, hadn't he? But what choice did she have? She couldn't just walk out the door and inform everyone that she was now Miss Lovelace again. Such a proclamation would forever sully her.

"Who is your witness, Counsel?" Judge Rice asked.

She stopped to watch the shifty man, wondering what he hoped to unearth. No one could contradict her account. Not Pastor Snow, not the conductor, not even Freida. No one could challenge her testimony.

"The defense calls Bailey Garner."

23

The framed copy of the Ten Commandments on the court-house wall made a fine tally sheet for Bailey as he checked off Pierrepont's multiple transgressions. The grim diversion was his only protection from Mr. Lovelace's tirade.

"It's outrageous that we don't get our say. We're her parents! What does that district attorney think he's doing asking you to testify?"

Hands in his pockets, Bailey kept his eyes on the plaque before him. Although Thomas Lovelace didn't expect a reply, Bailey wished he had one. Why was he called to testify? After the donkey he'd made of himself, he was surprised that Molly had requested his help. On the other hand, didn't he deserve a shot at the blackguard? Next to Molly, his future had been the most affected.

"Bailey Garner," the bailiff called.

Thomas stood as if to charge the courtroom but was intercepted by the bailiff, who held the door open for Bailey.

Bailey straightened his shoulders and prepared for battle, marching at a cadence until he'd turned into the box and had his hand on the Bible.

He was here, in the same room. Bailey's neck twitched as

he looked at the man who'd lain with his girl. Nothing Bailey could do to him would be bad enough. And there was Molly, looking as queasy as the town drunk. How he wished he could convince himself that she'd been kidnapped, abducted. How he wished she hadn't left him of her own free will.

He stumbled through the oath, not caring if the words were exactly right. He didn't need some lawman to remind him to tell the truth—not when God was there, waiting to exact vengeance.

Bailey grasped the arms of the wooden chair as he lowered himself into it. Ready for business. He'd been hard on Molly, but it was small potatoes compared to his feelings for the man seated across the room.

"Mr. Garner, would you please describe your relationship with Miss Lovelace." Pierrepont's lawyer stepped up to the bar looking like his chest had slid into his belly and got caught in his belt on the way down.

Bailey cleared his throat and tried to speak in the preacher voice he'd been practicing. "I've known her my whole life."

"But wouldn't you say your relationship has recently been of a more personal nature?"

"Recently? No, I haven't—"

"In the last year or so?"

Bailey leaned back in his seat and crossed his legs at the ankles. They were jumping right into the meat of his testimony. Didn't this expensive lawyer with the letters behind his name understand this was exactly what Bailey wanted to say?

"We were courting for over a year."

"With her parents' consent?"

Bailey frowned. "They didn't exactly approve, but there were no hard feelings. I work for them now."

"So Miss Lovelace deceived her parents to carry on a relationship without their consent?" Before Bailey could answer, the man fired another round in his direction. "Would you say that Miss Lovelace comported herself as befitting a lady during your relationship?"

"Of course. Mol . . . I mean *Mrs. Pierrepont* was well brought up."

"It's interesting that you'd say so, Mr. Garner, because I've discovered testimony that not six months ago you publically denounced her in front of your local congregation. Would you like to share your version of the incident?"

Bailey looked at Molly. Her expression looked a lot like it had that Sunday when he'd stood to unburden his soul. His heart lurched into his throat. "No, that's not why I'm here. Your man took her under false pretenses."

"Mr. Garner, you are here to establish her character, or lack thereof. Miss Lovelace has testified that she would not allow a man to trifle with her without the benefit of marriage. That is why your testimony is of particular interest to the defense. That is why we called you."

"You called me?" Bailey pulled himself forward. "I didn't come to help you. I came to put him in jail."

Without blinking, the lawyer turned to Judge Rice. "Your Honor, I'd like to point out that the witness is hostile, but we consider his testimony to be vital to our defense."

"You may proceed with the questions." Judge Rice's eyebrows lowered. "Mr. Garner, I remind you that you're under oath."

What could he do? Bailey looked for help, for counsel, but the district attorney was frozen like a scared possum. Molly's eyes were huge, shining with vulnerability, expecting the worse.

"Let's return to your proclamation before the church. What exactly were your words?" the lawyer asked.

Bailey scowled. "It wasn't Molly's fault. It was mine. I was confessing my own personal failings. Not hers."

"Did you ever force yourself on Miss Lovelace?"

"Of course not."

"So she freely allowed you liberties?"

"I didn't defile her, if that's what you're asking."

"But you are saying that all inappropriate contact between the two of you was consensual? That Miss Lovelace's claims of innocence are not accurate?"

Bailey swallowed hard. He'd sworn on a Bible, he who lived in a parsonage and opened up the meetinghouse twice a week. Did Molly understand, or would she think he was exacting his revenge? Too fast. Everything was happening too fast.

"It wasn't her fault. I take full responsibility."

"Seems to be a pattern of hers, doesn't it? She's never at fault?"

"You are leading the witness," Judge Rice warned. "Caution."

"Mr. Garner, if Miss Lovelace had as spotless of a reputation as she claims, she must have been humiliated by your confession before the church."

Bailey nodded. There was one response he could be proud of.

"Is it fair to assume that your relationship was not resumed? That she never again allowed you liberties?"

How did they know? Was it a lucky guess? Molly's cheeks flamed red, her eyes lowered. He wished she'd look at him. Wished she'd glare—or swear—or anything besides sit resigned as he bludgeoned her reputation.

Sheriff Colton coughed and raised an eyebrow. If Colton weren't there, Bailey would be tempted to fib on a stack of Bibles, but the man had caught them red-handed. He had to tell the truth or he'd be arrested for perjury.

His voice sounded weak, foreign to his own ears. "There was one incident."

He was lost. There was no redemption for him. Not only had he done his best to compromise her, but now he was exposing his near success to her enemies. Hell couldn't produce hot enough flames for him.

"One incident, you say. I won't ask for the lurid details, but are we to assume the . . . *ahem* . . . activity was more than a friendly gesture?"

Bailey sat mute.

"And when did this rendezvous occur? You weren't courting after you exposed her for her wayward behavior, but it must've been before she left town with Mr. Pierrepont." He leaned forward to peer at Bailey. "She enjoyed your company and then waited how long before skipping town with my client?"

Bailey crossed his arms. His jaw jutted out.

"Mr. Collins"—Judge Rice rubbed his forehead with a weary hand as he spoke to the district attorney—"do you wish to consult with your client, or should we continue?"

The District Attorney shuffled through papers. "I'm not sure how to proceed."

"Let's allow the witness to answer the question," Pierrepont's lawyer continued. "Perhaps the lady was innocently besotted with you. It took her a month, perhaps, before she elected to become the companion of another man?"

Why didn't Mr. Collins stop them? Bailey looked to the judge's bench, but there was no help coming from that direction.

"Not a full month, then? I *will* have your answer, Mr. Garner. Exactly how long did it take Miss Lovelace to turn her affections from you to my client?"

Since God hadn't graciously struck him mute, he'd have to answer the question.

"She left with him the next day—make that two days later."

Bailey had to clasp his fists together to keep from reaching over the banister, grabbing the lawyer by his fancy knotted cravat, and stuffing it into his satisfied mouth. He rambled on, but Bailey didn't catch all the words. Unfaithful, gold digger, cuckolding his client with other men—all charges brought against the solemn woman in the simple blue gown.

Mechanically Bailey rose as instructed and walked past her. Mr. Collins had finally voiced his opinion. There would be no trial. Bailey had ruined Molly's case, and Edward Pierrepont would walk out of Caldwell County not guilty. The married man who had bedded his sweetheart would go free.

All the guilt rested on Bailey.

24

The road between Lockhart and Prairie Lea had never seemed so long. No matter. Molly probably wouldn't be making this trip much in the months ahead. She was moving home.

From the back bench, she watched Bailey as he pretended that driving the surrey took his undivided attention. Ignoring her father was a skill she should've acquired years ago. Maybe then she wouldn't find it so difficult to keep from answering his questions. Thomas Lovelace wanted to know every word of Bailey's testimony, and Molly would do her best to ensure that he never did.

"I'd think the plaintiff's father would have some rights, but Judge Rice refused to tell me what was said." He bounced on the front bench of the surrey, forcing Bailey to steady the horse.

"I wondered what kept you so long." Adele was seated on the back bench next to Molly, but didn't seem too pleased about it. "Molly and I went to the boardinghouse right after the trial, packed her trunks, and still had to wait a half hour on you."

"I was giving Rice a piece of my mind, and I had some words for that snake, Edward Pierrepont, too," Thomas said.

Her mother's head snapped up. "They let you talk to him?"

"He requested a meeting, the fool. Believe me, I made him sorry he'd ever heard the name Lovelace." Her father mopped his brow with an already damp handkerchief. "What he did to us . . . Molly lost her job because of him. That requires financial compensation."

"But I understand the judge's decision." Her mother tucked an iron-gray curl into her bonnet. "You can't have an adulteress working for the law."

Bailey turned as if to speak and then faced forward again. So now he was silent? Too bad he hadn't gone mute in the courtroom—and what had her father said?

"Did you say compensation?" she asked.

Her father grunted. "It's hard to acquire a settlement without any leverage. I'm not sure how you destroyed your case, but I recouped what I could. One of my better negotiations, I believe."

The thought of taking anything from Edward Pierrepont made her ill. "I don't want his tainted money. You tell him we won't accept it."

"We've already accepted it. Hopefully the taint will be washed away by the interest it accrues in the bank," Thomas said.

Time might clean the money, but it wouldn't clean her. Molly had been shocked to hear herself characterized as an immoral woman. She had never considered herself lax in that department. She hadn't so much as kissed Edward before their wedding—or whatever that ruse was. As for Bailey, well, he was Bailey. That didn't mean she'd act so wanton with anyone else.

And how could she blame Bailey for the fiasco when everything he'd said was true? As soon as she heard each question, she knew what his answer would be. Had to be. He was too honest. Even if Sheriff Colton hadn't been present, Bailey wouldn't tell a falsehood, especially not for her.

Molly dropped her chin. Her gloves concealed a familiar lump on her ring finger. At the first opportunity she'd remove the shackle. Before, the ring had protected her reputation. Now it was pointless.

"This is why they shouldn't let women go under oath," her father said. "Their emotion, their sentimentality, is too easily manipulated. That lawyer had you cowed into submission from the very first question. Makes me wonder if you were as innocent as you claim."

"If I felt any guilt in my dealings with Mr. Pierrepont, I wouldn't have had him arrested. There's nothing else to be done, Father. The sooner it's forgotten the better."

"No one is going to forget." Adele lifted her chin and sniffed. "You were married, and now you're not. If he was in the wrong, where's the punishment for him? And how are we supposed to introduce you now? If you're not Mrs. Pierrepont, who are you?"

"I'm Molly Lovelace. That's always been my name."

And always would be.

"And exactly how are you going to occupy yourself, Molly Lovelace?" her father asked. "If Judge Rice doesn't want you at the courthouse, I'm sure as shooting not allowing you to flounce around the mill."

"I've been thinking about that," she said. "Perhaps I could make visits with Mother. There are women in Prairie Lea that need help, whether their husbands are incarcerated or they were affected by crime. I don't know anyone in jail now that Anne is free, but there's Mrs. Nimenko. Her husband was murdered. If I could do something for her—"

"I prefer visiting old maids and other unfortunates," Adele

said. "Or perhaps you could be an example to some young impressionable girl on the verge of making a similar mistake."

Did Bailey groan? No one else seemed to notice.

"I'd prefer to keep my calls to less personal subjects," Molly said. "If I can get them to come to church, then—"

"You don't plan on attending church, do you?" Her father turned horrified eyes on her.

"Why wouldn't I?"

"Don't you think it's hypocritical after running off with a married man?"

Molly's face burned hot, but her words burned hotter. "Isn't church the place for people like me? People who've ruined this life and have nothing to live for but the promise of the next? Would you keep even that comfort from your daughter?"

"Small comfort it'll be," he retorted. "You're mistaken if you think you'll be welcomed."

"How dare you!" Molly kept her voice low, even though town was behind them. "If it weren't for you, I would've never given Edward Pierrepont the time of day. I would have married . . ."

Only then did they remember their silent driver. The wheels creaked as they came down the last rise before they reached the home on the river. Thomas Lovelace's heavy breathing could be heard above the distant roar of the water falling over the dam.

"I don't know that I should go to church in my condition," he said. "My heart might not be able to withstand it. Perhaps on Sunday I'll feel better. Perhaps not."

"Thomas, what will I tell Reverend Stoker? He'll want to know why you aren't there," her mother said.

"You won't have to tell him anything." He rubbed his chest. "You'll stay home with me if I'm under the weather.

At least one woman in my family knows how to be a good wife."

Molly was crushed. What had happened to his deathbed resolve to treat her better? The compliments he'd heaped on her had been meaningless, just another maneuver for Thomas Lovelace to get what he wanted.

"I have a suggestion." Their driver finally found his voice. "You've been looking for a guard to watch the mill at night. I'll move into the watchman's quarters if you'll allow Molly to stay at the parsonage."

Molly sat upright. "Turn the buggy around. We've barely passed it."

"Do control yourself," her mother said. "It's a ridiculous suggestion. You can't live in town by yourself."

"What about Mrs. Cantrell?" Molly asked. "She lives by herself. And Louise? She lived by herself on the farm before she married Mr. Bradford."

Her father's mouth swished from side to side. Bailey lifted the reins. "If the answer's no, I understand. I'll be more comfortable in the parsonage, I guess."

"Wait." Thomas grabbed the lines with a meaty hand. "Let's not be hasty. Molly's a grown woman. Why can't she live alone?"

Molly turned hopeful eyes to her mother. "You'd be more comfortable with me out of the house. I know my presence distresses you."

"But where would we get the funds to furnish it? I haven't been inside in ages, but I don't think the décor is suitable."

"I won't change a thing. The house is in town, so I'll have neighbors, and it's right by the church. There will be plenty of people coming and going to check up on me."

"What will you eat?" Her mother's eyes narrowed. "You're not exactly a cook."

Molly's spirits soared. Were they really considering it? "But I can learn. I taught myself accounting. I learned shorthand with a little assistance. How hard can cooking be? Of course, I'd probably need to eat with you at first, but not for long. I can learn how to do it myself."

She was on the edge of the bench, eyes darting desperately from her father to her mother as they weighed the relief of having her out of their hair against the potential scandal the move might make. In the end, getting rid of her must have seemed the greater good.

"We could use a night watchman. If we're robbed, we'll lose more than fuel for a second hearth." Her father looked at Bailey. "But what will Reverend Stoker say?"

"Stoker I'll have to handle."

"Do you think she'll be at church, Ma?" Susannah called from the wagon bed as they turned into town.

Bailey rubbed his forehead and frowned at his little sister. "Don't stick your nose in the beehive. You'll get stung."

Since starting his job at the mill, Bailey always made it home to the ranch on Saturday evening and returned to town the next morning for church. This was the first Sunday since he'd moved into the watchman's quarters, the first Sunday since the trial forced Molly to return home, and he was glad for his family's company.

What would Stoker think about the parsonage's new resident? He would soon find out. It hadn't taken long to move Bailey's scant belongings out of the furnished cabin. He'd stuffed a saddlebag full of clothing and they'd swapped out the bedding that Mrs. Lovelace had brought up from the house, but in the confusion he'd taken Molly's pillow and left her his.

Big mistake. How could he get any sleep with her lilac scent reminding him of the best times of his life . . . and the worst?

And why was Molly protecting him? If she decided to tell her parents that he'd caused the case to be thrown out, he'd be looking for another job.

Not that he minded coming back to the ranch for a few days. The sheep's wool coats needed to be sheared soon, and the roundups were progressing as planned. With the cattle being rounded up for their journey north, there was plenty to do at the homeplace, but that wasn't his calling. Despite everything—despite Thomas's brusque manner, Molly's marriage, and now his accusations against her—Bailey was certain he was where God wanted him, but he wasn't sure he could endure it. He wasn't sure how to be the man he wanted to be while still dealing with the pathetic man he was.

Heaven knew how much he wanted to tell Reverend Stoker and his father about the hearing, but once again he couldn't clear his conscience without dirtying Molly's. Seemed like his mother saw right through his vague generalities, though. So Molly wasn't married? Pierrepont had charges against him, but he was free to leave? Didn't take Mary Garner long to smell trouble, and Bailey didn't need her stern warning. He'd done enough damage already.

"Poor Adele and Thomas," his mother fussed as he helped her down from the wagon. "I wonder how they're holding up. Reckon we're about to find out."

The churchyard did seem subdued, now that she mentioned it. Were the Lovelaces already inside, or had Thomas kept Molly away?

His cousin Eliza greeted them first. With a hug for his mother and a sympathetic look tossed his way, she whispered, "Did you hear about Molly?"

Mary Garner shooed her little girls inside and gathered her shawl about her. "What are people saying?"

Eliza bent over Bailey's short mother. "That he had a wife already. Molly and he were never married."

"But Mr. Mohle saw him in Luling leaving town. Isn't bigamy against the law?" Mary asked.

Eliza shrugged. "No one's talking."

Oh, yes they were. Everyone was.

Bailey's father joined the discussion. "We mustn't judge. Molly did what she thought was best to help her family."

"She did," Eliza conceded. "And even if she acted rashly, she surely didn't expect Mr. Pierrepont to be married."

Mary tucked her hand into the crook of her husband's arm. "And whatever we do or say, we've got to consider Thomas and Adele. They're surely plumb overwhelmed." She cast a significant look at Bailey and took his arm, as well. "What's done is done. We'll pray she doesn't get caught up in any more scandals."

Yes, his mother would pray fervently.

Before he could sit with his family, Mayor Sellers pulled him aside.

"You were there at the courthouse, I hear. Were you able to have your say?"

Bailey looked over his shoulder, relieved that no one was close enough to overhear. "It didn't go as I'd planned."

He started to turn, but Mayor Sellers caught him by the arm again and leaned in close, the scent of spicy tobacco seeping from his lips. "Well, I'm glad you didn't get your hands dirty. Not a nice boy like you."

Bailey twisted his arm away. "The music's started. Excuse me."

"Wait a second," Sellers said. "You haven't heard my news. Reverend Stoker isn't coming. He twisted his knee stepping off his porch and can't ride the circuit. He sent word for you to conduct the service."

"Me?" Bailey stumbled backward a step. "I'm no preacher. I can't do it."

"He warned me that you'd say that, but you can ask for testimonies, favorite verses, that sort of thing. The congregation will fill the time for you."

"No." Bailey was adamant. Here was one decision he would not regret. "I will not get up in front of these people as if I'm some sort of spiritual authority."

"Simmer down, there. I didn't expect you to be so uncomfortable. I can ask Weston to fill in, I suppose."

Bailey nodded his consent. Crossing the threshold, he felt as if he'd rolled in a cow pie. If Weston, his cousin, was holding a baptism service, he'd be the first candidate. Anything to wash the sludgy feel of unearned praise away.

As he entered the church, he saw that the pew normally occupied by the Lovelaces stood vacant, proof that Mr. Lovelace had gotten his way—again. Bailey took a seat next to his brothers and let his little sister Ida climb onto his lap. Mr. Mohle led the music while Mrs. Mohle, looking frailer than usual, pounded out the tune on the upright piano.

Bailey tried to follow the song, but between his jumbled thoughts and Ida's unsteady grasp on the hymnal, he had to skip the second and third stanzas. Could he put himself in Molly's shoes? How hard would it be to return to church? He flipped his sister's braid over her shoulder. He spent a decent chunk of time worrying about his reputation. What would he do if it was forever lost? How would he feel if he'd been denied justice by someone he'd once considered his best friend?

A jarring chord caught his attention. Mrs. Mohle jerked her eyes back to her music, and all heads turned to the rear of the church to see what had startled her.

Molly paused in the aisle. Gripping a Bible and her reticule, she took another tentative step. Her blue-and-yellow-striped gown set her apart, as did her plumed hat. If she'd wanted to sneak in unnoticed, she'd failed miserably. With all eyes on her she shouldered her way to the second row and took her solitary seat.

Typically the fourth stanza was sung with gusto, but the congregation couldn't get it together. Molly didn't sing. She remained unmoving, unblinking, staring straight ahead.

Over the din of the piano, Bailey heard quick footsteps coming up the aisle. Ida poked him and pointed. It was Rosa, Weston's wife. With a confidence borne by overcoming her own scandal, Rosa squeezed between the pews and sat by her friend after giving her a quick squeeze. At her heels was Weston himself, with little Luke tucked in his arms.

Bailey's throat burned. Good of them to welcome her. Of course, Rosa had stolen Weston right out from under Molly's nose, so she kinda owed her one. Maybe that's why she braved the whispers that accompanied her trip down the aisle. Ida waved at someone over his shoulder, and he turned to see Eliza pass with a child on her hip and a husband in her wake. Now, that was out of character. Eliza didn't brook any foolishness—unless it came from her husband, Jake. And if that weren't enough, Louise and Deacon made their way down front and joined the others, all trying to cram full skirts and long legs between the pews.

Bailey stole a look at Mayor Sellers. His nose flared and a drip of brown tobacco juice almost escaped his mouth before he sucked it back in. Others would disapprove, as well.

Flanked by his family, Molly's back lost some of the starch that she'd so painfully borne. No snide comment would reach her if she stayed safely wedged between Rosa and Eliza. The only person more formidable than those ladies was his mother.

He looked at his ma just in time to see her get to her feet. His father had already exited their section and stood aside to let Mary Garner pass. Not her, too. Now, instead of noticing who'd stood up for her, everyone would comment on who did not. Bailey clutched his sister and widened his eyes at his brothers. Tending his sisters would be his excuse to stay put. The pew was already as full as a twenty-piglet sow. No room for him.

They'd better stay put.

But when he looked up, he caught Molly watching him, and from the hurt on her face, she understood his veiled warning to his siblings. Bailey paled. There he sat, the one responsible for Edward's acquittal, and he couldn't support her. Do something that two-faced and God would strike him dead, sure as shooting.

Bailey determined to watch for an opportunity to support Molly. He wouldn't rest until he'd made up for the hurt he'd caused her, but until he could help her without stirring up gossip, he had to focus his attention on others. He'd continue making his visits, and in the meanwhile he'd encourage his family to give Molly the support he couldn't.

With that resolution, Bailey headed north to the Mohles' house the next day, following the grassy path until it wound to their place by the schoolhouse. The pounding from the carpentry shop announced that Mr. Mohle had a project underway, but when Bailey saw the mayor and heard the windy he was telling, he waved to Mr. Mohle and continued to the house.

Mrs. Mohle was reclining on a chaise lounge with a book in her hands and an afghan draped across her. When she saw Bailey through the open window, she lowered her feet to the floor.

"No need to get up," he said. "If you feel like having a visitor, I can let myself in."

She leaned back and pulled the blanket higher. "Thank you. I must have overexerted myself yesterday."

He closed the door behind him and took a seat. The smell of clean sawdust graced her tidy parlor. Her finely veined hands, so capable on a piano keyboard, fumbled with an embroidered bookmark. She made a spot for the book next to the potted philodendron on a marble-topped table.

"What brings you out?" Mrs. Mohle asked.

Bailey shrugged. "My evenings are long at the watchman's quarters. I swim, I fish, but it's pretty quiet compared to back home with the family."

"I was at church Sunday, remember?" Mrs. Mohle smiled. "I'm fine."

"You think I'm here because I'm worried about you? Maybe I want some company . . . or maybe I know that sometimes our physical healing is completed more quickly than our other hurts." Her downcast eyes were all the confirmation Bailey needed. "How are you really doing, Mrs. Mohle?"

She threaded her fingers through the loops of the blue afghan, studying it as if she were trying to find a loose end to pull and unravel every stitch. "I don't guess anyone knows what it's like until they've been here. You try not to get your hopes up, but every day you look forward to holding your baby in your arms. You pray for the child's future and prepare yourself for the hard times, because you know they'll be worth it." Her hands stilled. "And then even the hard times are ripped from you. The future vanishes. It's gone and you wonder where it went. The love you had has nothing to alight on, but you don't want it to fade. You don't want it to disappear."

"I don't believe love ever disappears." Bailey swallowed,

hoping he wasn't speaking out of line. "If you believe our good deeds will be rewarded in heaven, then you have to believe our prayers and God-pleasing dreams haven't perished, either. Those are the works of your heart, and that's precious in the sight of God. Prophecies will fail and knowledge will vanish, but love endures."

His words seemed to comfort her, but he had to ask himself if his life demonstrated the truth of them. Had his prayers for Molly gone unanswered? Was his love for her something that could only survive in the heavenly realm?

A silent tear rolled down Mrs. Mohle's face. "I would've been a good mother if I'd had the chance. All the love I felt for these children, all the plans I had . . ." Pink appeared on her pale cheeks. "Sometimes I feel like I'm being punished, but I have to decide that these trials won't be wasted. I didn't invite this sorrow into my life, but if it's here I'm going to use it to drive me closer to God and believe that He allowed it for my benefit."

Out of the open window Bailey caught sight of the azalea bushes—five of them now. It was a sobering thought that God loved His children thus—using sorrow to draw them nearer and build their dependence on Him. Had God orchestrated Bailey's situation to burn away his flaws? Without a doubt, Molly had changed since she said good-bye to him on Mrs. Truman's porch. Could he say with the same certainty that he'd matured, as well?

25

To Do List:

- *Convince Mother to visit Mrs. Nimenko.*
- *Distribute excess clothing culled from wardrobe.*
- *Wear boots on visits.*

Tuesday was visiting day. Molly crunched the cockroach under her slipper without mercy. Another good deed for the day—and not the most repugnant. No, her mother's condescending concern made her skin crawl more than the bugs. After carrying a basket loaded with day-old bread and wilted greens from house to house and noticing the disappointed looks on the women's faces, she knew the offering wasn't what they'd expected. Her family's finances had not improved, and yet Adele Lovelace still went on as if they were in high cotton.

"No need to thank us. We're doing our Christian duty—showing charity to those who've wandered from the chosen path," Adele said.

The spark from Mrs. Weems's countenance disappeared as she set the food on her wobbly table.

Molly could bear it no longer. "It must be difficult to raise a child on your own. I don't think I could manage half as well."

"Thank you, Mrs. Pier—er—Miss Lovelace."

Finally, someone who could sympathize.

"Precisely my dilemma. At least your husband had the decency to marry you before he left—and to marry only you."

"Molly!" her mother gasped.

A rueful grin appeared in Mrs. Weems's tanned face. "I suppose, but he'll get no thanks from me, not when he sends eight measly dollars a month to make ends meet. If he's working on the railroad like he says, he should be able to send more my way."

"Eight dollars a month?" Molly tilted her head. "You've got a prospering garden. Maybe you could trade some of your fresh produce for last year's canned goods at the mercantile and stretch your budget a little further. Let me get some paper and see if we can't find a way to improve—"

"Molly, that is quite enough. We must be going." Adele was on her feet, sliding her arm through the wide handle of the basket on the table.

"But Mrs. Weems and I have some ciphering to do. Her funds should be adequate if managed correctly. Then you wouldn't need to bring our dinner scraps."

"We are leaving." Her mother's mouth trembled as her face grew redder and redder.

"You best listen to your ma." Mrs. Weems didn't seem a bit disturbed by Mrs. Lovelace's disapproval. Molly almost thought her delighted. "But you're welcome anytime, with or without her."

Molly reached the door at the same time as her mother, who tried to squeeze through with the sturdy basket.

"Excuse me, Mother," she gasped.

Adele barged ahead, barely waiting to get a decent distance from the house before turning on Molly. "What pleasure can you possibly derive from equating your situation to that common woman's?" The feather on top of her hat danced like a cobra.

"Some similarities could be drawn. We were both abandoned by our men."

"You did not marry a low-class ne'er-do-well. You are not raising a child on your own."

"But I could be, couldn't I? And it wouldn't even be legitimate. Honestly, Mother, I don't see how you can pretend I'm more fortunate than she. At least she's married and has some degree of independence. I'm still a prisoner."

"Stop saying such dreadful things. Illness or none, your father is going to hear about this."

"Well, you'll have plenty to tell him, because I'm not finished. My next stop is Mrs. Nimenko's."

"You wouldn't dare. Haven't you heard what they're saying about her husband and that Tillerton woman?"

Ignoring her mother's indignation, Molly traipsed down the grassy path that she hoped led to the Nimenkos' new farm.

She remembered what the prisoner had said at the deposition about the man visiting Mrs. Tillerton for tawdry reasons. Who else thought the same? Did his wife have her doubts? It was one thing to lose your husband, quite another for the loss to be under ignominious circumstances—as she could testify.

Molly's approach was announced by scattering chickens and a bawling coonhound. A woman came to the door, followed by a son who was a head higher than her and half the width.

"I didn't expect callers." She scrubbed at her hands with her dish towel, her florid cheeks shining with heat from midday baking.

"I'm sorry to come unannounced. I'm Molly Lovelace. My parents own the mill."

Her mouth tucked up on one side. "You don't have to live in Prairie Lea long to hear of the Lovelaces. I'm Mrs. Nimenko. Why don't you come up to the porch? Ivan will bring you a chair."

"I hope I'm not interrupting."

"I just set the bread in, so it's no bother. I think I remember seeing you at the courthouse." Her mouth grew grim. "Have they caught him?"

"No, ma'am." Molly smoothed her skirt as she sat in the simple wooden chair. "Honestly, I'm not sure why I'm here. Ever since I heard about your husband, I've wondered how you were getting along. Not that there's much I can offer— besides friendship."

Gentle lines formed around Mrs. Nimenko's sad eyes. "Then you've come to the right place, Molly Lovelace. I was praying that God would send me a friend."

The fresh green shoots of prairie hay were almost as tall as the dry stubble that crunched under Bailey's boots. He would have to hurry to make it to the mill before his noon break was over. Delivering the charity account from the church wouldn't take long, but he also wanted to spend some time with Ivan Nimenko. The kid was doing a man's job running the ranch without his pa, and they were so new to the area that not many families had thought to help them.

The ladies on the porch saw him coming. Their voices faded in the breeze as they waited for him to get close enough to greet. If he hadn't known better, he could've sworn the woman with Mrs. Nimenko was Molly, but what would Molly be doing at the Nimenkos' ranch?

His steps slowed as the scene became clearer. He wasn't mistaken. Molly gripped her bag but seemed unable to escape.

"Ivan is bringing you a seat, Mr. Garner. Do you have time to visit?" Mrs. Nimenko asked.

It was too late for him to run. His hat was in his hands without any memory of removing it. "No, ma'am. I brought you . . ." Mrs. Nimenko wouldn't want Molly to know that she received charity. "If you don't mind I'll chat with Ivan."

"I wish you'd honor us with your company first." She nodded to the chair Ivan placed next to her, across from Molly. "I was telling Miss Lovelace how much I appreciate you. It seems like the rest of the world would rather we disappear until this mess is cleared up, but you haven't once made us feel unworthy."

Bailey eased into the chair and dropped his hat by his feet. "No one really believes those rumors, Mrs. Nimenko. Somehow people would rather spread a lie than the truth, but your husband's reputation will be cleared when it's all settled." He risked a glance at Molly. "Besides, I'd be the last person in the world who'd have the right to sit in judgment on someone." If a statue was still, she was immovable.

"Well, I thank you for spending time with the boy," Mrs. Nimenko said. "It's good for him to have an example like you. Not many young men have your wisdom."

Bailey felt sweat forming on his forehead. He hid his hands between his knees, surprised that Molly didn't correct her mistaken assessment. "I hate to think of you mourning here alone, Mrs. Nimenko. Would it be all right if I sent some women from our church to visit? They would love to make your acquaintance. My family in particular would be very welcoming."

Molly inhaled and looped her purse strings around her finger. "He's telling the truth. He comes from an extraordinary family."

Bailey's lungs felt too small for his ribcage. His family had rushed to her side while he hid in the pew.

Molly stood. "I should go, although I do hope you'll call on me at the parsonage, Mrs. Nimenko."

"At the parsonage?" Her eyebrows knitted into question marks. "Isn't that where he lives?"

Bailey choked. He pounded his chest to loosen the vise that refused to release his lungs. "No. I don't live there," he gasped. "Not anymore."

Mrs. Nimenko looked puzzled, but she let it pass. "Well, thank you for coming to see me, Molly. There aren't many who do. And I'm serious about what I said. I'd be proud to call you my friend."

Bailey rose as she departed, realizing how much he wished he still had that right.

Lola shot Molly a sympathetic look as she filled her glass of tea. Pretty desperate straits when the maid wouldn't trade places with you.

"And after she embarrassed me in front of Mrs. Weems, she went to visit that Nimenko woman, the one whose husband was caught at the Tillertons'." Her mother's voice rang off the polished surface of the long dining room table. "No telling how she disgraced herself while there."

"I was thinking about the settlement money, Father." Molly leaned forward, trying to draw his attention away from her mother's outraged sensibilities. "It's not doing anyone any good sitting in the bank. Why don't I use it to alleviate the concerns—?"

"That money will not be squandered on some unworthy women who didn't have the sense to marry well. It will be used for investments or to fund the mill if our balances get any lower. Buy a bonnet or some trifle to amuse yourself if you must, but the settlement—"

"A bonnet?" Molly's jaw dropped. "What's a bonnet compared to helping our neighbors? That is my money. You have no right."

"You will not speak to me in that manner, young lady." Her father smashed his fist against the table, causing the lid on the sugar bowl to rattle.

"Thomas, remember your heart," Adele said.

"She'd do well to remember," he said, his voice rising with every syllable. "She'd do well to remember that, according to God, she is not to provoke me to wrath with her disgusting behavior." His words rang against the pressed-tin ceiling.

"Sir?"

They turned at Lola's meek interruption to see Bailey standing in the doorway, his hands holding the account ledger tight, his mouth firm.

He'd heard. Molly tucked her feet under her chair. What did it matter? Bailey already knew the worst of her. Her father's tirade couldn't hurt his opinion.

"Mr. Lovelace, Mrs. Lovelace." He walked around the table and took the empty place setting. "Molly."

So he was acknowledging her now? She'd been invisible at Mrs. Nimenko's earlier that day. She didn't return his greeting but peered at the grandfather clock through the parlor doorway. Seven o'clock. Punctual. Molly had learned to wolf down her food so she could return to the parsonage before he arrived every evening. Unfortunately her mother's hysterics had delayed Lola's dinner preparation tonight, and there hadn't been time. Once again, Molly had no one to blame but herself.

Her father's chair groaned as he tilted the two front legs off the ground and crossed his arms. "Right on time, Bailey. I know you're here on a different type of business, but we could use a good word from you, if you don't mind. There are some in our midst who are disregarding the wisdom of the Lord. How about a little preaching before we crack open the accounts?"

How could you tell someone was looking at you when you couldn't see him? Molly didn't know, but the sensation was physical. She kept her eyes toward the parlor, but she couldn't control the heat creeping up her neck. Did Bailey wonder how he could've been so deceived? Did he chide himself for falling for a sinner like her? Would her skin stop tingling when he looked away?

"You want a good word, from me?" Molly heard the ledger drop to the table. "'And, ye fathers, provoke not your children to wrath: but bring them up in the nurture and admonition of the Lord.' I believe that's the verse. It's the father who's cautioned against riling up his offspring, not the other way around. We don't want to misquote the Good Book."

Molly bit her lip. She knew Bailey well enough to guess how his pulse was racing. He didn't correct his elders. He didn't start fights, but he'd stepped right into this one. And why? He was practically siding with her.

The floor thumped as the front legs of her father's chair landed. Thomas Lovelace didn't speak. He glowered at his wife as if she had something to do with Bailey's remark. Molly could almost hear the sweat popping out of Bailey's forehead. What was he doing? Didn't he like his job?

"Well," Thomas drawled, then beamed a relieved smile toward the young man, "I suppose you are correct. 'Bring them up in the admonition of the Lord.' That's the good word we need around here."

If an offering plate had been passed around the table at that moment, it would've come back full. God had worked a miracle. True, Thomas Lovelace had not admitted defeat, but neither had he insisted on the destruction of his challenger.

Molly glanced at Bailey and nearly laughed at the shocked look on his face. If he'd expected the worst, why had he spoken up? It wasn't like him to ruffle feathers.

Her plate was full, her stomach empty, but Molly rose. "If you'll excuse me—"

"Wait." Bailey stood. "You haven't eaten. I'll leave."

"But this is your supper. You shouldn't go hungry," Molly insisted.

"I don't mind."

She didn't understand. Was he being kind or was he avoiding her?

"Sit down, both of you. Supper is one of the perks of your job, Bailey. Don't let her discomfort trouble you. She's done her best to irritate all of us today." Thomas ripped some chicken meat off a leg and continued to speak around the bulk. "Did you bring Russell's latest balance?"

Bailey's vest flattened as he expelled a chest full of air and sat. "Yes, and it's low." He moved the salt cellar and opened the leather-bound ledger. "I've looked it over, but it's no use. Everything's accounted for."

"We are truly losing money?" Molly leaned toward her father. If only she could get a look at the page. "I thought Father's pessimism was at work again."

Thomas harrumphed and flipped the page. "What do you know about it?"

Enough to know the figure at the bottom of the column wouldn't make more than a month's worth of payroll. They'd be forced to liquidate some of their holdings at the bank to keep the company afloat. Courting Mr. Fenton hadn't been a complete waste of her time. She had charmed all sorts of helpful information out of him before he'd married Prue.

Bailey set his tea down. "Raw prices have remained steady. We haven't had any unusual expenses—no expensive machinery repairs, mules have been healthy, shipping hasn't gone up—and yet the balance is going down."

"Russell is robbing me blind. I knew it." Thomas spit a piece of fat into his napkin. "After all these years of trust, he betrays me."

"I'm not accusing Russell," Bailey said. "We need to know what is happening before we can know who is responsible."

Bailey met her eyes, although it seemed to pain him. "I'm no bean counter. Shouldn't we have someone else take a look at the books? Someone who's skilled with numbers?"

"Give me some time and I'll find it," Thomas said. "This goes to show you, Molly, every dime of that settlement needs to be reserved for the mill. You can't give away that money when I might need it soon."

The saws at the mill sat idle this time of night, moonlight reflecting on the teeth. The waterwheel continued its futile circling, never getting anywhere. Bailey jerked his fishing line through the dark water close to the waterwheel, and the roar of the water going over the dam drowned out the night sounds of crickets and cicadas.

He still loved her. When she'd left him, the thought of her with another man almost drove him to lunacy. But despite his hurt they'd found a working friendship that remained within the boundaries of her vows and God's law . . . until the trial had destroyed even that connection. Since then, Molly had clammed up tighter than an oyster, and he couldn't blame her. Maybe it was for the best. If she encouraged him, he might up and throw away all the good he'd done with Reverend Stoker.

But if he could be sure of her faithfulness, would it be worth it?

He watched as the strong current from the crashing water

carried his line to the middle of the dark river. Nothing was biting, but it didn't matter. The fishing pole was his excuse to linger after hours. The walls of the night watchman's quarters grew a tad tight if he went inside too early.

Something rustled nearby. Bailey shifted the pole to his right hand and half rolled on the grass to look down the bank. It was Molly. Pulling her shawl tight around her shoulders, she took another step toward the river and hurled something small and heavy into it.

Bailey caught sight of a glimmer of gold before it disappeared with a plunk.

Wordlessly she stood at the bank, watching the cascading waves dance over the edge of the dam. Bailey turned away and studied the fishing line as if he expected to reel in Jonah's whale at any moment.

But she saw him anyway. To his eternal surprise and slight discomfort, he could see out of the corner of his eye her white gown coming closer.

"Do you mind if I join you?" she asked.

Stunned, he pushed his newspaper-wrapped worms out of the way to make room.

Molly sat and pulled her knees to her chest. She slid her slippers off and tucked her gown around her feet. Was she getting ready to tear into him? Bailey's line went slack. He deserved a chewing out. Might as well get it over with.

"I don't even know where to start," he began. "I feel so bad about what happened at the courthouse. You have every right—"

"Oh, hush! You said what you felt you had to say. Why don't you be quiet and listen for once?"

Silence she wanted, silence she'd get. He went back to watching his line, every nerve pulled as tight as the strings on his guitar. Her hair was down. Occasionally a blond curl floated over to brush against his bare forearm. She might not notice, but he did. Of all the spots up and down the river, why did she come and sit by him?

To his surprise Molly flopped on her back, hands behind her head, and looked up at the stars.

"There's a lot I want to say, and there's no one I can talk to. Maybe that's my own fault. I'm trying to make friends, but it's too soon to pour my heart out to Mrs. Weems or Mrs. Nimenko. They don't know me—not like you do—and I'd like someone to listen while I sort this out."

"I don't think I'm the right person. I haven't been trustworthy—"

"I declare, Bailey Garner, you can't keep your trap shut for anything. Hush, now. I don't want to talk about the hearing. I don't want to talk about any of that. Believe me, Mother and Father have already done the topic justice."

One quick look at her, hair splashed across the grass, and Bailey knew he shouldn't look again. The desire to be near her, to find comfort together was overwhelming, but his desire had already destroyed her. He could listen without looking.

"I have to have something to live for," she said. "I won't be satisfied hiding in the parsonage or in Mother's parlor, arranging and rearranging knickknacks."

Her bare toes peeked out from under her gown as she let them stretch toward the churning water. He'd held her little foot and traced it at the cobbler's. He'd sewn the boots and tacked on the sole. He'd done the work, and in the end, the man with the money was the one who gave the gift and took the gift.

"I was reading yesterday," she began, "Isaiah 61. So many phrases of promise—to give 'beauty for ashes,' 'the oil of joy for mourning,' 'the garment of praise for the spirit of heaviness'—I know God can do that. I already sent Nick a letter about possible employment, but until I hear back, God must have something for me to do here—not anything important like help at the church or join a ladies' committee, but maybe I'm supposed to be a friend to people who need one. Even I could do that."

The water continued to roar and so did his love for her. People thought he was a saint, but Molly had shown him more grace than he would ever possess.

Something nudged his line. Bubbles appeared in the smooth pool protected by a fallen tree. Probably a giant catfish trolling for a midnight snack. Bailey drew in the line to check the bait. He could feel Molly's gaze on him as he pulled it up, hand over hand.

"I've always been so concerned about my future that I never stopped to see how anyone else was managing. Now that I don't have a future"—she swatted at a mosquito—"perhaps I could help someone I avoided before."

She rolled onto her side, propping her head up with bent arm. "You think they'd mind my getting involved?" She bit her lip. "Maybe I could use that settlement money for good. I could get Mrs. Weems started on the right foot, hire Mrs. Nimenko a farmhand so Ivan could go back to school. Small things like that?"

She looked so hopeful. Ready for the next challenge. Ready to move forward. He tossed the weighted line back out.

"Now I'm allowed to speak?"

She nodded.

"Then I'll tell you, you rolled onto my worms."

"Oh!" She sprang up and pulled a sticky folded piece of newspaper off her side. "Why didn't you tell me?"

"You told me to be quiet." Women. No pleasing them.

Molly scrubbed the wet spot on her dress with her shawl. "Revolting! They're ground into the fabric. Little bits of . . ."

She clutched her stomach as her eyes widened. Uh-oh. Bailey dropped his fishing rod.

"Don't get sick. Think about something else, Molly. Think about something else."

With a lurch his fishing pole parted the thick blades of grass and sped toward the river.

"Catch it!" he called, but Molly was in no condition to lend a hand.

Crashing through the brambles and into the river, Bailey chased his pole. Water filled his boots and splashed his chest, but he'd rather be in the river than next to a nauseous woman. He reached far and snagged the rod before it disappeared into the depths.

"It's a big one and feels like it's hooked good." He struggled against the pole, the water churning.

"Don't let it get in the branches. You'll never get it out." Molly's cheers confirmed that the worms were forgotten. "Oh, I saw it. That fish is as long as my arm."

"And a sight thicker." Bailey deliberately worked his way out from the bank, wading deeper and deeper. "I'm not going to be able to lift it with the pole. It's too big. Should be a net hanging in the scale house."

"I'll be right back."

Molly's bare feet skimmed over the cool grass. Her arm brushed against the slick spot on her dress, reminding her of the disintegrated worms, but she kept moving, not wanting to ruin Bailey's chances of success.

It'd been the right thing to do, leaving the parsonage that night. She hadn't known Bailey would be at the fishing hole, but when she saw him she couldn't stay away. Not after he'd stared her father down at supper. Only that gave her the courage to approach him.

Molly cut between the corncrib and the tack room, surprised to find herself out of breath, but when was the last time she'd actually run? When she'd worked at the courthouse, she'd rather incur Mr. Travis's wrath for being late than rush down the streets of Lockhart. She rounded the side of the scale house and stopped. Through the shadows she could see that the door to the mule barn stood open.

She paused at the scale house, squinting at the building across the gravel drive. Getting the net was her first priority. She could lock up the barn on her way to the parsonage.

But then she saw movement. A large figure crossed in front of the doorway, headed to the stall.

"Excuse me," she called. "What are you doing?"

He turned. It was Michael James. With a quick step to his left he disappeared into a dark corner of the barn.

Molly's heart lurched to her throat. That feeling—the feeling of being watched—descended on her again. He hadn't run off. He was waiting in the shadow. No mistake. He had come there for a purpose, and Molly might be all that stood between him and his goal.

Just like Saul Nimenko.

"Bailey," she called. "Bailey, come quick."

She could hear him, but his answer was unclear.

At the sound of a masculine voice, Michael darted from the building and sprinted to the shelter of the trees upriver. The saplings lining the banks shook as he passed through them until the darkness hid his progress. It didn't look like he'd carried anything away, but what if he wasn't alone? Molly kept her eyes peeled on the door and yelled for Bailey again.

She heard his boots sloshing across the yard. "What's the matter?"

"Michael James was in the mule barn. He ran over there."

She wrung her hands. "I think he was robbing us. Should I get a gun? You know he shot the last—"

"Shh . . ." He pulled his knife out of the sheath and turned to look upriver. "I wouldn't be able to catch him now. Let's make sure there are no surprises in the barn. Run to the house if he returns."

He squeezed her arm and motioned to her to wait outside the door. Poking his head in, Bailey looked both ways and then eased one heel at a time onto the straw as he snuck inside.

A mule snorted. She heard Bailey drop the pin into the latch. So the stall had been unfastened? Molly's chin hardened and her elbows tensed. How dare someone take something that didn't belong to him. How dare someone threaten the business she'd worked so hard to save.

The whole county was looking for Michael James, and she'd let him run away. Before she knew it she'd marched into the barn in search of a weapon. She made a beeline to the haymow and bent to retrieve the pitchfork. It was heavier than she'd expected, and when she finally pulled it free, she lost her balance and stumbled backwards.

Molly screamed as firm arms caught her from behind. A hand covered her mouth. She swung the pitchfork just as she realized who was holding her.

"Keep quiet or you'll wake the whole household," Bailey whispered.

He waited until she nodded before he uncovered her mouth, but his arms remained wrapped around her waist, her back pressed against his chest. She stilled, her anger forgotten. Did Bailey realize what he was doing? He was holding her, molding himself around her like they belonged together. She relaxed as the burdens she'd carried alone slid off her shoulders. With one hand Bailey took the pitchfork and tossed it aside before hugging her tight again.

He knew. He knew how much she needed him. He had to know how much she wanted him despite the fact that they could never be together.

His cheek pressed into her unbound hair. "Oh, Molly," he said. And that was all. She felt his lips against her crown. Molly closed her eyes and covered his hands with her own. She didn't want the moment to end. Every breath he took, every beat of his heart moved her—as it should. She'd ruined her chances, but nothing could ruin her love for him.

"I miss you," she said. "I miss us. I haven't been held like this since . . ." Was it the night of her father's spell? Yes, that was the last time they'd been together.

Bailey slid his arms apart. With a heavy sigh, he stepped away. She wondered why her reminiscing had upset him, and then it was clear. The last person to hold her hadn't been him.

"I think you'd better head to the parsonage before it gets any later." Bailey's shoulders slumped and he studied the dirt floor, looking like he wanted it to open and swallow him.

The shuffling of the mules filled the silence between them. Molly's arms dropped. He would never forget. No matter how much he cared for her, he couldn't forget.

The moment was ruined. When would she realize that Edward would always come between them? Her actions had put her forever out of Bailey's consideration. She was unclean in his eyes.

"I'll lock up," he said. "No sense worrying your pa till morning."

"Thank you." She stepped outside. Although the parsonage wasn't visible from the low riverbanks, she could find it while sleepwalking—as soon as she located her shoes. But she couldn't leave without trying to restore the moment they'd shared. "And thanks for letting me talk. Maybe I can come tomorrow night."

Bailey chewed his lip. "Didn't plan on coming out tomorrow. Maybe some other time."

She tightened her mouth briefly before forcing it into a smile. "Certainly. Some other time, then." But now she knew there wouldn't be one.

26

Bailey couldn't look at the mule barn without warmth creeping across his chest, and yet he'd found excuses to walk by it a hundred times that day.

Men waved from the back of a wagon as it rolled out of the lumberyard to take them home. Bailey returned the gesture, but he didn't have the heart to smile. No matter. They'd probably credit his melancholy to some deep contemplation of biblical scholarship, but his thoughts were occupied with a more earthly matter.

He entered the barn and saw that the pitchfork was still in the haystack where he'd tossed it. He inhaled the warm straw and animal scents, letting the memory of Molly in his arms return undiluted.

Why had he refused to meet with her? The answer was hidden somewhere between her past with Edward and their future. Could he forget her rejection when so many were eager to remind him?

The least he owed her was a sympathetic ear, but maybe another location would be better. His ear was attached to the rest of him, and there was no limit to the trouble found on a riverbank under the stars.

He latched the barn door and headed to the office to get the ledger. Thomas claimed to have gone over it like a mother searching for nits, but besides the low balance he could find nothing amiss. That wasn't good enough for Bailey. What if they were losing money because of him? He was the new man, and he wanted assurance that the dwindling profits weren't caused by his ineptitude.

Through the office window he saw Russell kneeling next to the woodstove. In his hand were what looked to be sales receipts. Russell swung open the square metal grate and stuffed the papers into the stove.

What in the world?

Striding through the door, Bailey snatched up the poker and stepped between Russell and the stove. He jabbed the rod into the blaze and tried to drag out the flaming paper, but it was too late to retrieve the receipts.

"What did you do?" He glared at the man crouched on the floor.

"I'm discarding the duplicate receipts. I didn't want them to get mixed in and cause confusion."

Bailey's fingers went as cold as the poker. Part of him wanted to accept the weak excuse, to turn a blind eye so he wouldn't learn anything he didn't want to know. But the truth was truth, even if it proved him wrong.

"Why would we have duplicate receipts?"

Russell stood, his bald head glistening from the heat. "I spilt ink on a stack of them, so I had to rewrite them all. We can't have two copies floating around." He shrugged easily. "Here's the ledger. Tell Thomas we had another busy day."

Bailey took the leather-bound book from his hand. The bright flames had returned to their normal height. Russell closed the grate and reached for his tan felt hat—the same color as the hands that grasped it.

Bailey's eyes narrowed. Russell's hands were clean. Bailey walked around the desk and found no deep stains marring its surface. The trash bin held no blackened rags. Everything was tidy.

Russell had his hand on the door before Bailey spoke.

"Have you seen your son lately?"

Russell turned to him, his face blotchy. "I should deny it, but yes, I've seen Michael. I see him every chance I get. Look, you've always treated me fair. You have to understand that I can't turn on my own flesh and blood. He's in a lot of trouble, and I can't refuse to help him."

"Even if he's a murderer?"

"But he's not. It's a misunderstanding."

"Like the mess of duplicate receipts?" Bailey's heart sank. "I've defended you to Mr. Lovelace. I've stood up for you."

"Mr. Lovelace doesn't deserve loyal employees. You know that if anyone does. We all saw how he treated you when you were courting Molly. You weren't good enough for his daughter, but that doesn't stop him from profiting off you."

"He gives me fair compensation."

"But does he appreciate you? Thomas Lovelace believes I'm a thief, whether I am or not. What do I have to lose?"

"Mr. Lovelace's opinion doesn't matter, not if your conscience is clean."

"My conscience doesn't trouble me. It's spotless." And the door fell closed behind him.

"As spotless as your hands?" Bailey replied to the empty room.

Night had fallen. Molly set the lamp on the table and picked up the dish towel. The cozy parsonage had seen more visitors than she'd expected. That morning Mrs. Weems had stopped in with little Charlie for a visit. With a pencil and the back of an envelope, Molly and she had compiled a list of her expenditures. There wasn't much excess, but with frugality she could make ends meet on the money sent by her errant husband.

By the time Molly had cleaned up her meager dinner, Mary Garner had appeared on the doorstep to school Molly in culinary skills that she'd been lacking for years. Molly smiled at the memory. Mary hadn't bothered asking what Molly needed to learn, but jumped in assuming she knew nothing—and she was right. Molly wiped out the basin. Despite her brusque manners, Bailey's mother had taken the time to help her, and Molly appreciated it. They got along splendidly, possibly because neither of them mentioned her son.

The dog next door barked, as if startled. Molly peered out the window, but her ears told her almost as much as her eyes did. She could barely see the man who veered into the neighbor's yard to pet the squirming animal. The chain rattled as the animal tried to reach its friend.

Molly went to the front door to pull in the latchstring when she heard the front step creak. The cabin was so small that whoever was on the front porch could tell that her lamp was lit and could probably see her through the lone window.

She took the globe off of the lantern and was pursing her lips to blow on the wick when she heard Bailey's voice.

"Molly, it's me. Are you still up?"

She straightened. "Just a moment."

Molly surveyed the cozy home, comparing it with how she'd found it the day she'd moved in. So far, so good. Just as clean as he'd left it and with the benefit of a woman's touch—three women if she counted her visitors today.

She smoothed the quilt on the bed and pulled the curtain over the corner where her clothes hung on their pegs, her curiosity running rampant. What was he doing here? Hadn't he refused to see her?

She swung the door open and held the lamp high. The golden light illuminated his boyish face and disappeared into the depths of his eyes.

"Won't you come in?"

"No, I won't."

The lamp flickered. Molly turned to hide her disappointment.

"I'd like to talk, if you have time," he said.

She motioned to the chairs. "We could bring them outside."

"Would you mind? I've promised myself . . . Well, I can't step foot inside unless it's daylight."

She handed him the lamp and without a word hooked an arm through each back and hoisted the chairs to the porch.

Bailey blew out the light and set the lamp by the door. "Don't want to attract bugs."

He sat. She sat. The dog barked once, probably wondering why the crazy man didn't go into his own house, but then it settled down, and the rustling of soft spring leaves could be heard.

Bailey didn't turn in her direction. As her eyes adjusted to the dimness, she saw the ledger from the mill on his lap. His fingers drummed against the leather cover.

Molly rubbed her hands together, itching for her turn.

"What's wrong?" he asked.

"Me? Oh, nothing. I need some cream for my hands, I suppose. They aren't accustomed to this kind of work."

"I thought I left the place clean."

"Spotless. It was spotless. And your mother came over today. She brought me some garden greens and introduced me to the cookstove. She was very helpful."

"I didn't know how you'd feel about her visiting."

"You knew she was coming?" Of course he did. "She's welcome anytime."

They fell silent again. Molly's impatience was growing. "Aren't you supposed to be guarding the mill?"

Bailey lifted his chin. "Ah yes. Now that you mention it . . ." He tapped the ledger again with his index finger. "I'm not usually this indecisive. There's something I'd like your help with, but it might not be wise to get you involved."

Molly's foot tapped against the floor. "What is it? Is it the accounts? Do you want me to look them over?"

His eyes smiled before his mouth did. "I should've known you'd be game."

She held out her hands. Bailey passed them over.

"As much as it pains me to admit it, your pa may be right. Russell James is acting suspicious. I pray we find there's an honest mistake. That would be best, but your father looked this ledger over again after supper and couldn't find a penny missing."

Molly had left her chair and was holding the ledger out from under the porch roof, trying to catch some moonlight on the pages. "So this is the record of the cash account—credits, debits, balance? I can keep this all night?"

"Yes, ma'am. I'll come by in the morning, but I'm not sure what your father would think about you double-checking his work."

"He'd be furious." Molly tore her attention away from the numbers to peer at the man. "You're risking your job. Have you decided you don't want to work there?"

"Just the opposite. I've decided to do everything I can to save the company—and the family—I care about."

"You're a good man, Bailey Garner."

He didn't respond.

Molly closed the book. "I want to help them, too. Help you. Help myself."

"At the river last night, you were talking about Mrs. Nimenko and Mrs. Weems. I know your mother is none too happy about your befriending them." Bailey stretched one leg out before him and wiped his palms on his trousers. "You've changed. The old Molly would've never noticed them."

Was she a better person now? Molly picked at a piece of wool caught on the roughhewn post. How could she be godlier yet less accepted than before? It didn't make sense.

"I pray I've changed. I pray that, given another opportunity in society, I won't forget those women and others like them." Molly leaned against the post. "I know what it's like to be friendless."

"That's not true." Bailey rose. "I've failed you in the past, Molly, but I won't again. As long as I'm alive, you aren't friendless."

He looked like there was more he wanted to say, but he didn't. Molly's eyes lowered. Friend was as good as he could offer. If they could recover the missing money and free up her settlement, she might be able to salvage a future for herself, but she wouldn't be able to restore the one relationship that meant the most to her.

# 27

Bailey woke with one leg hung between the slats of the mule stall, a barn cat nestled against him, and a sweet pillow under his head. No one would steal a mule on his watch. He didn't mind the discomfort as long as Molly was safe in the parsonage, out of earshot of her parents' frequently voiced disappointments. He watched the cat stretch, its back curving like the slender claws that emerged from its paws. What did Molly's parents have to complain about? If they had let her make her own choices instead of grooming her to catch the eye of a fop, her situation would be completely different.

Both of theirs would.

He extracted his leg from the slats and sent the cat scurrying. It was time to get the ledger from her, and he was taking off like a calf out of the chute.

Bailey turned off Mill Road toward Church Road, right into the path of Clara Cantrell, one of the old church ladies who'd probably knitted his mother a baby blanket before his arrival. From the way she squinted, she probably couldn't tell who he was until they'd come within a lasso's distance of each other. Then her eyebrows raised, her mouth twitched, and she gushed as only a lonely widow could.

"Bailey, what a pleasure to see you this fine morning. Shouldn't you be at the mill? Has working for the Lovelaces finally done you in?"

"No, ma'am. I'll be headed out there in a jiffy."

"Oh? Well, I want you to know I think it's a fine thing you're doing. If I've told Red once, I've told him a thousand times, 'That Bailey Garner carries himself above the fray. People may betray him, they try to drag him down, but he's got his eyes fixed on Jesus.'" She waved her hankie in front of her face as if overcome by the thought of her Savior. "If only that son of mine was half as righteous as you—"

"I'm sure Red appreciates the comparison." Bailey would have to steer clear of the man. Red could tear him in two if he had the mind. "People have been more patient with me than you know."

"I'll tell you what I know." She leaned in, her eyes now as clear as an eagle's. "I know no decent man would get caught up with that Molly Lovelace. She sashayed in from Lockhart, too good for Red or any of the other Prairie Lea boys. Now look at her. She certainly showed her colors, while her poor parents—"

"I'm afraid you don't know the whole story."

"When you're older you'll see things more clearly, son. I understand she's even been out to the Nimenkos' place. Can you imagine?" She tucked her hankie into her black sleeve. "Shameful the way she looks for controversy. Now, I won't keep you, although I did hear that Pastor Stoker is coming to town today. Please let him know that I prayed for his knee, and the fervent prayer of the righteous availeth much."

She almost trotted away, leaving Bailey smoldering over the injustice of her comments. He picked up a stick and flung it far from him. The morning was spoiled. Would people ever tire of maligning Molly? What would it take to clear her name?

Molly peeked out the window and shuddered. The sun hadn't cleared the horizon, but she could make out the despicable bundle at her door clearly enough.

Thank goodness Bailey was coming. Otherwise, who knew how long she'd be trapped inside, unable to step around the carnage? Who was that shadowy figure and why would he do this to her? Although the accounts had kept her up late, she'd woken early enough to visit the privy before Bailey arrived, but the sight of a man leaving dead animals at her door while it was still dark had terrified her.

Privy.

Outhouse.

She hadn't brought a chamber pot from home, and if someone didn't move those carcasses, she'd be in sorry shape indeed.

Molly didn't see Bailey until he'd almost reached the porch. She extended her arm out the window and waved.

"Bailey, it's me. Be careful."

"Of what?"

With a deep breath Molly pulled the door toward her, careful to remain hidden behind it.

He stood over the two dead rabbits, as if unconcerned. "What's wrong with you?"

"Don't you see them?"

"What?" He followed her pointing finger down between his feet. "The rabbits? Sure. You been hunting?"

"Of all the foolish statements. I've been trapped in this house afraid to set foot outside, and you think it's funny. Someone is trying to frighten me."

"No one leaves food on the doorstep to be scary."

"That's not food. It's a threat. Dead animals? I'm sure that's some kind of message in Indian."

Bailey rolled his eyes. Stooping, he picked up the rabbits by their hind legs and carried them past her into the kitchen, letting them swing in her direction when he rounded the corner.

"I thought you weren't going to come inside," she said.

"It's morning."

"So it is. If you'll excuse me."

"Where are you going?"

"It's morning. I haven't been outside yet." She twisted a curl around her finger.

He turned his back, giving her leave to . . . well, leave.

By the time Molly returned Bailey had the first hare spread on the cutting block and was washing his knife.

"Did you see who left them?" he asked.

"Not clearly. It was a man. Young looking."

"But not an Indian?" He cocked an eyebrow at her. "Whoever bagged these happens to be a good shot. Right through the head."

"I knew it. He's dangerous."

She looked away as he worked his knife around the rabbit's back leg above the foot.

"You might be more dangerous than the shooter." She shuddered.

Molly watched for Bailey to wink, to smile, but he did the grim work without his usual humor. He reached through the curtain covering the cabinet and pulled out a pot, for what Molly didn't want to know. Good thing he knew his way around this kitchen. She still didn't.

"I looked over the figures. Father was right. They add up, but what about the inventory record?"

"I keep it. I balance it with the lumber we have on hand every night."

"Could you bring it to me tonight along with the ledger?"

Bailey's brow wrinkled. "We haven't gotten that far yet,

but it's not a bad idea." He tugged on the rabbit's hide. "You sure you didn't recognize your rabbit slayer? Might have been a secret admirer."

She winced at the ripping sound as the hide separated from the muscle.

"He didn't look old enough for courting. Had an odd getup, walked like his boots didn't fit." Molly stopped. She dropped into her chair. "I know who it was—Anne Tillerton. Oh, fiddlesticks. I'm receiving charity from Anne Tillerton. Won't Mother be proud?"

With another firm tug, Bailey came up with a handful of fluff. "She needs a friend. You need food. Nothing wrong with that." He tossed the brown pelt to her.

Molly screamed and batted it away.

"Really, Molly?"

She smoothed her hair and eyed the brown fur suspiciously, then bent to pick it up with one finger and thumb. Molly loved rabbit skin, but she'd never had one so fresh before.

Bailey laid the naked rabbit aside and picked up the second one. "I'll get you set up for a pot of stew, and you can invite Mrs. Tillerton over to share it. That'd be neighborly of you."

Truly they were in very similar situations. Why had Anne married her schoolteacher? Had she fallen in love, or had her father pushed her toward him? At least Edward hadn't been abusive. Molly slid her fingers through the silky fur and wondered how much of Anne's erratic behavior stemmed from her treatment at Jay Tillerton's hands.

"One bad decision can change everything," she said.

Bailey dropped the second pelt to the floor and tapped his knife against the cutting board. "Are you talking about Mrs. Tillerton or yourself?"

She buried her hand in the warm skin. Anne was a widow.

Molly was an adulteress. No arguing over who'd stooped the lowest.

Bailey arranged the cutting board, then jabbed the point of the knife downward. The rabbit's carcass bounced into Molly's sight before disappearing again. He sawed forward, his face grim, then set aside his knife and grasped the edge of the cabinet.

At first Molly thought something was wrong with the rabbit, but Bailey wasn't seeing what lay before his eyes.

"Do you ever think of that last night on the road to Lockhart?"

Molly blinked. How many times had she relived every moment of their time together, asking herself if it had truly occurred? So many hopes appeared realized that night, so many dreams attainable, but by morning nothing remained. Just the shame.

Bailey continued, "Do you ever wonder what would've happened if Sheriff Colton hadn't ridden up?"

"Bailey, don't." She stroked the rabbit skin. "Now's not the time."

"Might as well be now. Let's hang out all our dirty laundry, all our bad decisions, and let the neighbors see. They know all yours, but mine are still hidden. I've got mistakes I repent of every day, but I can't decide what I regret more—my behavior or our location. I loathe what I did to you . . . and at the same time I'm sorry I didn't pull further off the road. I'm sorry we weren't hidden better." He pounded the cabinet top. "I've lain in that bed, in a parsonage, for crying aloud, and regretted I didn't come back to the boardinghouse, climb in your window, and carry you off."

What could she say? She'd watched at her window. She'd searched for him the next day with promises of love and commitment, but he'd left her behind.

"I thought I'd make you marry me," Bailey said, "but I felt guilty immediately. Then I thought I'd do the honorable thing and go to your folks. What I wouldn't give to change that decision. It was the biggest mistake of my life."

"You did right, Bailey. You turned around while you still could. Everything I've touched has been ruined. My dreams of freedom, of helping my family, even of having a career are destroyed. You're all that remains unscathed. I'm glad you're free. I wouldn't want your fall on my hands, too."

"But if it wasn't for me, you'd be cleared. Without my testimony Pierrepont would be in jail and you'd be justified. Instead, I'm holy and untouched, above reproach. And you . . ." He held out his hands and saw the blood on them. Turning to the basin, he lifted the pump handle and scrubbed like he was trying to take off his skin.

"Some have shown me kindness," Molly said, "but you can't touch me with a ten-foot pole. You've got what I always wanted, and you can't lose it."

Taking a towel, he turned to face her. "There's nothing I have that I wouldn't give you."

Molly looked into his dear face, proud to be his friend.

"You have respect, and that's something you can't share with me. Even if you can't walk on water, everyone here figures you'd float pretty well. That's all I hear from my parents, from Nick, from everyone. 'Bailey helped with this. Bailey said that. Bailey smote the rock and water flowed from it.' With me, no one expected me to amount to much. I was never meant to be of any consequence, but you can't disappoint everyone. They're too proud of you."

"If they knew my heart they wouldn't want anything to do with me. How can I be an example when I'm hiding who I am and what I want?"

His eyes roved her face desperately. He'd told her that he

wanted her before. He used to tell her every chance he got, and she'd taken him for granted. Now it was all she could do to stay in her chair and not run into his arms, but she was wiser this time.

"What does God want for you? What are His plans?"

"I prayed God's plans involved you, but not like this. Not after you ran off with another man." His chest rose and fell in long pulls. "I'm sorry, Molly, but people are always reminding me of what happened. It's going to be hard to explain to everyone that . . . that I still love you."

Molly sat, both feet pressed against the floor, both hands folded atop the rabbit skin. Her heart was leaping, but her joy was tempered by his angst. His feelings for her would cost him, and she knew she wasn't worth it. In some ways, their love was better left untested. She wasn't the same innocent girl Bailey had wooed before. If their relationship resumed, she'd be forced to face the personal consequences of her past. She would always be aware of his disappointment.

He turned to the cabinet and threw the rabbit meat into the pot. "The sun is up. I need to get to work." He filled the pot with water and showed her the correct seasonings to add. "Throw in some onions and celery. It'll be ready by dinnertime."

She walked him to the door and placed the ledger in his hands.

"Will you be back tonight to discuss the inventory list?"

His gaze burned steady. "I intend to discuss more than that."

28

Anne Tillerton spooned the last of the stew carefully. Had she not tarried so long, Molly would've thought her uncomfortable, but she was in no hurry to leave.

"Sorry I'm so quiet," Anne said. "Since you probably don't care how my traps are doing or that I found cougar prints at the creek, I'm at a loss. What do women talk about anyway?"

Molly folded her napkin and laid it on the table. "We talk about family. Tell me about yours."

"Not much to say. I don't plan on ever seeing them again." Anne stared into her soup.

Maybe family wasn't a safe topic. Molly wouldn't want to talk about hers, either.

"How about your farm? Your cattle were returned."

"And I sold them. What's the use of feeding livestock as long as Michael James is on the loose? If I caught him rustling I couldn't shoot him. No one would believe I had cause."

"Are you going to farm?"

"No, I put a notice in the paper to sell out. I don't know where I'll go, but I'll have enough to get started proper somewhere." She swirled the spoon in the empty bowl. "It probably isn't right of me to accept your hospitality when I'm leaving.

You shouldn't waste your time making friends with someone who won't be around."

"Nonsense." Molly rose and gathered the empty dishes. "Getting to know you isn't a waste. Besides, you provided the food. Maybe you shouldn't be wasting your hospitality on me."

Anne smiled. Her slanted eyes were enough to make her pretty despite her unruly hair. "I won't forget how you came to visit me at the jail. That was right Christian of you. No wonder they let you stay here at the church."

"What else are they going to do with me? My parents don't want me at home, and the only other person I'd want . . ."

Molly thrust the bowls into the sudsy water. She had to get those thoughts out of her head. As soon as Nick found a position for her, she could leave Bailey with all the conflicting emotions he stirred up. Over time, perhaps she could prove herself and they could have a new beginning, the two of them. Or if Bailey decided to leave Caldwell County, they could go where no one knew them.

"Someone's coming to the door," Anne said.

Bailey already? Dinner had just passed.

"Bailey? Are you in there?" a voice called from the yard.

Molly's mouth fell open. Reverend Stoker?

She stacked the bowls and opened the door. The pastor obviously wasn't a poker player. She could've read the surprise on his face from across the town square.

"Molly?" His brows lowered. "Where's Bailey?"

"He's living at the mill. Father asked him to stay on as a night watchman, so I moved here."

Reverend Stoker crossed his arms. "This is the first I've heard about it."

Anne stood shoulder to shoulder with Molly. "Do you need me to stay?" Anne asked.

"That's unnecessary." But she regretted her hasty answer as Anne slipped between them and made her departure.

Stoker looked past Molly at the dresses hanging and the slippers scattered in the corner. "Why aren't you with your parents?"

"We've had some disagreements. They don't approve of my new acquaintances, so Bailey thought it'd be nice for me to have a place of my own."

"He did, did he?" His forehead was creasing in deep furrows. "A place free from parental restraints where you could entertain?"

Oh dear. When he put it that way . . . "I'm talking about ladies like Mrs. Tillerton. Anyone who approves of me wouldn't be accepted at my parents' house. How can I demonstrate Christian hospitality if I'm exposing them to Christian hypocrisy in the same parlor?"

But he wasn't listening. "This won't do. Considering your past . . . er . . . friendship with Bailey, I cannot allow you to live in a house that is under his care. Surely you understand, Molly. Don't you realize how this will look to people?"

"But I'm at the parsonage. Where better to minister to hurting people than on the back lawn of the church?"

"I'm not talking about the women who might come here. I'm talking about the men. One man in particular." Stoker limped to the edge of the porch, removed his hat, and spoke without turning toward her. "Bailey wants what's best for you. He cares about you, perhaps to a foolish degree. I know you're repentant over what happened, but we mustn't let Bailey's reputation be blackened."

Molly gripped the doorframe with stiff fingers. "I want what's best for him, too. I wouldn't hurt him."

"Ah, but you have, haven't you?" He turned and the sympathy in his eyes softened his painful words. "You hurt him when you left. Now you're back, and any connection between the two of you will stir up a hornet's nest. I know you never intended to be in this position, but you have to think of him. What if God's calling him into the ministry? How could he serve if his family was tainted?"

A tainted family? Would even their children be judged for her mistake?

Molly could picture a dark-haired lad taunted by his peers. A blond child crying because she wasn't invited to a class-mate's birthday party. Was she dragging Bailey into a miser-able future? Was she strong enough to stay away?

She would for him.

"I lost my job in Lockhart. Nick is trying to find me a posi-tion, but I haven't heard from him, and I can't go home. Bailey spends every evening there. As long as I'm in Prairie Lea, I can't avoid him." She hid her hands in her apron pockets.

"I could refer you to an association in Austin. They might find employment for you there."

"But what about Mrs. Nimenko and Mrs. Weems? They were just beginning to trust me."

"I'm proud that you've befriended them." He crossed his arms. "We should've done more to help those women all along. You're leaving behind a legacy."

A legacy of care instead of shame? That was more than Molly had hoped for. Besides, in a city as big as Austin she'd find opportunities to get involved in, and hopefully there her involvement wouldn't ruin anyone's reputation.

Once she was certain her family was secure, she'd leave. Her presence in Prairie Lea could only bring trouble to those she loved.

"You're awfully anxious, Bailey," Mrs. Lovelace said. "Can't wait to catch a big one?"

It took him a moment to realize she was talking about fish. Mr. Lovelace was adding up the last of the accounts over dessert, but Bailey's thoughts weren't on the books. He was chewing over a more important matter. Should Bailey ask Thomas's permission to court Molly? Molly might not accept his suit yet, but he wanted to do it right this time. Getting her parents' approval would be a victory worth celebrating.

The grandfather clock struck eight. If they were courting, he'd meet her here at her parents' house. Everyone would know his intentions, and wouldn't they be surprised? Bailey swallowed. It might be hard at first. He could imagine what would be said behind his back, but he was tired of pretending. He was tired of wearing a reputation that didn't fit.

"Have they found the James boy yet?" Mrs. Lovelace asked.

"No," Bailey answered. "He's a fool if he's still in the county."

"He's still here," Thomas grumbled. "And I'll bet Russell knows where he is, too. I have to figure out how he is robbing me. It's probably been going on for years. Once a scalawag, always a scalawag."

On second thought, Bailey wouldn't ask for Mr. Lovelace's blessing. He'd already gotten it once, and there wasn't an expiration date that he'd heard tell of.

When Mr. Lovelace finally handed him the ledger, it was all Bailey could do to keep from bolting out the door. He reined in his enthusiasm, complimented Mrs. Lovelace on the pie that Lola had baked, and took his leave, patting his vest to insure the inventory booklet was safely inside.

What would Molly say? That morning she'd been reserved. She hadn't refused his declarations, but neither had she returned them. His long strides lengthened in his rush to get to the parsonage. He knew his Molly. She loved him, but convincing her to brave the storm of gossip they'd kick up was going to be tough. Especially since his old methods of convincing were now banned.

Reverend Stoker's horse was tied to the church's hitching post. Bailey halted. Maybe he should swing around the lawn. He didn't want his business with Molly to be delayed any longer. He would split open like an overripe watermelon if he didn't talk to her soon.

He backtracked to the street and removed the inventory booklet from his vest.

"Bailey, were you looking for me?" Stoker called through the open window of the church building.

"No, sir. Are you looking for me?"

"I guess you could say that, but you aren't easy to find these days. Come on in."

Bailey tightened his grip on the ledgers, wishing he had the nerve to make an excuse. He straightened his hat. Didn't matter much. From the sound of Stoker's voice, he wasn't going to get off the hook that easily anyway.

His pastor sat on the front pew and motioned for Bailey to join him. "You can imagine the fears that overwhelmed me when I saw that Molly had moved into the parsonage."

Looked like this was a conversation he couldn't avoid. Bailey sat on the second row and removed his hat. "You know me better than that."

"Yes, but I also know a young lady who has a history of bringing out the worst in you. I'm shocked you allowed her to live on the church's property."

With effort Bailey eased his shoulders down. It'd do no good to get riled at Reverend Stoker. The man had always been good to Bailey, but he needed to see where he was wrong.

"Her folks approved, but I should've asked you first. I'm sorry."

Stoker lifted his stiff knee and stretched his leg along the pew. "I'll help her move home tomorrow, but it'd be better if you didn't visit the parsonage until she's gone. If people see you together, they're going to question your character."

As well they should.

Bailey laced his fingers together. No matter how godly he lived today, he still had a past. God had forgiven him and with that forgiveness came the responsibility to live honestly. Not everyone needed to know his doings, but someone should hold him accountable, someone who understood how weak he was.

But how to get Stoker to really hear him this time?

Bailey's heart pounded, and he wiped his mouth. He was making things right with Molly, but how could he understand what she'd been through while he was still hiding his own failure? He had to speak now before he lost the gumption.

"Pastor Stoker, you know I enjoy serving here at the church. I don't think God will ever turn me into a preaching man, but that doesn't give me leave to stray from His path."

"Um-hum." Stoker rubbed his kneecap.

"I'm honored that you and the rest of the church trust me to keep the grounds up and go on visits."

Stoker grunted again and pulled out his pocket watch. No time to spare.

"If you have a minute, I would like your advice about a situation. There's a young man I spent time with this week who told me a shocking story. I don't know how to counsel him."

"Who is it?"

"I shouldn't say. I'd always thought him an honest sort. Trustworthy." Bailey's voice grew stronger as he found the story he needed to tell. He plunged ahead. "Turns out he's sweet on this girl, but she has her reservations. He told me he'd tried everything to win her over. Candy, songs, poetry. She was interested but wouldn't say yes."

"Someone here in Prairie Lea or in Lockhart?" Stoker's brows met over his puzzled face.

"That's confidential, and you'll see why. Not long ago he caught the young lady at a vulnerable time. She'd had a family tragedy, and she was feeling mighty low." Bailey's gaze dropped to the floor. He felt like he was disrobing in the pulpit. Naked for the world to see. "He thought that could be his chance. If he could ruin her, then she'd have to marry him."

Stoker's legs shot off the pew and hit the floor. "I refuse to do the ceremony. You can tell him that. She's under no obligation to marry him."

Bailey held up a hand. "Let me finish. He intended to compromise her. He got her alone, and then his plans fell through. Now, as far as God's law is concerned, I don't know what sin he's guilty of."

"You don't? Haven't you read about the seducers lying in wait? Doesn't the call for purity and holiness cover our intentions, not only our actions?"

Stoker was right. Finally Bailey was hearing the words he'd known were his due. Finally someone agreed with him on his sin.

"I can't stomach it, either. I don't know how he could justify himself." Bailey peeked at Stoker, still florid. "And then there's Molly, whose sole desire was to please her parents, but instead she's ruined. It dries up any mercy I might've felt for this man."

Stoker's eyes narrowed. "Molly used bad judgment. Had she prayed over her decision, surely God would've protected her."

"I agree that Molly made a horrible mistake, but while I was thinking about her, I thought that maybe I should introduce her to this man. He wants a wife and everyone seems to believe Molly is unmarriageable now. Perhaps——"

"Molly's misfortune shouldn't leave her at the mercy of ruthless men. She shouldn't be shackled to someone without a conscience." Stoker shook his head slowly. "I can't believe you'd suggest such a thing."

Bailey fell against the hard pew. He wasn't good enough for her. She wasn't good enough for him. Obviously they weren't fit for anyone else, either.

He'd made it through the account, and now it was time to take the blame. Bailey paused. Stoker's perception of him would change. Was he ready to lose his mentor's respect? And what if Molly refused to marry him? What if Nicholas found a job for her and she never returned? Was he making a needless sacrifice?

Bailey loosened his collar. He needed to deal with his hypocrisy even if Molly was out of reach. Besides, he'd do almost anything to clear his conscience. This secret had festered too long. It was time to come clean.

"Pastor, this is probably the hardest thing I've ever had to tell a soul. When I stood up in church that Sunday and asked y'all to pray for me, I didn't need protection from an enticing woman. I needed God to protect me from my own bad decisions. I cut Molly a wide swath in the beginning, but when I saw that Pierrepont fellow, I knew her parents would be hot on his trail. I knew Molly couldn't tell them no. So when the opportunity came, I tried to take advantage of her." He leaned forward, elbows resting on his knees. "That was *my* story I told."

Bailey hung his head, unwilling to watch the disappointment grow on Stoker's face. He'd told him. No going back. His pastor would never think of him in the same light.

"You didn't." Stoker sounded more hurt than anything. "You wouldn't."

"Mr. Lovelace had that spell and Molly looked to me for comfort. What did I do? Instead of offering her friendship, I pressured her. I knew what to say to earn her trust and silence her doubts. I told myself it was for the best because I was keeping her from making a mistake. If Sheriff Colton hadn't caught me—"

"You could've done her as much harm as Pierrepont did. Still could, if Colton talks." Stoker pulled out his hankie and mopped his face. Folding it carefully, he leaned back and sighed. "If Thomas Lovelace knew this, you'd be run out of town."

"But how do I make it right? I've been miserable hearing people talk about her, knowing the reason they can say such things is because I ruined her reputation."

"Are you talking about your confession last fall?"

"No, there's more. I'm the reason that Edward Pierrepont escaped jail. The trial wasn't canceled because Molly didn't have a case. It was canceled because of me. At the hearing, they asked me under oath to describe our relationship, to tell them about our last . . . encounter. Do you think she'd want this repeated at a trial with a jury and a galley full of people?" His voice rose. "He went free, I went free, and Molly bore all the blame."

And she'd borne it with grace while he'd cowered, unwilling to be counted with those who needed forgiveness.

Stoker's words stung. "If I was Molly, I'd never speak to you again. You've been prancing around scot-free while she's been scorned." He shook his head. "Even I've been unfair."

"I've tried to make it up to her. I've tried to help out when I could, but then people will hail me and cut her. I don't know why she's stood it. I don't know why she hasn't called me out." He watched Stoker for a reaction, but the man was still stunned. "I want to marry Molly if she'll have me. If that means I'm not cut out to help around here, then so be it. I'm willing to take my licks. It's not fair Molly's been taking them alone."

He'd bared his soul. It'd be hard looking Stoker in the eye for a while, but Bailey had no regrets. He finally felt clean.

"I'm glad you told me, son. I know it wasn't easy." Stoker paused before laying a hand on his shoulder. "I owe an apology to Miss Lovelace, as well. Unfortunately, I said some things to her today that, in light of your story, were unwarranted. I figured the trial would clear her, and when it didn't . . . well, I thought she was somehow to blame."

"We can go together to apologize," Bailey said. A first step toward bringing Molly back into society and taking him off his pedestal. "I was on my way to deliver these ledgers to her." He rose in time to see a horse thundering down the dirt lane. The roan flew by them with the rider crouched low, head inches from his mount's neck. Covered by a bandanna and slouch hat, Bailey didn't recognize the man immediately, but it rankled that he'd be as careless as to barrel through town.

"Who was that?" Stoker asked, peering out the door.

Before Bailey could comment, another rumbling was heard, louder than the first.

"Posse coming." Bailey could hardly contain his excitement. "That was Michael James."

"You take my horse," Stoker called. "I'll find another and be right behind you."

He nodded as Stoker hobbled to untie it from the hitching post. Bailey sprinted across the lawn to the parsonage and banged on the door.

"Here are the account books." He pushed the door open wider to see more of Molly's shocked face. "I've got to run. The posse. Be back in the morning."

And he clomped off in a rush to do his civic duty.

 29

The barking of the neighbor's dog woke her. Molly rubbed her eyes and groaned. It had been a late night, although a profitable one. She'd labored so long over the ledgers—trying one theory after another—that she hadn't felt like changing into her nightgown but fell asleep fully clothed. She blinked. Why was it still dark outside? Had morning not come?

Pushing the quilt aside, Molly stood and made her way to the window. What was bothering that dog? A firm knock on the door startled her. With a surprised laugh she smoothed her hair.

"Bailey, is that you?"

"Yep."

"You scared me coming over this early." She swung the door wide to see a pistol thrust into her face.

Grabbing the barrel, Molly tried to push it aside, but Michael James shoved her away, stumbled into the cabin, and fastened the door behind him.

Oh, how he stunk. Molly covered her nose, feeling ridiculous. Her life was in danger and her biggest concern was his hygiene. She'd better be careful unless she wanted her last breath to be the foulest. He motioned her to light the lamp while he pulled the curtain over the lone window. With shaking fingers she adjusted the wick and replaced the globe, only then getting a good look at the man who'd caused so many tragedies in their community.

Bareheaded, face haggard, and filthy gloves smeared in . . . Molly gasped.

Blood—bright and wet, with a dark crust already drying in the creases. His gloves were slick with it.

"Not Bailey. Please, tell me that Bailey is all right."

"Shut up!" He raised his arm as if to strike her but instead yelped. His arm dropped and he had to catch the back of the chair to steady himself.

"You're shot, aren't you?" Molly picked up the lamp and held it between them, only then noticing the thick dark fluid seeping through his shirt above his waist.

"I thought this cabin would be empty, since everyone is with the posse. Just as well. You can sew a few stitches to keep me from bleeding out."

Molly had avoided Michael for most of their childhood and had never thought to compare his looks with his father's. Even with her discovery over the account books last night, she still couldn't reconcile the connection.

"What makes you think I can sew? I don't even own a needle."

His lip curled, exposing a chipped tooth. "You are completely worthless."

The dog outside barked once, then whined in pleased recognition. Michael raised his gun.

"Don't open the door. Whoever that is, get rid of him." He turned a full circle. Then holding his side he shuffled to rest against the wall next to her bed.

"Molly, it's me," Bailey called through the door. "Is everything all right? I see your lamp is lit."

Her heart pounded. Bailey wasn't hurt, but he would be if she wasn't careful. "Yes, I'm fine. I'm looking over the account books."

When she heard his voice again, it was closer—as if his forehead was resting against the door. "Did you find anything?"

Should she tell Bailey what she'd discovered? If she didn't she might never get a chance to. Michael could kill her and burn the account books, and no one would know. Michael slid down the wall and crouched on his haunches, sweat gathering on his troubled brow.

"I found where Russell was cheating us." Her voice wavered, but she forged on. "He was selling oak planks, billing out oak planks but recording pine planks in the ledger. It's all here—thirty-six oak planks moved in the inventory book, thirty-six pine planks paid for. Again and again. Probably to help his son."

Molly broke her gaze from Michael's and looked at the two books laid out on the table. Hair ribbons of every color peeked from between the pages, blue ribbon in the inventory book corresponding with the blue in the account ledger. There were at least a score of ribbons, proof that once Russell had started siphoning the profits, he'd brazenly stolen at every opportunity.

Bailey's sigh could be heard through the thick door. "You know, I'd almost rather the loss was due to my mistakes than to hear that about Russell. What is Mrs. James going to do now with both her husband and her son wanted?"

Michael's face was gray. He'd given up all pretense of keeping his gun on her, appearing to struggle against pain and wooziness.

Well, he hadn't murdered her yet. Molly reached for a dishcloth, dampened it, and passed it over the bed to him.

"We can take care of Mrs. James. Michael has enough to think about without worrying over his mother."

The deep lines of agony around his eyes softened. He took the cloth and mopped his face, giving Molly a glimpse of the blood-covered arm that had been pressed against his stomach.

"Speaking of Michael," Bailey said, "he can't be far away. Got his horse shot out from under him. Colton said there's blood in the saddle, too, so be sure and keep your door latched. We're searching around town before we head to the James place."

Molly nodded.

"Molly, I need you to answer me, hon."

She swallowed. One more moment of silence and Bailey would bust in . . . and get shot in the process.

"I'll be careful. I'm just . . . I'm sleepy. Don't worry about me."

"I'll go, but some good news first. Michael's saddlebags were as loaded down as a Wells Fargo coach. That must be the money Russell stole. Your pa will be happy."

The pistol was lying on the floor now, although still in his grip. It was an odd-shaped gun. Her head cocked.

"And finding the gun will clear Anne of murdering Mr. Nimenko," she said.

"What?"

"The strange gun. The missing foreign gun of Mr. Nimenko."

Michael's head bolted upright. He lifted the gun and pointed it at her again.

"If you find it, I mean. If you find Mr. Nimenko's gun, then everyone will know that Anne is innocent."

Silence.

"I've got to go," Bailey said. "I'd better join the others." His fingers tapped against the door. "I love you."

Molly froze, unable to answer.

Michael's eyes turned into mean slits. "Answer him," he mouthed, "now."

She looked away and tried to forget the murderous weapon pointed in her direction. One slide of Michael's slippery gloves and she was dead. She might never have another opportunity.

"I love you, too, Bailey."

The tapping stilled. "Good night, Molly." And he was gone.

———

Bailey stepped off the porch but broke into a run as soon as he was certain his footsteps couldn't be heard.

As much as he'd enjoyed hearing the words come from her mouth, he knew that something was wrong. Nothing could've enticed him to declare himself through a door except the fear that he wouldn't get another chance. Her answer convinced him that she had the same concern. Michael James was inside.

Street by street the word spread and lookouts surrounded the cabin until Sheriff Colton was found. Every eye was trained on the only door and window in the structure. Soon Russell James joined the knot of men gathered behind the church. Then he drew his share of the glares.

"I hate to tell you, Russell," Reverend Stoker said, "but it looks like your boy has been shot."

"You think he's in there?" Russell ran his finger under his collar, even though no necktie was present.

Bailey stepped up. "I could be wrong, but the signs point to it. I spoke to Molly through the door, and something had her upset."

Russell's face paled. "Molly is with him?"

Bailey didn't answer. Why hadn't he thought of it sooner? Molly had told him about Russell's guilt with Michael listening. As a witness against his father, Michael had every reason to want her dead. Bailey should've kicked in the door at his first suspicion.

Russell put a hand on Bailey's arm. "Let me talk to him. He doesn't want to hurt Molly. I can get him out."

"I don't know," Sheriff Colton said. "He's facing murder charges. Why would you help us capture him?"

"To atone." Russell released Bailey's arm. His voice rose so no one in the posse would miss his words. "That money you found—I stole it. I've been robbing Mr. Lovelace so Michael could have a fresh start in Mexico. I'd ruin my life to give him a future, but I won't sacrifice another innocent person. I think I can talk him into turning himself in."

Colton looked to Bailey as the sole representative of the Lovelaces' interest. "I'll arrest Russell right now if you'd rather. We've got a clear confession."

Russell couldn't tear his eyes away from the lit window across the lawn. Bailey knew that Russell wasn't concerned about doing time, he wasn't thinking about escaping—Russell wanted his son to have the opportunity to get it right in the end.

Shouldn't Bailey, of all people, understand?

"I trust Russell. Let's give him a chance."

Spurs jangled in the darkness as the men fanned out and found barriers to hide behind. Bailey made it nearly to the porch and crouched behind the rain barrel.

"Michael! Are you in there? It's your father," Russell called.

A shadow passed across the curtain. Guns rose, but no one fired.

"Are you hurt badly, Michael?"

Bailey was close enough to hear his answer.

"It's bad, Pa, and I'm not spending the last minutes of my life being harassed by no lawmen. I've got nothing to lose."

Bailey knelt on one knee and dug his leading foot into the

soft ground. If he had to charge the door, he'd get a good sendoff.

"We could get Dr. Trench," Russell said.

"It's too late. Send everyone away."

"That's not going to happen," Sheriff Colton hollered. "If it's as bad as you think, don't you want to see your father before you pass?"

"You aren't going to let me," Michael called.

"Sure we will. Send Miss Lovelace out, and your father can come in to you."

The door moved. Bailey leaned forward, ready for anything. Michael James appeared, leaning heavily on Molly, his pistol pressed into her side.

With the light behind her, Bailey couldn't see her face, but her tiny steps told him that she was bearing Michael's weight. The man kept his right elbow pressed tightly against his stomach and was bent almost double.

"Send him in," Michael gasped. "She's my guarantee."

"Your father confessed to embezzlement," Colton said. "I'm not sending another criminal in for you to plot with until you release the girl."

"You'd better think again, Sheriff. You don't want her blood on your hands," Michael said.

Molly whimpered as he dug the gun into her side. Bailey gripped the rim of the rain barrel and half rose. If he could draw Michael's fire, someone would pick him off before he could shoot Molly.

"Her blood wouldn't be on the sheriff's hands." Russell took a step forward. "It'd be on mine. I'm the one who helped hide you after you were accused of killing Mr. Nimenko. I came between you and justice, and if you kill again, it'll be because I believed in your innocence. You said you had nothing to lose, but you do. You still have a chance to make things right. You could leave this world showing mercy, and you still have time to find mercy for yourself."

Michael panted, sweat rolling down his face. "I'm not ready to die, Pa. I want to talk to you . . . and Reverend Stoker. You promise they'll let me?"

"I promise, son. Let her go."

The gun dropped to the ground. Bailey was the first to reach Molly. But only after she and Russell had eased Michael to the porch did she allow him to lead her away.

———

"He wasn't going to hurt me, not after I tried to help him." Molly rubbed her arms, working warmth into them after her chilling encounter. From the way Bailey walked with his hands crammed in his pockets, she guessed that he disagreed. She might as well give up trying to convince him. Michael James didn't need her to defend or accuse him any longer.

The sun was rising on what promised to be a clear spring morning. Had someone wanted to track Bailey and Molly as they meandered in the meadow behind the church, the dewy grass held an easy trail. But anyone looking for excitement was still at the parsonage, talking over the dramatic events.

"I forgot the ledgers. Are you going back for them?" Molly asked.

"You're already thinking about the money?" He rolled his eyes. "That man—a murderer, remember?—held a gun to you. I gave Russell my sympathy and forgiveness, but seeing his son manhandle you nearly made me rescind my offer. I don't know how you can take it so lightly."

"I was worried at the time, but everything is set aright now. No more danger lurks, the money is recovered, Father's health will be preserved—everything we wished for has happened."

"Not everything," he protested. "Aren't you curious about how I knew you were in danger? It was because you'd never told me that you loved me before. So either you lied to send me a signal, or it was the truth and you had to tell me because your life was in danger." He took her arm and turned her toward him. "Which was it, Molly? Will you tell me that you love me when you don't have a gun to your head?"

"Bailey"—Molly pulled away as gently as she could—"I'm leaving, moving to Austin."

"Austin? Why now, when everything is falling into place?" He blinked. "Did Nick find you a job?"

She couldn't tell him about her conversation with Reverend Stoker, not if it would hurt the relationship between the two men. She shook her head. "Another friend."

He drew in a quick breath. She must have surprised him, but this time it wasn't pleasant.

"I've tried to atone for what I put you through. I understand if you don't trust me—"

"That's not it," she said.

"Then don't leave, not without an understanding between us. Last time we parted we had no pledge, nothing to hold on to. If there's the slightest possibility that we have a future, tell me now, so I have something to hope for."

Molly wrapped her arms around herself. She'd dreamt that someday their union could be blessed, but Stoker was right. Bailey was better off without her. Remembering that was the only way she could force the cold words from her lips.

"I know my mind. It won't change. I need to get away from . . . from everyone." Could he hear the blood coursing through her veins and crying out that she was a liar? Could he see the effort it took to disguise her love?

"If that's the honest truth, I'll go." His eyes never left hers, and when she refused to answer, he shoved his hands into his pockets. "I wish there was something I could do, could say, to persuade you."

Was she truly determined to release him? Molly knew the loneliness of going without his companionship. She'd suffered it once already, and putting miles between them wouldn't lessen her love. But if she'd been willing to marry Edward for her family, what wouldn't she sacrifice for Bailey?

And yet, he wasn't gone. He stood before her—broad shoulders that had shared her burdens even after she'd betrayed him, hands that had worked on her family's property to avert disaster, and a heart that turned to God and desired to do right, seeking Him even after failure. He was everything she wanted in a partner, but she couldn't have him.

"At least we can say good-bye this time." Had she meant to voice that thought aloud? Molly definitely hadn't counted on his reading her mind, but with her eyes straying to his lips, he could hardly miss her meaning.

One eyebrow rose. "If by a *good-bye* you mean a kiss, I think I can oblige—but only under certain conditions. We can't let this get out of hand."

Molly's face burned. The branches above them trembled in the early breeze. For all her brave talk, Molly had feared that she wouldn't see another morning. After surviving her ordeal, what kind of a risk was this? "It'll be all right."

"But we already know how quickly our . . . um . . . enthusiasm can—"

"Forget it." Molly threw her hands in the air. "It was just a kiss, but if you're going to carry on so . . ."

She spun on her heel, fully anticipating the warm hand that grasped her arm.

"It's never been *just a kiss* for me." Bailey tossed his hat on the fencepost and then took her hands. "This is what you want? I have permission?"

Molly stood tall and tried to calm her brittle nerves, determined to show him that she wasn't easily led astray. A quick survey of the meadow told her they were unobserved, so she nodded. She'd kissed Bailey before, so why did she feel like a maiden being led to the edge of a volcano? Why was this time different?

Her heart fluttered as he laid her back into the crook of his arm and bent toward her.

"No, wait," he said. "I might want you on this side."

Oh, he was a scoundrel. "Bailey Garner, what is wrong with you? Since when have you grown so particular with your kissing?" She was nearly woozy, and it hadn't even commenced.

"Since I know I'll have to remember this one for the rest of my life." He switched her to his other side, lifted her hair, and let it fall across his arm. He smiled down at her, so maddeningly close. "That's better."

Molly disagreed. The anticipation unnerved her, and when their lips finally touched, the dam broke, warmth rushing through her with a startling thrill. He filled her thoughts until there was only him. It'd always been only him, understanding and appreciating her. He moved across her mouth so slowly that she barely noticed his bristly stubble—didn't mind it, anyway—but he'd better hurry before she lost her resolve to do what was best for both of them.

Oh, fiddlesticks. Too late. She was his and always would be.

Molly wrapped her arm around his neck.

"No." He took her hand in his and held it against his chest. "You wanted a good-bye. Under the circumstances, I can't give you anything more."

He wasn't the boy she'd toyed with. He was the man who had her heart, and he was giving it back.

With one last kiss, so sweet that she wanted to cry, he released her. "I wish you the best, Molly, and I'm sure that's what you're going to find."

His cheeks were ruddy, but he stood his ground. Steady.

So this was how it would end? Molly wobbled to a walnut tree. "You're taking the books to Father now?" Her voice sounded as thin as a kitten's cry.

"I'll swing by the parsonage and get them. What are your plans?"

Molly leaned her face against the tree trunk. "I'll wait at Mrs. Weems's until the sheriff clears out, then I suppose I'll prepare my things. That position in Austin might come available at any time."

He took his hat off the fencepost and settled it on his head. "If I don't see you before you leave, take care of yourself."

She nodded. She'd have to, for no one else would care for her.

So she wasn't ready. Bailey could understand. Molly was a smart woman, and a smart woman wouldn't snatch him up at the first opportunity—not after the asinine way he'd been carrying on. The gravel crunched under his boots as he hurried from the parsonage to the Lovelaces' house. He'd be a sight more upset if it weren't for the good-bye. He smiled. That wasn't a good-bye—more like a *y'all come back*.

Bailey inhaled deeply at the memory, but the familiar shame didn't make an appearance. He'd demonstrated his feelings for Molly with respect and restraint. God knew how much it took for him to tear away, but his clean conscience was worth it.

As for her going to Austin, he didn't like it, but he understood her desire to get away. He'd travel to Austin if he had to, but visits would be more convenient if she was located closer.

Before Bailey reached the Lovelaces' house, he could hear the saw screeching down at the mill. He heard the mule drivers geeing and hawing at their teams, and, as always, he could hear the rumble of the water crashing over the impressive wheel.

Russell wouldn't be in the office this morning. Bailey hoped that Sheriff Colton would have mercy on him and allow him to bury his son before serving his time. His crimes were serious and could've led to more deaths had Michael escaped, but once his son's guilt couldn't be denied any longer, he had repented and persuaded Michael to do the same.

Lola let him in before he could knock twice. He found Thomas in the parlor pulling his socks on.

"Is it true? Did Russell confess to robbing me?"

"Yes, sir, and we recovered the money, too. Sheriff Colton said if we can show where it was stolen, they'll return it."

Thomas frowned. "His testimony will have to be enough, because we can't prove it. It doesn't show up in the accounts."

Bailey sat next to him and handed him the ledgers. "Yes it does."

He had to hand it to Thomas Lovelace. The man didn't need a lengthy explanation. He flipped through the books, mentally tallying the amount skimmed while Bailey wondered how Molly would tame her abundant hair with all her ribbons missing.

"Then we've been running in the black all this time." Thomas crashed his beefy hands together. "We did turn a profit this month."

"Yes, sir."

"And with the river up and the sales you're bringing in, we're set to clear record amounts."

"We were already, but the skimming hid it from us."

Thomas eyed him with a new appreciation. "I had my reservations when you offered to help, but I was wrong. Tell you what I'm going to do. When Colton hands over my money, you're going to get a nice chunk of it in appreciation for a job well done."

Now he was talking, but Bailey couldn't accept any more undue praise. "It wasn't me, sir. It was Molly."

Thomas laughed. "What did Molly have to do with it?"

"She's the one who put the two accounts together. I left the books with her last night, and she found his theft. See the hair ribbons? She should get the reward."

"That child? I can't go to the store without some busybody reporting on her doings. First she's having dinner with the Tillerton girl, and then she's harboring a fugitive. I'm glad she listened to Stoker and decided to move to Austin. I can't blame him for not wanting her at the parsonage."

"He talked to Molly?" Bailey frowned. Hadn't he been with the posse all evening? "Is that why she's leaving for Austin?"

"It's for the best. You obviously weren't comfortable with her here, and you've proven your worth at the mill. If you weren't my eyes and ears, I'd have to sell out."

Bailey didn't need any breakfast. He was going to swallow enough words to fill him up. "Forget Molly." If only it were that easy. "Is your offer of a reward still good?"

Thomas grinned. "That's my boy. Way to keep your eye on the prize. How about we hunt that sheriff down? Maybe he'll have my . . . er . . . our money in hand."

To Do List:

· ~~Pack bags.~~ *Done*
· ~~Clean parsonage.~~ *Done*
· *Move to Austin.*

A full day had passed, and Molly hadn't heard from anyone. Not Reverend Stoker. Not Bailey. Not her father. Her patience had worn thin. Clearly Stoker didn't want her to stay at the parsonage, but she wasn't going to drag her trunk to the crossroads and strap it behind the next buggy that appeared. With so much happening, she thought she would've heard some news by now. Her father could've at least stopped by to thank her. His health didn't keep him from piddling around town.

Molly drummed her fingers against the table. Nothing to do. No one to see. She'd made visits yesterday, but with her current social connections, it didn't take very long. The tiny cabin had been scrubbed and the dishes washed, and only the aroma of the weak coffee remained. All her worldly goods were assembled, waiting for a wagon to roll up and cart her away.

Austin. She clenched her hands together in a silent prayer. Would her lot be any better there? Would she meet the same characters with different faces? Faux friend Carrie, critical Mr. Travis . . . and the men? Molly groaned. What if she caught the eye of an eligible suitor? At what point during introductions should she disclose that she'd eloped with a married man?

The only man she wanted already knew.

Bailey had said his farewell—her pulse raced at the memory—*performed* his farewell was more accurate. No doubt when they encountered each other again, he'd wear the same distant expression he wore when meeting her publicly. No one would guess the reverend's perfect assistant harbored feelings for her. She wouldn't expose him. Not when he'd tried his best to forget her.

What was he doing now? Had he already told her father about the theft? After her ordeal it seemed like someone should check on her. Bailey had probably gone to Lockhart to retrieve the money, but she couldn't believe no one had been by to keep her abreast of the day's events.

Molly reached for her hat. Sitting around the cabin wouldn't satisfy her curiosity. Maybe the shop owner, Deacon Bradford, could fill her in on the town news.

Usually shopping cheered Molly. The smell of fresh merchandise invigorated her, but Deacon Bradford's store had the opposite effect. After the variety of Lockhart's emporiums, Prairie Lea's only store reminded Molly of all she'd left behind.

"Mr. Bradford, if I might trouble you—"

"'Bout time you made a visit. I bought a whole bolt of gingham I thought you'd like."

Molly coughed to cover her distress. Gingham! "How considerate of you. I'm not here make a purchase, but I wondered if you'd heard any news from my father or the sheriff recently."

"Your father? Ask him yourself. He's at the checkerboard on the west porch."

Molly barely remembered to thank him before clutching her skirts and whirling around. Her father was in town? He'd walked right by the parsonage without stopping to thank her?

Molly flew around the corner. A marked board balanced atop a barrel. Her father's elbows rested on his knees while Mayor Sellers chewed an unlit cigar with a scowl.

"Your move," the mayor said.

"Excuse me, Father." Despite her best efforts, Molly couldn't keep her boot heel from tapping on the porch floor.

"Can't you see I'm busy?"

Her stays grew tight as she drew in a long indignant breath. "That's it? You're not pleased that I'm safe or that we recovered the money?"

The mayor's eyebrows rose, and he removed his cigar. "Of course he's pleased. He's not laid into anyone yet this morning, and it's nearly noon. Happiest I've ever seen him."

"I'd be happier if I knew what Bailey was up to," Thomas said.

Molly tilted her head to better see her father's face bent over the board. "Isn't he at the mill?"

"Hasn't been there since I promised him a reward. He agreed to take Russell's position, but then he skipped town."

"Why are you rewarding Bailey?"

"Because he found the embezzlement. Without him we couldn't prove how much had been stolen." Thomas jumped a goober pea they were using as a checker.

"But he didn't discover the embezzlement. I did."

Mayor Sellers clasped his cigar between his teeth and grunted. "That's a doozy of a story, young lady." He double jumped two pecans and dropped them into his pocket.

"It's the truth. Bailey brought me the books. I spent the whole night going over them, and he's taking the credit?"

The two men exchanged amused glances.

"Child, if you were that intelligent, I wouldn't have to keep you on an allowance or manage your settlement."

He leaned forward to move his pecan, but Molly was quicker. Her hand darted to the board and plucked it out of his reach. "And about my settlement . . ."

Thomas ran a finger under his collar. "Well, we shouldn't need it now that the books aren't being skimmed, but you never know. We might want to invest in a cotton gin. We could run a belt from the waterwheel to a gin and have a whole new—" Her scowl stopped him. "Do you have a better idea? I hate to see you fritter the money away on pretties."

"Pretties?" Molly snatched her bonnet off her head and held it before her. "I've worn the same old hats since I returned because you insisted our family was broke." Molly threw her hat to the ground. "It's my money, and I'll buy a hat if I want to."

"Sounds like we best call this game a draw." The mayor rose to his feet with creaky knees. "See you tomorrow." He ambled away as quickly as his high britches and short suspenders would allow.

Thomas rocked in his chair. "You should invest the money, save something for the future. To tell the truth, I've dipped into it time and again to meet expenses, but the money recovered from Michael James should pay it back. That is, if Bailey hasn't run off with all of it."

She gritted her teeth. Bailey had kissed her good-bye. He'd said he might not see her again. "No wonder I fell for Bailey. He reminds me of another man I've tried to love my whole life."

"Don't get all emotional. I'm taking care of you, aren't I?"

"You're taking care of yourself. I'm just your baggage." Molly took a handful of nuts from the board and stomped through the curious shoppers exiting the store.

So Bailey had taken the credit and the money? Somehow whenever a man decided to help her, she ended up pocket poor and still in their debt. The peanut shells disintegrated in her hand. She chewed furiously as she walked, the top of her head burning under the midday sun, her hat lying forgotten at the store. No matter. A vast selection of hats in Lockhart awaited her pleasure.

Too angry to wait for a ride, Molly headed out for Lockhart on foot, with plans to accept the first method of conveyance that presented itself. She didn't care if she reached town in a turnip wagon. All that mattered was getting her hands on her money and on Bailey Garner. He could keep the reward if he needed it, but by george, she would rain curses on his head until he stood toe-to-toe with her father and admitted who had really saved the business.

 30

The trees lining the streets disappeared as the road wound over the prairie. Molly would be as red as a sausage before she reached Lockhart. The waving grass offered no protection from the sun. Her lawn dress was wilting as quickly as her coiffure. Molly walked faster. If she was blistered and freckled, it'd be Bailey's fault. Another misdeed to harangue him over.

From behind, a horse approached her at a fair clip. Disappointed it wasn't a buggy, Molly swerved into the right wagon rut to make room, but the rider didn't pass.

"Where are you headed?"

Molly turned. It was Anne, with a wide-brimmed hat casting shadows over her fair complexion and curly hair.

"To Lockhart, actually." Molly's steps didn't slow. "And you?"

"The same. I got word there's a buyer for the farm. That notice in the paper did the trick."

"Congratulations." She'd be happy for her friend later. She didn't want to lessen her fury until Bailey had borne the brunt of it.

"You wanna ride?"

Molly pulled her skirt out of the cockleburs. Which was worse—riding into town on a horse behind Anne Tillerton or arriving beet red and bedraggled?

"Thank you."

Molly could barely climb on, even with Anne's help. She sat astraddle and wrapped her arms around the smaller woman.

"Hang on." How Anne managed to hold on to the reins with Molly's weight sliding from side to side, Molly couldn't guess. The girl must have arms of rawhide, but at least she wasn't talkative.

"Take me to the jailhouse, please," Molly said. "I have unfinished business with Sheriff Colton."

"Don't we all," Anne said.

The jailbirds called out to them through the bars as they approached the prison, adding to Molly's general sense of displeasure. She straightened her legs and then groaned when she realized her skirts only reached her knees.

"Men," she said. "Those fellows better hope they never let women serve on juries, or I'll hang them all."

Anne braced herself as Molly slipped off the side of the horse, and then adjusted her errant clothing.

"Miss Lovelace, I wondered what the commotion was." Sheriff Colton stood in the lone unbarred doorway in the building.

Anne wrinkled her nose at him before riding away.

"I came to inquire about the money you recovered." Molly caught the eye of Russell James before he stepped into the shadows of his cell. To think, all those years working faithfully for her father and he'd be remembered for his thievery—all on account of his son.

No fear of Thomas Lovelace endangering himself on his children's behalf.

"It's been collected. Bailey was here earlier."

"You gave him all of it?" Molly placed her hand against her forehead to shield her eyes.

"Sure did. He had a letter from your father." The sheriff stepped into the blinding sunlight. "That was a letter from your pa, wasn't it?"

"Yes, sir." You could torture her with a hair iron and she wouldn't air her suspicions before the interested, incarcerated audience. "Thank you for your time."

Molly lifted her lawn skirt and trotted across the street, unwilling to satisfy the curiosity that'd appeared on Sheriff Colton's face. She hoped she could return and visit Russell James later, but right now she was on the trail of a true scoundrel. Would Bailey have gone to his uncle and aunt's house? Molly stepped into the shade afforded by an awning at the bank. He wouldn't run away with all the money. She trusted him to bring her father's share back, but what about hers? Did he really believe he deserved the reward for bringing the books to her?

The door to the bank opened behind her.

"I thought I recognized you." Prue stepped out in a rose-colored dress of the same simple cut she'd always favored, but with more color and finer fabric. Before Molly could pinpoint how the changes had worked such a transformation in her appearance, Prue had thrown her arms around her, making further inspection impossible.

Who would've thought Prue would want to be seen with her? Of course, Prue's primary flaw had always been indiscriminating grace.

"I guess this is your bank now?" Molly asked.

Prue's serene smile brought refreshment to the heat. "I help Mr. Fenton when his mother doesn't require my attendance for callers, but I'd be happy to retire. Staying home to raise a family will be my first priority."

At least there was one tragedy Molly had avoided. No matter how fine Prue's dress and the house on San Antonio Street, Fenton could have never made Molly happy.

"I didn't expect you so soon," Prue continued, "but I suppose he told you about our offer. There's no reason for you to go all the way to Austin to find work. We'd be honored if you'd work here at the bank. I know you've got a talent for bookkeeping, and Mr. Fenton has long admired your charming manners with customers."

If the words were coming out of Carrie's mouth, Molly would've known they were meant to hurt, but Prue had no ulterior motive.

"Work for you? Here at the bank?" Molly took in the impressive brick structure with a real second story behind the front. So Reverend Stoker had found her a job closer to home? "And Mr. Fenton doesn't mind?"

"He knows you'll work hard and be an asset to the company. Why don't you come in? He'll tell you."

Molly lifted her chin. Could she live this close to her parents and Bailey and keep her sanity? Did she have any other offers? Nick's answer hadn't come yet.

"I will," Molly said. "As a matter of fact, I have an account that I need to inquire after. I understand a settlement was deposited in my name." She crossed her fingers in the folds of her gown. *Please, God, let it be at Prue's bank.*

Prue's knit her brows. "Yes, it's here. Justice should have cost him more, but it's a large sum nonetheless."

By the time Molly got a look at the number in her account she could almost reconcile herself to taking employment there. The bank was stately, the bookkeepers clean and efficient, but she wasn't ready to think that far ahead. A black-hearted con man needed to be dealt with first.

"Are you going to meet Bailey now?"

"What?" How did everyone know her business better than she did? "Have you talked to him?"

Prue's mouth crinkled in a whimsical grin. "Yes, of course. He's looking to lease a little house over by Father's smithy."

Molly's lips tightened. "So he thinks he can take the reward money and leave Father shorthanded? Not on my watch."

Molly spun on her heel and stomped toward the barred door, ignoring Prue's sputtered protests. That man was as worthless as a breeding pair of mules. Hadn't she told him she was moving to town? True, she'd thought she was going to Austin, but her biggest reason to relocate was to avoid falling for him again. Now here he was making his own arrangements. Lockhart wasn't big enough for the both of them. That fact had already been proven.

Her temper grew hotter with every step under the blistering sun. She strode past Mrs. Truman's boardinghouse before she had time to worry about crossing paths with Carrie. She skirted around the clanging hammers of the blacksmith's shop, unwilling to run into Mr. McGraw and Prue's easily amused brother. Before she'd realized it, Molly found herself on the porch of the little white house they'd perused long ago.

She wasn't surprised that the door was open and a familiar voice echoed through the empty building.

"I have the money, don't worry about that, but I'm not sure about the terms. Can you give me a week to think it over?"

Molly had reached the kitchen before her eyes adjusted to the shade.

"What are you doing?" she demanded.

"Molly?" He couldn't have looked more shocked if he'd been struck by lightning. "How did you get here?"

"Did you think I was going to sit by and let you run off with my money? Let you take credit for discovering the theft and leave me behind?"

A throat clearing from the corner of the kitchen startled her. Molly turned to see a scowling man.

"Mr. Garner, I'll let you think over my offer. No hurry. Just get back to me."

"He's not getting back to you. He doesn't have any money." Her hands were on her hips as she did her best to block the doorway. "Tell him, Bailey. Tell him you're broke."

"I'll tell him no such thing." He didn't look the least bit ashamed. "Get out of his way."

"Not until you set this right. You have my money, and this man is my witness that you refuse to give it back."

The man held up his hands in surrender. "I didn't witness anything. I'm not taking sides."

"Sorry about this, Matthews. I'll let you know what I decide," Bailey said as the man angled past Molly. Bailey didn't even act sympathetic when Matthews bumped into her. "Now, what's this about?"

"You told Father that *you* found the discrepancies in the ledger," she said.

"I told him you did, but he didn't believe me."

"That doesn't justify what you've done."

"What? Missed a day of work? I think I have a good excuse."

"How do you have the nerve to act so smug? You know I'm talking about the reward—money that should've gone to me," she said.

"It should've gone to you, but your father wasn't going to give it to you. He offered it to me instead."

"How convenient."

"Not really. I've spent all day trying to get that money for you and set you up. I didn't expect such a strong show of gratitude."

"I don't know what you're talking about."

"Because you haven't asked."

The only sound in the room was their gasps for air and Molly's whalebones creaking as she tried to catch her breath. Bailey was having the same difficulty.

"I—"

"You—"

They stopped.

"Ladies first," Bailey said.

"If you didn't plan to keep my money, why are you moving to Lockhart?"

"*I'm* not moving. *I'm* the manager of the mill—replacing Russell James, remember?"

Molly gestured to the house around her and then raised her shoulders.

"I'm trying to help a good friend of mine, who told me that she couldn't live in Prairie Lea anymore. She wanted to move." His voice dropped to a more reasonable volume. "But I don't want her to go all the way to Austin."

"Oh." Molly tried to swallow, but the sunburn had traveled from her face and neck to her throat. "But you shouldn't spend my money without my permission."

"I wouldn't touch your money. I've saved enough of my wages to get you started, and I talked to Prue about your working at the bank."

"*You* talked to Prue? I thought it was Reverend Stoker."

"No. I got you a job, a place to live, and money from your pa that you earned fair and square. And I wasn't going to sign anything with Matthews until you'd looked over the contract. I figured you could probably negotiate a better deal, although after he witnessed that childish display, I'm not so sure."

Molly tapped her foot. "You came here for me? That's what you've been doing?"

Putting his hands on the countertop, Bailey hopped up

on the counter and leaned against the pump handle. "Yes, ma'am."

She shouldn't be surprised. He'd procured the parsonage for her. He'd done everything he could to help her, as long as it didn't sully his reputation.

A cocklebur scratched at her ankle. She bent, caught the hem of her dress, and tried to make sense of his actions. "Keep your wages. It wouldn't look right for you to spend your money on me."

"I don't care. There shouldn't be a conflict between doing the right thing and looking good." He must've watched her for a moment, for he was quiet. Then he added, "If you're determined to move, I'll support your decision. If you decide to go home to your parents, I'll carry your trunk to the front porch. I'll do anything for you, even if you don't return my regard."

"What do you mean by that?" Molly ripped out the cocklebur with vigor, stabbing her finger in the process. She threw down her hem. "You can't say I don't have feelings for you. Haven't you noticed all I've done? I could've told everyone what a hypocrite you were, but I didn't. I could've told Father about your testimony on the witness stand and had you fired, but I didn't."

"Why didn't you? I had it coming."

"Because I *do* love you, you dunce. Maybe Michael James had a gun pointed at me and forced me to say it, but that doesn't mean it wasn't the truth, so don't sit there all righteous like you've suffered alone. I've done my share. I asked your mother to teach me how to cook your favorite dishes. I even burned my finger." She held up her hand and pointed at the damaged digit. "And she laughed."

Bailey hopped off the countertop. "I worked for your stinking pa so I could marry you. I kept the job just to see you once in a while. If that's not suffering—"

"I wanted nothing more than to be your wife, but I stayed away so you'd have a chance at some nice girl."

"But I don't want a nice girl. I want you. Staying away had to be easier on you than it was on me. Else you would've given in. You don't have the patience."

"I guarantee I've got the patience. You wait and see. Reverend Stoker told me it'd be better if I left, and I'll do it because I want what's best for you. If I come home to visit, I'll barely speak to you. That'll show you how much I love you."

Bailey's face creased in confusion. "Reverend Stoker said that to you? When?"

"Thursday after you picked up the ledger."

"*Hmm* . . . before he talked to me." He stretched a suspender away from his chest and let it snap while he studied her. "You're sunburned."

"Yes, well, I was in a hurry and forgot my hat."

"In a hurry to find me?"

"I'm hungry, too. Give me my money so I can buy something to eat," she said.

"I might keep it."

"That's what I thought, you swindler."

"I'm keeping it until you answer a question for me." A grin teased at the side of his mouth. "If you weren't trying to out-love me, what would you do?"

"You mean if I was going to be selfish?"

"If you can imagine such a scenario."

Molly lifted her chin in the air. "If I was going to be completely selfish, I'd get decked out, fix up my hair, and go after you like a bear after honey. Every corner you turned, I'd be there waiting. I wouldn't care how much people disapproved or how much they pitied you for getting tangled up with me. I'd count myself lucky and ignore everyone else."

"Sounds like a good plan, if you were selfish."

"But I'm not." Molly crossed her arms, daring him to contradict her.

"You have your moments. Unfortunately you usually repent before anything comes of them. Stop glaring at me. All I'm saying is it sounds like we're both trying to be good by sacrificing what we most desire. Isn't that true?"

Molly's cheeks pinked at the word *desire*, but she didn't protest. He knew her too well.

"Do you know how badly I wanted to marry you?" Molly asked. "How much I regret that I didn't?"

Bailey couldn't believe the words coming out of her mouth. The dust motes in the abandoned house caught the sun, giving the room a dreamlike quality, but she was really there saying words he'd wanted to hear for years.

"When it didn't work out, I contented myself with loving you from afar." Molly's inky lashes fluttered against her cheeks as she lowered her eyes.

Bailey's head spun. His chest felt filled with cottonwood down. She'd said that she had wanted to marry him, but did she still?

He cleared his throat. "What if us being apart isn't the best? Could it be that God gave us this love for each other because He wants us to be together?"

She looked like his suggestion halfway scared her.

"Are you after my money?"

"Sweetheart, there's not enough money in the world to make messing with you worth it—not unless I was plumb crazy about you."

From opposite ends of the room they watched each other—a standoff—wondering who would be the quickest to draw. Molly flinched first.

"You can't be a preacher married to me. Imagine what people would say."

"I've never stood behind a pulpit on Sunday, but I think I've preached enough sermons already. Besides, I think we'd be so busy visiting sick folks, helping widows and such, I wouldn't have time. As far as my reputation, I've already told the reverend everything. I'll make an announcement from the church steeple if you'd like."

"You're staying in Prairie Lea?"

"Unless you want to live here with the haint." He smiled. "I do enjoy working at the mill, though."

"I wouldn't mind staying in Prairie Lea. I didn't want to leave my new friends." Her face took that calculating look that usually meant a counteroffer was pending. "Wait a minute. What exactly are you proposing? Never again am I going to assume—"

She didn't need to finish her statement, for Bailey had no problem declaring his intentions.

"Molly Lovelace, will you marry me?"

"When?"

"I don't know. Tomorrow? The next day? As soon as possible." Could they really do that? Could it really be that simple?

"Who'd do the ceremony? It must be someone I know personally. No more anonymous parsons."

"Absolutely! Reverend Stoker approves now that I've explained to him, or I could ask Judge Rice. Even better, I'll ask them both." His heart pounded against his ribs as she considered his offer. That was his girl. Not going to enter into a contract without reading the fine print.

"I have an idea," she said.

"I've got lots of ideas." He didn't take a step closer, but somehow she read his mind.

Her head tilted and her mouth pulled down in exasperation.

"Behave yourself. We've got some business that needs attending. If you disapprove, you'd better speak up."

"You know I will."

Bailey barely got the door pulled shut behind him before she had reached the road and was marching toward the square.

"Slow down, will you? I think I have a right to escort my fiancée."

"I'm not your fiancée. I'm not accepting your proposal until I'm standing before a bona fide minister of the gospel or a justice of the peace. I've got to be legally wed before you take any more liberties."

"Then it'll be a short engagement."

Molly sailed into Fenton's bank like she owned it, unaware of her ragged appearance. Behind the counter, Prue's eyes traveled from Bailey to Molly and then back again. A gentle smile crossed her face. "Back so soon?"

"I need to get my money out of the bank."

Bailey's eyes widened. She wasn't playing for peanuts.

"But the settlement is in Mr. Lovelace's keeping."

"It's my money, and if everything goes as planned, he'll get it soon enough." Even Molly's bedraggled dress couldn't disguise the strong lines of her figure. Stonewall Jackson had nothing on Rockfortress Lovelace. "I need to find a representative to make an offer on the mill in my behalf." With a firm jaw she amended her statement: "In our behalf."

31

Two days later Molly's sunburn was at its pinkest. Her skin had prickled at the cool water in her basin that morning, but she felt cleaner than she had in a long time. Her parents couldn't shut the door in her face when she arrived the night before with her trunk on the porch, so they accepted her return with grace stretched thin over their many disappointments.

She ran her hands over the smooth tablecloth and inhaled the rosy smell of Lola's supper ham. Such a feast, and it seemed like she was still full from dinner. "It's good to be home."

"I should've known you wouldn't be gone long. Not with my luck." Thomas Lovelace's silverware clinked together over his plate.

"Thomas, don't be cruel," her mother said.

"What? She knows I'm joshing her. Isn't it the tiniest, most helpless kitten that's the most adorable?"

Molly closed her eyes and said a silent prayer. Surely they loved her, but they had no idea how to be the support she needed. Praise God, He'd sent someone who did.

She raised her eyes to meet Bailey's across the table. If he didn't stop grinning at her, her parents would suspect something. Molly stretched her foot out until she found his, and then gave him a good kick in the shin.

The boyish glee didn't leave his face. He merely winked and tucked his napkin into his collar. "Y'all must be glad to have Molly home."

She tried not to let her voice become too chipper. "I can resume my charitable visits with Mother."

Mrs. Lovelace frowned. "Maybe you should go with your father to the store and play checkers."

"No. She always beats me." Mr. Lovelace pushed a thick slab of meat between his teeth. "But I'll tell you this, I'm practicing. Now that I don't have to be at the office every day, I have time for more gentlemanly pursuits, like checkers."

"And horseshoes," Bailey added.

"Yes, horseshoes. Did you hear that I beat your father? First person to trounce George Garner in a decade."

Bailey was smiling at her again. She tried to look stern. Hopefully he'd be gone before the offer arrived, because at this rate he would ruin everything.

They each had warm slices of sweet potato pie on their plates when a horse pulled up the drive. Molly dared one last look at Bailey and then allowed an expressionless mask to settle over her face.

"Who is that?" her mother asked.

Before her father could make it to the window, Lola had escorted the man inside.

"Good day, Mr. Lovelace. You might remember me from Lockhart. I'm Augustus Mooney, attorney-at-law. May I have a minute of your time?"

Mr. Lovelace scowled. "*Humph*. What is this about? Do I get to testify against Russell James?"

"I couldn't say. My business doesn't involve any criminal

proceedings. Rather it's an offer that I've been retained to present to you, an offer for your business."

Her father took a step backward and wiped his hands on his napkin. "An offer to buy the sawmill?"

Mrs. Lovelace fingered her pearl necklace as though it were a rosary. "You could sell it? We'd get money and you wouldn't have to worry about it anymore?"

"Not so fast, dear. Don't forget we have our children to consider. We'd be selling their legacy." He eyed the man's portfolio, as if he could read the numbers through the leather.

"Nicholas doesn't want the mill. He's too busy," Adele said.

"But there's Molly to consider. I dote on the gal. Can't seem to keep anything from her." He flashed a quick wink at Molly out of the attorney's sight.

With well-practiced ease, the lawyer spoke. "Do you mean to suggest that your daughter could manage a sawmill?"

"Father, I can't allow you to mislead this man. As you've pointed out numerous times, I can no more balance a ledger than I can shed my skin." She scratched at a patch on her sunburned nose.

"But Bailey can," Thomas said. "I'm not saying that I'm rejecting your offer, Mr. Mooney, but it'd have to be a rich one indeed. We have hopes for Bailey and Molly, here. There's more than one way to keep the business in the family."

"Actually, Miss Lovelace and I are getting married this week." Bailey's smile was wider than the San Marcos River.

Molly's mother gasped. "It's the first I've heard of it."

"*Shh*, Adele. You shouldn't be surprised." Thomas beamed at Bailey. "All our worries about the business will be set at rest. Any offer made now would have to soothe my conscience if I snatched this moneymaker from the hands of my son-in-law and daughter. Now," he said, rubbing his hands together in anticipation, "what is your offer?"

"First let me offer congratulations to Miss Lovelace and, er . . . Mr. Bailey."

Pretending to forget Bailey's last name? Molly choked on a giggle. My, but he was good.

"This might be a conflict of interest, but if Mr. Lovelace doesn't accept this bid, I'd like to offer my services to write up the transfer of the business to you. A wedding gift, if you will. We could even do it tonight."

"Whoa, there. Let's not get ahead of ourselves," her father said. "I'd like some time to think it over. Let's go into the study, where we can have some privacy."

Still clutching the portfolio, the man followed Thomas out of the room.

"That man," her mother huffed, "has no conscience at all. And you, Bailey, you're just as corrupt. Scaring me like that."

Molly leaned over her plate. "Mother, we are getting married. Bailey wasn't playing along for Father."

"You can't be serious," she said. "What about our objections?"

"If anyone could object, it'd be Bailey's family. Not ours."

Although she never came close to touching the back of her chair, Adele's slouch was visible. "How did we get here, Molly? I'd hoped for more." She blinked at the tinkling chandelier. "We'd all hoped for more."

"You were hoping for the wrong more. That's what led me astray. I didn't stop to consider what was important, and I've paid for my mistake. But if we have a second chance, then the sooner we get started the better."

Bailey laid his hand on the table, palm up. Molly grasped it. Then he offered Adele the other hand. She looked uncertain.

"I'm sorry we've been rough on you, Bailey. I hope you don't take it personally."

"Makes me feel like one of the family, Mrs. Lovelace."

She took his hand and squeezed.

The dishes hadn't been cleared before Thomas danced into the dining room. A chair fell over as he brushed past it to embrace his wife. "I'm doing it. I'm selling the mill."

"You are? I thought you were giving it to Molly and Bailey."

"That's what I wanted him to think, and they did a fine job convincing him. Brilliant." He beamed at them. "Bailey, I hope the new owner keeps you on. You're a real hand."

"So you like the offer?" Bailey asked.

"I could wish for more, but I'm ready to retire. The deposit will give us a nice nest egg, and then we'll get a share of the profits for a decade."

"Do you trust the new owners?" Molly tried to keep the edge out of her voice, but her father didn't notice when she failed.

"Their credentials are impeccable. They've worked at a mill similar to ours and run it successfully. Surely they can hold it together for ten years. They do the work and I'll take my share."

Bailey stood. "I'd best get to the office and lock up for the night. You probably don't want me to mention this to anyone."

"Absolutely not. I'm going to Lockhart to sign the papers Thursday."

"Perfect," Bailey said. "That'll give me time to get the wedding ceremony planned."

Before Thomas could say a word, before Molly could protest, Bailey leaned over the table and kissed her firmly on the lips—on the lips, in the dining room, under the crystal chandelier that swayed when she opened her eyes.

"Bailey, I told you that until we're wed you're to pretend there's no agreement."

"Must've forgot." He picked up his hat and strutted out the door before her shocked father could stop him.

It was a beautiful day for a wedding, but this wedding wouldn't be beautiful. Instead of getting a new dress and making sweets for a reception, Molly had been reading contracts and arranging funds. Trying to do it without arousing her parents' suspicions had consumed most of her time.

"When are you supposed to meet with Mr. Mooney?" Molly asked for the hundredth time.

"Four thirty," her father answered, slowing his team as they rolled into Lockhart. "Too bad we can't sign the papers first. It'll be hard to concentrate on your wedding until the deal is sealed."

"I don't think this wedding will take much concentration," her mother said. "A few words before the judge hardly qualify as a grand occasion."

"Still, I wish you and Bailey all the luck, and I sincerely hope the new owners allow him to stay on. I worry, though. They seem set in their ways. Even after being told about our daughter's wedding, they still insisted on the afternoon appointment."

Molly watched the buildings as they passed. It was incredible. She was getting married today to the man she loved, yet she wasn't allowing herself to believe it. Hopefully she'd believe it later, when he took her home to the parsonage. If she didn't get it through her blond head that they were joined in holy matrimony by nightfall, Bailey was going to be put out with her for sure.

Her heart twisted. Her trepidation couldn't be ignored for much longer. She'd thought that she'd put her disgrace behind her, but now she realized that the worst was still ahead.

She straightened her back. First there was business to conduct. A few words with Judge Rice, and then they'd await her father's arrival at the attorney's office.

"You look nice, Molly," her mother said. "It's a crying shame no one will see you, but under the circumstances it wouldn't be fitting to have a big to-do."

"Bailey will see me. That's enough."

Thomas smiled at his wife, still reveling in his good fortune. "You know, we were wrong about that boy. Molly should've married him in the first place."

Molly dug her fingernails into her palms and swallowed any words that would mar her blessing. "Thank you for approving. I'll be proud to be his wife."

"We hope he's proud of you, dear." Her mother adjusted her hat and performed a minuscule nod at a woman crossing before them. "It was wise to have a modest proceeding, nothing showy. Perhaps that'll give everyone time to get used to the idea." She craned her neck over the crowd before her. "Why are you stopping here?"

"Open your eyes, woman. The road is blocked. As soon as I find a hitching post, we'll get out and walk."

"What is everyone looking at? It's not market day. I'd hoped the square would be vacant. Oh dear," Mrs. Lovelace sighed, "we're sure to run into an acquaintance and will have to explain our meeting with the judge. I'd hoped to avoid sharing your news myself."

Her father handed the two women down and took her mother's hand in his, dragging her along as she frowned at the abandoned wagons on the side of the road. Mrs. Lovelace unfurled her fan as they approached the courthouse lawn and saw what was responsible for the crowds.

A white tent covered the northwest corner, and under its shade stood an arbor covered in pink roses. "How beautiful!" Mrs. Lovelace said.

Molly was impressed, too. People were milling at the edges of the tent, clumping together and whispering in wonder.

"What's the arbor for?" Molly asked a man nearby.

"Someone told me it's a wedding. I don't know the happy couple, but they said I was welcome to attend." He smiled, showing teeth that looked like he'd gnawed on gravel. "After the ceremony there'll be cake."

Looked like he'd eaten too many sweets already, but maybe she and Bailey could sneak some. With one last longing glance at the festive tent, she followed her parents to the courthouse steps.

Judge Rice met them inside the door. His kind blue eyes sparkled when she gestured at his corsage.

"Do you wear that to all your civil ceremonies?" Molly asked.

"For the important ones." He grasped her by the shoulders. "May I kiss the bride?"

She nodded and accepted a peck on her forehead. "Is Bailey here already?"

"He's been here since dawn."

"Then let's get this over with," her father said. "We have important business waiting."

"No, don't go that way." Judge Rice motioned to the gathering on the lawn. "He's out there—inside the tent."

Of course he was. Bailey never passed up a party. Molly followed Judge Rice through the milling crowd, searching for her fellow. What would he be wearing? It shouldn't matter, but she'd worn her favorite silk gown with the princess Basque. She'd feel foolish if he was wearing his dirty canvas britches and an old vest.

As they approached the white tent, flaps blowing on the edge of the shelter, Judge Rice stopped them.

"Mrs. Lovelace, if you'd allow me to escort you to the front, we'll let Thomas do his task."

"She can't leave," her father protested. "We're supposed to go to your office."

Molly's attention was drawn from her parents to the man standing under the arbor. He was obviously the groom, decked out in a ready-made suit. She smiled. His bride probably wouldn't recognize him, for he'd obviously never worn those clothes before.

A man stepped up to the groom, and Molly gasped. Reverend Stoker? What was he doing? Then her hand flew to her mouth and her stomach turned inside out. It couldn't be. But it was. The uncomfortable groom wearing the hurriedly stitched suit was Bailey.

She took in the whole scene—the flowers, the hastily constructed shelter, the white sugar cakes on the table in the shade of the oak trees. Her wedding.

"We mustn't," her mother said. "It's too extravagant. What will people say?"

"They'll say that a man must love a woman very much to plan this on his own," Judge Rice said. "There's a place for us up front. Let's go."

What could Molly do? She touched her hair, suddenly insecure about her appearance. Did she look like a woman who deserved a wedding on the town square in the middle of the day?

Then Bailey saw her.

His smiling eyes blew her concerns away like dandelion fluff. She was marrying Bailey. It was going to happen. Right here. Right now. Her father took her arm and directed her to the center of the tent. No music, no chairs, but the curious crowd parted, pushing those on the farthest rim out of the shade.

Why would Bailey do this? It was enough that he'd give her his name. He didn't have to act proud of it. But he certainly didn't look humble. His chest rose, and he tugged downward on his satin vest with a satisfied yank. His smile widened, and he took a breath as if preparing to call out to her, but with a sheepish look he contained his enthusiasm.

She was moving toward him, pulled by her father before she knew what was happening. A hand extended between strangers to thrust a bouquet of pink roses at her. Molly peered over their shoulders and saw Prue on tiptoe. She didn't have time to say thanks, because after years of dragging his heels, Thomas Lovelace was dragging his daughter to the altar. He didn't even pause when Rosa stepped in her path for a quick hug. Molly squeezed her quickly and smiled at her impulsiveness. Leave it to Rosa to hug the bride on the way down the aisle. If Rosa was there, that meant Bailey's whole family couldn't be far away.

How had he pulled this off without raising a hint of suspicion?

They stood before Reverend Stoker as her father placed her into Bailey's care. So many questions for him. So many things to say, but Molly couldn't speak. She let her eyes do her talking for her. Over the noise of the Lockhart commerce and curious latecomers, they repeated their vows, Bailey struggling to keep his composure under the rose-scented lattice.

As suddenly as it'd begun, the ceremony ended, and he leaned forward to give his first kiss as her husband—and it was the best one yet.

"Y'all enjoy the cake and punch," Bailey announced to the crowd. "We've got plans."

"Bailey!" Molly clutched his arm and turned last year's shade of pink as guffaws erupted. Molly chewed the inside of her cheek. What was she going to do? She probably didn't have to say anything. She had no secrets from Bailey, but could she move on without acknowledging the past?

He offered his arm and steered her through the well-wishers. "Only a few more hours."

She wouldn't think about it. Not yet. "First we have an extremely uncomfortable appointment with our lawyer."

"Do you think your parents are there already?"

"I'm certain of it. If Father had his way, he would've walked out as soon as he gave you my hand. He's anxious."

"Makes me wonder if we offered him too much."

Molly glared. "I know how to figure a fair bid for a business based on profit and capital. The market—"

"*Shh.*" He covered her hand. "Let's not have our first spat before we leave the wedding party."

"No one would be surprised."

As they neared the attorney's office, Molly grew even more thoughtful. Justice allowed her—nay, required her—to carry out this coup, didn't it? To prove to her father in grand fashion that she was capable? After today he could never deny it again. Here was a maneuver that would leave him breathless, but would it be with anger or with appreciation?

The closer they came to the office, the more her doubts grew. Was she honoring her parents? Would they resent her secrecy?

Her legs stopped moving. Bailey pulled her a full yard before he realized she was digging canals with her feet.

"What's wrong?"

"I don't know if we should do this. It doesn't seem right."

"Are you pulling my leg? Have you seen how happy your pa is? If we back out now, he'll be disappointed."

"But he'll feel foolish when he realizes we tricked him. What about his heart?"

"Taking the business off his hands is the best thing we could do for his heart. He can finally relax. Let's go."

Holding on for dear life, Molly moved lead feet up the steps to the front door of the solicitor's. Her heart pounded when she spotted her parents' surrey parked at the side. Where had her sense of triumph gone? All she anticipated now was her parents' anger.

Bailey held the door open for her and ushered her inside the gleaming office. The foyer was deserted. On their last visit Molly had noted the shelves of stuffed folders lining the walls above the cushioned benches. Now she wondered if each of those deals wrought the same level of emotional turmoil that hers did.

"They're in the office." Molly couldn't tear her eyes from the closed door.

Bailey took a seat. "If you want to change your mind, it's not too late. He keeps the mill, you keep your money. We've already settled the important matter."

The door opened. Molly jumped, but it was only Mr. Mooney. He closed it carefully behind him, not allowing any stolen glances to reach the foyer.

"Mr. Lovelace has signed the contract and is more than a little pleased with himself, although naturally he's trying to disguise his glee."

Bailey rose and stood at Molly's side. "Have you told them we're here?"

"Not directly. I told them the new buyers might meet with them today to facilitate a smooth transition. Are you ready?"

Bailey leaned over her shoulder and whispered in her ear, "Nobody can keep your father happy. At least make him proud."

Bailey was right. She'd tried all her life to please her father. She'd worked to fit his expectations only to learn that he was trying to mold her into a person he couldn't respect. She was doing nothing illegal or immoral, and as Mr. Mooney had pointed out, her father was pleased with the deal.

With a tight nod from her, Mr. Mooney opened the door wide.

"I didn't expect to see the two of you here." Her father laughed. "Did you come to meet the mysterious new owner? Beg him to keep you on at your position?"

Molly's doubts shriveled up like feathers in a flame. He wasn't worried about their future. He didn't know how to worry about anyone besides himself. Her allegiance belonged to Bailey.

Mr. Mooney had pulled two more chairs into the room and crowded them around the rectangular table.

"Don't bother with those chairs, Mooney," Thomas said. "I don't want a whole gaggle of people in here when the investor arrives."

Mr. Mooney straightened and raised an eyebrow at Molly. It was time.

Using all the grace her mother had pounded into her, she lowered herself into the chair. "No one else is coming, Father. Your offer came from us."

The silence was rancid. He almost began to laugh, but he looked at Bailey and stopped. His chin jutted out as his belief grew. Molly had expected a storm, and it seemed that one was brewing. He reached for the papers on the table, but Mr. Mooney reached them first.

"Of course, once Mr. and Mrs. Garner have signed the contract, you'll be able to take a copy with you."

"This is preposterous." He turned to Adele, who couldn't hide her astonishment.

"Molly, how could you? You foolish girl," her mother said.

"Consider the terms, Mother. Father is content with the amount. Wouldn't you be uncomfortable going into business with strangers?"

She closed her fan. "Well, I suppose it would be better to have family on the property."

Thomas's eyes ran over the contract in Mr. Mooney's hand again. He leaned back in his seat and swung one boot across the other knee. "I have half a mind to nullify the contract. I never consented."

"You signed it to an anonymous bidder," Mr. Mooney said.

"But they aren't anonymous. I know them." When no one answered he tried a different tact. "Where'd you get the money?"

"From my settlement," Molly answered. "That was enough for the down payment."

"Your settlement?" He rolled his eyes. "I shouldn't have put that money in Fenton's bank."

"It's my money, and I'm not squandering it as you feared."

"You're not? Seems like you lost every penny. Why buy the mill when you knew I was going to give it to you?" He squirmed under the disbelieving looks from every person in the room. "I would have . . . eventually."

Molly leaned forward and rested both hands on the table. "Father, we worry about your health, and nothing made me happier than to see your relief when you got our offer. Can you hold on to that joy? Can you remain pleased that you no longer have that responsibility?"

Bailey took her hand as they waited for his reply.

His mouth grew small and his nostrils grew large. "My concern is that you're going to constantly ask me for help. There's more to it than either of you realize. You won't manage very well without my years of expertise."

"We'll do quite well," Molly huffed, but Bailey interrupted.

"But we'd do better with your counsel. What if, once a week, say, we got together, maybe over a game of checkers, and you could advise me."

"I'm not sure if once a week would be enough. You'll probably be harassing me for more."

"No, I promise." Bailey raised his hands in surrender.

"Once a week over checkers. I solemnly swear I won't allow you to be tricked into giving advice anywhere else or at any other time. I'm firm."

Molly sat amazed. How could Bailey handle her father so easily when she still couldn't manage him? But then he had a knack for taming strong-willed Lovelaces.

"My misgivings haven't disappeared," Thomas said, "and I'm trying to look out for your best interests, but if you're absolutely sure . . ."

"Anything we can do to protect your health," Bailey said. "So, Mr. Mooney, if you'll hand us a pen, let's make it legal."

Besides the scratching of the metal nub on the paper, the room was silent. Bailey handed Molly the pen and she had *Molly Parmelia* written when he halted her with a gentle touch to her back.

"Don't forget your new name."

"Oh, you're right." She bit her tongue and scripted out *Garner* with a flourish. "How's that?"

"Beautiful." But he wasn't looking at her penmanship.

"So what now?" her mother asked Mr. Mooney. "When does it change hands?"

"Immediately. I have a note for the full deposit. Bailey and Molly will make payments to you as agreed upon. You retain the house and the lawn directly surrounding. The Garners now own the business, all the equipment, and the property associated with it. The accounts at the bank will be transferred to their name by the end of the business day."

"So really, Thomas, not much has changed," Adele said. "Bailey will be there working, and you'll be free to come and go from the house as you please."

"And you won't have to go over the books every evening," Molly added, "although I'd still like to come over for supper. I'll miss Lola's cooking while living at the parsonage."

"Of course, dear," her mother said. "Now that you're married, it'll be easier on all of us."

Molly felt the familiar discouragement creeping up on her, but before it could settle, Bailey stepped in.

"Time to go, my bride. We have a long ride home."

"You might as well take our surrey," her father said. "Since I'm now a man of leisure, I'd like to take a few days to enjoy town. You, on the other hand, better scurry back to work."

Molly rose and ran her hands down her silk wedding gown. If she could survive the humiliation of the night ahead, they'd be fine.

32

The last time Bailey was alone with Molly in this surrey, he'd determined to make her his wife. It'd taken much longer than he'd expected, but he'd finally done it right.

Besides an axle that needed grease, the surrey was quiet. The waving swells of tall grass rustled in the evening breeze. Occasionally Bailey threw out a juicy remark, hoping to entice Molly into a conversation, but she only nibbled. What was she so nervous about anyway?

Since she'd chased him and the money up to Lockhart, Molly had conducted a tightly organized campaign to secure the mill. She'd been so focused on the business that she'd never questioned his plans for their wedding. Had she expected him to back out? Was she only now realizing the permanence of their vows?

She looked lovely in her fancy getup. He'd feared that she might not appreciate the extravagance of a public wedding, but his gamble had paid off. Molly always dressed to be the center of attention, whether it was her wedding or not. She had seemed pleased with the ceremony, so what was bothering her now? He snuck a sideways glance at her. One by one, she pulled the petals off her rose bouquet, leaving a trail like bread crumbs to find her way home.

"It's been a long day," he said.

"*Um-hum.*" Her fingers faltered as she tried to catch another petal while the surrey bounced.

"We're almost home."

She didn't answer.

Bailey rested his elbows on his knees and watched the horse's ears twitch, dodging the mosquitoes that were rising from the creek banks as the sun set.

Was she nervous? They weren't strangers. She trusted him. At least until last winter she'd trusted him, but then things had changed. They both had changed.

It wasn't until he saw the horse's ears rotate toward him that he realized he'd sighed. He straightened to take a look at Molly's decimated bouquet. Was she thinking of Edward? The thought soured his stomach. Maybe he was better off not knowing.

The horse required a tug to convince it to turn onto Church Street instead of Mill Street. Molly resisted even more.

"Can't we go to the mill?"

"Tonight? No one is there."

"But we own it now. Don't you want to see it?"

"There's another piece of property I'm more curious about." He gave her the beguiling smile that usually earned him a half-hearted reprimand, but Molly wasn't looking. His heart sunk further. "It's your day, my dear. Let's go to the mill."

His fears multiplied with each moment that she failed to reassure him. The reasons Molly had refused to marry him in the first place returned to mock him. He wasn't rich and she'd always wanted to handle investments and property. Was he merely a means to that end? Had she settled on running her parents' mill and needed his help to make it a success?

They rolled toward the riverbed. The buildings and machinery, the belts, the stacks of lumber, the barns holding wagon teams should have thrilled him, should have filled him with the pride of ownership, but he was more concerned by the distance growing between his new bride and him.

Bailey stopped the wagon by the vacant office and came around to help Molly step down. As soon as her feet touched the gravel drive, she strode toward the river, leaving him behind.

"Molly, I don't know what's upset you, but I'd think you could at least talk to me about it. If you want to be alone, I understand." He followed in her wake. "All right, that's a fib. I don't understand, but I'm willing to hear you out."

At the riverbank she stopped. She pulled her hatpin out from her hat and let the plumed creation float to the ground. She reached behind her and fumbled with the buttons at her waist, her eyes filling with frustrated tears.

"What are you doing?" Should he thank his lucky stars or have her put into an asylum?

She wrestled her overskirt down to her ankles and pulled her white petticoats free. Her hands stretched behind her shoulder blades as she tried to jerk more buttons loose. "Are you going to just stand there and stare?" she asked.

"Yes, I am."

Probably not the best answer. She was upset and deserved a more sensitive response, but his manners had plumb given out.

She spun away, leaving a lacy trail behind as she marched to the thick undergrowth on the bank. He barely got a peek at her chemise cover before she disappeared from view.

"How about I'll wait here until you tell me what to do?" he called.

The branches swayed violently. Bailey tried not to imagine what articles of clothing she was wrestling off, but what was he supposed to do? This didn't sound like any honeymoon story he'd ever heard.

———

Molly loved Bailey. She wanted to marry him like nothing she'd ever wanted before, but since their engagement she'd forced it from her mind. Once they were married, she knew this moment would arrive. Unavoidable. She'd tried to forget, tried to pretend that something would intervene and it wouldn't be as difficult as she feared, but here she was and it was worse. Her hurt couldn't be removed. Bailey couldn't be spared.

With shaking hands she shed her boots and stockings and stepped off the steep bank into the river. The cool water swirled around her knees. Her chemise floated as she waded deeper—waist high, shoulder high. Until this moment she didn't know what she was going to do, but once here it seemed natural. Years had passed since she'd last taken a dip in the river. She'd forgotten what it felt like to be this free, but she also felt exposed.

Wrapping her arms across her chest, she hovered upriver behind the stand of bushes where her gown lay, refusing to let the water carry her any further. She was exposed, and not for the first time. This wasn't the first time, and Bailey knew it. She hadn't been forced. She hadn't been abused. She'd been willing.

And now she had nothing to give Bailey that was new. She had nothing left.

A shadow fell across the water. She lifted her head. Bailey stood on the bank, his jacket and shoes removed. Molly didn't have to drop much further for the water to hit her chin, but she did anyway.

"I love you, Molly."

He didn't ask. He didn't require an explanation. But he deserved one.

"I wish . . ." She let the water cover her mouth. Her hair floated in front of her, wrapping around her neck. She pulled the tendrils away. "I wish this water could wash away every bad thing I've done. I wish the memories could float away, over the dam and out to the sea."

"It's not water that cleanses us. You know that."

Yes, praise God, she knew that. "I've been forgiven, but I haven't made it right with you. I can't make it right. All I can do is promise that I'll be faithful to you from this moment on."

"And that's enough."

She watched the ripples pass, savored the caress of the water as it glided across her skin and tugged on her petticoats. She released her arms and let her fingers spread, dividing the water into ribbons as it slipped through. God had forgiven her. Bailey accepted her. Could she forgive herself?

Since returning home, Molly had found the courage to keep living. She'd learned to soldier on, to fight for her future, but she had forgotten how to be vulnerable.

Molly took a deep breath and submerged herself completely. Her scalp tingled as the air bubbles floated from her locks. She was weightless, innocent in this hidden world where no one could accuse her, no one knew her past. But she couldn't stay forever.

She lifted her head and waited for the water to clear from her face before opening her eyes. But at a mighty splash she had to peek. Bailey had disappeared, and the ripples in the water gave her a clue as to his whereabouts. They moved in her direction, bubbles outlining a path that was coming uncomfortably close. He emerged a few feet away and waited, as if watching for her reaction.

"Oh, Bailey. Your suit! It's brand-new."

"Don't worry. The expensive parts are hanging over there on the bushes."

"Good. I didn't want you to ruin—" She stopped as he stood his full height. His white shirt clung to him like wet paint. She hadn't realized how bright the moonlight was.

He seemed unaware of his effect on her but watched the river as it swept past them. "I think you have the right idea, Molly. We need a fresh start. You aren't the only one with a past to repent of."

"Who? When?" To Molly's knowledge, Bailey hadn't seriously courted anyone besides her.

"I'm not talking about another woman. I took liberties with you that I had no right to. Even if you'd never met that other man, I still treated you with disrespect. I didn't protect you as I should have." His hands skimmed across the water's surface. "So here we are, both needing forgiveness, and both forgiven. If doubts ever return, we can look back at tonight and remember releasing our mistakes and letting them float away. Cleansing every touch that ever dishonored you, mine included."

"As far as the east is from the west?"

"So far hath He removed our transgressions from us."

Once again, Molly closed her eyes. The crickets' song echoed above the roar of the water flowing over the wheel. The tension in her neck eased. Water couldn't come back up a dam. It was gone forever. And God was so good to give her this second chance, to give her one who understood her and loved her anyway.

Bailey touched her cheek, and she almost slipped to the bottom of the river, so great was the shock. The stream had lulled her as she floated in an ethereal cloud, but she wasn't alone. A real-life flesh-and-blood man was with her—waiting.

"Steady now," he whispered. His eyes were so full of love she'd come closer to drowning in them than the river. "I'm ready to let go and begin anew. Are you?"

Molly nodded. Their paths had covered unwelcomed terrain that had left them both tarnished, but between the two of them there would never be another stain.

He stroked her cheek with the back of his hand. Trailing his finger down her nose, Bailey outlined her lips and pressed his fingers flat against them, covering them completely. Molly tightened her mouth against the pressure, giving him a silent kiss.

The water sped as it coursed between them. He stepped closer. The current quickened as it rushed through the narrowing channel, and then it was no more. Warmth replaced the cooling stream as Bailey closed the gap. He lowered his mouth over hers as rivulets cascaded off of him and mingled with her tears. She wrapped her arms around his neck and anchored herself on his strength, no longer alone in the fight against the current that could carry her away.

Love and security. Molly had offered one to get the other and had almost lost both. But once the counterfeits were removed, she could appreciate the man who'd been there all along—the one who even now was trying to catch his breath, forehead pressed against hers, droplets sparkling in his lashes.

"I've tried to be a cowboy, a blacksmith, a minister, and a cobbler, but I finally found my calling."

"And what would that be?"

"Partnering with you to take on the ills of the world, making our corner of Texas a better place, and keeping you somewhere between bliss and exasperation."

"I'm dangerously close to one extreme." Molly brushed the water from his face. "I couldn't tell you which, but the rest of your plan sounds perfect."

He smiled. "Then it's time to take you home."

Holding her hand, he led her to the riverbank, never giving

her a chance to argue—and that was fine. As she climbed out, her wet clothing was heavy, but her heart was light. She would follow him through thick and thin, but there was no need to follow him home.

She was already there.

Regina Jennings is a graduate of Oklahoma Baptist University with a degree in English and a minor in history. She has worked at the *Mustang News* and at First Baptist Church of Mustang, along with time at the Oklahoma National Stockyards and various livestock shows. She lives outside of Oklahoma City with her husband and four children.